"It takes courage to experience and write about the war described herein. The reader can only imagine the pain and suffering to live and write about such a compelling war story. A reader will find a heroic struggle of man's capacity for brutality and discover with the author the gift of life—a capacity for strength and kindness amidst our national moral tragedy."

—**Edward W Beal, MD, Clinical Professor of Psychiatry, Georgetown University School of Medicine, Captain, US Army 1967–69, Author,** *War Stories From the Forgotten Soldiers*

"Having interviewed hundreds of Vietnam veterans and gotten to know many of them and their families, I've learned a good deal about their experiences, both in the war and in the decades after their return. Each story is different, yet common threads connect them. *Poisoned Jungle* weaves many of those threads together, while also containing unique images and experiences of the sort that cannot be invented by someone who had not gone through them. The first section, set during the war itself, reads like a memoir, and the rest of the novel opens out from there as the characters struggle with the physical, psychological and moral injuries suffered during the war and try to find a place in a world that is supposed to be home, but is often unwelcoming or uncomprehending. Through it all, a spirit of hope and humanity shines through. The wounds of war never entirely disappear, but it is possible to move past them. James Ballard has created a remarkable work that will ring true to many Vietnam veterans and their families and do much to educate the rest of us about them. As someone who has never been to war, I know that I will never fully understand what these veterans went through, but as an interviewer, I have found that listening to them helps close the gap between us. *Poisoned Jungle* tells a story well worth listening to."

—**Dr. James Smither, Director, Grand Valley State University Veterans History Project**

"Some wars don't end when the fighting stops. In *Poisoned Jungle,* James Ballard forcefully captures a medic's fears, confusion and strength on the ground in Vietnam in prose that mirrors the best of Tim O'Brien. But his story goes deeper, in the eloquent depiction of the struggle to readjust to stateside life, a flight to find oneself, and an eventual landing spot away from the clatter of the guns. James Ballard's work represents in tones that are eminently human the timeless quest for peace, one that transcends all wars, both external and internal."

—**Greg Fields, Author,** *Arc of the Comet,* **2017 Kindle Book of the Year Nominee in Literary Fiction**

"Reading *Poisoned Jungle* was difficult at times because it truly depicts the way it was in the Nam."

—**Tom Bradburn, Vietnam Veteran, 1st Marine Division, 1968–69, Author,** *Luck of the Draw*

"I had the privilege of reading the author's original manuscript of *Poisoned Jungle.* I found myself drawn into the events that form the backdrop for the book James Ballard has written.

The circumstances of what happened in those jungles and the experience these young men faced in the aftermath as they returned home was compelling. *Poisoned Jungle* will give the reader an appreciation for what veterans of Vietnam experienced, from the horrors of the battlefield to the uncertainty of returning to civilian life.

"The descriptive and visual nature of the writing is excellent. I was immersed in the story to the point that I could almost taste the tepid water from Andy's canteen. The subtle insight into the effects of defoliating chemicals used in Vietnam, continuing to affect both military and civilian populations to this day, is written in a compassionate and understanding narrative."

—**Don Levers, Author,** *Loot for the Taking, Our Fathers' Footsteps*

Poisoned Jungle

by James Ballard

© Copyright 2020 James Ballard

ISBN 978-1-64663-311-1

Published by

 köehlerbooks™

3705 Shore Drive
Virginia Beach, VA 23455
800-435-4811
www.koehlerbooks.com

POISONED JUNGLE

a novel

JAMES BALLARD

VIRGINIA BEACH
CAPE CHARLES

For Greg, and Terry

Because you were there

For all those touched by the Vietnam War

May we all find our own peace

AUTHOR'S NOTE

WRITING TRUTHFULLY ABOUT war is painful—beyond the killing, lifelong physical and psychological disabilities are created. Complicity spreads a wide net in this destruction of lives. Participating in it challenges every moral precept of what it is to be human. Surviving war leaves an indelible question at the forefront of one's being—*Why me? Those more worthy, brave, compassionate, and innocent were destroyed while I have been spared.*

Restoring the damaged parts of one's self is painful and often unattainable. The impact of war is not only transformational on the human psyche, but ongoing.

If not irrevocably damaged by witnessing what human beings are capable of inflicting on one another, it is also human to try and piece together the fragments of a shattered perception of humanity. The alternative is chaos—of the mind and of civilization.

As a medic in my war, there was a horrible irony and agony to the frantic efforts to treat casualties who only moments before were healthy human beings. Sometimes this was an enemy soldier; more often it was Vietnamese civilians caught in the crossfire. Most often, I treated American combatants too young to vote who were caught up in a war not of their making, but of their country's. When efforts failed and a person became permanently maimed, or a corpse, it set in motion powerful psychological consequences. Finding equilibrium with those forces became imperative.

While fictional, it is hoped the characters in this novel will resonate with readers and provide a glimpse into one war, and its lingering and complicated repercussions. Certainly, the political realities should not be ignored; on the surface there are winners and losers. Beneath that, all sides have suffered the tragic consequences of man's capacity for brutality.

PART I

MEKONG DELTA

CHAPTER ONE

Mekong Delta, Vietnam
1969

WHITE HENRY WALKED point as third platoon moved through part of a dead and decaying jungle. Twenty men followed his lead, spread out, careful not to bunch up too close.

From near the rear of the platoon, Andy Parks watched Eli and the Professor struggle to get enough traction to ascend a steep knoll. The herbicide used to spray the forest killed enough vegetation to make it a hard slog through the rotting slime. Dead birds and the corpses of monkeys, furry mounds now, littered the ground where they'd fallen from their perches high above. Difficult to breathe in the stench, unbearable in the mid-day heat and humidity, Andy repressed the urge to gag.

With skeletons of trees hovering over them, and goo clinging to their boots, the platoon trudged on. Weighted down with seventy pounds of gear, the straps on Andy's pack cut into his shoulders. He tried adjusting them as he kept moving, loosening them, cinching them tighter. Nothing helped.

Sweat poured out of Andy, saturating his fatigues, and dripping off his face. Mosquitoes buzzed around his head, incessant in their pursuit of a landing spot. Some of the rotted slime got on his hands and he accidentally smeared it on his brow when he wiped away sweat and swatted at the bugs.

On a forced march to rendezvous with first platoon, a tree line loomed ahead where the deadly spray ended in its quest to deny cover to the enemy. A rifle shot dropped the platoon to the ground to return fire. A half-hearted firefight ensued, and when it ended an eerie quiet remained. The distinct smell of gunpowder from the spent cartridges littering the ground mingled with the rotted jungle.

"Charlie's jus' messin' wid us," Black Henry said to a new guy. "Jus' lettin' us know he knows we's here." His Alabama accent imbued with a speech impediment created an unusual cadence difficult to understand at first. The newbie nodded, at least pretending to comprehend.

"Welcome to the Nam, boy," White Henry chimed in. "I'm so short I don't belong out here with the rest of you geniuses," he said, referring to the few days left on his twelve-month tour. Some guys got a little spooked towards the end of their tours. White Henry remained unfazed.

"Ya see, way I figure, we're all a bunch of dumb fucks for bein' here."

Every member of the platoon was painfully aware they had drawn the worst shit detail possible just being in the Nam, let alone wandering around in the boonies looking for a fight with Charlie.

"Ya gotta come to the Nam and mess with that little fucker harder than he's gonna mess with you," White Henry said.

"An' jus' how you messin' wid Charlie right now?" retorted Black Henry, having heard it all before. The two feigned irritation with one another but were in fact inseparable.

White Henry persisted. "Just sayin' how you can survive the rest of your tours without me here to look after your sorry asses. But, hey, I'm so short you won't even be able to see me in a few days."

Andy pulled himself up from the muck. It covered the front of his fatigues and seeped through and burned where it mixed with his perspiration. After drying, the slime chafed his skin with every movement.

Static from the field radio broke the silence. Pinto, the radio telephone operator, handed the receiver to Lieutenant Howitz. After surveying the platoon's position while he listened, he made a decision.

"Saddle up and let's get moving. First platoon's gotten Arty involved. We're no longer needed. Let's get outta this shit and back into the cover of the jungle."

An hour later, the men came to a stream, and each squad took turns washing the dried rot off their clothes and bodies while the others stood guard against an ambush in the dense jungle. As the platoon's medic, Andy checked on two of the guys with dysentery. Weak and miserable, they rested on the sloped bank hoping to regain some of their strength before resuming with the patrol. Andy filled their canteens.

"Thanks, Doc," said Arsenal. Already skinny, the kid could not afford to lose any more weight. Andy would have liked to send him back to the rear, but the platoon, shorthanded and deep in hostile territory, needed his expertise on the M-60 machine gun.

White Henry continued on point after the break. Andy marveled at the way he remained so calm with only a few days left in country. Reaching higher ground after rinsing in the stream, Howitz ordered the platoon to dig in for the night.

"That was some shit we went through today, Doc," said Sammy, Andy's best pal in the platoon. He already had several shovelfuls of damp earth piled around the outside of the foxhole they were digging. The medic tried to help him with the nightly task but was often pulled away to treat the maladies of soldiers in the field.

Jungle rot kept him busy; then there were a plethora of rashes and infections from the swamps and jungles. If the men could have just been able to keep their feet dry, it would have helped, but this was the

Mekong Delta, Vietnam's rice basket. Not very high above sea level and submerged under a massive river system emanating from the Mekong, its major tributaries fed the streams and canals throughout the region. Before reaching the sea, water filled every low-lying area, the swamps the platoon had to traverse. Lovely for the mosquitoes, which carried malaria, and ideal for the leeches, which took a lot of blood before Charlie got to them. Blisters formed before becoming calluses, and leeches somehow found their way to bare skin.

White Henry approached with one of the new guys limping behind him. It took two weeks for most newbies to get in shape. Nobody packed seventy pounds of gear and ammo in the heat and humidity without suffering, especially in the beginning. Dehydration took its toll. Good sources of water, hard to find, soon tasted of plastic from sloshing around in warm canteens. Never refreshing, iodine purification tablets added to the ugly taste.

"Calhoun here's havin' some trouble, Doc," White Henry said, motioning for the new guy to sit down on the mound of dirt positioned around their foxhole.

The kid looked scared and miserable but pretended nonchalance. Andy could tell by looking at the thin sheen of sweat on his pale skin, and his shortness of breath, that he had heat exhaustion.

"Let's get you cooled off," Andy said, touching the new guy's forehead with one hand, and his arm with the other. Clammy to the touch. The medic asked, "You feel weak, a bit nauseous?"

The kid nodded. "I'll be all right," he said. "Just need to rest, catch my breath some."

Andy took a cloth and poured water on it from his canteen. He wiped the young soldier's face, then had Calhoun take his fatigue shirt off and continued with his chest and back. Opening his aid bag, he handed the kid a handful of salt tablets.

"Try and drink as much water as you can," he told him. "Get some rest, get cooled down. You're dehydrated. Let's make sure your heat exhaustion doesn't turn into heat stroke."

After White Henry left with Calhoun, Sammy sat next to his friend. The two shared a foxhole most nights they were in the field. Sammy took a green can of C-rations from his pack and used his opener. "Pound cake," he stated, unenthusiastically. "Fucking pound cake in a can. Can you believe it?" He broke it in half and gave a piece to the Doc. Sammy examined his portion before taking a bite. "Fucking ugly and tastes like shit. Got some good news, though, Doc. The LT says we're outta here in the morning."

Andy chewed on his half of the cake and watched as the platoon sergeant organized placing the claymore mines around their nighttime perimeter. "I guess that's it, then, for White Henry. His last night in the boonies."

"Guess so," said Sammy. "If anyone deserves surviving the Nam, it's him. For our sakes, I hate seein' him go."

✳ ✳ ✳

Back at base camp in Dong Tam, White Henry went around and said goodbye. A compact man, not overly tall, his hands were large and strong. The platoon depended on him.

Sammy and Andy walked with White Henry to the airstrip, shaking hands before boarding the helicopter that would ferry him closer to the rear and out of the Nam. "Watch yerself, now, Doc. Pleasure knowin' ya. Ever in Missouri, come look me up."

White Henry looked at Sammy. "Goes for you, too, bro. Look out for one another. Get back home safe."

Ten months into his own tour, Andy could not remember crying in the Nam. He struggled to suppress the tears forming at White Henry's departure. A pensive Sammy watched the Huey lift into the sky.

"There goes one tough motherfucker," he said. Andy knew what he meant. They felt alone and vulnerable without him. White Henry had gotten the platoon out of some serious jams.

Later, still thinking about White Henry's departure, Sammy sat on his cot and sipped on a warm can of beer. "Be different not havin' him out there," he said, referring to the endless patrols third platoon spent trudging through the Delta. "Saved my ass a time or two."

"All of ours," Andy added, remembering one of his worst days in the war.

❊ ❊ ❊

The soldier nicknamed Boy Red had arrived in the platoon five months after Andy. Red-headed and with boyish features, he looked younger than his age. Whatever adjustment problems the kid had he kept to himself.

Andy learned more about Boy Red from inscriptions printed on his helmet than anything the kid had told him. His camouflaged cover had a four-leaf clover drawn on one side with the word *IRISH* printed beneath it. *NINA* stood out in bold letters on the other side. The kid never spoke of her, but Andy knew it referred to his girl. Nobody wrote their mother's name on the side of their helmet.

On a patrol, third platoon came to a swampy patch in the jungle and waded into the leech-infested muck. The water line reached the middle of Andy's thighs. Even though Andy couldn't feel them, he knew the leeches would be feasting beneath the surface.

Boy Red didn't feel the trip wire concealed below the water when his leg dragged it, pulling a grenade with its pin already removed out of a tin can.

Shrapnel exploded into Boy Red's upper body. Not far behind him, Andy's ears rang from the sound and the concussion of the grenade detonating. Alive when he got to him, Boy Red's face was unrecognizable. Bleeding from the neck profusely, he sank into the swamp's filthy water. Andy wrapped his arms around Boy Red to prevent him from submerging in the muck.

With one hand, Andy felt along his neck, slick from the bleeding. He knew by then the kid would die. Desperate to keep his head above the water, he slipped the straps from Boy Red's pack off his shoulders and got him to an embankment nearby.

Andy heard White Henry shout, "Don't nobody move!"

The platoon had walked into an intricate spider web of trip wires interwoven with an assortment of booby traps connected to each other. Andy froze and looked in White Henry's direction. With only his head above water, White Henry felt with his hands for the wire he had brushed up against. He cut it with his knife, creating a safe spot for the rest of them to step.

White Henry continued to wade through the water, snipping trip wires and making sure the platoon knew exactly where to follow. More booby traps concealed in the trees and shrubs were spotted, and some of the guys froze. White Henry assured them he would take the lead, finding all the trip wires for them. If he missed one, he would suffer the brunt of an explosion or the tip of a sharpened bamboo stake. In this way, step by step, the platoon moved through the swamp.

Andy took a field poncho and wrapped Boy Red's body in it. Sammy took one end while Andy held the other, dragging the corpse along the murky surface. Eli and Black Henry, the Professor and Minnesota took turns carrying him out. Everyone feared dying in the Nam and being left behind.

The kid's helmet, blown off in the blast, hung in the brush. The word *Nina* had a line through it. Andy figured Boy Red must have received a letter from his girl breaking it off with him. Such letters only flowed one way in the Nam.

By the time the platoon reached higher ground, the web of booby traps had ended. Charlie, eerily prescient in his craftiness to inflict pain and instill fear, had been nowhere in sight, but the platoon felt his presence with every step it took.

Exhausted and encrusted with mud, the platoon emerged from the swamp shivering from the fear, cold, and exertion it took to survive its booby-trapped ordeal. As they picked the leeches off one another, too tired to say much, each man, in turn, nodded in White Henry's direction. No spoken words were necessary.

Some of the men smoked, or milled about with dazed looks, feeling relief that the worst was over. Only White Henry's bravery had prevented more casualties.

Andy cleaned Boy Red as best he could, wiping some of the blood and mud from his body before wrapping the poncho around him for the final time. Later, when the rotors of a helicopter could be heard approaching the landing zone hacked out of the jungle, some of the platoon helped load him onto the Huey.

As the medevac lifted off, several members of the platoon stood in the LZ not ready to resume their activities as grunts in a war that had just taken one of their own. Like an unrehearsed ritual, each man watched, alone in the reverie of his thoughts, mesmerized by the distinct sound of the rotor blades beating the air. They looked at the sky as the helicopter grew smaller until it disappeared along with their fallen comrade.

Wishing they were on that bird flying out of the Nam—*but alive*—leaving the forsaken jungle for the last time, nobody stirred until the LT gave the order to saddle up. They would return to humping through the swamps of the Mekong Delta now, overburdened with gear, looking for Charlie, but hoping not to find him.

CHAPTER TWO

ANDY "DOC" PARKS shared a hooch with Sammy Donato when the platoon stood down in Dong Tam. Headquarters for the Ninth Infantry Division, the base sat on a square mile of swamp filled in with silt from the My Tho River. The massive tributary of the Mekong flowed northeast along Dong Tam's south border. At the river's edge, deepened by dredging, wooden docks provided mooring for the Navy's contribution to the war effort. Patrol boats bobbed in the mud-brown water next to the armored troop carriers used to insert the division's Riverine Force. Time spent at the camp offered respite from the dangerous and grueling patrols in the field.

The two men slept in an old Army tent intended to be temporary. A single light bulb hung from a wire that dangled from its peak. Only leaking during the worst downpours of the monsoon season, the drab green tent offered comforts not found in a foxhole. It even had a door.

While the platoon searched for Charlie in the Ca Mau, their barracks had been damaged in a rocket attack. Rebuilt, it had been assigned to others during another long stint in the field. Comfortable enough, the two friends were content to stay put. They weren't in base camp all that much.

Not long after White Henry rotated out of the Nam, Black Henry walked into their hooch. The Professor and Yardly, the platoon's Montagnard Tiger Scout, followed him in. Unassuming, but never far from the Professor's side, Yardly took a seat on the floor and crossed his legs. Black Henry remained standing and got right to the point.

"Doc, need ya ta look at dese rashes."

Sammy protested the intrusion. "Don't you guys know how to knock?"

"What, we 'pose ta wait in de entryway for da butler?" answered Black Henry.

"What's wrong with hoofin' it down to Battalion Aid and havin' them take care of you? Doc's busy."

"Don' look busy ta me. 'Sides, it's kinda private. Me an' da Professor got dese rashes all over includin' our behinds. Need da Doc ta take a look."

"You barged into our modest abode so the Doc can take a look at your ugly butt?"

"And da Professor's. 'Sides, you live in a tent, muddahfucker, in dis shithole Vee-et Nam, and dat's only when you ain't humpin' you's ass off in de boonies. Don' be gettin' all uppity wid me." Finished making his point, Black Henry stood with his hand on hips, glaring at Sammy in mock consternation.

The Professor, silent, but nodding agreement, plopped himself down next to Andy. He'd completed one year at a community college in Ohio, more education than any of the other grunts in the platoon. A pair of glasses with thick black frames was the most prominent feature on an unremarkable face. The Professor's nervous habit of constantly pushing them higher on his small nose made the spectacles even more pronounced. His nickname emerged when the guys learned he'd been to college.

"Doc, we really do need you to look at these rashes," the Professor said when he finally spoke. "I pretty much have this shit all over my body." He opened his shirt, exposing some lesions and tiny black dots. His face had them, too. Andy looked at his back and could see cysts beginning to form.

The medic knew Vietnam had a myriad of bacteria and fungi causing all manner of skin rashes and infections. Nasty parasites caused similar problems. It didn't end there. Bites and stings from insects turned into ugly sores from unsanitary conditions in the field. Cuts from sharp-edged grasses and barbed plants contributed to an array of skin problems in the tropical climate. The infections, difficult to keep dry and clean in the swampy terrain of the Delta, festered before they could heal.

As third platoon's medic, it fell on Andy to fix everything. Or at least try. It didn't matter that his training included mostly emergency battlefield procedures. The guys depended on him to know how to treat their minor ailments, too. All the medics in the battalion shared information. Andy learned as much as he could from them. Before rotating home, his predecessor, Doc Woski, gave him some advice.

"These guys are depending on you. Don't let them down. But don't ever bullshit them."

Andy soon discovered a fine line between inspiring confidence and admitting ignorance. His aid bag contained antibacterial and fungal creams and their oral counterparts. A lot of the time he got lucky and the creams helped clear up rashes and infections of nineteen and twenty-year-olds with healthy immune systems. Sometimes they'd be out there for three weeks sleeping in foxholes every night and eating a diet of C-rations—meals in a can devoid of much nutrition.

The Professor's symptoms worried Andy. "How long have you had this?"

"Pretty much since we came back from our last patrol. Black Henry's got it too."

Black Henry turned away from Sammy and unbuttoned his shirt so the Doc could have a look. Muscular from working as an Alabama farmhand since the age of fifteen, the Nam had trimmed twenty pounds off his powerful frame. The black dots were harder to see on his dark skin but were the same as the Professor's. Black Henry ignored Sammy's razzing and dropped his pants so Andy could have a look at the rest of him, exposing his backside to Andy's hooch mate. Nobody wore underwear in the heat and the humidity of the Nam.

"Ya got anything for dis, Doc? It's drivin' me crazy wid de itcin' an' tinglin' an' all."

"I'll give you some creams, guys, but maybe get a doctor at Battalion Aid to look at you, especially if it doesn't clear up before we head back out on patrol."

Sammy smiled after they left. "Fuckin' dorks in Vietnam. They probably had Yardly lookin' at their butts and comparing notes about their rashes."

"Very funny," Andy said. "But did you get a good look at them? I'm not sure I've seen that before."

Sammy shrugged. "There's bigger problems to worry about, Doc. They don't need to be runnin' to you with every blemish on their tender skin."

Andy appreciated Sammy's concern. The two had grown close during their tours, sharing everything from their C-rations in the field to the packages of food their mothers sent from home. Misery and combat in the Nam deepened their bond. "Friends forever," Sammy often stated. "We do whatever it takes to get each other home, bro." Andy always nodded, grateful to have such a good friend looking out for him in the Nam.

Andy Parks grew up in the small town of Afton in northeastern Oklahoma, where remnants of the Cherokee Nation remained. His family identified with their Native roots going back to Nanye-hi on his dad's side. His grandfather, Jacob Parks, spoke the language, and lived with the family before his death. One-quarter Cherokee, Andy was influenced by Jacob's connection to the tribe.

Before receiving his draft notice, he'd never been farther than Tulsa, a two-hour drive from his home. His father, Henry Clay Parks, had seen some of World War II but never talked much about it. Named after the famous senator who had tried to protect the Cherokee from their forced removal, the elder Parks never said much about Vietnam, either. He told Andy he'd never heard of the country before America went to war there. He didn't want to see his son have to fight so far from home, but like his own war, the elder Parks figured the country must have a good reason for being there. Oklahoma boys didn't dodge the draft.

Sammy Donato, the Italian-American kid from the Mohave Desert town of Barstow, California, had an urgency to prove himself. Born in the US, his parents were immigrants who still spoke English with an accent. Caught between two worlds, he refused to avoid the draft, which would have amounted to sending someone else in his place. Showing a willingness to risk making the ultimate sacrifice for his country would prove he belonged, Sammy figured. Stocky when he arrived in country, the hardships of the Nam pared him down to sinewy proportions.

Sammy quickly became a member of the platoon the guys depended on. His nickname, "Sammy Do," reflected his steadiness and resolve over months of being in the rain, wading through the swamps, suffering in the heat, and experiencing the agony and terror of combat.

On a night ambush, Sammy had confided to Andy, "Doc, whether I'm goin' back alive or dead, it's not as a coward."

Andy had not confessed—even to best-bud Sammy—how overwhelmed he felt as the platoon's medic. After ten weeks at Ft. Sam Houston, Texas, where the Army medics trained, he had a brief posting in the emergency room at West Point. By the time he received his orders for Vietnam, Andy had at least seen some traumatic injuries and dead bodies. But nothing stateside prepared him for the wounds suffered in combat, wounds beyond repair. Each life lost took a part of him, and left him wondering if he could have done more.

Andy arrived in Vietnam in late October of 1968, two weeks before Doc Woski rotated home. He got little information from the medic who'd survived a year in the Nam. Woski would sit and gaze outwardly, showing little emotion, never saying much. Uncommunicative, his focus internal, he simply showed Andy the basics of what he needed to know. A year in the Nam and all the guys Woski had been closest to had finished their tours, some in body bags. Now deeper into his tour, Andy understood how the war seeped into a grunt's psyche, rendering words inadequate to explain the Nam. He now understood Woski's stoicism.

Enormous pressures burdened him. Andy had an entire platoon—some twenty-five men—to look after, and not just their battle wounds. When he arrived, the platoon was just as apprehensive about him, waiting and watching to see if he would be any good. Tensions developed fulfilling his responsibilities. In charge of handing out the anti-malaria pills, the weekly one, large and hard to swallow, gave almost everyone the shits.

Eli, a member of the platoon who'd survived extreme situations, burned with a ferocity none of the guys liked to disturb. The first time Andy gave him his malaria pill, Eli said, scowling and unapproachable, "Think I take that fuckin' horse pill, Doc, when all the Army feeds us is the C-rats? Get me a decent meal and I'll consider it." He took his weekly dose and tossed it on the ground behind him. "I have my preventive means right here," he said, pointing at the supply of bug juice strapped to his helmet. He reeked of the mosquito repellant, and nobody messed with Eli.

Arriving in country two months before Andy, Eli remained a mystery. Nobody knew where he came from or much about him. His entire focus on surviving the Nam, he kept to himself. He'd lost his entire squad, down to five men, soon after joining third platoon. Charlie had killed the point man and took out two more by booby-trapping the body. Only Eli remained after his squad leader rotated home days later. Or the night the VC swarmed over Eli on

a listening post, and he emerged ghost-like in the morning, nobody
understanding how he could have survived.

The superstitious stuck to Eli, someone who'd survived situations
that left most others dead. Law-of-averages types in the platoon,
certain that danger caught up to you, avoided him. None of it mattered
to Eli. By himself, or surrounded by others, he remained alone.

Andy suspected some of the platoon wanted to contract malaria
to get out of the field. Andy tried to warn them, told them disease
could kill them, too, or cause brain damage. There were many forms
of brain damage in the Nam.

Andy's aid bag contained an assortment of field dressings, IV
solution, tourniquet pegs, epinephrine, tubes of morphine, and a
tracheotomy kit, along with more mundane medical supplies for
treating minor ailments. His training emphasized the need to keep
the casualty breathing, stop the bleeding, and prevent shock. In the
Nam, getting a medevac also made a crucial difference. Sometimes
they were not available.

Andy, not a month into his tour, lost his first killed in action that
way. The platoon, deep in the Delta, had dug in at dusk. A steady
drizzle set in during the night. They were cold and uncomfortable.
The clouds obscured any light from the moon. Andy learned Charlie
could fight in the rain, and the dark. The enemy probed their
position. Two claymore mines detonated on their night perimeter,
and a firefight erupted at close range. Charlie tossed some grenades,
and one of the blasts caught a guy they called Square One.

Andy got to him right away, but the casualty struggled to breathe.
Andy couldn't see well enough in the dark to know the location of
all his wounds. He ripped Square One's fatigue shirt off and felt with
his hands along his chest, slick with blood turning sticky as some
coagulated and dried on Andy's hands. Fearing some shrapnel had
penetrated the lung cavity and punctured its vacuum, Andy placed
a large petroleum bandage over the entry points on his torso and
wrapped it tightly. The wounded man continued gasping for breath.

Andy stayed with him the entire night, agonizing that the weather did not clear enough to get a dust-off in. With Square One's veins collapsing, Andy made a mess of getting an IV started. At first light, the young medic discovered a small wound on the side of his head, making his other efforts to save him futile. Square One died just after dawn as the drizzle lightened.

Ben Moses helped Andy put the dead man in a body bag. It had stopped raining. The platoon, soaked to the skin, shivered from the cold and the close encounter with Charlie.

"You know," Moses said, "the brother wasn't such a bad guy. The Nam fucks with everybody in different ways." He patted the body bag before rejoining the rest of the platoon readying for the day's hump. "Rest in peace."

Square One had been a total pain in the ass since Andy had been with the platoon, figuring him for a cracker with his Oklahoma roots. No way Square One accepted the new medic before he'd proven himself. Andy resented the hostility. He had enough to contend with without one of the guys not trusting him. Andy knew the history of his own people, the Cherokee, and they had suffered too. And maybe he didn't have enough Indian blood to impress the full-bloods back home, but in the Delta, cold and shivering with the rest of the platoon, he faced the same discomfort and danger from Charlie. Andy didn't have it in him to hold a grudge like that, not with a man's life at stake. But doubts surfaced in him about his abilities. Maybe he could have done more to save Square One if he was a better medic. *Too late for that now.*

Andy's thoughts, interrupted by the sound of the rotors on an approaching helicopter, had one other casualty to get on the dust-off. Minnesota had a frag wound on his forearm that would need surgery at the 29th Evacuation Hospital in Binh Thuy.

"A wound like this ain't gonna be good for too long outta the boonies, now is it, Doc?"

Andy shook his head no.

"Be good for a rest, anyway," Minnesota said, before boarding the Huey. "See you guys in a couple of weeks," he added, already walking towards the medevac that would ferry him out of the worst part of the war for at least that amount of time.

CHAPTER THREE

ANDY'S DAYS OF trudging through the swamps, rice paddies, and jungles of the Mekong Delta searching for an elusive enemy created a deep fatigue. Charlie knew the terrain better and could blend in with the local population, surfacing when he sensed an advantage, lying low when he did not.

Most of the humping just wore everybody out. Bodies under constant stress, without sleep and proper nutrition, developed sores that did not heal. Simple cuts became infected because of unsanitary conditions. Immune systems weakened with the constant grind of an infantryman's life in the field.

Water, so plentiful in the Delta, emanated from the mighty Mekong and diverged into its major tributaries. The My Tho branched into the Co Chien and Ham Luong, flowing through the provinces of Ben Tre, Tra Vinh, and Vinh Long, all before emptying into the South China Sea. The saturated landscape could not absorb all the water. Andy marveled at how the rivers and canals, their channels so full, appeared to have no banks when observed from the shore. Jungle, dense with flora, grew to the water's edge. Flooded rice paddies, surrounded by mud dikes, held more water. And the swamps, so prevalent on their patrols, were saturated during the monsoon rains, but never dry during the dry season.

Water everywhere, but so much of it not fit to drink, resulting in more health issues for the platoon. Bacteria survived the purification tablets the Army provided and wreaked havoc on intestinal systems. Dehydration sapped stamina and caused heat exhaustion, sometimes heat stroke. Andy could not keep enough salt in his system; his abdomen ached from the cramping.

Some of the illnesses encountered were of the Army's own making. Twenty million gallons of chemical defoliants were dropped on an area the size of Massachusetts, with 500,000 acres of crop land thrown in for good measure. The rationale—to deny cover and sustenance to the enemy—lacked precision.

Early in his tour, Andy had overheard the company commander say, "Let Charlie hide behind that. If we poison the jungle enough, then maybe some of it will rub off on him."

Charlie absorbed some of the poison, along with the Vietnamese in the countryside. Members of third platoon did as well. When moving through parts of the damaged jungle, they filled canteens from streams and pools of water accumulated from runoff after heavy rains, or during the monsoon season when all low-lying areas were saturated to overflowing.

Grueling and monotonous, the days ran together, the sequence of events jumbled in Andy's mind. Patrols turned deadly and terrifying the instant contact with the Viet Cong occurred. The medic's worst days in the war were seared into an ugly collage of wounded platoon members struggling to survive their tours. The randomness of who lived and died in the war zone penetrated deeply into the psyche of the young medic. Andy's responsibilities, and his expectations of himself, were impossible to meet.

❊ ❊ ❊

Camel's death hit the platoon hard. Andy's second KIA was the first friend he had to put in a body bag. Already with the platoon when Andy arrived, Camel helped the new medic adjust to the rigors of a grunt's life in the Delta. Patiently showing Andy how to efficiently pack his gear, advising him what to take on his first patrols, Camel exhibited a kindness the new medic appreciated.

"Just remember it's just as dark for Charlie," he'd told Andy before his first night ambush. "You'll get used to it. Fall in behind me in the formation, Doc. Third platoon looks after its medics." Camel accepted him into the unit and made him feel he belonged. His assurances meant a lot. Andy would do his best for them. Camel never doubted that.

"Bring lots of bug juice for the Ca Mau," he told Andy before a long patrol. "You'll be miserable without it." The mosquitoes were bad everywhere, but worse in the Ca Mau.

Talk about a nickname fitting like a glove. No matter how burdened with gear and ammunition, Camel packed the weight. No matter how tired, hungry, thirsty or scared, the man kept going. With a stoop to his gait creating a slight hunchback at the base of his neck, his physical features suggested his nickname. And he smoked—like a chimney—Camel cigarettes, of course.

Andy had frantically tried to stop Camel's bleeding. He died clutching onto Andy, fully conscious, sensing death, his eyes pleading for life.

The patrol, similar to so many others, had been uneventful into the third day. The VC, camouflaged and waiting for a quick hit and run behind the last paddy dike before the safety of a tree line, opened fire. Third platoon, exposed, but spread out as Lieutenant Howitz insisted, found cover behind the mud walls of the dikes built to contain the water necessary for cultivating rice. Walking on top of them made it easier to move through the paddies, not damaging the green shoots of the seedlings, while the men had the hope of keeping their feet dry.

The platoon found cover easily, returning fire from behind the mud dikes, which formed walls of rectangles and squares throughout the cultivated area. The instant Andy heard the first shot he dove behind a dike. With his adrenaline surging, he barely noticed the coldness of the water. Squatting, he peered above the embankment.

Andy looked for casualties and listened for shouts of help. Hearing nothing but the platoon's M-60s already set up and firing towards the tree line, along with the M-16s everybody else carried, he didn't see any wounded. The distinct sound of the enemy's AK-47s on automatic, and a lone RPD machine gun, added to the intensity of the firefight.

Andy undid the straps of his aid bag, which held it to the frame of his pack. If there were any wounded, he would get to them taking only his M-3 aid bag, compact with thirty pounds of medical supplies. He'd memorized the contents of the three compartments so he could find what he needed without fumbling.

Ahead of Andy and to his left, Lieutenant Howitz spoke into the receiver of the field radio, giving coordinates for artillery in range and calling for the support from gunships. Charlie would not hang around once the heavy guns emerged.

It surprised Andy how many rounds from automatic weapons were fired without hitting anybody. With every step, Andy kept a continuous watch for where to find cover if a firefight erupted. The surge of adrenaline when under fire and the deep fear in his gut of a single bullet ripping into him was not something he got used to.

Hundreds of rounds zipped through the air and embedded themselves into trees and mud banks. Others whizzed by Andy's ears, close enough to hear, or whizzed overhead as his body hugged the contours of a depression in the ground. His senses instinctively calculated angles with precision, desperately seeking protection behind objects capable of absorbing a bullet, or a low spot depriving them of accuracy. Sometimes the enemy, or a platoon member, could not find cover quick enough, or miscalculated. And that was when Andy, boy medic, needed to treat a casualty.

After the initial intensity of the firefight, the Viet Cong had no interest in waiting for the gunships to arrive, or an artillery barrage to change the dynamics of their contact with third platoon. They retreated into the trees, leaving a rear guard to cover their movement.

It was during the platoon's pursuit of Charlie retreating that Camel took a single gunshot wound to his liver.

Fully conscious when Andy got to him, Camel told him through his shortened and choppy breath, "Doc, I'm hit bad." Then asked, "Am I gonna make it?" Camel's eyes were desperate for reassurance, but still not complaining. Andy worked quickly, ripping his fatigue shirt open and applying a pressure bandage. He secured it with an elastic wrap. Desperate to stop the bleeding from a liver shredded by an AK-47, Andy tied and taped it all in place.

The medic remained silent, unable to speak. While his hands worked quickly in a desperate attempt to stem the flow of blood, the physical Andy functioned, treating a wounded platoon member. But his mind froze. His hands were steady, even under fire. But his mind could not think of any words to say to a friend, a dying platoon member. Andy failed as a medic and a person.

With blood everywhere on Camel's abdomen, soaked into his fatigues, and all over Andy, the medic knew there were too many blood vessels severed in the liver to stop the bleeding. No amount of pressure would do that. The damage internal, Andy replayed that moment over and over in his head. He failed to give Camel the only thing of value he could have—a sense of hope—even if it wasn't the truth.

Camel clutched Andy with all his remaining strength until it ebbed out of him like his life itself. Slipping into the nether realm only the dead can enter, Camel's grip loosened in death.

The platoon watched from behind the mud dikes to avoid the debris from shelling now pounding the retreating enemy, which flew from the shattered trees. Andy viewed the artillery barrage with his dead casualty. Andy couldn't stop repeating in his mind what he should have said to Camel before he died.

"Dust-off's on the way, Camel; we're getting you outta here. Soon you'll be home sipping drinks with all the lovely girls you left behind, man. Meantime, we got you covered. No way we're letting you die out here in this shithole of a rice paddy."

After the firefight, and after the artillery had finished demolishing the trees nearest to the rice paddy, Andy continued to function. Feeling empty, his emotions in a jumbled mess, Andy looked for Camel's dog tags. He found them tucked in the upper portion of his boot, like every infantryman is instructed to do. He needed to know Camel's real name to complete the field medical card, the medic's responsibility before putting a dead man in a body bag. Michael Gene Harris—known only as Camel to the platoon.

Andy never asked his real name. He'd never paid attention to the tag, now stained with blood, with HARRIS sewn in black letters above the bulky shirt pocket on his jungle fatigues. He had no idea what part of the country Camel came from, how many brothers and sisters, aunts and uncles, friends and lovers. Those closest to him would still be worrying about him, pulling for him, hoping for his safe return from the Nam.

In two or three days, official representatives from the Army would arrive on the doorsteps of his parents' home to inform them of their son's death. Impeccably attired in their dress greens, an officer and a chaplain would perform their macabre duty. First, Andy had to finish his own set of morbid responsibilities. He tagged the body and zipped up the ugly green bag with Camel a bloody mess inside of it.

Even then, the rest of the country would only know him as a number, part of a statistical accounting of young men dead in the war zone for the week, then month, then year. Business would be normal for most of the country. In a couple of days, not for Camel's family.

The futility of the war penetrated the numbness in Andy. A lot of the guys vented their rage blindly at the Vietnamese, all of them *gooks*, *dinks*, or *slopes*, none of them to be trusted. Vietnam was, in their view, nothing but a worthless shit-filled bog of rice paddies, swamps, and jungles full of hazards waiting to prevent them from returning home to a normal life.

The members of third platoon, empty and spent, and suffering, watched a helicopter ferry another one of their own out of the war zone. Andy thought, *Maybe that's the whole point of war, making each other suffer. Somebody will eventually give up, and those that are left can stop trying to kill each other and get back to living.*

❆ ❆ ❆

Third platoon also knew how to inflict pain.

Dong Tam, sitting on its square mile of filled-in swamp, offered a permanent target for the Viet Cong mortar and rocket crews. Ninth Infantry night ambushes tried to intercept them.

Andy preferred night operations, once he adjusted to being in the dark, understanding the enemy operated in the same conditions.

The best part was that sometimes the platoon only spent the night in the field, setting up just a few hundred meters from base camp, returning in the morning to sleep on their cots, eating meals in their mess hall, not out of a can. It was a preferred option over spending two or three weeks on patrol, sleeping in foxholes and humping heavy packs through leech-infested swamps.

A lot of nights went without incident. The Viet Cong mortar teams might be pounding Dong Tam, but from a different part of the jungle. The platoon would sit and listen, unable to do anything about it. Sometimes they'd hear a firefight erupt, some other platoon having encountered Charlie somewhere beyond Dong Tam's perimeter, the *rat-tat-tat-tat* cadence of automatic weapons rhythmic from a distance.

Andy learned the sounds of the jungle from the nights when no contact occurred, listening for a human presence, a snapping twig, a palm leaf rustling unnaturally. Each evening the platoon tried anticipating the route or positioning of the Viet Cong. Charlie needed to be within three kilometers of the base, the normal range for the most common types of mortars. Third platoon and the VC varied their patterns in a deadly guessing game.

On a muggy night thick with mosquitoes, the heat of the day not fully dissipated, a four-man VC mortar crew walked right into their position. The platoon set up, waiting, night discipline in effect, no smoking, talking, flashlights, unnecessary sounds. Andy thought the VC ought to be able to smell them, the mosquito repellants, the sweat from overheated bodies, or hear the pounding of hearts beating faster and louder when the platoon realized the enemy had walked into their ambush.

But the Viet Cong also had their preoccupations, breathing heavy and struggling with the weights they carried. Empty, the 82 mm mortar weighed 123 pounds. Broken into three pieces for transporting through the jungle, each of the shells, hanging from slings and pouches, added another seven pounds to their loads. The four-man team, badly outnumbered, and overburdened with the munitions they intended to hurl at Dong Tam, had no time to return fire.

Andy caught a glimpse of a young man struggling with the weight of the base plate and several mortars just before the platoon opened up. Young men packing too much weight to carry without effort, perspiring heavily, exhausted, scared and uncomfortable. How many times had Andy been in that situation?

Over in seconds, the team had no time to react, not even to experience the terror of their fate. The platoon could not have been positioned more perfectly. Somebody guessed right, Howitz, headquarters, or blind luck terminating four Viet Cong lives in a few seconds.

Lieutenant Howitz organized the disposal of the munitions. Judging by the circular base plate and size of the tube, and that four VC were walking it through the jungle, an 82 mm mortar unit. At least twenty-five rounds were scattered and being assembled in stacks. Once they were set up, a good team could drop-fire that many of the seven-pound shells in a few minutes.

Andy checked the bodies for any signs of life. Twisted into unnatural positions in death, the darkness lent them an eerie dimension. He noticed a checkered bandana around the neck of one of the soldiers. Kneeling to get a closer look, he could see a long and thick braid trailing from behind the skull. Andy took it in his hands. Vietnamese women had such beautiful hair when they allowed it to grow long. Hard to tell the age, but the corpse was clearly that of a young woman.

Andy had long since grown accustomed to seeing dead bodies in the war zone. Once he had injected a dying Viet Cong soldier with enough morphine to hasten a less painful entry into death, then worried what he would do if one of his platoon members needed it. There were always decisions to be made in the Nam.

There would be no difficult decisions on this night. The platoon worked quickly, readying the enemy's weapons for destruction and checking the bodies for any documents that would yield information. Still in hostile territory, second squad searched the dead soldiers while the others guarded against a counterattack.

Sometimes the killing went too easily. Success in the war, measured in body counts, had third platoon up four to zip, at least on that night.

CHAPTER FOUR

IN THE PROVINCE of Tra Vinh, third platoon prepared to enter Anh Cam. Andy's stomach tightened. Dreading the encounter, he took one last drink from his canteen and strode towards the village. On the banks of a canal, a single row of thatched dwellings sat ten meters from the muddy waterway, looking peaceful and picturesque from a distance. Andy knew the Vietnamese in Anh Cam would be expecting them. Like all villagers, they hated the way the Americans intruded into their lives.

Enmity existed both ways. Second platoon had been ambushed near the village the day before. Initially greeted with strained smiles and assurances of "no VC, no VC," the platoon came under heavy fire less than a klick from the village. With two of the grunts in the lead squad dead, and three other platoon members wounded, the new lieutenant rushed forward for a better look. Wanting to prove his mettle, he became the third KIA when a quick burst from an AK-47 sent three rounds into his chest. Charlie vanished. No enemy bodies were found for the count, the measure of success in the Nam.

Angered and humiliated by the heavy losses to one of his platoons, and with no dead VC to justify it, the company commander ordered third platoon to conduct another search.

They entered the village quickly. Ordered outside of their dwellings, the villagers clumped together in small groups. Holding crying babies, fidgeting with their hands, faces drawn tight with suppressed anger and fear, the Vietnamese watched the young men rummage through their belongings. Andy knew they wouldn't find anything. This was payback for the ambush of their sister platoon.

Also fearful, and reeking of mosquito repellant and perspiration, smelling of the swamps and rice paddies, the young Americans looked for signs of Charlie. Locked and loaded, they entered each thatched hut in two-man teams, routing out any remaining Vietnamese while checking the meager contents of their household items.

Andy watched Eli. Jittery, and on his last patrol before rotating out of the Nam, the rifleman kept an eye on an older couple while Ben Moses went inside. A young child, wide eyed and terrified of the Americans, hung on to the leg of the woman. Eli, glaring at them, didn't give a shit. The child could drop dead of fear for all he cared, one less gook to worry about.

Printed in bold letters on the side of his helmet, a single question summed up Eli's feelings. *WHAT ARE THEY GOING TO DO, SEND ME TO VIETNAM?* Battalion disliked the helmet graffiti, but Eli had it right, at least about that. There was nowhere worse than an infantry platoon in the Nam to send the disgruntled young man.

Howitz didn't care about the graffiti on the helmets. He left the men alone about it and focused on the important stuff—like getting them back home. The men respected him for that.

Andy liked the lieutenant. Instructed to stay close to him while they were in the villages, Andy sensed Howitz disliked the searches as much as he did. But orders were orders, and higher command insisted on them.

There were usually some maladies for Andy to look at, which amounted to throwing a few pills down the throats of the Vietnamese in a feeble attempt at appeasing them for the intrusions into their lives. Andy hated that too. Fake medicine fooled nobody, certainly not the villagers. Following the ambush, there wouldn't be any fake goodwill today.

Ben Moses emerged from the hut shaking his head, indicating there were no larger-than-normal pots of cooked rice, or hidden weapons—signs of Viet Cong activity. Inscribed on his helmet, the word CLEVELAND stood out, a city that the black preacher's son had rarely been out of before his tour in the Nam.

They were poor boys hassling poor villagers—all in the name of freedom. Scared and often in danger, none of the draftees in the platoon were free to go home. None of them had asked for this war or understood it. Survival became the goal. Not once had Andy heard any of them discuss freedom, other than to be free from the brutal realities of the Nam.

Andy sensed the villagers wanted to be left alone to farm their rice crops. The platoon intruded on that, as did the Viet Cong. Both sides brought them fear and disruption—not freedom.

Halfway through the village, Sammy came out of a hut and stopped to take a swig from his canteen. Looking weary and already perspiring in the midmorning heat, he moved towards the next dwelling to inspect. The Professor tagged along. Two eyes drawn on the back of his helmet, complete with spectacles resembling the real ones he wore, peered out at Andy as he followed Sammy. Andy wondered what the Vietnamese must think. Maybe they were just as war weary as the guys in the platoon. Thinking too much only complicated the situation and wasted energy, more likely to get someone killed than do any good.

"It just pisses them off, you know," Sammy told Andy after one of their searches. "I mean, how many times have we found anything? All we get out of it is a bunch of angry rice farmers who hate our guts."

An inverted peace sign adorned the front of Sammy's helmet. Two fins were drawn in, making arrows out of the lines hurtling towards the ground. Andy remembered the day he drew it. Sitting on his cot, he looked up with that quizzical grin of his and said, "Sums up the war effort pretty good, Doc, don't it?"

❋ ❋ ❋

The one time they found something, Andy had Sammy aim his rifle at the head of a wounded Viet Cong soldier.

In a village near Soc Trang, an overanxious family could not hide their fear, speaking rapidly and in short choppy sentences. Even the young Americans knew the Vietnamese were nervous.

Minnesota and Eli, fingers on triggers, loaded clips in their M-16s, rushed into the hut. Hiding under a cot, the wounded VC had no time to react.

In one motion, Eli jabbed the man in the ribs with the point of his rifle, causing enough pain to temporarily immobilize him. Eli dragged the soldier, gasping for breath from the severity of the blow and clutching his side, out of the hut and into the light of day. Not through with him, Eli smacked his face with the butt of his rifle before pressing the end of the barrel against his forehead.

"LT," he shouted, "got somethin' for ya." Straining to control his anger, and just itching to hurt the Viet Cong soldier some more, Eli rocked back and forth, keeping his rifle firmly against the man's head.

"Let's get him searched," Howitz ordered. "Make sure he's not armed."

Dressed in the *ao baba* common to the VC, the so-called black pajamas hung loosely on the man's frame, muscular for a Vietnamese. Minnesota ripped the shirt open. The man winced while glaring at the troops surrounding him. A large scab on his shoulder oozed pus. Minnesota, careful not to miss anything, continued the search by checking the baggy pants that covered all but the man's bare feet. Satisfied, Minnesota nodded at the lieutenant.

"Doc, have a look at him," the LT ordered. "I'll see what headquarters wants to do. He might have some rank."

Older than most of the Viet Cong soldiers Andy had seen, the man made no attempt to feign neutrality. The intensity of his glare unsettled Andy.

Self-preservation kicked in. He called for Sammy. "If he makes one move for me, you blow his fucking brains out."

"I got it, Doc. Don't worry," Sammy said, positioning himself so if he did have to shoot him, there would be no chance of hitting Andy.

Several days old and badly infected, the scab covered much of the enemy soldier's right shoulder. Treating him in the glare of the sun, with the dust swirling around and flies landing on the wound, seemed like a bad idea. Andy shook his head.

"The man needs a hospital, Lieutenant. It'll only make it worse, tryin' to treat him under these conditions."

Normally, Andy would have administered some form of painkiller, maybe even a bit of morphine. Given the man's hostility, his eyes burning with hatred, the medic hesitated, not wanting to give him any pain relief that might embolden him.

Leaning in to have a closer look, Andy dabbed at the edges of the scab with some gauze. The wound fizzed where Andy poured part of a bottle of hydrogen peroxide over the scab.

Sammy, uncomfortable with the situation, moved closer, rifle still pointed at the Viet Cong's head. "Careful, Doc," he said, also affected by the intensity of the malevolence in the man's eyes.

Andy, embarrassed about being fearful of a wounded man, especially with a rifle pointed at his head, worked quickly. He'd never experienced that degree of hatred, so palpable, like a cornered animal knowing it will die but willing to fight to the death.

The LT, having made radio contact with higher command, returned his focus to the captured man. Accepting Andy's assessment of the VC's wound, Howitz called it off.

"All right, Doc, battalion's got a Huey on the way to take him to the 29th Evac. They'll treat him before turning him over to the ARVNs. Sammy, Eli, get him bound, feet included. Command doesn't want him jumping out of the chopper before they get a chance to interrogate him."

❋ ❋ ❋

Going into the villages reminded Andy of his Cherokee roots. A whole people had been rounded up and forced from their homes by the Union Army—the US Army that Andy had been drafted into and now searched the homes of Vietnamese farmers at gunpoint.

Andy had ancestors on the Trail of Tears. In 1838 over 16,000 people were forced into guarded stockades, then made to walk through the winter months to a new home. One-third of them perished along the way, remnants of his family arriving in northeastern Oklahoma before it became a state.

His grandfather lived with Andy's family for a time when Andy was a young boy. The elderly man, short and slender, took his hand and walked with him every afternoon. Sometimes his mother joined them. She had no Indian in her but grew fond of the older man.

Fluent in the Cherokee language, Jacob Sequoia Parks spoke it with the full-bloods they sometimes met. Straddling two worlds, he fascinated the boy. In northeastern Oklahoma, the history of the Cherokee was a part of growing up, visible in the faces of the people, and in the historical landmarks so prevalent in the region.

❊ ❊ ❊

The village search over, Howitz got on the radio and spoke with the company commander. With first platoon nearby, the captain ordered the lieutenant into one more village before digging in for the night. Military Intelligence insisted a VC battalion operated in the area. The captain wanted his company to find it.

Sammy fell in with Andy at the edge of the village, the thatched huts in a long row along a widened path packed with rounded stones sunk into ground with only the tops visible. Palm trees grew tall above the roofs. A wind blew briskly through the fronds high above the simple dwellings, the setting picturesque and idyllic if not for the poverty—and the war.

Always the war. Nobody in the platoon wanted to be there.

"LT says we gotta search one more village before we dig in for the night," Sammy said. "The captain's pushin' hard to find somethin'. If you ask me, we oughta be diggin' in for the night before then."

Overhearing, Eli, never missing an opportunity to express his disdain for being in the Nam, said, "They're not askin' ya, Sammy Do. Captain thinks he's gonna win this war. Fuck that shit. Think I give two hoots about winnin' this war? Charlie can have his shithole of a country, his leech and mosquito-infested swamps and jungles. Nothin' but pain and a world o' hurt out there for us motherfuckers, nothin' but a shitload o' misery. It's not like I'm ever comin' back."

The three walked a short way alongside one another before the need to spread out dictated more distance between them. As a parting verbal shot at being in the Nam, Eli mumbled, "I'm too short for this shit."

Before Sammy took up a position farther from Andy, he told him, "Winning is makin' it back home, Doc."

"Amen to that," said Andy.

After crossing a series of flooded rice paddies, the platoon entered jungle terrain between the villages. Staying off the main path to avoid predictability and the likelihood of an ambush and booby traps, first squad hacked a path through the thickest part of the brush and flora. Towering trees, their branches growing like tentacles with a profusion of leaves sprouting from them, provided a canopy above the jungle, blocking any direct sun. Hot and humid, the cover failed to provide any relief from the afternoon heat.

Two hundred meters in the jungle thinned by a previous napalm strike. Blackened trunks of trees, scarred from the burning onslaught, struggled to regain their vibrancy. Parts of the jungle spared from the worst of the bombing looked sick, the grasses drooping and yellowed. Leaves on the shrubs and fronds on the young palm trees tinged with brown unable to regain a healthy vitality.

The platoon moved with ease now through the damaged jungle. Andy paused for a moment to drink from his canteen and allow for

Sammy to put a few more paces between them now that they were more visible, the need to spread out instinctual at this point in his tour.

Andy realized he'd been here before. Vaguely at first, but then distinct images emerged. Memories of another bad day in the war two months ago flooded his mind, the day of the actual napalm strike—and the only time he'd clashed with Howitz.

❋ ❋ ❋

The platoon, on a break two klicks from a village likely to be VC friendly, sat in small groups, talking quietly, smoking, trying to down enough warm water from foul-tasting canteens to stay hydrated.

Andy, in his normal position near the rear of the platoon, sat on the ground and leaned his back against his pack. Black Henry rested near him, initiating a conversation. Andy mostly nodded in response to what he said, too weary from the day's humping to want to talk.

The break, turning unusually long, provided a nice respite from having to continue hacking their way through the thick jungle. Some of the guys even dozed, waiting for the LT to pass the word to saddle up and continue with the patrol.

Seconds after a plane swooped low, Andy heard an explosion, then saw a huge orange fireball form amidst an oily black smoke. Moments later a second explosion and fireball set the jungle on fire.

Startled out of their complacency, some of the guys shouted, "Get some, get some." With VC in the area, planes dropping loads of napalm on Charlie hiding in the jungle lessened the danger to the grunts on the ground.

Word passed through the platoon to look for any stragglers fleeing the burning inferno. Men readied their weapons and found cover while waiting for further orders from the lieutenant. Nothing happened.

Guys kept their rifles ready, but some lit cigarettes and fidgeted with their gear. More time passed.

Finally, word came down the line. "LT wants the Doc up front, ASAP."

Andy grabbed his aid bag and hurried past the platoon members in front of him in the formation. As he came closer to where the giant fireballs erupted, he could smell gasoline mixed in the stench of the burning jungle, an ugly black smoke billowing into the air.

At the edge of the jungle six small bodies were laid out in a row. Five of the children were already dead, their torsos a hideous mess from the napalm. Huge burn blisters formed on their exposed legs. Parts of their clothing had burned into their flesh. Their faces, contorted and disfigured in death, made it impossible to reveal their genders.

At the end of the row a girl of about nine clung to life, struggling to breathe. Her lungs, probably seared from the napalm, could not get enough oxygen.

Andy shook his head. There was nothing he could do but relieve her pain. He took a tube of morphine from his aid bag and injected it in the girl's thigh. Howitz looked away.

"This little girl's not gonna make it," Andy said. "But just in case I'm wrong, Lieutenant, get a medevac in here right away."

"Dust-off's on the way, Doc. Clearance for the airstrike came down from headquarters."

Something snapped in him over these dead kids.

"These children are hardcore VC?" Andy shouted. "Fuck headquarters! Fuck this war!"

"Air strikes have saved our asses, Doc. You know that as well as anybody."

"Yes sir," Andy said with a tinge of sarcasm.

The lieutenant let Andy's comments linger without responding. Andy knew the LT must be hurting, too. But he had called in the air strikes, and just like that the jungle was on fire and six kids were dead. Andy knew he was just trying to get the young men under his command back home alive but wasn't ready to give him a pass on these kids.

Maybe their parents, fearing the Americans would be searching their village soon, sent them into the jungle to hide before the platoon hassled them in their never-ending search for Charlie.

Andy kneeled beside the little girl. Conflicted, he wondered if he should give her a lethal dose of morphine to end her suffering. Deciding not to, he struggled to make sense of the strong emotions raging in his head. The futility of the war pressed in on him. His hands shook when he went to touch the little girl's face.

Angry and frustrated at his inability to put life back into the dead bodies the war kept taking, no medical options remained. Realizing his impotency for restoring life, he was unwilling to end one by giving the girl enough morphine to kill her. He experienced a numbing sense of hopelessness over his choices.

Andy looked at the dead children again. On parts of their bodies where the napalm burned deep, a tar-like residue remained. In an instant the jungle had been set on fire. Eternity would not restore all that was lost.

Napalm, a jelled gasoline dropped at low altitudes, detonating on impact with the ground, created massive fireballs that sucked all the oxygen out of the air. Carbon monoxide poisoning occurred rapidly. The children were probably asphyxiated before their burning flesh killed them. Andy had seen it before.

Headquarters advised there were likely VC in the target zone set up and waiting for them. Walking into a Viet Cong ambush was deadly, guaranteeing casualties and likely dead platoon members. The only bodies found that day were those of the children.

Later, tucked into their foxhole for the night, Sammy, sensing his friend's distress, asked him what had happened.

Quiet for a long time, Andy finally told Sammy about the dead kids, and the little girl that he put on a dust-off. "The kind of thing that will haunt us for the rest of our lives," he said.

Sammy, not knowing what to say, asked, "S'pose headquarters'll add those kids to the body count?" Realizing the answer before he'd finished asking the question, he blurted out, "Fuck headquarters! Fuck this war!"

CHAPTER FIVE

WAITING FOR A Huey to pluck Eli out of the war, several platoon members stood near the edge of an LZ. Some of the men smoked and fidgeted, quietly envious that it was Eli about to leave the Nam. Andy stood next to Sammy. Ever gracious, Sammy shook Eli's hand and congratulated him on surviving his tour. The Professor and Black Henry waited their turn to say goodbye.

Dirty from another night in a foxhole, the Professor wiped his glasses with a camouflaged cloth he kept tied around his neck. Andy supplied the platoon with the green cotton material. Tightly packed in tiny cardboard boxes marked as field dressings, they served a more useful purpose as bandanas. It kept the perspiration out of the men's eyes during the heat of the day.

Eli never wavered in his hatred of the war, or anything Vietnamese. Andy wondered if his fierceness helped him survive, or if blind luck made the difference. Looking at the young grunt as the sound of the rotors from the approaching Huey grew louder, Andy wished him well. Eli's last days in the war ended as they had begun—on a patrol deep in the Delta.

Andy noticed the growth of a blondish stubble protruding through the accumulated grime of a last patrol as Eli waited for the helicopter. Looking frail, the final efforts to survive his tour had diminished him physically. His eyes remained wary of any last-minute catastrophe.

True to his personality, he made sure the LT and everyone else in the platoon knew his rotation day out of the Nam. In a parting shot, more to the war than his fellow platoon members, he told the assembled group as he boarded his helicopter, "So long, motherfuckers. It's been a nice war."

Andy knew otherwise. Sarcasm and bitterness, the results of an infected soul, oozed out of Eli as pus does from a festering wound. The medic knew Eli had not always been so cynical. He'd been in the shit too long. Andy stood with the others watching as the helicopter revved its engine to create enough lift for the bird to ascend and take Eli into the sky.

※ ※ ※

Arriving in country, Eli appeared as normal as anybody else. Scared and unsure of himself, he'd been assigned to Tut's squad. Originally, the squad leader's nickname had been King Tut, but by the time Eli arrived, it had been shortened and nobody remembered his real name.

Tut never wanted to be a squad leader. Only through attrition did he assume the position, reluctantly. Tut never forced any of the others to walk point. Shorthanded, and with only new guys, he assumed that responsibility. It became his habit. But with a week left on his tour, Tut got the jitters. Scheduled to be the lead squad the following day, he gathered the men around his foxhole and leveled with them.

"I been walkin' point every time for our squad. I only got six days left in country, and I got a bad feelin' about this one. Can't do it anymore."

The men nodded. They understood. Up front with the guys, and him being so short, the squad decided to draw straws to see who walked point. Eli had participated in the draw but gotten a long straw.

A kid from Massachusetts ended up drawing short. He'd been in the Nam a few months, but never walked point. Scared, but knowing he had to do it, he led the patrol the next day.

The kid got off easy to start with. The morning included the search of a village. In the afternoon, the platoon entered terrain thick with brush and scrub flora. When the platoon came to a bamboo grove, the point man entered. He disappeared. Tut's bad feeling emerged. The platoon searched for two hours before finding the kid tortured and dead.

Charlie wasn't through. He'd had enough time to kill the kid in a cruel and painful way, then booby-trap the body. Tut had seen that before but didn't have time to warn the two squad members who found him. Tut heard a grenade explode when they cut the point man loose from the trunk of a tree where Charlie had tied and tortured him. It killed one of the rescuers and wounded the other. Tut blamed himself.

The medevac landed and took three of his squad members—two to the morgue and one to the evacuation hospital. Tut sat staring straight ahead, blinking occasionally, but not seeing anything. His hand held a cigarette that he kept tapping against the barrel of his rifle before lighting it. Sometimes it would shred from the tapping before being lit. Tut would unconsciously reach for another and continue the tapping.

Eli, new in the Nam and seeking guidance and reassurance, approached his squad leader. Tut had nothing more to give. Whatever remained of Tut was trapped deep inside, or tapped out like his mashed cigarettes. He felt hollow; only the shell of his former self remained. Sometime during the night, he realized he might be able to leave Vietnam, but the Nam was never going to leave him.

❉ ❉ ❉

Andy was with the platoon the second time Eli got stranded out on an LP. Within sight of the Seven Mountains during the day, every time the platoon got near them, they took casualties. The end of the infamous Ho Chi Minh Trail, Charlie dug in and fortified beneath them. Whenever they wanted to, the VC came out of those mountains like ants leaving their nest.

Surrounded, and without air or artillery support, the platoon found itself in serious trouble. Howitz, expecting the worst, had the foresight to insist they pack extra claymores with their gear. The platoon set every one of them. With 700 pea-sized steel balls in each, it saved them from being overrun.

Green tracers from the enemy's AK-47s punctured the dark of night, while their own red ones answered back. The colors of war. *Who decides the color of a tracer?* Andy wondered. *Is it a form of Psy Ops, too? Are there advantages to one color over another? Or does somebody just like the color green, or red?*

Andy thought he would die that night. They had not even been able to dig in properly. The water table too shallow, by the one-foot mark, pools of it formed and filled their foxholes. The guys, desperate to drain them, tried everything.

During lulls in the battle, Charlie conducted his own version of psy ops. The US Army had dropped millions of *chieu hoi* leaflets in the Delta. Andy had seen a couple of the pamphlets. *Chieu hoi,* meaning "open arms" in English, offered amnesty and a reward for information after coming over to the South Vietnamese side. Now, in the dark, Viet Cong soldiers eerily chanted their own version of open arms: "*Chieu hoi,* GI, *Chieu hoi!* Tonight, GI die! *Chieu hoi!*"

Andy heard Charlie taunting the platoon. Some soldiers on both sides were cruel; the Vietnam War brought that out in men. The eerie threats would have bothered him, but there were casualties to treat. The lulls in the firefight provided opportunities to get to guys without getting shot. A dead medic was useless to his platoon.

With all the dying, Andy became a decent medic. Certain of his death, his hands stopped shaking. Running towards the shouts for help and splashing into the partial cover of saturated foxholes, Andy's psyche transformed into a deeper, mysterious zone. The uninitiated might attribute it to the adrenaline surging through his system. Andy knew it to be more than that. He could not fully comprehend or explain how he changed that night.

With the light of dawn, Andy continued tending to the casualties in his care. Finally, gunships were available, and a dust-off. As quickly as Charlie had emerged from the mountains, he retreated into them. Not liking to leave his dead any more than the Americans, every Viet Cong soldier packed one wounded or dead man back into the mountains. Charlie could not take all his corpses with him.

Eli emerged bloody but alive. He had spent the night on a two-man listening post a hundred meters beyond their perimeter. Nobody ever knew how he survived. Not wanting to be mistaken for an enemy soldier in the dark, he waited until dawn to emerge from hiding. Caked in dried blood from the fight, he walked back to their perimeter.

"Don't shoot," he yelled. "It's Eli. Don't shoot." Those were the final words he spoke that day.

"Eli?" one of the grunts posted as a guard asked. There were always guards posted, and they were jittery after a night the platoon thought it would be overrun.

"Fuck, man," the grunt muttered. "You're lucky I didn't shoot you. How'd you survive last night, man? We didn't expect to see you alive."

Andy, seeing Eli covered in blood and expecting him to be wounded, came over and had him sit near the casualties waiting for the medevac. "You hurt anywhere, Eli?" There'd been so many bullets flying through the air that night, it made no sense that any of them were alive. So how could Eli possibly emerge unscathed when he'd been 100 meters beyond their perimeter? Like an apparition, he'd appeared, the second time he'd survived an LP that had been overrun. Legends are born of such experiences.

The medic looked for wounds underneath the blood and mud on Eli's fatigues. Not meeting Andy's gaze, Eli continued to stare past his shoulder. Not finding any wounds on Eli, Andy turned his attention to his casualties. Anxious for the medevac to arrive so they could be treated at the evacuation hospital, he moved among them, making sure that shock had not set in and that the bleeding had stopped.

Four bodies lay wrapped in ponchos. Second squad, or what was left of it, weary and wary, looked for a fifth beyond their perimeter. Eli's dead partner on the listening post needed to be retrieved.

His platoon decimated, Howitz convinced headquarters to send some slicks and ferry the survivors back to Dong Tam. Eli never said a word to any of them. Nobody was in the mood for talking. An eerie quiet settled over them, including Andy. He only wanted to get back to the relative safety of Dong Tam and collect his thoughts, set his emotions in order. Nothing but a mud hole during the monsoons, Dong Tam afforded the only safety he could expect for now.

Boarding the Huey for the ride back to Dong Tam, Andy watched as the mountains faded from view. They never would from his mind. His jungle fatigues stained with the blood of several platoon members, Andy noticed how peaceful and pastoral the Delta looked from the air. As a medic, his baptism was not only of fire, but of blood.

Thirteen platoon members remained physically unscathed after their foray near the mountains. How it affected their minds, who could say? Standing down in Dong Tam, Howitz came and spoke with each member of the platoon privately. The twenty-three-year-old lieutenant thanked them for how they had held together that night, told them it saved them from being overrun. He asked how they were. Andy, along with the rest of the platoon, received a bronze star for his actions that night. The five dead men received theirs posthumously along with their purple hearts.

CHAPTER SIX

A MIST HOVERING over the rice field restricted visibility and added an eerie feel to the early morning quiet. Andy had been awake since pulling night guard duty. Unable to sleep after his shift, the medic sat with his field poncho wrapped around him, trying to ward off the damp chill. He strained to see in the shrouded light before dawn, while his mind sought clarity through the fog of his fatigue. Just a few weeks separated him from his rotation date out of the Nam.

Tired before the day even began, Andy reached into his pack and opened a can of C-rations, not bothering to look at the writing listing the contents. Food in the tins provided nourishment for survival, the choices mundane and uninteresting. Andy ate them cold, always too busy or tired to bother heating them. Most of the guys ignited a small piece of the putty-like C-4 explosive to warm the drab meals, quicker than the heat tabs provided with the rations. Sammy dozed fitfully beside him, curled into a partial fetal position beneath his poncho, his body leaning against the wall of the foxhole.

Andy sensed some of the platoon stirring, but with sound and light discipline in effect, only a gentle rustling of the leaves in the trees behind him broke the predawn quiet. Shrieks and cries from jungle birds punctured the nocturnal silence just as the first rays from the sun began penetrating through the layers of mist.

Yardly, the platoon's Montagnard Tiger Scout, approached Andy's foxhole. The brown-skinned boy soldier looked younger than his sixteen years. Andy scarcely noticed anymore. The war had seeped so deeply into his being that the absurd reality of a boy facing the awful and heartrending effects of combat was nothing unusual. The destruction of lives normal, surviving unscathed became a crippling fantasy the young medic avoided dreaming about, fearing it would render him soft and powerless to face the last weeks of his tour. Age had no meaning to psyches wizened by obscene brutalities so whimsically spewed out among the war's combatants.

"Come, come, *bac si*. Must come." The Montagnard, using the Vietnamese word for doctor, motioned with his hands to hurry. Andy set down his can of C-rations, grabbed his aid bag, and followed the boy. The kid led Andy to the foxhole he shared with the Professor.

Rescued by third platoon after a bloody fight in the Seven Mountains, the boy showed his gratitude with a fierce loyalty, particularly to the Professor. Called "Yardly" by the platoon, a name he could not pronounce, the Montagnard knew enough English and Vietnamese to act as a scout and interpreter for the Americans. During the battle, the Professor helped Yardly drag his badly wounded cousin to safety behind a boulder at the base of the seventh mountain, but only to die before a medevac arrived to ferry him to a hospital.

Lt. Howitz refused to make the battle a slaughter for the platoon by advancing stupidly on fortified Viet Cong positions strategically tiered on the mountain. If B-52 strikes and Cobra gunships could not dislodge Charlie, suicidal assaults by third platoon were not going to. As soon as one air strike ended, Viet Cong machine guns fired on advancing troops. Upset with stupid military tactics, Howitz provided what cover he could for the Montagnard forces assaulting the mountain. Helpless to prevent the slaughter, platoon members helped gather the indigenous troops' dead and wounded.

Andy, his aid bag depleted with the number of casualties, worked quickly. He improvised by ripping fatigue shirts into dressing-sized strips. Ignoring minor wounds, he treated a Montagnard soldier whose hands, covered in blood, held his intestines in place as he looked wildly at Andy. The medic forcibly removed the soldier's hands while placing a shirt over his abdomen, tying it in place with the sleeves. A precious minute wasted, Andy knew he should not spend time on hopeless cases. He moved to a soldier bleeding from a gunshot wound in his thigh, a large chunk of flesh hanging by a shred of skin and tissue where the bullet exited.

Yardly's cousin, another of the dying Montagnards, would join the line of dead soldiers laid out in a clearing after the battle. The Professor sat with the boy while air strikes pounded the mountains, sending VC deep into their subterranean complexes to nurse their wounds and regroup for another battle. Yardly and the Professor crouched behind a boulder with the dead cousin. Their bond initiated during the intensity of the fight, Yardly only left the Professor's side when duties required a parting.

This is what the platoon learned of the Montagnard's story.

❊ ❊ ❊

Yardly began his life as a soldier at the age of fifteen. The Montagnard men of Dak Son, organized into a militia to fight the Viet Cong, returned from his first mission to find their village obliterated. Piles of smoldering ash were all that remained of their dwellings, built on pilings above the ground in the Montagnard way. Charred bodies, grotesque and unrecognizable, were left bloating in the heat. Near the remains of a hut that could have been Yardly's, a woman lay on her back, all the hair burnt off her body. Her face, too charred to identify, concealed her gender. Her breasts, burnt but intact and pointing skyward, did not. Legs bent at the knees and obscenely spread open showed her female part fused from the heat.

There were only women and children in the village, and the aged too feeble to fight. No match for two Viet Cong battalions angry that Dak Son sided with the Americans, the grisly lesson given with automatic weapons and flamethrowers burning alive anyone hiding in their huts. Two hundred and fifty-two bullet-riddled and charred bodies lay rotting. The burning, with hand-held flamethrowers, a cruel and twisted irony—napalm Viet Cong style.

Yardly had vowed revenge at seeing the corpse that might be his mother. Killing VC became his life's purpose. Only an uncle and a cousin remained of his family, fighters now, and like Yardly fierce in their resolve to avenge the massacre at Dak Son.

Yardly's uncle Glun, seeking relief from his despair, killed Viet Cong with a ferocity matching his grief. Seeing a grenade land at his feet, Glun grabbed it, attempting to throw it back at the enemy. It exploded in his hand. Yardly watched his uncle's torso disintegrate into a pulpy mass of blood and tissue, and the explosion render every facial feature unrecognizable. Cousin Jum took a round from an AK-47 in the chest. Missing the heart, passing through the lungs, the bullet left the boy drowning in his own blood. Yardly had watched the last of his family perish.

With hatred begetting hatred at the base of the seventh mountain, the Professor sat with the Montagnard after calling for Andy to treat his cousin's wounds. He would add the body to the memory pile of dead ones, feeling impotent in the pursuit of life while death became more normal than living.

※ ※ ※

At his foxhole, Andy found the Professor curled into a ball and shivering beneath two poncho liners. Andy hopped in beside him and sat him upright against the earthen wall. Damp from his own perspiration and a night in the mist, Andy removed the Professor's dirty glasses and handed them to Yardly. Andy felt his forehead. The gesture provided comfort more than an attempt at diagnosis. The

Professor needed a clean bed and some decent nutrition, some rest. There were maladies galore to choose from—infections, malaria, dysentery, dehydration—none of them curable on a patrol in the Delta.

"Doc?" The Professor squinted at Andy through unfocused eyes. "Ya got anything for this?"

"Let's see what your fever is," said Andy.

The guys were ever hopeful Andy could fix their ailments with a pill, an ointment, or mysterious concoction.

Andy stuck a thermometer under the shivering Professor's tongue. Yardly looked on with concern. The kid had experienced intense combat by the age of fifteen but looked more distressed about the Professor's condition than in the aftermath of any firefight he'd experienced with the platoon.

With the Professor's temperature at over 103 degrees, Andy would have to speak with Howitz. The grunt could not continue. Andy wiped his face and popped three aspirin into the Professor's mouth. He then peeled away the ponchos and opened the Professor's shirt, finding his chest a mess of boils, infected scratches, and pimple-like bumps filled with pus. The Professor shivered uncontrollably.

Andy attached a bag of saline solution to a sterile pack of tubing. He disliked starting IVs in unsanitary field conditions, but the Professor would need to begin replacing fluids. Yardly helped steady the Professor's arm while Andy inserted the intravenous needle. Andy made sure the saline solution flowed into the vein and taped it securely in place. Before leaving to find the lieutenant, he looked at the Professor, frail and vulnerable. Andy remembered the Professor's arrival in the Nam, so afraid his teeth chattered.

❋ ❋ ❋

The Professor was fortunate to be assigned to White Henry's squad; the experienced grunt took the new, frightened, bespectacled kid aside and told him a few things about surviving his tour.

"We're gonna look after you as best we can," White Henry had begun. "But we need every man to function out beyond the wire. Can't do it without your help, neither."

The Professor nodded, trying to steady himself.

"Let me see your rifle," White Henry said. The squad leader took it in his large and steady hands.

"First off, you need to know this rifle, how to keep it clean in the muck out there. Take it apart and reassemble it in the dark when you need to. And this here," he said, tapping a finger on the barrel. "Make Charlie eat the shit that comes outta here if he messes with you or the platoon. Think you can do that?" he asked.

The Professor nodded some more. Just to make sure, White Henry added, "Third platoon needs every man to be functioning, lookin' out for one another. No weak links in the chain. That's how we try an' get everybody back home again. Understand?"

Without waiting for a response, White Henry handed the Professor his rifle. "Just remember we gotta stick together out there. Charlie don't care. He'd like to see ya go home in one o' those aluminum boxes. All we got is each other. Welcome to third platoon."

Everybody arrived in the Nam afraid. The Professor just had more trouble covering it up. Andy sympathized with the new grunt but didn't know how to make his entry into the platoon more manageable. Each man had to find his own way of facing the possibility of dying. Mind-numbing fatigue helped with the transition. And after the first combat, when it was fully understood that Charlie wanted to kill you, the war began to seep into a grunt's being. The Professor did not have long to wait.

❊ ❊ ❊

Forays into the Ca Mau peninsula were wet, miserable and dangerous. Charlie controlled most of the region and had many places to hide when he wanted to avoid contact or set an ambush.

White Henry had instructed the Professor to fall in behind him on the patrol, his terror so palpable the platoon could feel it. Burdened with gear, the Professor's fear propelled him forward. Ankle deep in water, the platoon marched through a marshy area where the reedy grasses grew chest high. Their sharp edges sliced into hands and arms exposed where sleeves were cut off or rolled up in the heat.

Andy felt exposed in the grassy marsh. It would neither conceal them nor stop a bullet from an enemy AK. Leeches thrived and Andy watched the Professor pick one off his arm. Unnoticed by the Professor, a round-headed snake glided behind him in the shallow water. Andy only caught a glimpse as it slithered through the reeds.

The venoms in some of Vietnam's snakes were so poisonous that the platoon killed any they saw. With one hundred and forty species, only thirty were deadly. Andy knew that most of the round-headed snakes were harmless but did not know many of the species by name. Snakes were just another of the many hazards of the Nam. This one glided effortlessly through the reeds.

By midmorning the heat reached ninety degrees as the platoon entered terrain more swamp-like with dense brush growing on the higher patches of ground. Howitz ordered a break once the men were half a klick beyond the reeds.

Andy checked on the Professor, now miserable enough to be struggling with each step. Breathing heavily, he sat with his back against his pack, looking for any remaining leeches while he tried to catch his breath.

"How you doing?" Andy asked. "Better take a couple of these," he said, handing the Professor some salt tablets. "You got plenty of water? Don't let yourself get dehydrated."

The Professor just nodded and didn't answer, either not wanting to waste any energy talking or not knowing what to say.

At the point position, Eli halted and took cover. About to take a drink from his canteen, he abruptly crouched lower. He signaled for the platoon to be quiet by tapping his lips with two fingers. The men passed the signal down the formation.

Howitz motioned for White Henry to come forward and check with him. After meeting with the LT, White Henry left to check on Eli, taking Arsenal with his M-60 machine gun and his assistant gunner with him.

"What is it, Doc?" the Professor had asked quietly, sensing the escalating tension in the platoon. Andy tapped his lips and shook his head, indicating the Professor should not speak. The slightest sounds of twenty men could magnify the presence of the platoon to the Viet Cong. Andy's stomach tightened., but he maintained a calm exterior for the Professor's benefit. Everybody needed to be functioning. The medic motioned for him to have his rifle ready. As a precaution, Andy undid the straps fastening his aid bag to the frame of his pack.

Andy could see Howitz take the headset from the RTO and speak into it. The lieutenant motioned for the platoon to move forward and take cover. The experienced guys knew Eli spotted something on point. The new grunts, tense and unsure, copied their actions.

The platoon edged forward to Eli's position and spread out. The potent odor of a familiar sauce the Vietnamese used to flavor their rice permeated the air.

Andy watched the Professor take up a position a few meters from him, making sure he had cover and a clear line of fire. The Professor had looked at Andy for reassurance. The medic nodded back, focused now, calm yet hyper alert, readying himself for whatever happened.

The Viet Cong near, Andy had no idea if the enemy knew of the platoon's presence, nor how large a unit was cooking lunch on the other side of the brush.

They waited. Andy knew Howitz had probably requested air support. Deep in the Ca Mau Peninsula, the platoon was vulnerable without it.

Andy desperately hoped for the Cobra gunships to arrive with their lethal arsenal to spare third platoon a bloody fight on their own. Their firepower resided in the automatic weapons of twenty guys. Every grunt packed an extra belt of ammo for the M-60s, the platoon's most important weapons—the extra weight a nuisance until needed in a fight.

Andy listened for the sounds of an approaching helicopter. Too faint at first to be sure, then distinctive in the way the rotor blades chopped at the air, creating sound but not yet visible. The enemy would hear them too, interrupting lunch and creating havoc for the VC. Swooping in above the treetops, the first ship fired a volley of rockets, each leaving a vaporized trail visible from Andy's position on the ground. The Cobra's Gatling guns simultaneously fired on the Viet Cong unit on the other side of the tree line.

Andy had his aid bag at his side and his M-16 on automatic, not knowing which he would need first. The Professor had looked at Andy for guidance, but the medic only nodded in the direction of the gunships. Traveling in two-man teams, the Cobras possessed enough firepower to shred the jungle of life where they aimed their arsenal of rockets, grenades and the large-caliber rounds from their Gatling guns firing 4,000 bullets per minute.

The first Viet Cong soldier Andy saw emerged from the trees fifty meters from his position, close enough to see the terror on his face in fleeing the firepower of the gunships. Several rounds from the platoon penetrated his chest.

Hoping to gain speed in fleeing the ravaging gunships by running alongside the tree line, more enemy soldiers broke free of the dense thicket. Third platoon put dozens of rounds of small arms fire into their bodies.

Viet Cong commanders, desperate to establish a defensive position to return fire, organized a squad-sized group of soldiers just inside the tree line. It would be the only resistance third platoon encountered that day. While the Cobra gunships circled in the air readying for a second deadly pass on the VC positions, the enemy's AK-47s fired at third platoon. The firefight ended when one of the gunships unleashed its Gatling guns on the VC engaged with the platoon. The trees, no protection from the firepower of a Cobra, were shredded along with the Viet Cong soldiers.

Andy listened for a call that he was needed. *Nothing.* No more VC emerged from the tree line. The Cobras continued to fire on Viet Cong soldiers desperately fleeing the death machines raining fire on them from the sky. Unable to hide or outrun 4,000 bullets per minute, the slaughter continued beyond Andy's view. He waited with the rest of the platoon. Not quite believing there were no casualties on their side, he took his aid bag and went to make sure. Familiar faces, strained with tension, nodded as he passed, the stress of combat etched on unshaven faces grimy with sweat and Delta muck. Andy nodded back.

Howitz ordered the platoon towards the tree line. Locked and loaded, they approached the first of the bodies lying still and silent, their death an inevitable conclusion in a showdown with the gunships. Instinctively, Andy looked for enemy survivors. Seven bodies lay just inside the trees, which were unable to protect them from the Americans' overwhelming firepower.

Part of the jungle died with that kind of destruction. Smaller trees, their broken trunks shattered, lay toppled over the Viet Cong bodies. Andy knew from the shredded corpses there were no survivors.

A meadow came into view on the other side of the trees. Dozens of bodies lay twisted into grotesque postures, death grimaces on some of the faces. Andy moved quickly through the clearing with the platoon, checking for signs of life while the others made sure there were no survivors capable of continuing the fight.

"Hey, Doc," Sammy shouted, "this one's still alive." Removing the weapons from the wounded soldier, he waited for Andy to arrive. "Looks like a whole fuckin' company got wasted, Doc," he said before moving on to check more bodies in the clearing.

Andy kneeled on the ground next to the dying soldier. Barely conscious, the wounded man's focus internal, the struggle to breathe consumed his remaining strength. Blood spewed out of his mouth with each short and desperate breath, spraying Andy's face. One round had penetrated his chest, and another had shattered his pelvis. Andy knew the quickest way to end his suffering would be to put a bullet into his head. Instead, he took a tube of morphine and injected it into the man's arm. Hoping to ease the soldier's last moments into death, he worried one of his guys might need it before he could replenish his aid bag.

Andy looked up for a moment at the carnage lying before him— at least fifty bodies. He was sickened by all the dead before him but elated at having survived.

Andy noticed the Professor staring at him a few yards away. Their eyes locked before the newest grunt continued with the search of the meadow. Andy sensed the Professor would be okay now. It was always good for a new guy to get his first taste of combat, get shot at and transition into the reality of the war.

Andy's thoughts were interrupted by Howitz calling for him to have a look at another enemy soldier who had somehow survived the firepower of the gunships. Andy left one dying Viet Cong soldier to go and tend to another.

Numbed and overwhelmed by the devastation before him, Andy couldn't help thinking how the killing and wounding was so much easier than putting bodies back together after the frenzied violence of combat. But as Black Henry had commented once, "Best not do too much thinkin' in de Nam. Get yerself wasted dat way. Lotta time fer thinkin' afta de war."

CHAPTER SEVEN

ANDY KNELT BY the Professor at the edge of the LZ waiting for a helicopter. Eleven months into his tour, Andy had lost track of how many medevacs he'd waited for to rescue young grunts damaged by a war not of their making.

Yardly, ever faithful to the Professor, helped Andy tend to their sick platoon member. Sammy and Black Henry stood nearby ready to help get the Professor on the approaching medevac that would lift him out of the jungle and take him to a field hospital. As the helicopter landed, Andy squinted from the hot wind churning up dust from the Huey's rotor blades. Out of the corner of his eye he saw the pant legs of the grunts' bulky jungle fatigues flapping against their legs.

Andy handed the improvised intravenous pole to Black Henry and told him to keep it above the Professor's head. Yardly and Sammy lifted the sick man to his feet, and he hobbled towards the medevac. The dust-off medic, a tall, thin kid with greyish blue eyes, crouched at the side door waiting for his patient. His manner friendly, his eyes expressed weariness with the war. His faded and tattered jungle fatigues hanging on his thin frame suggested he'd been in the Nam a while.

"Hey, Doc," he greeted Andy. "What you got for us?"

"High fever, unknown origin," Andy answered. The noise from the rotor blades made it difficult to communicate. "How far to the evac hospital?"

"Twenty minutes out," he answered.

Andy hopped into the helicopter and helped the other medic pull the Professor into the Huey and took the bag of saline solution from Black Henry.

"We got him, Doc," the dust-off medic said, positioning the Professor on a field stretcher.

"Take good care of our guy," Andy said, before hopping back out of the helicopter. He recognized the medic from a previous medevac but couldn't remember where.

"No worries," he said. "We'll have him in the hospital soon."

Andy retreated to the edge of the LZ and watched the chopper lift off. He felt some relief the Professor was out of the field and would probably be fine, but an empty feeling also overcame him as the dust-off disappeared in the sky. Often Andy would never see the wounded soldier again, and he rarely knew anything about their condition until returning to Dong Tam. The Professor, halfway through his tour, would likely be back with the platoon.

Feeling alone as the medevac disappeared into the morning mist of the Delta sky, Andy reflected again on the Professor's first combat.

※ ※ ※

The platoon called it the "Slaughter in the Ca Mau." A team of Cobra gunships turned a vulnerable situation for the platoon into the destruction of a company of Viet Cong. All of the ugly nicknames of the heavily armed helicopters—Spooky, Death Angel, Puff the Magic Dragon—affirmed in the one-sided battle. Andy had watched the killing machines with the conflicting emotions of relief and horror. Seventy-seven VC bodies were found on the battlefield. Several more blood trails vanished in the swampy terrain beyond the clearing where most of the killing occurred.

Andy, near the Professor in the formation, had watched the new grunt adjust to his first combat in the Nam, and his first dead bodies. While tending to three dying Viet Cong soldiers, he watched the Professor vomit at the edge of the clearing. Adrenaline surged through their bodies, temporarily alleviating the fatigue.

All of the guys Andy felt closest to had been at the battle. Eli, on point for the day, picked up the scent of Viet Cong preparing rice for a midday meal. Beyond Andy's vantage point, a VC sentry, distracted by his hunger, got careless. White Henry and Arsenal had taken aim at the enemy while Eli circled behind and stabbed him with his knife, the slaughter able to proceed because of the silent killing of the sentry.

Sammy and Black Henry moved through the bodies in the clearing and kept an eye on Andy while he tended to three dying Viet Cong soldiers. The killing so easy, it had hardly seemed real anymore. The bodies became numbers for higher command. With the danger receding, Andy's adrenaline surge dissipated, and fatigue returned. With it came the emotional numbness as he measured the slaughter.

Andy looked at the sky where the helicopter carrying the Professor had disappeared. Aware of his emptiness, but not conceptualizing its cause, he turned and walked slowly towards the platoon's nighttime perimeter. Howitz disliked being visible and predictable two hours after daylight. He'd already organized for the day's patrol with the squad leaders and was anxious to get going. Andy strapped his aid bag to the frame of his pack and fell in with Sammy in the formation as the platoon moved out single file, each man allowing a few yards' distance between them.

By midmorning the platoon had traversed the swampy terrain near the edge of the rice paddies and entered a banana grove growing naturally on slightly higher ground. Overlooking a slow-moving stream below it, Howitz halted the platoon for a break. The early morning chill dissipated with the rising sun in the sky; Andy's perspiration darkened his fatigues. Leaning against the trunk of a banana tree, he took a drink from his canteen. Sammy walked a few steps towards him and eased the weight of his pack off his shoulders before sitting near the medic.

"Look at that poor kid," Sammy said, nodding towards Yardly, sitting by himself and looking distressed.

"He's worried about the Professor," Andy said.

"What's he even doing out here?" Sammy asked.

"His village was destroyed, wiped out. Where's he gonna go?"

"So, he finds a home with an American infantry unit? The kid's only sixteen. I gotta tell you, Doc, this war has some crazy shit."

Andy only nodded, not wanting to add anything to the discussion.

"Come to think of it," continued Sammy, "what're any of us doing out here?" He reached for his canteen and unscrewed the lid. Before taking a drink, he asked, "The Professor gonna be okay?"

"Eventually, if the war doesn't kill him," Andy said. "He's quite a mess."

Neither of them spoke for a while, and Andy remembered them sitting in White Henry's hooch a couple of months earlier in Dong Tam sipping on warm cans of beer.

❊ ❊ ❊

Black Henry was there, and Sammy. The Professor, healthier then, was at ease and an accepted member of the platoon, and like the rest of them glad to be out of the field on a break at their base camp.

Late in that evening, with everyone relaxed and having drank enough of the warm beer to have a buzz, Charlie began lobbing mortars on Dong Tam. Not close at first, the four of them had continued drinking and enjoying the break. As the mortars started landing closer, nobody wanted to be the first to suggest heading to the sand-bagged protection of the bunkers. Perturbed their rare evening of relaxation was being interrupted by Charlie, they sat in

White Henry's hooch longer than was prudent.

Finally, White Henry had turned to the Professor and asked, "What do you think we should do?"

"Me?" the Professor questioned. "I guess we better get our butts in the bunker, but kick Charlie's ass the next time we see him."

White Henry nodded his approval. Sammy had grabbed the last of the warm beers on the way to the bunker. Dank and dark inside, they could hear a firefight erupting beyond the perimeter, where first platoon was on night ambush.

"Dat be a first," muttered Black Henry. "Dose muddahfuckers disruptin' Charlie."

About the time the warm beers were finished, the mortars ended. The war having intruded on a night in base camp, the four had wandered back to their hooches too tired for anything but sleep.

❋ ❋ ❋

Andy's thoughts were interrupted by the LT giving the orders to saddle up and get moving again. He took a last gulp from his canteen and prepared to move out. Sammy winked and smiled.

"Feel better?" he joked, extending a hand to help his medic get to his feet. Andy wondered what it would take to get him down.

"We better check on Yardly," Andy said, "see how he's doin'. I'm so used to him being with us I forget how young he is."

"Can do, Doc," Sammy said, shouldering his gear. "He can double up with us tonight in our foxhole. He ain't very big." Still smiling, he moved out to take his place in the formation.

By afternoon, the platoon walked across some rice paddies on narrow mud dikes and found itself at the edge of more jungle. Howitz, wanting to go farther before ending the day's patrol, had the platoon enter the densely growing terrain at the edge of the last rice paddy.

With vegetation so thick, the platoon's progress slowed as they hacked and slashed their way through parts of the jungle. After 200 meters the growth thinned, and they skirted several ponds of standing water where clouds of mosquitoes swirled around their heads. Andy, sweating profusely, began to cramp from a lack of salt. Swallowing two saline tablets with a drink of warm water from his canteen had him slightly nauseous. Two hours of humping remained before the platoon would set up camp for the night.

The distinctive burst from an AK-47 on the formation's right flank interrupted Andy's physical misery. He dove for cover and crawled to a fallen log and listened. One of the platoon's M-60 machine guns returned fire along with bursts from several M-16s.

Sammy crawled towards Andy and hollered, "I think it's only a squad of VC, Doc. I'm taking Yardly and Black Henry with me and am going to see if we can't outflank them."

Sammy moved out, and Andy took his aid bag and rifle and prepared to move towards the firefight. On his way, he heard someone shout, "Medic! We need the Doc up front, pronto."

Andy crouched low and ran towards the sound of the voice calling him. Thirty meters from his position he dove to the ground and crawled the last distance to Pinto, the platoon's RTO, writhing in pain, and bleeding from two gunshot wounds. One bullet had shattered his collarbone and torn into his right shoulder. Another round had penetrated the fleshy part of his thigh, blood pulsing from an artery. Andy decided to treat the thigh wound first, bleeding enough to require a tourniquet. He needed to calm Pinto to stop him from thrashing around.

"We got you, man," Andy yelled in his ear. "I need you to try and hold still enough for me to get the bleeding stopped. Think we can do that?" Andy knew it usually helped to get the casualty focused on helping him, working with him to get stabilized.

"It fuckin' hurts, Doc," Pinto shouted.

"I know, man, I know. I got somethin' for your pain, too, but I gotta get the bleeding stopped first. Think we can do that?"

The combination of Pinto focusing on getting some pain relief and the medic treating his wounds calmed him. Andy worked quickly. He'd memorized every part of his aid bag and could find anything he needed even in the dark.

It took a minute to get the tourniquet placed and adjusted—not too tight, but Andy needed to know it wouldn't be jarred loose. Already, they were calling for him to treat another casualty.

Satisfied he'd stemmed the bleeding sufficiently in the thigh, he took a tube of morphine and injected it into Pinto's other leg before tending to the shoulder wound.

"I gotta go, man. You'll be okay now. It won't be long, and the morphine will ease the pain. I'll be back to check on you as soon as I can."

With the firefight ebbing, Andy moved forward with ease and without worry. He saw two platoon members standing by a hole in the ground trying to lift Minnesota out of it.

"Get me the fuck outta here, you crazy motherfuckers," he was shouting. "Don't you know they put all kinds of shit on those punji stakes. Hurts like a son of a bitch."

Andy moved the young grunt away from the pit. The sharpened point of a bamboo stake remained embedded in his boot. Minnesota leaned back with his hands on the ground and stared at Andy looking at his foot.

"Let's get this out of you," Andy said, taking hold of the sharpened bamboo stake. "Ready?"

Minnesota, taking his wound well, nodded his consent. Andy grabbed the shaft of the stake and gave it a tug. Not enough of the shaft remained to get a good grip, and his hands slipped. A second try failed as well.

"Let's undo your boot and try it that way," Andy said. With the laces undone, the medic took hold of the boot with both hands and pulled it off. The stake came with it.

"Lucky I didn't lose my balance and fall in on my chest," Minnesota said. "Fuckin' Charlie. A hundred ways he'll kill ya."

"Aren't you lucky," Andy said, holding the boot and feeling for the point of the stake inside of it, wanting to know how deeply it had penetrated Minnesota's foot. Finding the point with his thumb, he felt a sharp prick, and guessed about two inches. "This time you'll be out of the field for a longer stay in the hospital."

"No shit?" he said, suddenly pleased with his wound. "You sure those stakes ain't got no snake poison on 'em?"

"You'd be dead by now if they did," Andy said.

That brightened Minnesota's mood even more.

The grunt's hardened rubber sole on his jungle boot prevented most of the stake from penetrating deep into his foot. Andy smeared some antibacterial cream over the puncture wound and wrapped it with a bandage.

"I gotta go," Andy said, needing to get back to check on Pinto. "The LT will have a medevac soon. You want some morphine?" Andy asked.

"Naw, it just makes a guy goofy. It don't hurt that bad, especially without any snake poison or any of that shit on them punji stakes."

"You are one happy casualty," Andy heard one of the grunts tell Minnesota as he was leaving to check on the RTO's wounds. "I'll bet the Doc wished they were all as cheerful as you."

The thrill of being alive in the aftermath of a firefight caused giddiness in some of the guys.

❋ ❋ ❋

In their foxhole that night Sammy said to Andy, "You're too short for this shit, Doc."

"Ain't too short for nothin', bro. Get thinkin' like that and I'll get myself a one-way ticket outta here in a body bag."

"Just a little longer, Doc. You'll make it. We'll see to that."

"We're down to seventeen guys. Two medevacs today. First the Professor, then Pinto and Minnesota."

"They were tracking us, Doc. You get a good look at that pit Minnesota fell into? Hastily dug and constructed. Not very deep.

Not many stakes in it. A quick hit and run. Just a squad of VC. I don't think we wounded any Charlies."

Andy leaned his back against the damp wall of the foxhole. "Sometimes I can't even remember what life was like before the Nam. Know what I mean?"

Sammy leaned towards him and spoke softly. "Let's just make sure there's one after Vietnam, Doc. Just a few more weeks of this and you're home free."

CHAPTER EIGHT

ANDY DOZED IN his foxhole, his field poncho wrapped tightly around him to ward off the light drizzle. His rifle lay diagonally across one of his legs ready for his guard duty at 0200.

Yardly, finishing his watch, approached the foxhole he shared with Andy and Sammy.

"*Bac si, bac si,*" he whispered to Andy as he gently shook his shoulder, using the Vietnamese word for doctor. "Time for you watch."

Yardly stood in the foxhole and offered his hand to help the medic to his feet. Andy had slept lightly, wondering if he'd ever really slept since his first night in country eleven months before.

Andy winced as he took Yardly's hand. His right thumb throbbed. Too dark to see, he felt its swollen contours with his fingers as he walked towards the guard post. The platoon packed empty sandbags with them to the field, filling them each night to build a temporary bunker. Andy took his position behind them and looked into the darkness, listening for any sounds out of the ordinary.

Already chilled from the dampness, Andy laid the wet side of his poncho on the ground and knelt behind the short wall of sandbags. His thumb, twice its normal size, made it hard to grip the stock of his rifle. Charlie's prowess for taking advantage of any carelessness had achieved mythical proportions, and Andy would not get complacent so late in his tour.

❈ ❈ ❈

Returning to his foxhole after the two-hour guard shift, Andy remained awake. His thumb throbbing, he waited for first light. He would get Sammy to help him lance it and drain the pus. Taking a syringe and a vial of lidocaine from his aid bag, he injected the painkiller into his infected thumb, now more than twice its normal size.

"Morning, Doc," Sammy said when he awoke. Seeing the aid bag open, he moved closer and watched Andy preparing to lance his thumb with a scalpel.

"What's wrong?" Sammy asked.

"Infected thumb, full of pus," Andy answered. "I need you to give me a hand."

"How'd that happen?" Sammy enquired.

"Not sure," Andy said. "Maybe from the punji stake I pulled out of Minnesota's foot.

"You sure you wanna do this here, Doc?"

"No choice. I need to drain the pus and get it bandaged. I can't grip nothin' the way it is."

Andy held the scalpel awkwardly in his left hand and pushed the point of the blade into his thumb before making an incision an inch and a half long. Pus oozed out as he squeezed the thumb with his left hand.

"Let me help you with that, Doc," Sammy said as he took a piece of gauze from Andy. Wrapping it around the thumb, Sammy gently squeezed. "That hurt?"

"Not yet," Andy answered. "Keep squeezing. I need to get as much pus out of there as possible."

By midday, Andy realized he'd made a mistake in trying to treat his thumb in the field. The pain from the incision shot up his arm.

Losing his balance in the mud at the edge of a pond, his bandaged hand caught his fall, but soaked up water from the swamp.

Physically miserable, Andy couldn't reconcile his discomfort with all the dead and wounded from his tour in the Nam. Feverish, ghosts haunted his thoughts. *Had Camel complained? Not even when he was dying.* Boy Red's bloody and mangled face appeared in his memory. Hideous images of the children in the jungle scorched and blistered from the napalm. Montagnard bodies formed a long line at the base of the Seven Mountains. The dead from the slaughter in Ca Mau jostled with the face of Square One, the first casualty he had failed to save. All the dead—friend, foe, and innocents—vied for his attention. Andy would not go back to the rear with an infected thumb. The platoon, always shorthanded, had begun the patrol with twenty men. Seventeen remained. They could not afford to lose their medic.

Seeing Andy struggling and in pain, Sammy spoke with Howitz during a break. Andy, embarrassed by his difficulty with a thumb injury, would not. With Andy near collapse, and not able to make sense of his jumbled emotions through the fog of his misery and fatigue, the lieutenant intervened.

Weak and humiliated, Andy passively looked up as Howitz strode towards him. Without saying anything, the LT took the injured hand and removed the bandages. Andy's right thumb, a pulpy infected mess of blood and purplish skin, oozed more pus from the site of the incision.

"Better get you to a hospital, Doc," is all Howitz said, before calling for another dust-off. Too tired and uncomfortable to resist, Andy laid his head on the ground and closed his eyes.

❋ ❋ ❋

The medevac approached from the south. Like every helicopter, the sound of its rotors whacking at the air announced its presence before landing in a natural clearing the platoon utilized as an LZ.

Sammy walked with his friend to the opened door of the Huey.

"Get some rest, Doc," is all he said before Andy boarded. "The war will still be here when you get back. You're short now. Too short for any more of this shit," Sammy added, shouting to be heard above the sound of the rotors churning through the air.

Sammy stood in the LZ and watched the helicopter fade into the sky the same way Andy had on so many occasions. Andy watched from the air as his friend waved and disappeared from his view. The dust-off medic looked at Andy, his only passenger. Used to seeing everything from sucking chest wounds to missing limbs, he looked puzzled at Andy's apparent health.

"You short or somethin'?" he finally asked.

His sheepishness returning, Andy held up his bandaged thumb.

As the helicopter approached the 29th Evacuation Hospital, Andy saw two rows of Quonset buildings joined by a covered hallway which one end of each Quonset butted up against. The medevac landed on a pad fifty meters from the triage unit. An asphalt path ran from it to a set of double doors at its entrance. A medic from the hospital dressed in jungle fatigues greeted Andy and led him through the doors. Fully ambulatory, he walked into the building and was surprised to see a woman, also dressed in fatigues, with a stethoscope hanging around her neck.

"What happened to you?" she asked. "You look in a lot better shape than most of our visitors." She smiled and took Andy's hand to have a better look. Her sleeves were rolled up above the elbows, and her dark hair, not very long, was tied into a ponytail behind her head. Lieutenant's bars, the rank at which nurses entered the Army, were in black on her collars. Her name tag said BRANDON, and her accent suggested somewhere in the Carolinas.

"Not exactly sure," answered Andy. "I just woke up with my thumb infected. It got pricked with a punji stake yesterday. Could be from anything."

"I'll get Paul to look after you," she said, as she wrote something on a chart.

A sandy-haired medic approached and said hello. "Lay down here," he said, pointing to an Army-green field stretcher sitting on two stands resembling sawhorses. "Normally we cut the clothes off our casualties, but let's hold off on that until you're ready to go into surgery. One of the doctors will be in to have a look at you soon. I do need to get an IV started and get your vital signs."

Andy lay on the stretcher and looked up at a metal bar running the length of the room. Bottles of saline, IV tubing, stethoscopes and blood pressure cuffs dangled from it. Five sets of the stands, also Army green, but empty, occupied the rest of the triage unit.

The medic took a blood pressure cuff from the pole and wrapped it around Andy's arm.

"Where you comin' in from?" he asked, before putting a stethoscope in his ears. The name tag on his fatigues said VOIGHT.

"Somewhere in Vinh Long," Andy said.

"Grunt?" he asked.

"Grunt medic."

"No shit? Welcome to the 29th Evac." His manner friendly, Paul Voight continued the conversation while he readied to start an IV on Andy. "How long you been in country?"

"Eleven months."

"You're short," he stated.

"I guess I am," said Andy. "It feels like I been in the Nam forever. You?"

"Nine months, now. I was in the field for a while," Voight said as he inserted a needle into Andy's vein. "Got hit three months in and was transferred here after my platoon got a new medic."

"Which is better?" Andy asked.

Taking a blood sample before hooking the intravenous tubing to the needle in Andy's arm, Voight taped it securely in place while answering.

"Depends on the day," he shrugged. "Nothing worse than wandering the boonies looking for a fight with Charlie, but here, there's never a lull in the war. We get casualties every day. Even when it's not you guys from the Ninth Infantry, there's civilian war casualties, and the Montagnard units. Every time they try and take the Seven Mountains it's a mass casualty situation. Last time, they were bringing Chinook-loads of the wounded. We had field stretchers lined up into the hallway. Piles of blood-soaked fatigues. So much blood on the floor it was hard to keep your footing. A total clusterfuck."

Andy remembered the day the platoon rescued Yardly. "I was at one of those battles," he said. "Nothin's gonna dislodge Charlie from those mountains. The B-52s pounded those rocks for hours and he came up fighting. Must be dug in pretty deep to take that kind of pounding and still put up a fight."

"I guess so," Voight responded. "Listen, we don't get too many conversations with our patients in here. I rarely see a casualty after they leave triage. How about I come and find you on one of the wards in a day or two? We can have a coffee and I'll show you around. Doctor Waters has been notified and should be here soon to take care of that thumb. They'll get you into surgery right away if it stays quiet."

Andy lifted his head and looked around the room. Shelves of medical supplies took up the entire wall behind him. Voight disappeared out the set of doors that opened into the covered hallway. He carried the vial of blood taken from Andy when he started his IV. The lab would verify his blood type.

Andy rested his head on the stretcher and waited for the doctor. Voight returned from the lab and busied himself restocking supplies on the shelves. A radio at the far end of the room crackled and a voice broke through the static.

"This is dust-off seven-seven. We've got six casualties on board, four stretchers and two ambulatory, two serious, ETA twenty minutes."

"Roger that, seven-seven. You know where to find us."

Voight returned to Andy's side. "I guess that postpones your surgery for a bit," he said. "They'll want to see what comes off the medevac before taking you into the OR for a minor wound. I gotta move you over there," he said, pointing to some chairs lined along the wall opposite the medical shelves. He walked Andy to one of the chairs and hung his intravenous bottle of saline on a stand next to it.

Andy heard the medevac land on the helipad. A half minute later a gurney burst through the doors with the first casualty. Three more followed in quick succession. Andy watched Voight and another medic lift the field stretchers off the gurneys and immediately begin cutting the clothes off the wounded before getting blood pressures and pulses recorded. Two nurses worked on the other stretcher-borne casualties. Andy watched Voight start an IV on a wounded grunt. Two ambulatory patients, one limping, walked in with a third medic. He got them situated on field stretchers before helping one of the nurses with a more seriously wounded patient.

A doctor arrived in jungle fatigues and asked Nurse Brandon what had come in on the dust-off. Without looking up she said, "We've got a sucking chest wound, Doctor. I'll set up for a chest tube." She wheeled a cart with a large glass bottle with rubber tubes protruding from a stopper that sealed it. A small motor powered the device. Brandon opened a sterilized package of instruments for the doctor, who was already gloved and tending to the patient.

"I'll put the chest tube in first," he told the nurse. "Let's get him stabilized. Finish that cutdown," he shouted to another nurse on duty tending to the other seriously wounded casualty. "Verify his blood type and let's get some in him."

The doctor made an incision between the ribs and inserted his finger into the chest cavity. He suctioned off some of the fluids, and inserted the chest tube, suturing the skin tightly around it. Nurse Brandon turned the machine on, which drained excess fluids out of the chest cavity and helped restore the vacuum in the lungs necessary for breathing. The whole procedure took just a few minutes.

The other seriously wounded patient writhed in pain on his stretcher. It looked to Andy like he'd lost a lot of blood from a wound in his upper thigh. The cutdown enabled the nurse to get an IV started even with his veins collapsing from shock and a loss of blood.

"Hang in there," she told him. "We've got you now. Everything's going fine. We'll have you into surgery in just a few minutes and get things fixed up. Just have to get another IV started and some more blood in you and it all gets better from here. Can you hear me?" The patient nodded that he did. "You will be fine," the nurse reiterated. He nodded again.

Andy realized the nurse was telling her patient all of the things he had failed to tell Camel. Gloom descended on Andy as he watched the medics in triage keeping their patients alive, doing for their wounded what he had not done for his.

The grunt with the sucking chest wound was the first to be wheeled out the doors of triage and into surgery. A few minutes later, the casualty with the cutdowns followed.

Andy looked around the room, no longer neat and tidy. One of the casualties on a stretcher looked at Andy and asked, "You hit?"

"Naw," Andy said. "Just my thumb. Bad infection."

"No shit?" the grunt said. "Maybe they can amputate, get you out of the Nam."

Andy had not thought of that possibility. *Would losing a thumb be enough to get me home?* "I doubt it's that bad," he said.

"How long you been waiting?" the wounded grunt asked.

"Not long. Just about to go into surgery when the call came in announcing your arrival."

"Sorry about that," he said. "Motherfuckin' Charlie, set up and waiting. That was our point man, with the chest wound." He gestured with his head in the direction of the doors leading to the hallway. "Charlie jumped the gun a little or it could have been worse." Meaning the VC hadn't let the point man travel beyond the ambush, allowing for more of the platoon to enter the killing zone. "Maybe our guy spotted something . . . You got a smoke?"

"Sorry, man," Andy said. "They probably don't want you smoking in here anyway."

Unperturbed, the wounded grunt looked around some more before uttering, "I'm too short for this shit. Couple more months and I'm outta here."

"Who's your medic?" Andy asked.

"The other guy already in surgery. I tried to keep him from going after our point man, told him we'd get to him. But they're tight, so he went anyway. Now they're both fucked up."

Voight interrupted. "You're next," he said to the grunt. "They'll be ready for you in the OR in just a few minutes. I'm gonna wheel you out in the hallway for now so we can get things ready for the next set of visitors."

"Can I smoke out there?" he asked

"Suit yourself," said Voight. "What are they gonna do, send you to Vietnam?" He winked at Andy.

Two hours later, after all six casualties from the medevac were out of surgery, the same doctor who Andy watched put the chest tube in the wounded grunt operated on his thumb.

"I think we can save it," Andy heard him say just before the anesthetic took hold. "Be easier to just cut it off, though," he joked. "Probably get you out of the Nam."

"Thanks," Andy mumbled. "But I think I'd like to keep it if it's not too much trouble. I'm pretty short already, you know."

CHAPTER NINE

ANDY AWOKE ON a hospital ward, dark except for a light at the nurse's station at the far end of the room. As his eyes adjusted, he made out a row of beds on each side of the Quonset. Twenty were occupied. A lone figure sat at a desk where the light illuminated a stack of medical charts.

Andy shifted to his side for a better look at the ward. The nurse, sensing his wakefulness, walked over to his bedside.

"Hi," she whispered. "I'm Lieutenant Renwicki, but just call me Wilma. There's no need for any formal military protocol on the wards. Are you in any pain?"

Andy shook his head. "It's just my thumb," he said, still groggy after the anesthesia.

Renwicki smiled. "I'm going to check your temperature and pulse and get a blood pressure."

"I'm sure they're fine," said Andy, not wanting to be a bother when there must be seriously wounded patients for the nurses to tend to.

Ignoring Andy's concern, she got his vital signs and entered them on a chart. "Good," she said, "just a touch of fever left. Let me know if you need anything. Dr. Waters will be by in the morning. He can answer any questions you have about your surgery. It's about four in the morning. Things will get busier in a couple of hours. Until then, try and get a little more sleep. I'll be on shift until seven."

Andy looked around the ward again, trying to locate any of the guys from third platoon. Too dark to see well, he laid his head on his pillow and dozed.

At six o'clock the lights came on in the ward, waking Andy.

"Good morning," the patient in the bed next to him said cheerfully. A slightly older man, probably in his thirties and career Army, sat facing Andy with his feet dangling over the side of his cot. A large bandage wrapped in gauze covered his upper left arm.

Nurse Renwicki arrived, and the patient turned his attention to her. "This is the prettiest nurse in the hospital," he said, winking at Andy.

"You must be feeling pretty good, Sergeant. Pesky enough to return to your unit soon," she retorted. "Behave yourself in front of our new patient." She looked at Andy and smiled. "I think Sergeant Wilkie is recovering nicely."

"Truth be told," the sergeant responded, "I'd like to stick around longer and get fattened up a little before returning to my unit."

"I didn't realize the food was that good here, Sergeant," she said.

"It beats the steady diet of rice and a few bony fish I have to scrounge to eat in my unit," he said. "It's uncouth, what I have to live on."

"It must have rubbed off and affected your personality," she stated, without missing a beat.

Wilkie laughed. "She's great," he said after Renwicki left, "but it's all true, about the rice and fish, and some powerful-tasting Vietnamese sauces to flavor it, and maybe a few vegetables thrown in."

Andy wondered what kind of unit had to scrounge for its meals. The C-rations provided for third platoon were tedious and bland but easy to access. "So, who are you with?" he asked.

"A mobile advisory team," he said. "MAT for short. We're out in the villages with the Vietnamese Popular Forces, a local militia. We help train and equip them and go on operations together. Want to see where I live?"

Wilkie pulled a set of photographs out of an envelope on the bedside table and handed them to Andy. "We live right in the village."

Wilkie's living quarters looked like a fortified bunker. The roof, a thick plate of steel with thick rows of sandbags stacked on top, sat on more bags of sand that surrounded the structure.

"Very homey," the talkative Wilkie continued, "but I'm not in a hurry to get back. There's just the five of us. We hardly ever see another American. Don't really know who to trust besides my other team members. As you can see, we're heavily fortified."

Andy stared at the photographs. "What part of the Delta you in?" he asked.

"Bac Lieu Province, very remote out there. Our PFs are all farmers who would rather be tending their rice fields than fighting Viet Cong. We can't convince 'em they need to fight and secure the area first, then they can farm. I think they resent our presence. Who knows what side deals they have with Charlie, paying him off with rice to leave them alone to farm. Unfortunate, but it don't work like that. First the VC take their rice, then their young men. I think the villagers play both ends trying to avoid the war. We don't sleep too sound out there."

"Sounds risky," said Andy. He'd never heard of a MAT team before. "So how'd you get hit?"

"On a night ambush," answered Wilkie. "I'm not sure who found who? We had quite the firefight with Charlie. When it was over, the local militia had retreated and hardly fired their weapons. Makes you feel kind of vulnerable."

❋ ❋ ❋

The patients on Andy's ward were in the last stages of recovery before returning to their units. Most were Ninth Infantry grunts, either with minor wounds or just about healed from more serious ones.

Still hooked up to an IV, Andy spent his first morning writing a letter to his family, then pretending to doze to avoid Sergeant Wilkie's incessant need for talking. Andy's ears, the closest set available, absorbed stories about Wilkie's tour with his MAT team, and how it differed from his first tour in Vietnam with an infantry unit. The sergeant's dialogue continued until interrupted by Dr. Waters's arrival to check on Andy. Wilkie wandered off in pursuit of someone else to talk to.

Waters, a surgeon in his early thirties, looked at the thumb. "We caught the infection before it moved into the bone. Another day and we'd have amputated. We'll keep fighting the infection with antibiotics administered intravenously for a couple of days, then give them orally. Any chance of keeping it clean when you return to your unit?"

"Not much," answered Andy. His thoughts turned to Sammy, Black Henry, Yardly, and the rest of the platoon. They would have another medic with them in his absence. Strange how he missed those guys, worried about them.

After Dr. Waters moved to another patient on the ward, one of the grunts from a sister company recognized Andy and came over to say hello.

"Hey, Doc," he said. "Where'd you get hit?"

It took a few seconds before Andy recognized him in the blue hospital pajamas. "Mac?"

The grunt nodded. "Just an infection," Andy said. "You know who the Professor is?"

Mac nodded again. "Everybody in the battalion knows who the Professor is," he said. "Can't miss him with those glasses."

"You seen him in the hospital?" Andy asked.

"I think he's on one of the wards across the hall, next to the Vietnamese ward," Mac said.

"How about Pinto and Minnesota?" Andy continued.

"No, don't know Pinto, and I haven't seen Minnesota. You guys get ambushed again?"

"Partly," Andy answered. "The Professor's just real sick. Thanks, man," Andy said.

"No problem, Doc. Catch you later."

Andy's second day on the ward began with Wilkie's complaints about his MAT team's supply problems. "We're so far out in the boonies headquarters forgets we're even there. Have to threaten supply with bodily harm to even get enough ammo. 'Bring me a VC flag,' they say, 'and we can get you anything.' VC flag my ass," he continued. "Let one o' those fat-ass REMFs go and get one from Charlie."

Andy nodded, the best way of responding to Wilkie. He was going to do most of the talking anyway.

Voight arrived on the ward mid-afternoon. "Feeling better?" he asked.

Something about the triage medic appealed to Andy. Wounded three months into his tour, and assigned to the 29th Evac after recovering, Voight remained soft spoken, and exhibited a kind manner with the casualties.

"Not bad," Andy said. "I might get this IV disconnected tomorrow, make it easier to walk around."

Voight thought for a moment. "I'll tell you what," he said. "I think we can do better than that. Give me the set of jungle fatigues you came in with and I'll get them laundered and bring them back tomorrow. The staff won't mind. Then I'll show you around. Be good for you to get off the ward."

"Thanks," Andy said. "I hate to ask," he continued, "but can you check on a couple of guys for me? They would have come in the day before I did." Andy had to think a moment to remember Pinto and Minnesota's real names. "I'd like to know how they're doing."

"I know what you mean," said Voight. "I still think about the guys I was with, wonder what happened to them. When I was hit, we were on a night ambush in a large rubber plantation. The trees were in such straight rows. It was so dark I couldn't see a thing until the muzzle flashes of the VC when they opened up on us. I wasn't hit immediately. I was trying to get to my friend. Patch, we called him. He died right after I got to him. I had to feel for his wounds. As near as I could tell, a round must have hit him between his neck and shoulder and traveled into his lungs, maybe his heart. Before I could do anything more two rounds from an AK caught me. One of them smashed my collarbone and the other tore through the flesh on my upper arm and grazed my chest. I don't know why I wasn't medevaced out of country to recuperate. The wound to my collarbone made it impossible to carry any gear in the field, so they assigned me here."

Voight rubbed his shoulder, then smiled when he saw Andy looking at him. "It still hurts sometimes," he said. "Maybe I shouldn't talk about it and it wouldn't. I can check on your guys for you."

❄ ❄ ❄

The next morning Dr. Waters came onto the ward and looked at Andy's thumb before instructing the nurse to remove his intravenous. Andy asked about the Vietnamese ward, knowing the Professor would be next door. Finding him asleep, he stood and watched him breathing, deciding not to wake him. Andy noticed the Professor's glasses on the table next to the bed.

The nurse on duty came and stood quietly behind Andy. "A platoon member?" she asked.

Startled, Andy nodded.

"He'll be all right," she said, in a Midwestern twang. "We don't know everything that's wrong with him, but he's doing better."

"Can you tell him Doc was here to see him? He doesn't know I'm in the hospital. Came in the day after he did," said Andy.

"You're his medic? Martin has talked about you."

Andy had forgotten the Professor's first name. The nurse's eyes welled up with tears.

"My brother was a medic. I guess it runs in the family," she said, trying to suppress tears. "Killed over here just a year ago. I'm sorry," she said, gently crying. "You boys are all so young, so very, very young."

Not knowing what to say, Andy said nothing, even though he felt he should. Feeling tongue-tied, he finally uttered, "I'm sorry, too, ma'am, about your brother."

"Oh, here I am crying," she said, dabbing at her eyes and trying to pull herself together. "I'm the one who's supposed to be looking after you, and here I am crying. I'll be sure and tell Martin you were here."

❃ ❃ ❃

True to his word, Voight arrived with Andy's jungle fatigues freshly laundered. "Put these on," he said, handing them to Andy. "I'll show you around."

Andy changed quickly, anxious to see the hospital compound. They walked through the hallway, passing the doors of several wards on both sides before exiting into a small courtyard. The mess hall was on the right, and the company orderly room to the left. The medics' barracks, two-story wooden structures, were beyond the company orderly room, and the doctors' and nurses' quarters opposite it. Heavily sandbagged bunkers, like the ones in Dong Tam, were next to every barracks. Looking like giant armadillos overloaded with protective armor, they stood as a fortified reminder of the war.

"Not much to see," said Voight, "but it will do you good to get some fresh air. On the way back we can get some coffee in the mess hall and have you back on the ward for supper."

The 29th Evac had its own compound surrounded by a twelve-foot-high wire fence. Three guard towers, spaced evenly along the north side, rose thirty feet in the air. They overlooked a field of reeds between the hospital and an Air Force base. A downed Chinook helicopter not worth salvaging lay in ruins outside the perimeter.

"Charlie sneaks in and lobs a few every so often," said Paul, pointing at the field of reeds. He was referring to the Viet Cong mortar teams prevalent in Vietnam. "I don't know why the two compounds are separate. Gives Charlie a space between them to slip in and do some damage. He doesn't like to stick around long, though. The gunships put on quite a show at night trying to take him out."

Voight pointed beyond the perimeter to the northeast. "The Basaac River is just over there. The Navy has a small base with some river patrol boats. Our dust-off unit is located there."

Voight stopped beneath the middle guard tower and hopped up and sat on the wall of sandbags surrounding its base. "Have to pull a four-hour shift in these a lot of nights."

Andy sensed something on his mind. Andy felt a strong affinity with Voight, one of those people in life a person develops an immediate connection with.

"It's mostly a boring four hours but gives you a chance to think. Not always such a good thing."

Andy rested his good hand on top of the sandbags and let him continue.

"We had a young boy medevaced in last night. The kid was only about three. A bullet shattered his pelvis and deflected into his intestines. He was quite a mess, but he just lay there, fully conscious, looking up at us with his large dark eyes while we worked on him. His whole family came in with him. Not a whimper from any of them. They watched as we tried to stabilize him."

Voight looked at Andy before continuing. "I don't know how he was wounded. We only treat noncombatants we wound by mistake. I've treated a lot of civilian war casualties since I've been here. Children and the elderly are not spared. Such a stoic people, the Vietnamese. I wonder what they really think of us."

Andy had wondered the same thing. It was something he didn't like to think about.

Voight stared out at the compound, his back towards the field of reeds. "I don't know what to think about this place. You kind of lose perspective being cooped up in triage. That small room has seen every kind of misery. I don't have to tell you about all the war casualties we see. There's other stuff, too—suicides, and civilians, like the little boy last night."

Andy remembered the six napalmed kids and putting the young girl on a medevac. "You treat a little girl, maybe nine years old, about three months ago? Her lungs were probably seared from a napalm strike."

"I can't remember, man. There have been so many kids come through triage. We try and stabilize them for surgery, get them into the OR as quick as possible. I don't have many conversations with patients like this. I rarely know what happens to anyone after their surgeries. I have treated many little girls. By the sounds of it, she probably died en route and was taken directly to the morgue. That's it over there." He pointed to a small nondescript building standing by itself not far from the helipad.

"There's an Army mortician that runs it, a kid, really. I don't know what his training is. He's a bit of a pothead, and some of the medics like to smoke weed inside the morgue because it's air-conditioned. Brass rarely hassles them in there."

The two medics walked back towards the hospital. Paul continued.

"I've gone out on the PBRs a few times to do what's called a MEDCAP. We set up a clinic while the river patrol boats cruise the canals. We see a lot of cleft palates and deformities in the young kids. I go out because I want to do something positive while I'm here. But I know it doesn't make much of a difference. We hand out a few pills, drain and bandage a few infections, but it's impossible to do any follow-up. Maybe we're just a propaganda tool.

"Sometimes we set up in a school if a village has one. A long line forms and we look at each person. Some of the villagers just want the pills we hand out, while some mothers are looking for miracles for their deformed babies.

"They are poor, and there's a war going on, so there is nothing we can do. By late afternoon, the PBRs are done patrolling, so we return to their base. They are not on the canals after dark."

Voight stopped walking and looked at Andy. "At this point in my tour I can't make any sense out of it. Can you?"

"Just trying to make it home again, man. Maybe we can sort some of it out then," Andy said, remembering a similar discussion he'd had with Sammy.

Reaching the mess hall, they entered and proceeded to a coffee urn next to the chow line. Dr. Waters, seated in the area designated for officers, noticed Andy and waved a hello. *Silly to have segregated eating areas in the war zone,* thought Andy, *but that's the Army for you.*

"He's one of the good ones," commented Voight. "The doctors and nurses have their own thing going and are not very military. Most of the doctors are draftees, too, and want to get out as bad as the rest of us. Some of them are pretty arrogant and get cranky, take out their bad moods on the medics. A couple of them always ask if the incoming casualties are American or Vietnamese when summoned to triage. It's kinda like applying the Hippocratic Oath hypocritically."

The two sat by themselves in the nearly empty mess hall.

"The nurses and medics pull twelve-hour shifts. I'm on nights right now. Most of the nurses are good to work with, a few are difficult. I guess it's like anywhere." Voight paused for a moment. "Three months to go."

"Then what?" asked Andy.

"Honestly? All of my focus has been on getting out of Vietnam."

❋ ❋ ❋

Returning to the ward, Andy found Sergeant Wilkie eating.

"Thought you might miss supper," Wilkie began, talking even while he ate. "Need to fatten up before I go back to the boonies. Looks like you could use a few pounds yourself."

It was true. Nurse Renwicki insisted on weighing Andy, and he was surprised when the scale showed him at 145 pounds, thirty less than when he'd arrived in country. He'd noticed the deterioration on some of the other guys but not in himself.

Unusually reflective that evening, Wilkie admitted to Andy he felt guilty about being away from his MAT team for so long. "There's just the four of them out there right now. Every man makes a difference in such a small unit," he said, "especially when the villagers aren't all that friendly."

Andy related to that. Awake for a long time that evening, Andy worried about the platoon as he dozed off.

A *whump, whump, whump* woke Andy. The sound of the mortar rounds, not close at first, intensified as they landed closer. A real war was much louder than the movies, one of the first distinctions Andy noticed.

Nurse Renwicki, on duty for the night shift, began getting the patients to lie on the floor along one of the walls. A three-foot-high row of sandbags placed along the outside of the Quonset provided some protection from the mortar rounds, landing closer with each blast. Pulling mattresses off beds, the nurse began placing them over the patients. She had lots of help on the ambulatory ward, full of mobile patients used to combat situations.

The closest explosion sprayed sand and debris against the Quonset wall facing south. "It doesn't usually last long," she said, trying to assure the patients, forgetting for a moment they had all seen enough combat to get wounded. "The gunships will put Charlie on the run. The Viet Cong are usually more interested in the Air Force base across from us."

"Fucking Charlie," a muffled but familiar voice stated from underneath a mattress. "Hate that motherfucker. The stupid shithead is wasting his mortars on a hospital where everybody is already out of commission."

Of course, it was Sgt. Wilkie initiating a conversation during the mortar attack.

"I'd feel a lot better with an M-16 in my hands," offered one of the grunts.

"How good are the medics at protecting us?" another one shouted.

Someone laughed. "My medic doesn't even carry a weapon." The grunt referred to having a conscientious objector for his doc. Not required to bear arms, the Army still conscripted them for duty as medical corpsmen.

"He wouldn't be much good in this situation," another stated.

Sensing some disrespect for his medic, who had been with him on every patrol suffering the same dangers and hardships, the grunt defended him.

"I didn't say he was a bad medic, just that he doesn't carry a weapon."

"What do you think, Doc?" Mac asked.

Andy pretended not to hear. The mortar attack subsiding, he tuned out the continuing banter and began helping Nurse Renwicki put the ward back together.

Wilkie appeared from underneath a mattress. Intent on having the last word, he said to no one in particular, "Might as well head back to my unit in the morning where I will at least have a fucking weapon to protect myself."

Noticing Nurse Renwicki was close enough to hear his profanity, he apologized. "Sorry, ma'am," he said, looking at her.

Odd, thought Andy, *for Wilkie to think that profanity might offend a nurse who has seen every kind of grotesque wound in Vietnam.*

CHAPTER TEN

ANDY SAT ON the edge of his bed reading *The Stars and Stripes*. The only newspaper readily available to soldiers in the war zone contained upbeat stories about the US military in Vietnam, intended to be a morale booster for the troops. Andy read about the latest *Bob Hope Show*. Nothing in the paper reported the war he knew.

Voight arrived for his daily visit. "I checked on your guys," he said.

"Terrific," said Andy, tossing the paper aside. "Are they still here?"

"Only the Professor, but you already knew that. Your RTO, the guy you call Pinto, was medevaced to the 24th Evac in Long Binh, a bigger facility better able to treat his wounds long term. His leg is really fucked up, lots of complications from the arterial damage. You saved his life, man."

"And Minnesota?" Andy asked.

"A more interesting case," Voight said. "He's also at the 24th. Whatever that punji stake was smeared with, it caused an infection that antibiotics are having a problem controlling. They might have to amputate his leg."

Andy thought for a moment. "I barely touched the tip of that punji stake with my thumb," he said.

"Then you are lucky, my friend. Charlie can kill you in a hundred different ways."

❊ ❊ ❊

The Professor, still being treated intravenously, looked at Andy sitting in a chair at his bedside. "They don't know everything that's wrong with me, Doc. You have any ideas?" His glasses back on his head, he looked hopefully to Andy for solutions.

That's exactly why I feel so much pressure, thought Andy. *The doctors and nurses don't know everything that's wrong, but the Professor thinks I do . . . and I keep losing people.*

"Don't rush coming back," he began. "Make sure you feel strong enough."

"I am feeling better," the Professor said, "but whatever's wrong has still got me feeling bad. I'm worried some of the doctors are starting to think I'm faking it to avoid going back to the field."

"Don't let 'em rush you," Andy said. "That's one thing they don't know about—what it's like packing all that gear out there."

The Professor nodded.

"I know the one nurse I talked to likes you," Andy said, trying to lighten the conversation.

"Her brother was a medic over here, you know," said the Professor.

"I know," said Andy. "And he got killed about a year ago."

"I didn't wanna tell you that part," the Professor said. "How long you gonna be in the hospital, Doc?"

"Not much longer," Andy said, ignoring the advice just given the Professor, and feeling the need to return to the platoon.

❊ ❊ ❊

Voight reemerged on the ward looking tired.

"Another rough night in triage?" Andy asked.

Voight nodded. "A platoon of grunts got ambushed humping through a rice paddy. Happened just before they were gonna dig in for the night. Some of their guys were hopping mad about it. Figured they shudda already been dug in instead of trying to cross the paddy. Once it got dark, they had to crawl through the water in the flooded rice field to get to some better cover. Charlie had that all figured out and started dropping mortars on their position. Nine wounded in triage. Don't know about their dead."

Voight and the triage staff worked on the wounded during the attack on the hospital. "We just closed the doors and only used the lights we absolutely needed. The barracks next to mine were damaged. One of the first rounds landed beside the building and wounded two medics who were sleeping on the bottom floor. Everybody else was on shift or able to get to the bunkers. We were already working on some Vietnamese civilians. How crazy is that? We wound them with our firepower, medevac them to the 29th, and Charlie starts lobbing mortars on them."

❋ ❋ ❋

Andy, scheduled to be discharged from the hospital one week after arriving, went for breakfast with Voight. The triage medic, coming off another busy night, looked stressed and weary. He picked at a dry piece of toast while drinking a cup of coffee. He rubbed his throbbing shoulder.

"It never ends," he said. "I was so thankful to be out of the field when I first got here. But the war just keeps coming at you. We lost a casualty in triage last night. Maybe it's for the best. We had four cutdowns going, one in each limb. The pneumatic cuffs were forcing four pints of blood into his veins, and he was convulsing from the shock of everything. The guy's face was blown off. Blinded, and his testicles shredded, he struggled to breathe. We tried hard to save him, but a part of me was asking 'Would I want to live with those kinds of injuries?' Honestly? I don't think so."

"Maybe it's best," Andy said.

"Folks back home have no idea how messed up some of these wounds leave people, do they? How much pain and suffering they cause."

"You did what you could."

"We did, but it's never enough, is it." More statement than question, Andy felt the same way.

"I'm being discharged today," Andy said.

"Dr. Waters told me." Voight reached in his fatigue shirt pocket and pulled out a slip of paper. "Here's my parent's address in California. Look me up if you get a chance."

"Sure thing," Andy said.

"Take care of yourself out there in the boonies," said Voight, a sadness in his voice.

"Sure thing," Andy repeated.

At the gate to the hospital compound the guard pointed Andy in the direction of the main road. "Stick yer thumb out and an Army truck'll give ya a lift. Can Tho Army Airfield's only a few miles that way," he said, pointing south. "From there it should be easy catchin' a flight to Dong Tam. No need ta worry about Charlie during the day. Around here, he only comes out at night."

Andy walked the hundred meters to the main road, and as the guard predicted, got a ride on an Army deuce and a half. Sitting in back and looking out the rear of the canvas-covered truck, Andy saw several open-front shops busy with commercial activity. On both sides of the congested roadside, Vietnamese displayed a variety of wares. Stores with brightly colored ceramics neatly arranged sat next to motorcycle repair shops with spare parts strewn across dirt floors. Soup cafes, busy with customers, were next to coffin makers and bamboo shops.

The vibrancy of the activity interested Andy. Can Tho, on the banks of the Hau River, a major branch of the Mekong, was the largest city in the Delta. Cyclos, bicycle-powered and motorized, competed with small motorcycles flowing in and out of the city. Army trucks lumbered along amidst the congestion.

The truck stopped in front of the entrance to the airfield. At the end of a roadway, a flight tower protruded incongruently out of a small terminal building. Andy walked towards the entrance. Two Cobra gunships, surrounded by sandbagged walls, sat just off the steel-matted runway.

Inside the terminal Andy approached a soldier about a flight to Dong Tam. Without saying a word, he pointed to a skinny kid in jungle fatigues sitting at a desk, the only piece of furniture in the building.

"Anything to Dong Tam?" Andy asked.

"Oh yeah," the kid responded. "Charlie hit a bullseye last night and blew up the ammo dump. Lots o' flights to Dong Tam. Hang around and I'll let you know when somethin's goin' out."

"Thanks," Andy said, looking around. With no chairs to sit on, and the floor filthy, he told the soldier, "I'll be right outside."

"Suit yourself," the kid answered while looking at a clipboard.

Outside, Andy found a wall of sandbags near a small palm tree providing some shade. Nearing noon, and the temperature rising, he sat facing the runway under the partial shade of the palm fronds. Perspiring, he watched for helicopters or cargo planes landing at the airfield before proceeding to Dong Tam. Soldiers hitched flights in Vietnam like they did cars in the US.

Three helicopters landed within the hour. The last one dropped off a major with a Ninth Infantry unit patch and cut the motors. Andy noticed a door gunner sitting in the opened bay casually smoking a cigarette. When the rotors stopped, Andy approached the Huey.

"Where you heading?" Andy asked.

"Beats me," he said nonchalantly. "They don't tell me nothin'. I'm on board to man this baby." He tapped the M-60 machine gun mounted in the doorway of the Huey. "Dong Tam eventually. Don't know before that."

Andy recognized the accent. "You from Oklahoma?" he asked.

"Sure 'nough. Been in this shithole long enough and would like to get back there. How 'bout you?"

"Afton," Andy responded. He recognized some Native characteristics in the high cheekbones and rounded face. His eyes were a dark brown and his skin had a reddish tinge. He wore a small leather pouch on his neck along with his dog tags. A feather engraved in the leather and three bright-red beads on the strap that held the pouch around his neck, Andy recognized it for a medicine bag.

"Northeastern part of the state," Andy continued. "Not a very big place."

"I know where it is," the door gunner said. "We used to kick your ass in football every year." In Oklahoma, even a town with just 900 residents fielded a high school team.

"I never played," Andy said.

"Never?" The door gunner looked at him like he was some kind of weakling.

"Not my thing." Andy shrugged. "My brother plays," he added, attempting to save face. In fact, he enjoyed the solitary sports more, inspired by the track and field exploits of Jim Thorpe, the athletic Indian from Oklahoma. Of course, he played everything, including football, but stories of his Olympic success had left an impression on Andy.

Satisfied, the door gunner told him, "Hop aboard if you like. We'll eventually get you to Dong Tam. Wouldn't be in a hurry to get back if I were you. Motherfuckin' Charlie blew the ammo dump last night. Rocked the whole base. Fuckin' Charlie. Sick o' that motherfucker, too. You a grunt?"

"Grunt medic," Andy said.

"Spent my time in the boonies," he said. "Now I take care of Charlie from the air." He patted his M-60 machine gun again. "Had enough of that motherfucker, and the entire Mekong Delta for that matter. What you doin' in Can Tho?"

"Just getting out of the hospital," Andy said.

"Twenty-ninth?"

Andy nodded.

"Been there, too. Been everywhere in the Delta. Charlie can have it. Too many mosquitoes, leeches and snakes, too wet during the monsoons, and too hot when it ain't rainin'. Glad to be up in the air now. Nearly lost a couple of toes from the jungle rot, I had it so bad."

Andy nodded again.

"The major'll only be a minute. You can sit over there." He pointed to a pallet of ammo crates in the cargo bay of the helicopter. "We'll be dropping that off someplace, then we should be on the way back to Dong Tam."

The door gunner noticed Andy looking at his medicine bag. He took it in his hands. "Gotten me through a lot o' shit," he said, fondling it. "Motherfuckin' lieutenant in my first unit joked about it, then started gettin' suspicious 'bout what I carried around in it. Thought maybe I had some dope. Made me open it for him when we was back in camp. Motherfucker bought it our next patrol."

Andy knew the significance of a medicine bag, a private thing, the contents known only to the individual.

Andy looked at the gunner's helmet on the floor of the Huey behind him. A black handprint, large and prominent, adorned one side of the camouflage cover, what a Cherokee warrior would paint on his face before battle.

"Tahlequah," he said. "That's where I'm from. Seat of the Cherokee Nation."

"I know where it is," Andy said. "You used to kick our asses in football."

Before Tahlequah could respond, the major showed up with a captain in tow. When the helicopter started and the rotors whirred with the revved engine, Tahlequah turned and shouted in Andy's ear, "New company commander. Welcome to the Nam," then winked knowingly.

The Huey lurched into the air, quickly rising several hundred feet. Tahlequah remained seated with his feet dangling over the side. The Delta was beautiful from the air, the massive waterways and contour of the rice fields interspersed with the swamps and jungle.

❊ ❊ ❊

After dropping the pallet of ammo for a company on a sweep not far from Dong Tam, the Huey rose again and headed for the Ninth Infantry's base camp. Not pretty, the camp came into view, and still smoldered where the ammo dump had blown from a Viet Cong mortar round getting lucky. As the Huey got closer Andy made out some shirtless figures with sprayer packs strapped to their backs. On the edge of the browned-off area beyond the perimeter, they worked on widening the dead zone around Dong Tam.

Touching down only long enough to let the officers and Andy out, the helicopter kept its engine revved, making it difficult to hear. As he got off, Andy placed a hand on the door gunner's shoulder and shouted "*wado*" in his ear, meaning "thank you" in the Cherokee language.

Surprised, the Indian smiled and gave Andy a thumbs-up as the helicopter lifted off the ground.

The major, seeing a Jeep already there to give him and the captain a lift, offered Andy a ride.

"Thank you, sir," he said. "I need to get back to my platoon."

CHAPTER ELEVEN

AFTER A WEEK in the hospital, Andy returned to Dong Tam. Three weeks remained on his tour. Third platoon had returned to base camp soon after Andy had been medevaced, too shorthanded to effectively remain in the field. The platoon stood down for two days while it resupplied and took a needed break, then resumed a series of night ambushes close to Dong Tam. Andy's replacement was among five new guys assigned to the platoon. Andy being restricted to light duty while his thumb finished healing, the company commander ordered him to spend time with the new medic, then go on a final field operation with him.

On the eve of Andy's last patrol, scheduled for a week of humping west of Dong Tam, Sammy sat on his cot across from his hooch mate. In his friend's silence Andy sensed a hesitation to speak, a fear of saying the wrong words. The mood, normally somber before a patrol, intensified when all that remained between returning home and living a normal life was a few days in the jungles and rice paddies of the Mekong Delta.

"You know, Doc," Sammy finally began, "we've gone through a lot of shit together. I don't know why they're makin' you go on one more patrol. They oughta be cutting you some slack. You've done enough for the platoon. Someone else's turn."

Andy shrugged. He assumed he would be with them until his tour ended. Expending so much concentration and effort, he felt like he'd been in the Nam forever. Andy attempted to treat his last patrol like any other hump beyond Dong Tam's perimeter, trying not to get too spooked about being so short

"You're the best friend I've ever had, Doc," Sammy confided.

Before Andy could respond, Black Henry and Yardly walked into their hooch. Yardly took a seat on the floor, too shy to sit on one of the cots in the tent. Black Henry stayed for a warm beer and cautioned Andy how to approach his final days in country.

"I seen it befo," he stated. "Get too spooked you's start ta hes'tate jus' dat lil bit." He held up his thumb and index finger with a small gap between them. "Charles be watchin' fo' dat, grease you's ass no matta how short. Make no difference to dat muddahfucker."

Andy had heard it all before. *Thanks, Black Henry*, he thought. *I wasn't too spooked until you reminded me how short I am. You are all hovering around me like I'm certain to get wasted on one of my last days in the war.*

※ ※ ※

The platoon assembled at the wire and prepared to walk beyond the perimeter. Howitz conferred with the point man, giving him a last set of instructions. A lone sentry manning the M-60 machine gun sat shirtless on top of a sandbagged bunker. Exchanging light-hearted banter with some of the guys while he smoked a cigarette, he wisecracked about the platoon's ineffectiveness in finding Charlie.

"It's more like he finds you, and greases your sorry asses," he mocked.

Some of the platoon rested on the ground before the final order to saddle up, eyes closed, not in sleep, but in concentration and reaching internally for the mental fortitude to face another week looking for a fight with Charlie. Others, already resigned to what they faced, finished last cigarettes while staring at the ground or looking beyond the perimeter. Andy and Sammy stood by themselves, the banter of no interest to either man.

When the order came to "lock and load," the point man stepped beyond the wire and the patrol began. Turning serious because he'd been there, too, the guard manning the M-60 at the bunker uttered a "good luck, guys," and nodded in their direction. Sammy fell in the procession just before Andy, determined that nothing would prevent the Doc from finishing his tour and going home.

※ ※ ※

Scheduled to spend a week of night ambushes and daytime patrols, the platoon settled into a familiar routine. No contact with the enemy occurred as the week progressed. The worst incident involved a cache of cooked rice the platoon found in one of the villages. Too much for a family to eat before spoiling, Howitz had Yardly question the household about its need for such a large quantity.

The boy soldier, fierce in his hatred of the Viet Cong, strode past the family and took a close look at the large cauldron of cooked rice. Pacing back to the family gathered outside of their thatched dwelling, he stopped in front of the household's head, a middle-aged Vietnamese dressed in a ragged shirt and pants cut off above his knees for working in the rice paddies. Yardly jabbed questions at the man in Vietnamese. Nervously, he stood and answered without looking directly at the Montagnard. Yardly paced after each exchange, thinking what to ask next, stopping and glaring into the older man's face. The farmer remained standing, not shifting his feet, answering in short bursts of Vietnamese, then longer explanations while Yardly grew impatient.

Sneering, Yardly turned to Howitz and offered his translation. "Man say need much rice, feed many family. No VC, hate VC, take many young man, and much rice." The Montagnard boy looked towards the family, scowling, before blurting, "This man lie. Much rice for VC. Family cook rice for VC."

Standard procedure required the LT order the rice destroyed to keep from feeding the Viet Cong. Instead, Howitz ordered a thorough search of the village.

"If we find any weapons, torch the rice with them," he ordered. "No weapons, the family keeps the rice." The son of farmers, the lieutenant understood the intensive labor of cultivating and harvesting rice.

Andy watched the search. Spared from participating directly, he tended to an old woman with an infected foot. Warily, she watched Andy with eyes that gave no hint of her emotions. *Should I lance and drain her foot?* There would be no follow-up. Andy, weary of practicing bad medicine, looked at the woman's leathery skin, bronze and weathered from a lifetime of working in the rice paddies. Her teeth, stained from betel nut juice, worn stubs in her mouth. Clothed in rags, her poverty obvious, Andy deadened the foot with lidocaine and pulled a thorn embedded in her infected heel.

With no weapons found, the platoon moved out of the village and into the rice paddies nearby. Walking on top of the dikes, Andy, glad to leave the village, took his place in the formation behind Sammy. The heat from the sun, feeling good at first as it dissipated the morning's chill, had Andy perspiring. Perhaps that would be the last village Andy would search with the platoon.

After a midday break, they skirted the edge of a swamp, reminding Andy of the day Boy Red triggered the booby trap that killed him. More rice paddies followed. One hundred meters in front of them Andy noticed five Vietnamese tending to their crop. The stooped figures wore conical hats common to the farmers in the Delta. Not wanting to attract attention they continued with their work, not looking at the platoon as they got closer. Howitz, seeing no need to interrupt their labors, looked in their direction but kept the platoon on a course that would pass no closer than twenty-five meters from the Vietnamese.

Andy heard a helicopter's rotor blades approaching from behind. Turning for a look, a lone gunship appeared as a speck on the horizon. Flying low and just above the treetops, it made one pass on the platoon's left in the rice paddy before circling back towards the trees. Some of the guys waved, acknowledging their presence. Circling again before making another low pass above the rice fields, it flew directly towards the Vietnamese tending their crops.

One of the Vietnamese stood and looked at the approaching gunship. The farmer and four other workers bolted from the approaching helicopter. The Cobra fired its Gatling guns, mowing down all five. Andy couldn't believe what he witnessed. Howitz motioned for him and Sammy's squad to move out and check on the Vietnamese now lying still in the shallow water of the paddy.

Andy knew what he would find before reaching the bodies. Nobody out in the open escaped the deadly firepower of a Cobra gunship. Andy arrived at the first casualty. Not bothering to unfasten his aid bag, he threw off his pack on top of a mud dike and waded towards the still figure. Lying face down in the water, Andy turned the corpse over and looked at the dead face of a woman. Eyes open, Andy laid her back down in the water and avoided her horrified expression by closing her eyes with his fingers. Sammy checked on another corpse a few meters away.

A standard Huey approached from a different direction and landed. The five dead lying blood-covered in the muck were in full view. A lieutenant colonel stepped out of the helicopter and strode towards where Andy and the squad hovered over the corpses. Sammy, as the squad leader, approached the colonel.

"What have you found, son?" the officer asked.

"Five dead, sir," Sammy responded, "all women. Can't find any weapons."

Andy recognized the battalion commander, Lieutenant Colonel Bolt. He'd never had a conversation with him.

"What were these women doing, son?"

"Working in the rice paddy, sir. We were on patrol and they were just working. We weren't very close. A gunship appeared and went straight towards them. When they started to run, it opened up."

Colonel Bolt got on his radio and into a discussion with someone on the other end. At first, the battalion commander sought clarification, but the conversation turned heated. Lieutenant Howitz arrived, and they all listened to the colonel's part in the call.

"Who authorized the air strike? No need? There are five dead Vietnamese women and no weapons found. They were working in their goddamned rice field. What do you mean, 'Were they running?' Of course they were running. They had a Cobra gunship bearing down on them."

The colonel paused for a moment before speaking again, at first in a softer voice, incredulous at what he was hearing.

"Did I hear that correctly, sir?" he asked. "If they were running, they must be VC? Add them to the body count?"

Bolt paused again, weighing his words carefully. "I did not come to Vietnam to kill innocents indiscriminately. What do you mean they were probably VC anyway? One of my platoons was nearby and saw nothing out of the ordinary. No, sir, I am not telling you how to command your brigade. I am not telling you how to conduct the war. I am telling you how I am not conducting my battalion. Is that a direct order, sir? Yes, sir."

Bolt put down the receiver. He knew as a career officer he had crossed a line difficult to erase.

Howitz approached. "Sir, is there anything to be done?"

"Done? I think we have done enough here. Headquarters has ordered to leave the bodies where they lay. 'Let the VC deal with their own dead,' is how it was put to me. You have done a fine job commanding your platoon, Lieutenant. I fear we have sunk into an abyss with this war. The rot that is emanating from our conduct is palpable. The killing has come to be too easy. We now unleash it on anyone in sight." He looked at the lifeless bodies lying in the paddy water.

"Your men—boys, really, when they received their orders for Vietnam, mostly draftees. This is not the United States Army they should have to be a part of. The nation should not be making them participate in such barbarism. This is not my first war, Lieutenant. It is not my first tour in Vietnam."

"No, sir," Howitz responded.

"When I returned from Korea, I was proud of my service, felt like I had made a positive sacrifice for my country. I wanted to stay in the Army. My family has a military history that goes back to the Civil War. I had ancestors at Bull Run and Gettysburg, and in every war since."

"Yes, sir," Howitz said.

"There is always tragedy in war, Lieutenant, innocents getting killed. But this shooting of anything that moves and calling it a dead VC is something we will come to regret. I never thought I would see my nation participate in this kind of killing. God help us. I have said too much."

The battalion commander paused. "Good luck, Lieutenant. And to you, son." He nodded to Sammy before turning and walking to his helicopter.

Bolt knew headquarters wanted bodies, dead ones, tallied on a gruesome score sheet, now the measurement of success in the war. Andy knew if it was a measurement of anything, it was of their failure as an Army, a nation, and as a people.

In Dong Tam, the lieutenant colonel was relieved of his command.

❊ ❊ ❊

Andy, numbed to his core by one more slaughter, waited in silence for Sammy to speak. His friend, more agitated than he'd ever seen, weighed his words carefully, not wanting to speak until sure of what he wanted to say. Denied any euphoria about going home because of the ugly and senseless deaths on his last patrol, he waited silently for Sammy to talk about what they witnessed prior to returning to Dong Tam.

"You know I'm not a coward, Doc. You know we've seen some killing and I've always held up my end. This was something different. I didn't come to Vietnam to be killing unarmed women working in their rice fields."

"But we didn't kill them," Andy offered feebly. Feeling the same way, he spoke the words for his friend's sake, not because he believed them. Andy felt complicit in the killing, somehow, just as he had when the children were napalmed. It had ceased to matter what side the dead represented, whether they were enemy soldiers, civilians, children, or his fellow platoon members.

Is it worth surviving in the aftermath of witnessing all of the death I've seen? Is living a prize to be valued? It was our side doing the reckless killing, and not just some Cobra pilot in a murderous rage. It is sanctioned and encouraged at the highest levels.

With each new commander itching to put his stamp on the war, wanting their strategy adopted for winning it, the quagmire deepened. Andy and third platoon had carried on while headquarters kept trying to figure it all out, over a lot of dead bodies—American and Vietnamese, Viet Cong and NVA Regulars, rice farmers, ARVN, Army Infantry, Marines.

Andy reflected on Voight's answer when asked if he'd remembered the little girl after the napalm strike. *"I have treated many little girls. Sometimes I pull a shift and see only civilian war casualties."*

Sammy shifted on his cot. He had the dazed but penetrating look a lot of guys had after a firefight, or some near miss like the day White Henry led them out of the booby-trapped swamp.

Frustrated, he summed it up. "Somebody ought to tell them they can't win what they can't win," Sammy said. "You know what I think, Doc? I think the killing's gotten too easy for some of us, especially if you don't have to look someone in the eye while you're doing it."

CHAPTER TWELVE

ANDY STOOD NEAR one of Dong Tam's perimeter gates as the platoon prepared to go on patrol. This time, Andy would not be with them. Elated about surviving his tour, yet confused by an accompanying emptiness, he felt conflicted. While returning to the certainty of a future in Oklahoma, guilt gnawed at his conscience about abandoning friends in the Nam.

As the men filed by nodding and shaking hands, Andy bade them a final goodbye.

"Good knowin' ya, Doc," Black Henry told him.

"Good luck, Doc," said the Professor, now back with the platoon.

"Bye-bye, *bac si*," Yardly said. "*Fini* Vietnam."

And then Sammy, the only man smiling, happy for Andy's survival, grabbed his hand to shake and put his other arm around him. Pulling him close, combat gear and all, he said, "See you back home, man. Two months left and I'm out of the Nam and the Army."

Not knowing what dangers the platoon would face, Andy watched them exit the gate and begin another patrol.

He'd said his goodbyes to Sammy the night before, the friends making sure how to find each other after the war. Not feeling right about the celebration of a short-timer's party on the eve of another combat patrol, Andy had spent his final night with the platoon visiting quietly.

As he walked back to his hooch, alone, the platoon moved deeper into the jungle—without Andy as their medic. Worried and concerned, Andy realized he would not have any news about the men for several weeks. Sammy promised to write, but letters from the Nam traveled slowly and spoke of events no longer current.

Prior to his boarding a Huey to ferry out of Dong Tam, the faint sounds of a firefight beyond the camp's perimeter reverberated. Nothing unusual, except Andy had no way of knowing if it involved third platoon. He suppressed his anxiety. The platoon, without him, would cope. The new medic, a kid from Texas and new to the Nam, would have to as well.

Andy's flight out of the Delta, deceptively serene and peaceful high above the irregular contours of rectangular rice paddies and jungles below, showed many shades of green that looked like paradise. Andy marveled at the beauty from the air. Far above the muck of the swamps with their leeches, mosquitoes, snakes and Charlie, all wanting to take some blood, a pastoral view prevailed. He took a last look before descending into Tan Son Nhut where his orders stated a flight would return him to US soil the next day.

Andy had no problem catching a supply helicopter to the sprawling American base near Saigon. The military city, with a thirteen-mile perimeter, was a major staging area for supplies and men arriving and leaving the war zone.

After landing, Andy found his way to the point of departure for American military personnel, crowded with men anxious to return home. Hundreds of soldiers milled about the grounds near the barracks used for temporarily housing them.

Two large and informal groups gathered a short distance away. After reporting in and receiving the details of his departure, Andy wandered towards the crowd of men. Not knowing anyone, he hung back from the celebrations, feeling strangely pensive. On one side soldiers smoking marijuana dominated the gathering, the potent odor emanating from the smaller groups within the larger one. A more boisterous crowd on the other side mostly drank cans of beer, an inner core highly inebriated and whooping it up.

Feeling separate, Andy did not participate. Nearer the barracks, solitary figures deep in their thoughts smoked cigarettes or sipped on fifths of whiskey straight from the bottle, staring at nothing in particular. Some, squatting Vietnamese style, leaned against sandbagged bunkers not comprehending that they were safe now, deep in the bowels of the large military installation. Expecting the next mortar attack, the fear from their deadly struggles still palpable, their blank but penetrating stares gave no details but told a lot about them.

Unsettled, Andy set out to explore the large base. Near Saigon, but totally American, he walked a long ways on the tarmac without seeing an end to flight hangars, supply depots and barracks to house the thousands of support troops. Walking easily without any gear to pack, Andy continued late into the afternoon.

Tiring of the military installations, Andy found the perimeter and walked along it, browned off for miles with the chemical sprays. He meandered back towards his staging area. At the edge of a runway he spotted two odd-looking planes being worked on by a crew of men. Curious, Andy walked towards them. As he got closer, he could see an array of tanks and piping attached incongruously to what looked like C-123 cargo planes. When he got near enough to read the large block letters on the fuselage, Andy understood: *ONLY WE CAN PREVENT FORESTS.*

Strangely depressed that evening, Andy lay on his cot in the crowded barracks and stared blankly into the dark towards the ceiling. He tried thinking about returning to Oklahoma, seeing his family and the warm homecoming he'd receive. Thoughts of the platoon dug in somewhere in the Delta intruded. They'd be at the edge of a rice paddy or deep in the jungle.

Not expecting his life to be any different after the war, Andy tried focusing on familiar images from home. Like all the men, he should have been fantasizing about the meals his mother would cook, and the girls he'd meet. Instead, his mind returned to the war, wondering if the platoon was safe, if Sammy and the Professor were okay. *Will the new medic look after them if they're hit? Should I have extended my tour until Sammy rotates home? What about Black Henry? It's crazy to consider staying in country until everyone goes home. And what about Yardly? He's in the Nam for good.*

Finally, exhausted, Andy closed his eyes and dozed fitfully. In sleep, a year of images presented themselves—Camel pleading for Andy to save his life; Boy Red unable to speak because of his injuries; Square One, Andy's first KIA; the napalmed children; the slaughter in the Ca Mau; the burned skin and innocent eyes of disfigured children; faces and limbs blown apart; leeches, infections, lesions, puss . . . the five dead women in the rice field.

Waking in the morning, Andy tried to clear his mind. Not feeling rested, he looked around him. Crowded, and amidst the noise of many men preparing for their flights out of the Nam, he felt insecure and lonely. *My last morning in Vietnam.* His head throbbed. *Strange to be having withdrawal symptoms about leaving Vietnam.*

Not hungry but anxious to get out of the barracks, he followed some of the men to the mess hall nearby. Filling a cup with coffee out of a large urn, he found an unoccupied seat at the end of a long table near some soldiers who appeared withdrawn and uninterested in conversation. He sat near them, thankful for their aloofness, drinking coffee until it was time to catch his flight.

Army buses transported them to the edge of a runway to wait for their departure. A Boeing 707 landed, and 180 troops in new jungle fatigues strode by to the cheers of some of those going home. Not everybody participated. Too aware of the hardship of the Nam, Andy knew not all the new guys would make it home.

Now their turn to board, Andy walked up the portable stairs and took a seat in the middle of the large plane. *How modern,* he thought. American stewardesses ushered them in, wholesome in their health and eyes sparkling with vitality. Their clean dresses contrasted sharply with the drab green and faded fatigues of soldiers still smelling of the jungle. Andy entered a world that should be familiar but felt foreign.

Wasting no time, the 707 taxied, revved its engines and sped down the runway. At liftoff a spontaneous cheer erupted from the throats of the men aboard. Despite his inexplicable gloom, Andy participated. A distinctly physical sensation of a mighty weight being lifted from his shoulders surprised him as the plane soared higher above the Nam. Hurtling towards a future that had been in doubt for a year, Andy was on his way home.

PART TWO

WAR WITHOUT END

CHAPTER THIRTEEN

THE JUBILATION FOLLOWING takeoff settled into a subdued and reflective mood as the plane achieved cruising speed and altitude. Solitary thoughts replaced any need to talk for most of the soldiers on board. A flight of twenty-two hours separated the men from a return to their homeland after a year's tour of duty in Vietnam.

Andy, exhausted, but too keyed up to sleep, sat and thought about his future—now that he had one. Three days before, he'd seen his last dead bodies in the Nam. He had no idea of the final body count of the deaths he'd witnessed during his tour. Seventy-seven alone from the slaughter in Ca Mau; dozens more in the battles near the Seven Mountains. Eluding death, he pondered what to do with life. He had twenty-two hours to think about it.

After brief layovers in Japan and Alaska for refueling, the plane landed at Travis Air Force Base and rolled to a stop while the soldiers leaned towards the small aircraft windows for their first glimpses of a homeland not seen for a year. Andy felt a rush of excitement despite his uncertainty about the changes within the country and himself.

Travis, tucked between oak-studded hills and the eastern reaches of the San Francisco Bay, looked welcoming from the air. Geographically situated for returning American soldiers from their war, the large and sprawling installation provided miles of runways for its fleet of military planes. With eleven square miles to choose from, placing the out-processing center at the edge of the base near a main thoroughfare made logistic sense for returning an army from Vietnam—also convenient for several hundred anti-war protestors. They gathered outside the building and along the eight-foot-high chain link fence at the edge of the tarmac.

The soldiers, forewarned Army style, were told how to deal with it. A sergeant came on board and gave them instructions to ignore the demonstration. Protestors had their democratic rights and the soldiers had their orders.

Andy heard a rhythmic chant when the doors on the plane opened. "NO MORE WAR, NO MORE WAR." Andy wanted no more war. He thought he'd left all that in Vietnam. Descending the portable stairs from the aircraft, he saw the protestors pressed against the fence at the edge of the base. Signs with anti-war slogans waved in the air above the crowd.

The chanting intensified when the demonstrators saw the soldiers begin to walk off the plane. "PEACE! NOW! NO MORE WAR! PEACE! NOW! NO MORE WAR!" Repeating the phrase over and over. The returning veterans had to walk within a few feet of the hostile crowd to reach the out-processing center. Jeering protestors screamed obscenities at them.

A few of the soldiers, willing to disobey an order, glared at the gathering. They shouted angry words of their own. Andy saw a grunt with an Air Cav patch yell at the protestors, then shrug before saying, "What are they gonna do, send me back to Vietnam?" After a year of facing the NVA and Viet Cong, the long-haired hippies were unintimidating.

Andy looked at the demonstrators out of the corner of his eye. A bearded young man in frenzied anger hung on the fence shouting. Pretending to climb over and confront the soldiers, he pushed his weight against the chain link barrier. A soldier, unfazed, took a run at him and tried to hit the man's fingers. The crowd backed away on the other side. Smirking at their cowardice, he returned to the line of soldiers.

"Just what I thought," he said, "bunch of fucking pussies. Send them to the Nam and let Charlie have a go at 'em."

Uncomfortable in their presence, Andy just wanted to get inside the building beyond their gaze and the noise of their shouting. He caught glimpses of signs. Peace symbols adorned the air above the jostling. Andy heard another soldier comment, "What are they so pissed about? It's us just back from the Nam, man. You ask to go there? I sure as hell didn't. Should be their turn if you ask me."

His buddy, quieter, told him, "They ain't askin' you, man. If they were, we wouldn't be here."

Andy spotted a sign with the familiar MAKE LOVE, NOT WAR. Remembering the helmet graffiti of Minnesota's, Andy recalled the bitter inverse stating *MAKE WAR, NOT LOVE.* War-making cost Minnesota a leg from a punji stake smeared with some nasty shit Charlie knew how to scrounge from somewhere in the jungle.

Another sign expressed some barely comprehensible flowery hippie bullshit. WAR IS NOT HEALTHY FOR CHILDREN AND OTHER LIVING THINGS.

"Tell me about it," some war-weary grunt proclaimed, marching towards the processing building still yards away. "They gonna tell me somethin' about the war? Fuck it, man. It don't mean nothin.'"

Andy glanced at the crowd with just a few yards to go before entering the building at the edge of the base. A girl with a green headband holding her long red hair in place stared at him. Heavy set, but pretty, their eyes locked for a moment. Her glare expressed contempt for Andy. She gave him the finger.

Not back from the war five minutes, the soldiers received their first lessons in returning from the Nam. Andy, age twenty, and too young to even vote, knew some of the country's anti-war sentiment would be directed at him. Thoughts of Sammy, the Professor and Black Henry in a Mekong Delta jungle flooded his mind. Not one of them had asked for this war. Maybe Camel had found some peace in death.

Andy kept walking but continued looking at the red-headed girl with the long hair. Her green eyes matched the color of her headband.

Inside the building tailors fitted the soldiers with new dress greens, necessary for Andy after a thirty-pound weight loss. Anxious to be on their way home, lines formed for receiving orders, pay vouchers, insignia and ribbons earned in the war zone. And, for the lucky ones with less than five months' military service left, discharges. Andy missed the cutoff by two weeks.

Three hours after landing, with everything he needed for a thirty-day leave, Andy exited the double doors onto the street. Seeing none of the protestors lingering nearby, he found his way to a bus station and asked for a ticket to the San Francisco Airport.

Autumn in northeastern Oklahoma had always been Andy's favorite time of year. Summer's heat gradually dissipating into the cooler weather of October and November were a relief from temperatures often reaching 100 degrees. The large deciduous trees lining the streets of his hometown of Afton had turned from green to bright yellows and reds, dropping to the ground and swirling in the late-October wind. As a boy, he loved the sound of the leaves crunching underneath his feet as he walked to and from school.

Returning from the war, the massive trunks branching into smaller and smaller limbs bare of any leaves triggered an unexpected bleakness in Andy. He'd never noticed the shabbiness of the small town before. The lovely trees and well-kept yards of summer covered up the dilapidated porches and crumbling foundations of houses once grander, but now gradually descending into states of disrepair. Peeling paint on wooden siding matched the barren trees—and Andy's mood.

The expected euphoria of surviving the war never quite materialized. Brief flashes of it lightened Andy's mood only to be intruded on by a deep foreboding that confused him. During his tour, the men all fantasized about returning home. They shared versions of living happily if they could survive their tours. Only the war stood between them and a return to a normal life.

Instead of joy, an emotional flatness permeated Andy. He was fatigued from all the travel and unsettled by the scenes on American soil.

Andy's mother, Rebecca, joyous at his return, flung her arms around her boy while the rest of the family patiently waited their turn to greet him. Everybody crowded around, smiling, the men pumping his arm, the women tearing up and wanting a hug.

Andy smiled complacently. Politely acknowledging everyone who gathered in the family home to welcome him back, manners learned growing up remained intact. Inwardly claustrophobic at the attention, he maintained a cordial exterior.

Henry Clay Parks, proud, but mostly thankful to have his son back, ushered in the guests crowded into the modest house on Fourth Street. Typically more reserved, the elder Parks talked with the men, keeping the conversation light while the women fussed over Andy and gave him more hugs. Noticing the weight loss without commenting, plates of food appeared. The instinctual nurturing of the women proceeded with amazing rapidity.

Rebecca's sister, Ruby, sliced into two pecan pies, her specialty from growing up on the nut orchard ten miles from town. Andy's aunt Lucille from his father's side, setting out a bowl of potato salad, gathered utensils and chatted excitedly. "We are so glad to have you back, Andrew, safe and sound where you belong. Do you have to go back to the Army?"

"I do," Andy said. "I have a posting in San Francisco. After my leave I'll have about four months left in the Army."

"San Francisco," Louise Thornbill commented. "I didn't know there were Army bases in a big city. How nice to see some of the country." The preacher's wife, good friends with Rebecca, poured coffee into mugs for the men.

"Letterman's Army Hospital is at the Presidio in San Francisco," Andy explained, "with a lot of wounded men from the war recuperating. I'll be a medic there until I'm discharged."

Andy joined the men in the living room. His uncle Roland, Ruby's husband, made a spot for him on the couch. Andy wanted out of his uniform, away from the formality, but didn't know how to disengage for a while without appearing rude. The men, smiling, also uncomfortable dressed in suits worn mostly for church, drank their coffee and chatted. Wanting to ask Andy about Vietnam, but not uttering a word about it, small talk prevailed.

"It's good to have you back, Andy," Fred Sixkiller, Lucille's husband, remarked. His son and Andy's cousin, Freddy, nodded a hello. "Probably glad to just be back and get on with your life, right? A lot of young men are getting their draft notices now. Freddy's wondering if he should just join up and get it over with."

Freddy, his hair longer now, looked younger, and more Native. Lucille, in marrying a Sixkiller, increased the amount of Cherokee in her family. Both sides in the marriage had genealogies linked to Nanye-hi. The famous warrior, then peacemaker, distinguished herself in battle by picking up the fight after her husband, Tsu-la Kingfisher, died in a 1755 battle with Creek Indians. Cherokee bloodlines had been diluted in the Parks family but remained important.

Andy pretended not to notice the implied question, which he had no intention of answering. Dreading any talk about the war, he retreated deeper into silence. Trying not to appear impolite, he struggled to find words to contribute to the conversation.

Nothing changed in the house during the year of his absence.

Loosening his uniform tie and then pulling it off completely, Andy tried to keep from fidgeting on the couch. Already uncomfortable, caught between learned manners from the past and the need to be alone, the dreaded question emerged.

"What's it like over there?"

Paralyzed by the question, Andy felt cornered. His mind returned to the jungle—and the guys in the platoon. The tongue-tied medic, not knowing how to answer, stared blankly at no one. Panicking over a simple question, one without answers, he didn't give any. *How do you sum up in a few words a year in the muck of the swamps of the Mekong Delta, the death, the stench, the cruelty, the fear, the barbarism?*

"Hard to say," Andy mumbled feebly. "Hard to see the big picture. Maybe now that I'm home—"

Without prompting, his mind dredged up one of the battles near the Seven Mountains. Five in the platoon died the night his hands stopped shaking, the night he became a good medic.

Andy sat in the familiar living room surrounded by people he'd known his entire life. But he would not have felt more ill at ease with total strangers. He concentrated on patterns of behavior learned by rote, on common phrases, their superficiality understood by all. Sensing his distress, Rebecca and Henry Parks intervened.

After thanking everyone for coming, the elder Parks turned to Andy. "It's been a long day for you, son," he said.

"And a long year for all of us. We are so thankful to have you back with us, dear," Rebecca added. Andy could see the concern in her eyes. "You must be exhausted. I've made up your bed for you. We can talk more after supper."

Andy could hide the sores and boils from a year in the swamps and jungles beneath his clothes. He worried the other scars of war, the invisible ones, would show in his eyes. His mother would notice that.

Relieved to be alone in his old bedroom, he changed out of his uniform and hung it in the closet. None of the clothes in his dresser fit, the shirts hanging loosely on his lean frame, the pants needing his belt notched three holes tighter. Crawling under the freshly laundered quilt on his boyhood bed, Andy felt a moment of peacefulness, safe for the first time since going to the war. Falling into a deep sleep, Andy rested for the first time in over a year.

❃ ❃ ❃

Waking four hours later, troubled, but not knowing why, Andy bolted upright in bed. Alarmed at allowing himself to fall into such a deep slumber, it took a second to comprehend. He felt the bed around him in the dark. Realizing he was in Oklahoma and not Vietnam, he let out a breath and relaxed his tensed muscles. Taking a moment to orient his troubled mind, he told himself, *You are home now. No need to worry.*

CHAPTER FOURTEEN

HOME A WEEK, Andy visited with his mother while she fried potatoes and took biscuits out of the oven. Sitting at the kitchen table with a cup of coffee, he reflected on similar mornings growing up. Rebecca Parks insisted on few things in life, feeding her family a good breakfast before church every Sunday being one of them. Resigned to attending the morning services, Andy obliged his mother.

Aware his year in Vietnam was difficult on the family, Andy attempted to hide his growing sense of isolation. Feigning interest in local events—who was getting married, having babies, building a house—he participated in conversations by rote. Bumping into friends and former classmates, he declined invitations to go out or have coffee. A constant anxiety gnawed at him about the fate of the platoon still waging war in the Delta. With growing frustration Andy watched the people in Afton go about the mundane events of their daily lives while friends in Vietnam remained in danger. Confused about his feelings, he dismissed them. Unable to interpret his emotions, how would anyone else?

Andy suspected his mother knew the war had changed him. Every time she looked into his eyes, he noticed concern on her face.

She mostly listened, careful not to pressure him into talking about painful experiences before he was ready.

Andy spoke of the beauty of the jungle, where the variety of flora grew in layers high into the sky. Shades of green, his favorite color, stunning in the variety and shapes they defined, and intricately entwined with the plants weaving around one another in search of nutrients and light. He described the rice paddies, the seedlings swaying above the flooded fields, the farmers in conical hats always bent over tending their crops. He talked about the Vietnamese villages along the canals, the massive rivers and saturated landscape of the Mekong Delta. Andy mentioned the swamps and even the mosquitoes—but never combat.

The family learned about Sammy, Black Henry, and the Professor. They were fascinated to hear about Yardly and Montagnard ways. How they built their houses secured to posts above the ground and were an indigenous people with their own language and customs different from the Vietnamese. Yardly's bond with the Professor, and his fierce loyalty to the American soldiers he found a home with. They never heard about Camel dying, Boy Red, the napalmed children, and the dozens of corpses Andy failed to save as a medic.

Sometimes Andy would speak, and his mind would drift off for a few moments thinking about the war, but he never talked about it.

What the family could not see was something Andy kept hidden, something even he could not conceptualize. The shame and complicity of participating in so much violence and death, surviving what so many others did not. This feeling became normal for Andy, the source obscure, deep, and difficult to decipher.

✱ ✱ ✱

Only two things bothered Andy about his mother—her devotion to the church, and the fact that she had named him Andrew.

Prior to the war, Andy found church excruciating. Home again, he attended only for his mother's sake. The elder Parks also went to please Rebecca but had negotiated a deal with his wife. He could watch football on Sunday afternoons in exchange for devoting the morning to God.

Saying hello and visiting with members of Trinity Baptist Church before the services began, Andy sat between his parents in a pew near the front and off to the side of the pulpit. Louise Thornbill waved a gloved hand at them in greeting. Andy politely nodded back.

Horace Thornbill walked to the pulpit and the congregation rose for a prayer.

"Our Heavenly Father who watches over us not only in our daily needs, but throughout the trials and tribulations of our lives, we wish to thank thee, Dear Lord, for your Grace and Compassion in protecting one of our own children. Andrew Parks has returned from the war, sound of body and of mind. We thank thee, Heavenly Father, for answering our prayers, and the prayers of this young man's family. Amen."

"Amen," the congregation repeated.

Horace Thornbill looked at Andy and began clapping. The parishioners remained standing and followed his lead. Rebecca cried and hugged Andy, who wished to shrink and disappear from the attention.

Seven days prior he'd returned to Travis Air Force Base with hundreds of angry protestors screaming obscenities at him. Home one week, and Trinity Baptist gave him a standing ovation for surviving the war.

Before leaving church, and at the request of Rebecca Parks, the congregation prayed for the safe return of Sammy, Black Henry, the Professor, and Yardly. Not believing in the efficacy of prayer, Andy wondered what they were doing at that exact moment.

Andy knew the church filled a void in his mother's life, lonely after losing her mother to pneumonia at the age of four, bereft and orphaned when her father died before her eighth birthday. Hauling produce to market as the foreman of a pecan farm, Arnold Elrod's brakes failed on the loaded truck descending Frick's Mountain near Grand Lake.

With three children on the farm and no parents to look after them, the kindly but older owners of the orchard did their best. Rebecca, the youngest, stayed with them. Ruby, four years older, went to live with friends on a neighboring farm. Andrew, sixteen and old enough to work, struck out on his own. Rebecca had lost not only her parents, but a brother who doted on his younger sister.

Andy's mother often spoke about his namesake, the uncle he'd never met. She told stories of how he used to build things for her and showed Andy drawings, which she still had. The sketches of rural Oklahoma depicted scenes in the orchard, loading crates of pecans onto trucks, and shaking nuts from the trees. Cows grazed in the oak-studded hills of the area. An eagle perched on a stout branch, then soared into the sky, gradually disappearing in the sequence of drawings, much like Andrew had faded from Rebecca's life.

World War II began, and Andrew had joined the Navy, rescuing him from the drudgery of farm labor and a working poverty. Rebecca knew little about those years of her brother's life. Returning from the war, marrying, drifting away from Rebecca, Oklahoma, and a bad marriage, Andrew disappeared before his sister gave birth to Andy.

The missing men in Rebecca's life became Andy's namesakes. Christened Andrew Arnold Parks, Andy was the best he could salvage from a name like that.

The Parks side of the family identified with the Cherokee, the Native ancestry passed down through Andy's grandparents. Jacob, fluent in the Cherokee language, forged his links to the past by listening to aunts and uncles recounting the hardship of *nunna-da-ul-tsun-yi*, "the trail of their tears." They spoke of babies wailing from hunger and succumbing to exposure and pneumonia, crossing rivers and streams, their banks frozen with ice and accumulated snow. The gnawing hunger and bitter cold killed the frail and vulnerable. Trekking 900 miles without enough food or warm clothing, children starved, and died of whooping cough. Many aged, unable to withstand the hardship of walking every day, gave up and died. Long after the tears dried, a palpable anguish remained in the telling by the survivors of the forced trek in the winter of 1838, leaving an indelible impression on the Cherokee boy.

Jacob, his father dying before he really knew him, was raised by an aunt after his mother remarried. She never returned for the boy, her fate remaining a mystery. Abandoned or orphaned, Jacob never knew.

Perhaps the similarity of not having parents to raise them, and of family members who vanished, drew Rebecca and her father-in-law into an unlikely bond. They adored one another. Jacob becoming the father Rebecca lost, and the Parks the only family she knew.

Living with them for the final years of his life, Jacob told Andy the stories he had heard as a boy. One-quarter Cherokee, and having no grandparents from his mother's side, Andy identified with the Parks.

Names were important to the family. Sequoyah, the inventor of the Cherokee alphabet, was Jacob's middle name. Henry Clay, Andy's father, named after the famous senator who opposed the forced removal of the Cherokee, bore his name with pride.

The Cherokee hated Andrew Jackson. Fighting alongside him at the Battle of Horseshoe Bend, they helped defeat the Creek Indians in 1814. By 1830, the newly elected president had endorsed and passed the Indian Removal Act sanctioning the eventual removal of the Cherokee from their original lands. The tribe never forgave Andrew Jackson for the betrayal, which led to the Trail of Tears.

The Sixkiller side of the family refused to carry a twenty-dollar bill on their person because it bore the seventh president's picture. Andy would have changed his name except for the hurt it would cause his mother.

❋ ❋ ❋

Ten days into his leave, Andy took $400 and bought a used Chevrolet station wagon. With nothing to spend money on in

Vietnam, even on Andy's $278 per month rate of pay, he saved money. For risking his life in the Nam, he received an additional $65 a month combat pay.

Using his vehicle as a pretense for visiting family outside of Afton, Andy drove. Taking Route 59 to Copeland, he crossed Grand Lake on the bridge and continued through Grove. Farther south, he entered Tahlequah and traversed several streets in the town. Seeking a connection with his previous life, he felt a certain peace in just driving. Revisiting the landscape of his youth, he reflected on what to do with his life. Maybe his remaining months in the Army would give him some time to figure it out.

Leaving Tahlequah, Andy traveled northeast towards Ballard, the countryside full of landmarks to the Cherokee's forced migration into the area. Mostly, Andy found serenity in the landscape, the winding rivers and rushing streams, where cows grazed amongst the oak trees on the rolling hills of northeastern Oklahoma.

Stopping at the Sixkiller cemetery close to the Arkansas border, he remembered some of the headstones his father pointed out on previous visits while retelling stories heard from Jacob Parks.

A train crossed a trestle over a creek within sight of the graveyard. Andy looked up and waved when the locomotive's horn signaled its presence with two prolonged blasts. Listening to the clacking of the steel wheels on the tracks, Andy wished for a moment he could hop on the freight train and let it take him to some unknown destination. Maybe he could start a new life and avoid the pitfalls that ensnared him in this one. As the rhythmic sound of the southbound train's steady momentum faded, the juxtaposition of hope and melancholy intermingled in Andy. Unable to connect with the life he'd had before the war and not knowing why, he supposed his could take a path in either direction.

Ten miles outside of Afton, Andy arrived at the graveled drive of his aunt Ruby's. Winding through the neatly planted orchard, he parked in front of the farmhouse and got out of his car. Greeted by Pal, the farm's overly friendly border collie, Andy felt a twinge of familiarity.

Ruby, an older, stouter version of his mother, came out of the house and met Andy on the porch.

"This is a surprise," she said, giving her nephew a hug. "I didn't expect to see you all the way out here for a while. I woulda thought you'd be blowin' off some steam in town after what you've been through."

Also more direct and gruffer than Rebecca, Ruby stood back from Andy and looked at him. "Come in where we can have a decent chat," she ordered, "and I'll get you something to drink and maybe a snack or two. You're awfully thin. Roland's out somewhere tending to his darn orchard, but he should be back soon."

Andy followed his aunt into the house and to the kitchen where Ruby already had a coffee pot on the stove. "Coffee good?" she asked. "If you want something stronger, I'm sure I can find some of Roland's stash of whiskey. Says he only keeps it for medicinal purposes." She shrugged. "Don't believe it for a moment."

"Coffee's fine," Andy said. His family never kept alcohol in the house, and he'd never developed a taste for it.

After setting two mugs on the kitchen table, Ruby sat opposite her nephew. Childless, she and her husband often had her nieces and nephews out for visits. Andy had fond memories spending parts of summer holidays helping his uncle Roland in the orchard.

"So, how are you, really? Your mother's worried about you," she said, getting right to the point. "She very nearly worried herself to death the whole time you were gone in Vietnam."

Andy knew that. Unable to explain, he avoided the topic.

Sensing Andy's reluctance to talk, Ruby approached it from another angle.

"Rebecca's worried you'll just up and disappear like your uncle did."

The comment confused him. "Why?" he responded, looking at his aunt. "What does Andrew have to do with my being back?" Andy knew his uncle had been in the Navy, but that was all. How would being on a ship in his war mean anything?

"He was just never the same, is all," answered Ruby. "He was a medic, too, you know."

Andy didn't know. "Mom never mentioned it," he said.

"She had no idea. When Andrew returned from the war it was all so crazy for everybody. People were just so glad the war was over, and Andrew, like everybody else, didn't want to talk much about it. When he left, we just figured he wanted to get away from his wife and all. They were fighting something terrible.

"A few years later, one of Andrew's buddies from the war shows up looking for him. Says he never got a chance to thank him properly for saving his life. It's important that he find him. He left a photograph. It's the only one we have from Andrew's time in the Navy. Here, I'll go get it," she said.

When Ruby returned, Andy looked at the photo. He stared and stared, stunned. It could have been a scene from the jungle in Vietnam. Three helmeted Marines, looking weary but smiling, sat close to one another on the ground in front of a small palm tree. Andy saw the family resemblance in the man in the middle. An aid bag, similar to what he carried in Vietnam, lay on the ground in front of his uncle. Andy understood now, more than his mother or aunt could know.

"This is in the Pacific somewhere," he commented. "Do you know where?"

"We have no idea," she said. "All we knew is that Andrew joined the Navy, and then that fellow shows up saying he was with the Marines."

"Navy corpsmen are their field medics," Andy told her. He knew that from Vietnam.

"He looks a lot like you," Ruby said.

❋ ❋ ❋

Andy gathered with the family on the eve of his departure. His leave had required three Sundays of church attendance and numerous visits by relatives and friends. He looked forward to the long drive from northeastern Oklahoma to California. The compact station wagon allowed him to find refuge in the countryside every afternoon. The serenity provided enough of an emotional release to help sustain a polite exterior. Fitted with a sleeping bag in the rear, and a supply of canned goods, Andy prepared for the trip to his posting in San Francisco. Scheduled to report for duty in one week, he planned on seeing part of the country along the way.

Henry Clay stood in the family's living room. Arms folded, he struggled for the right words to address his family. Worried about Andy, he expressed it with concerns over his son's trip. Hoping Andy might reconsider his decision to leave a week early, Henry Clay made a final pitch.

"It seems like you just got here and have to leave again. I wish you weren't so determined to drive all that way across the country. Make sure you're careful and get there in one piece."

Andy nodded. After avoiding thousands of bullets, hundreds of mortar rounds, and an unknown number of hidden Viet Cong booby traps in Vietnam, his father worried about him driving to California. Andy couldn't wait to hit the road.

Unable to hide her concern, Rebecca tried not to cry. Mostly succeeding, she summed up her feelings about Andy's departure.

"I hope you are okay, dear. Something is bothering you; a mother can tell. At least we know you are safe now and can get on with our lives knowing you are home."

Andy's sister, Nancy June, sat on the couch next to her husband, Ben. Pretty, and in the romantic stages of marriage, she leaned on her husband's shoulder. Bubbling over with happiness, she chided her brother.

"We've barely had a chance to see you, Andy, but I guess you'll be back in no time, right?"

"Soon as I'm out of the Army," he said.

His sister was named after two other Nancys in the family, an anglicized derivative honoring the ancestral lineage to Nanye-hi.

June, a reference to the month of her birth, complemented her sunny disposition and sparkling dark eyes.

The family concocted names that way.

George Washington, Andy's younger brother, sat next to his mother on a small sofa. Born on the first president's birthday, and embarrassed by his middle name, he rarely used it. Andy hadn't visited with him much, either, George being busy with school and playing football for the high school team. Andy picked him up from practice a few times. Worried about the draft, George asked him about the war.

"Avoid it," Andy told him without elaborating. "No good will come of you going."

Able to avert any overt rudeness during his leave or swearing with every other word as they had in Vietnam, Andy drove west out of Afton. Excited to be on the road to California, Andy drove out of Oklahoma.

CHAPTER FIFTEEN

ANDY CROSSED THE California state line and headed for the coast. Taking five days to drive from Oklahoma, he observed parts of the country incognito, stopping at roadside cafes for coffee, overhearing conversations about the lives of strangers. He watched families and friends interacting with each other, enthusiastic about their communities, speaking of weddings planned, local sports teams winning and losing, and weather forecasts predicting sunshine or rain. Andy observed, but never participated. Not understanding why he felt so out of place, he had a vague sense of wanting to be a part of conversations—someday, somewhere—but didn't know how.

Looking forward to seeing the ocean for the first time, he stopped at a secluded beach south of San Francisco, deserted in late November. He walked for miles on the shore, the scent of the ocean in the light breeze blowing in from the sea. Gathering driftwood and building a fire in the sand, Andy fell asleep to the sounds of the waves' rhythm.

Waking in the night, he kept the fire going, the heat enough to warm him in his sleeping bag. Never dozing more than four hours at a stretch since returning from the war, he listened to the cooing of birds nesting nearby disturbed by his presence.

On his second day, he found a secluded perch among the jagged outcroppings overlooking the sea. With a sandy patch level enough to make a camp, he gathered more driftwood to keep a fire going during the night. A shallow cave worn from centuries of storms eroding the rock formations during high tides provided Andy with shelter from the rain when gales blew in off the ocean. Exhilarated, he stood in the wind while waves pounded the rocks below him.

Climbing the cliffs before dark for a panoramic view of the coastline, its uneven contours stretched for miles in both directions. The power of the sea, persistent in the constant shaping of stone, left craggy remnants protruding from the sand. Glimpsing eternity in the continuity of nature's steady renewal soothed Andy, providing him a sense of hope.

At dawn, gulls circled overhead, and sanderlings fed on the shore, running on spindly legs avoiding the waves, stopping just long enough to pierce the wet sand with long beaks probing for some hidden morsel.

Due at the Presidio before noon, Andy pulled a set of rumpled dress greens out of his duffel bag and dressed. Taking the coastal highway into San Francisco, he drove through the busy streets, glancing at rows of brightly painted houses built without space between them. Apartments stacked on top of each other contributed to the congestion, while sidewalks full of pedestrians moved like ants in each direction.

Highway One took him right to the Army post in the city. Turning onto the base at the Presidio Boulevard entrance, he pulled into a scenic lookout and got out of his car. A view of the ocean extended for miles. The Golden Gate Bridge spanned the entrance to the bay, its orange pillars poking through remnants of a morning fog dissipating with the heat of the day. Smoothing out the worst of the wrinkles on his uniform, he prepared to return to life as a medic.

The US Army, at the Presidio since taking it away from the Mexicans in 1846, sat on 1,500 acres overlooking San Francisco Bay, a spectacular setting for a military base. At ten stories, Letterman's Army Hospital, with 550 beds, towered above the other buildings on the base. Amputees, burn patients, and the paralyzed occupied its therapy rooms and rehabilitation centers. With each patient a testament to the prolonged and lasting agonies of war, their battles were now waged regaining function in unusable limbs and with the fitting of prostheses from missing ones.

At the northwest point, a massive pillar of the Golden Gate Bridge anchored the southern span of the famous gateway to the bay. Nearby, the Presidio's stockade housed another form of misery. Misfits of the Army, its rapists, killers, and deserters, were crammed into a jail too small for all the transgressions occurring during an unpopular war.

Finding the company orderly room near the hospital, Andy entered a small redbrick building. A lone occupant sat at a desk conducting a telephone conversation. Gesturing with his free hand and nodding to Andy, he indicated he would be with him when the call ended. Dressed in the semi-formal tan khaki uniform, the man's rank insignia of a master sergeant showed prominently on his sleeves, the unit's top NCO. The printed name tag above his shirt pocket read HASTINGS.

Ending the call, he grabbed a file from a stack on his desk. The first sergeant stared at Andy for a moment before welcoming him to the unit. Relieved that Hastings did not take issue with his rumpled appearance, Andy stood at ease. Career military, slender and with a brush cut flat on top, the sergeant opened Andy's file.

"Andrew Parks, says you're just back from Vietnam, Ninth Infantry. We can use some experience on the wards," he said, closing the folder. "I think you'll find this a plum assignment. I'll give you a couple of hours to get settled in the barracks. Report back here at 1300 hours."

Another brick building housed the company's medics. Nice on the outside, the sleeping quarters lacked privacy. A long row of bunks along each wall, without partitions, contributed to Andy's disappointment. Clean and sterile, linoleum floors glossed to a high shine, evident even in the darkened room, smelled of floor wax and antiseptics. Devoid of any other activity, medics pulling night shifts dozed in some of the beds. Andy organized a footlocker assigned with his bunk, showered in the latrine, and hurried outside to escape his growing sense of claustrophobia.

Back in the orderly room at 1300 hours, the company clerk, a young-looking kid, greeted Andy.

"Hi, Top says I'm to take you over to the hospital and introduce you to the staff on the ward you'll be working. My name's Renaldo."

Andy nodded a hello.

"Top says you're just back from the Nam. See some bad shit over there?"

Not knowing how to respond, Andy shrugged.

"I mean, what's it like?"

"It's hard to explain, Renaldo," said Andy, not intending to be rude, but wanting to end the conversation. "Maybe you should volunteer and see for yourself."

"Fuck that shit," said the brash young clerk. "I guess we should get going."

"That's probably wise."

At the hospital, a dark-haired WAC sat at a reception desk making entries into a logbook.

"New medic for you," said Renaldo, seeming to know her. "I'm supposed to take him up to the quad ward and introduce him. Care to go out tonight?"

"In a word, Renaldo, no, not tonight, and probably never," she answered. "You know where the quad ward is?"

"Yeah."

"Then you should probably get up there."

Renaldo winked at her as they left. "She won't go out with me," he said. "The girls in San Francisco won't have anything to do with us Army guys, so we're stuck with the stuck-up WACs. Not many options," he said, surprisingly cheerful despite his gloomy dating situation.

Taking the elevator to the fourth floor, they emerged in a small lobby. Andy followed Renaldo through a pair of swinging doors with a nurse's station on the other side. Two young women in traditional white dresses abruptly ended a conversation and looked up. Neither nurse had rank insignias or military designations.

"New medic for you," said Renaldo. "Guess I better get back to the orderly room."

One of the nurses, a pretty blonde, stared at Andy long enough to make him uncomfortable.

"Hello, Parks," she finally said, looking at the name tag on his uniform. "Do you have a first name?"

"It's Andy," he responded. "That's what I go by."

"Well, Andy, this is Matty," she said, looking at the other nurse, "and my name is Marilyn. We're hired as civilians because there are not enough Army nurses. This is the quadriplegic ward, and all our patients are paralyzed from the neck down. You must have seen some bad stuff in Vietnam, but do you know anything about quadriplegia?"

Andy shook his head no.

She explained that quadriplegia was impairment or absolute paralysis of all four limbs. Varying degrees of torso function could be present, and some patients were ventilator dependent.

"We requested a medic who is also a Vietnam veteran be assigned to the ward. We need help with a specific patient who is not adjusting well to his paralysis. He's hostile to the nurses, and none of them like going near him. He keeps swearing at them and mumbling about us being rimps, whatever that means?"

"He could be referring to REMFs," Andy said, "rear echelon motherfuckers."

"Well, whatever," Marilyn said curtly. "That's why we've brought you in, Parks. If you Vietnam guys have your own way of talking, you can help us out with that, too."

Andy suspected the nurse was one of those pretty girls used to the world acceding to her every whim, and when it didn't, she got irritated.

"What's the patient's name?" Andy asked.

"Calvin Lake," Marilyn answered, "but he doesn't like going by his name." She rolled her eyes.

"What does he like to go by?" Andy thought he might have a nickname from the Nam.

"We don't understand that, either," she said. "Something about an eagle; maybe you can figure that out, too."

Not on the ward five minutes and Andy disliked Marilyn.

"I suppose we should show you around," she said. "You can start tomorrow. Stop by the laundry and get the white smocks you will need."

Andy followed Marilyn through another set of double doors. Entering a large ward, a different reality emerged. Patients lying in the middle of circular frames filled the room. Each device, with a diameter taller than Andy, held a man immobilized by their injury. Ventilators, breathing for patients without even that basic function, were the only sound Andy heard besides their footsteps. He and the curt nurse were walking among dozens of men who could not.

An eerie sense of dread seized him at the sight of so many tortured bodies back from the war lying inert and unable to function. His mind detached itself, similar with a combat situation. Images of the slaughter in Ca Mau flooded his mind.

The damaged bodies lying prone and immobile slammed against the inside of his head. The steady rhythmic sound of the ventilators breathing had a grotesquely hypnotic effect, immobilizing Andy emotionally.

"This is our acute ward," Marilyn explained, "where our most severely paralyzed patients are kept. Each man is assigned to a Stryker frame, capable of rotating three hundred and sixty degrees. The wheels at the base can be unlocked for easy transporting of the entire unit."

Andy heard her words, but his mind reached back to Nam.

"At best," Marilyn continued, "we hope they can regain some function in their arms and be able to utilize their fingers enough to eventually work the electric controls on a wheelchair. Most of the patients on the ventilators have deteriorated to the point where it's only the machines keeping them alive. We don't expect a lot of them to survive. For the patients able to breathe on their own, we are trying various forms of therapy that we hope will gradually restore more function to their arms and fingers. Calvin Lake is over here," she said, as if his paralysis had also made him deaf. The nurse approached the patient cautiously.

"Calvin, I have someone here I would like you to meet," she said. Andy thought she acted like Calvin might jump up and do something besides lie there paralyzed.

"Fuck off," a voice from the frame said. Andy could not see his face, just the back of his head, shaved, with light-brown hair growing in tufts where lacerations healing produced scar tissue.

"Calvin, this is Andy. He's going to help look after you."

"If he's another one of your REMF bastards, you can both fuck off."

"Actually, Calvin, Andy's just back from Vietnam, too."

Andy cringed and turned to Marilyn. "I'll stay and get acquainted with Calvin, if that's okay?"

"Certainly," she said, and left, her footsteps steady and echoing through the ward.

Andy moved to the floor where he could look at Calvin's face for the first time. Lying prone and on his stomach, sandwiched between two padded supports on the Stryker frame, two bluish grey eyes alertly locked into Andy's gaze.

"So," he said, pausing, "you're Andy. Just what is it you expect to be able to do for me?"

The direct question caught Andy by surprise.

"I don't know, man. What is it you'd like me to be able to do for you?"

"Miss Prissy gone?" Calvin asked.

"She is."

"You back from the Nam? I see it in your eyes, man. Infantry?"

"Grunt medic," Andy said. Looking at Calvin's face, Andy noticed scars from three more lacerations.

"At least you been there. We'll discuss what you can really do for me later. For starters, I need to get off this fuckin' ward once in a while."

"I think I can manage that. They'll want me to take you to therapy. Have you started any yet?"

"Fuck the therapy," Calvin huffed, angry at Andy's obtuse response. For some reason Doc Woski's instructions to Andy when he arrived in the Nam popped into his head. *"Don't ever bullshit these guys."*

"You wanna know what you can really do for me?" Calvin continued. "Finish the job."

Andy didn't respond.

"There's no way I should have made it out of the Nam, Doc, and I don't wanna live like this. You like to know how this happened? I remember most of it."

Andy nodded for him to continue.

"Been in the Nam five months, 101 Airborne, and we was always in the shit. Big battles with NVA Regulars pouring over the DMZ. Walked into it real bad on one of our patrols. We were overrun so completely the LT was calling for air strikes on our own position just to get the motherfuckers off us. That much I remember.

"I was hit and must have been unconscious for a long time. I woke up when a couple of the guys from one of our sister platoons put me on a stretcher. They told me mine was wiped out, only a handful of the wounded left alive. The LT was dead for sure, and the platoon sergeant. Some of the wounded survived by playing dead, but I don't know who made it out. I couldn't move, so here I lay."

Andy, still on the floor, shifted positions. Calvin Lake's gaze never wavered, looking through Andy like he could see all the way to eternity.

"So, here's the deal," he continued. "Before I kill myself, and I might need a little help, I need to know what happened to my platoon members. Think you can do that? If not, get the fuck out of here and go tell Miss Prissy I don't care if you're just back from the Nam or Pluto. I want somebody who can help me with what I need."

Andy shifted uncomfortably. Calvin Lake's intensity was the worst kind of scrutiny, but Andy found his voice.

"I'll be honest with you, man. I can help you with the first part, but I'm not gonna be able to help you kill yourself."

"We'll see," Calvin mocked. "We'll talk more about that later. Find me a way off this ward tomorrow that doesn't involve therapy. If monotony could kill somebody, then I wouldn't need help doing it. I don't wanna spend months in therapy just to get a little movement in my fingers back."

Andy knew what Calvin was talking about. They had all dreaded the worst kinds of wounds in Vietnam, the ones worse than death. Some of the guys even devised elaborate pacts with each other. *"Shoot me if I'm blind and my balls are shredded, I'm paralyzed, or burned bad from the napalm."* That sort of thing.

Calvin spoke again, interrupting Andy's thoughts.

"And one more thing, Doc. Bring a bottle of Wild Turkey with you tomorrow. It'll help with the monotony."

Andy took a moment to comprehend.

Not missing anything, Calvin picked up on Andy not knowing what he was talking about. "Let me guess," Calvin mocked. "You don't drink, either. Aren't you a piece of work."

CHAPTER SIXTEEN

AN INNER VOICE screamed at Andy when he left the hospital. *I'm sorry, sorry, sorry, Calvin. I can't do anything for you and the other men lying beside you.*

Overwhelmed, Andy walked towards the company barracks with his head pounding and full of twisted feelings. The afternoon sun of a beautiful San Francisco day had him squinting against the brightness, trapping images in his mind of damaged bodies lying immobile on the quadriplegic ward.

Incapable of sorting it out, Andy entered the barracks and sat on his bunk. Other medics milled about, visiting quietly in small groups, strangers to Andy. In the Nam he'd had Sammy to lean on, and White Henry, even Black Henry and the Professor. Intensely alone, Andy changed into civilian clothes. More isolated than he could remember being in Vietnam, he walked outside, the urge to flee overwhelming.

At his car, he sat gripping the steering wheel, hoping something familiar would help sort through his confusion. Safe now, he just needed to settle in, finish his few months in the Army. Inside, his emotions churned. *How am I going to complete even a few weeks on the quad ward? I can't help anyone there. And what am I going to do for Calvin?*

Andy drove off the base. In Oklahoma driving helped him during his leave, the winding roads through the countryside calming him.

Andy welcomed the anonymity of San Francisco. The congestion of the city swallowed him. Nobody questioned him amidst the crowds and bustle or paid attention to the boy medic home from Vietnam.

At dusk he pulled into a Union 76 service station, the bright orange on the neon sign a familiar image in a city full of novelties to the small-town boy from Oklahoma. After filling the gas tank, Andy parked on a hill and watched the skyline come to life with electricity. One flashing *LIQUOR* reminded him of Calvin's request.

Entering the store, Andy stood mesmerized by the wall of choices with colorful labels. The clerk picked up on his uncertainty. "Can I help you find something?" he asked.

"Wild Turkey," Andy stated, trying to pretend he knew something about drinking. His only experience was with an occasional beer to be sociable. Not liking the taste, he'd never been able to drink enough to get anything but a light buzz.

"Down by the bourbons and whiskeys." The clerk pointed towards the back of the store.

"Thanks." With so many choices, Andy stood gawking at the shelves, wondering about the difference between bourbon and whiskey.

"A little bit farther," the clerk said, arriving to assist him. "Here you go," pointing to a yellow label with a bird on it.

"Nice picture," Andy said awkwardly, reaching for the bottle closest to him.

At the counter the man asked, "You twenty-one?"

"Almost," Andy said. "It's for a friend."

"Law says you gotta be twenty-one, son."

Andy stood for a moment, his ingrained manners not knowing whether it was appropriate to just walk out of the store or put the bottle back on the shelf.

"For a couple dollars more I guess we can let it slide. Since it's for a *friend*," he added sarcastically.

Having enough of the city, Andy drove back to the Presidio. Still restless, he returned to the barracks, sitting on his bunk with his back propped against the wall. One day back in the Army and it felt worse than Vietnam. He fidgeted with the bottle of liquor he'd bought for Calvin Lake. He remembered seeing wild turkeys in the hills of northeastern Oklahoma.

It was stupid to buy this for Calvin, Andy admonished himself.

On impulse he twisted the cap off the bottle. Desperate enough to try anything to obliterate the painful emotions raging, he took a swallow. He coughed and sputtered on the first burning sip. Figuring there must be a reason so many people drank the stuff, Andy persisted, taking progressively bigger swigs, just like his buddies had in Vietnam.

A warm glow reached his brain, easing the worst of his thoughts. Just then, Renaldo appeared.

"The first sergeant doesn't like any drinking in the barracks."

Startled, the intrusion angered Andy. "What's he gonna do, send me to Vietnam?" That's exactly where Andy wished he was. Worried about Sammy, he should have extended his tour until his friend was able to come home with him. Bad decisions were becoming a habit.

"Just letting you know," Renaldo persisted.

"Fine," said Andy. "I've been warned."

"You drink like that in the Nam?" the company clerk continued.

Andy didn't respond.

"If you like, we can go over to the Enlisted Men's Club and drink there."

Wanting to tell Renaldo to fuck off, Andy checked himself, remembering an encounter with an ugly drunk. "Maybe some other time, Renaldo."

"Suit yourself," said Renaldo as he left.

His senses dulled, obliterating some of the worst images in his mind, Andy dozed off, exhausted.

An image of the little napalmed girl emerged. Struggling to breathe, her efforts focused on inhaling enough oxygen to stay alive.

Andy, distressed, knew there was not enough in her damaged lungs to sustain life. The jungle burned all around them. Desperate for a remedy, anything that might work to alleviate the suffering, he looked for his aid bag. In the flames beyond the girl, it caught fire, becoming a useless pile of ash as Andy watched.

The Viet Cong girl with the long black hair glared at him, demanding he do something. Paralyzed, Andy looked at where his aid bag had disintegrated.

Calvin Lake appeared, his head, detached from his body, useless to him now. *"See, Doc, there is no life for me without a body, not one I want to live. Do the right thing for once. Put me out of this misery. Would you wanna live like this?"*

Bolting awake at three in the morning with his head feeling like it would explode, Andy rushed to the latrine. Barely making it to one of the sinks, he vomited. Gripping the sides of the wash basin for support, he stared at his ashen image in the mirror, bloodshot eyes peering back at him. Shaking, he turned the faucet on, washing the vomit down the drain, retching twice more.

Not rested, and dehydrated, he splashed some water on his face and drank from cupped hands. Finding a bottle of aspirin in his footlocker, he swallowed four tablets before lying on his bunk. Shivering, he pulled the Army-issue blanket over him and waited for the aspirin to take effect.

When he stopped shaking, Andy got up and showered. Still wobbly and nauseous, he craved something to quench his thirst. Expected on the quad ward in three hours, he needed to pull himself together.

Craving liquids, Andy dressed and walked to the mess hall. Orange juice and coffee helped alleviate some of his symptoms. Renaldo sat across from Andy with a heaping plate of sausages and eggs.

"Hungover?" He smirked. "You smell like a brewery. The first sergeant isn't going to like it if he finds out you been drinking so much."

Worried about the smell of alcohol oozing out of his pores, Andy returned to the barracks and showered for a second time. Brushing his teeth thoroughly and gargling several times, he'd run out of time to prepare for his first full day on the quad ward.

※ ※ ※

Calvin Lake's impairment, severe in all four limbs, left him dependent on the hospital personnel for basic bodily functions. Urinary catheters, relatively simple, took care of the body's liquid waste. Bowel movements were more complicated.

A medic named Kenny, assigned to help Andy with learning the basics of caring for Calvin, showed him how to induce defecation.

Wearing surgical gloves, Kenny reached into Calvin's rectum. "It's best to achieve some regularity," he explained. "Without it, the chance of infection increases if the fecal matter sits there too long."

Imagining himself in Calvin's place, Andy remembered times in the Nam when he'd avoided death and serious injury. Moving too soon, or too late, miscalculating an angle, in a split second a life of normal expectations was shattered. Sometimes, it was just bad luck. Understanding the patient's humiliation increased Andy's guilt.

Calvin, not taking the procedure passively, goaded and berated the young medic as he attempted to stimulate a bowel movement.

"Hey, Kenny, got your orders for the Nam yet? See what it can do for you. Become the man you always wanted to be."

Silent, Kenny ignored Calvin's taunting. Unable to induce any natural function, he continued removing fecal matter with his hands.

An hour and a half later they washed in the lavatory and took a break in the staff cafeteria.

"Any questions?" Kenny asked. "I think they've got Calvin scheduled for some therapy today. Check with the nurses when we get back."

"Thanks, man," Andy said. Still shaky from his hangover, he'd recovered enough to function, but just wanted to get through the day.

"The nurses are hoping since you're a Vietnam vet you can establish some kind of rapport with Calvin. He's not the only patient wanting to commit suicide, but he's the most persistent. Nobody likes having to deal with him. You just back from the war?"

"One month," Andy said. "How long you been on the ward?"

"About six months. Some of the other medics have got orders for Vietnam. I'm hoping they need to keep some of us around now that we know how to take care of these guys."

The Army used on-the-job training to fill in the knowledge gaps of its medics.

"Is the war as bad as they say?" Kenny asked.

"Sometimes," Andy said. The ward full of quadriplegics spoke to the question better than he could.

Back with Calvin, Andy rotated him on the Stryker frame so he could see where they were going and unlocked the wheels. Needing off the ward, he figured Calvin must as well.

"Hey, Doc, I thought you didn't drink."

Embarrassed, Andy shrugged, knowing his pores must still be oozing booze.

"You can't tell me you'd want to live like this," Calvin ranted, "having strangers pulling shit out of your asshole."

"I thought you wanted me to find out about your platoon members?" Andy said, attempting to deflect some of his anger.

"I do, but then I want some help ending this nightmare."

"Give me some names," Andy said. "I've got some ideas how we can get started."

At first, Andy just wanted a way to communicate with Calvin about something that wouldn't create a confrontation. He remembered trying to get casualties in Vietnam working with him to ease their pain and any fear from being wounded. He tried the same with Calvin in hopes it would stem some of the rage.

"Who should we look for first, the guys in your squad?"

"We were down to about nineteen men in the platoon when we

were hit so bad. I have it all in my head."

"Good," said Andy, "I'll start jotting down names. I've got to take you to therapy now. The nurses are insisting."

"What, they're worried about my limbs atrophying?

"And blood clots," Andy said. "Just go along for the ride; then we can work on finding your platoon members."

❋ ❋ ❋

"Eagle One was my nickname over there," Calvin began. "I walked point quite a bit. Didn't mind it as much as some of the guys. The platoon thought I had good eyes, and, hey, we were the Screaming Eagles of the 101 Airborne. Some guys joked that we were the puking buzzards because of the eagle having its mouth open on our insignia, but we were proud of that patch."

"What's with the controversy over your name?" Andy asked. "Marilyn told me you didn't like going by Calvin."

"I was just messin' with Miss Prissy," he said. "I was a little bit goofy with the meds, too, but everybody around here is so stupid about the Nam. The medics who haven't been are petrified of going, and the nurses don't know shit."

As usual, Calvin had a point, but if one's impressions about Vietnam came from a duty posting at Letterman, fear of going was reasonable.

Andy wheeled Calvin to an elevator, and they perched themselves on the tenth-floor solarium. Calvin's Stryker frame tilted so he could see out the windows, Andy took notes while Calvin talked.

"Our doc was a kid from Idaho. Not the same medic as when I arrived in the platoon. The first one got greased early in my tour and Timmy replaced him. His name is easy to remember because we just called him Doc Barker. The whole battalion was going through medics. I mean, none of our life expectancies were good, but man did we lose some medics. But Timmy was still there the day I got hit."

Andy put *Timothy Barker from Idaho* on the list for Renaldo to check. He'd had a chat with the company clerk about tracing the names Calvin gave him, putting him to work on something besides reiterating what the first sergeant did or didn't like. The kid agreed, but for a fee, of course, using the Army channels of communications in ways he was privy to.

"One of the guys in my squad I liked was a Puerto Rican from New York City. Spoke with an accent, so I don't know if he was born here, but he was dependable in a firefight. I guess that was the important thing in the Nam. I'm pretty sure his last name was Delgado, first name Pedro. Brown Bird, that's what we called him, was still alive when I was wounded."

Pedro Delgado, Puerto Rican, aka Brown Bird went on the list.

"I know the LT didn't make it out, and our platoon sergeant, a lifer from somewhere in the South. He was a tough motherfucker. I give him that. Not the brightest bulb upstairs, but a good sergeant, never let us down.

"Like I said, we were down to nineteen guys, never had enough replacements. There were five newer guys I never got to know, so I don't need any information on them. One of our M-60 machine gunners was a black guy from Ohio somewhere. We called him Black Eagle, which he kinda liked for a nickname. His last name was Edwards, Delmer Edwards. A guy in the same squad as Black Eagle, Ron Mortimer, Morty for short, I liked him."

Three days on the ward, and Andy had eleven names on the list. He'd invited Renaldo to the Enlisted Men's Club for drinks to go over his notes. While looking at the names, he thought about third platoon. On three occasions Howitz's leadership spared them the annihilation Calvin experienced—the slaughter in the Ca Mau, the battle at the base of the Seven Mountains where Yardly appeared, and the night the VC came out of those same mountains and nearly overran them. Waiting to hear from Sammy, the worry about his friend was constant.

Renaldo ordered a beer. Andy, drinking whiskey, already had a light buzz. Drinking was becoming a self-medicating painkiller.

"Finding out about the dead guys should be easy," Renaldo said. "The Army has good statistics on them. Any of those recently discharged we'll know are alive and made it home. Finding out where guys are still in the system may take longer."

"Can you do it?" Andy asked.

"Absolutely," he said. "I just have to be careful the first sergeant doesn't find out about me using unauthorized channels."

"Why should he care?" Andy asked. "You're just finding out where guys are for a badly wounded patient. Why's everybody so afraid of Hastings, anyway?"

"Just don't get on his bad side."

Andy shrugged.

"Oh," said Renaldo, "I almost forgot. Here's a letter that came for you today."

CHAPTER SEVENTEEN

ANDY'S HAND SHOOK as Renaldo handed him the letter. Plain as day, Sammy's name appeared in the left-hand corner. It meant he was okay, as of a week ago when the note left Vietnam.

Andy rushed back to the barracks to open the envelope.

Hello Doc,

I'm not used to writing you letters. It seems strange not having you in the hooch after our patrols. Strange not having you out there with us, too, but I'm glad you're back in the World not having to worry about Charlie and surviving the Nam. I'm down to one month now, pretty short, but I guess you know that. Be back around Christmas, and be discharged to boot as I'll have less than five months left on my draft commitment.

I've got some bad news. Three days ago, we were back in the Ca Mau after a stint of night ambushes near Dong Tam. Everybody was wore out from humping through the swamps. The Professor was on point and took a round in the gut. He must have spotted something, and Charlie shot him before he could take cover. Yardly went after him. We tried stopping him, told him we'd get to the Professor, but the kid went anyway. The VC wasted him. By the time we could get to the Professor, he was dead too.

Sorry for the bad news, but I thought you should know. Black Henry has hardly spoke since the Professor and Yardly bought it. Thinks he should have been on point. I thought the Professor might make it, but you never know in the Nam. Be glad when this fucking war is over.

Bye for now. And see you soon.
Sammy

Andy rummaged through his footlocker for a bottle of Wild Turkey to dull the gut-punch news. He chastised himself for thinking the war might stop taking platoon members because of his absence. Unable to reconcile his safety while the Professor died an ugly death in a remote part of the Delta, Andy felt the hopelessness he'd experienced in the Nam. *I should've been there to help.*

In Vietnam mode, where death shadowed life, Sammy gave a matter-of-fact account of the Professor's demise. Yardly, being Montagnard and loyal to a fault, had tried to rescue him. *Stupid kid, what was he thinking?* It never made sense to him that the boy was out there with the platoon.

Andy remembered the Professor arriving in country so afraid of the Nam he shook. Maybe he'd known all along he wouldn't make it out. Andy pictured him lying there, afraid, bleeding, in a lot of pain, the firefight intense around him, pleading in his mind for the guys to get to him before his life ebbed out of him.

At least it's over now, the suffering for the Professor. And Yardly, what was he ever going to do when the Professor left the Nam? Not a problem now with them both gone.

Andy sipped the whiskey. He had tried staying away from the stuff, at least cutting down. Ashamed of his drinking, of whatever weakness created the need to blot out with alcohol, Andy felt worse in the mornings when he had to face another day on the quad ward. The news of the deaths took him back to Vietnam.

Due on the quad ward, Andy was in no shape to function. He'd really overdone it with the drinking for the last couple of weeks, ever since hearing about the Professor and Yardly. Still partially drunk, the thought of facing the day caused him to vomit. Showering before his shift was not enough to revive him or flush the alcohol from his system.

He considered going on sick call, the Army's equivalent of phoning in ill. That would leave Kenny to fend with Calvin. Swallowing a handful of aspirin, he dressed and headed to the mess hall for coffee. Only one shift remained before two scheduled days off.

Calvin noticed the hangover. With bloodshot eyes and pores oozing alcoholic waste, Andy's breath still smelled of whiskey even after gargling with mouthwash.

"Be a little easier if you didn't hog it all yourself," Calvin said. "Be nice if you shared a little."

"Not a good mix with the painkillers you're on," Andy told him.

"Right," Calvin mocked. "Not good for my body. What about my mental health? Since my body don't work no more, the head is all I got. I'd rather have the alcohol, a double dose of blot out."

"Look, man," Andy said. "I got some bad news recently. We lost a couple more people in the Nam. Guys I was close with. I'll figure out something, okay?"

"Sure," said Calvin. "How are you comin' on the list of names I gave you about my guys?"

"Renaldo's workin' on it. Says it won't take much longer."

"Nothin' like a company clerk workin' the angles."

Worried about the nurses noticing his condition, he asked Calvin, "You up for getting off the ward for a while?"

"Anything you say, Doc."

"I'll be gone for a couple of days. I'll get Kenny to look after you. Try not to give him such a hard time. He's a good kid."

"Scared shitless of the Nam, Doc. He should try and be more manly about it."

"Like us?" Andy said.

Andy didn't believe in fate. Who got orders and who didn't came down to luck.

Andy had them hiding out on the tenth-floor solarium in a corner away from the elevator doors. He pretended to write in his note pad when anyone came near. The nurses wouldn't bother him while busy with Calvin.

A double amputee in a wheelchair approached—Morrelli, 101 Airborne, legs missing at the knees. The airborne guys had a knack for finding one another. In separate battalions in the Nam, they had not known one another, but he and Calvin linked up in the hospital.

"I thought I might find you here," said Morelli. Letting his hair grow, and a beard, he'd been at Letterman's getting fitted with prostheses and learning to walk. Proficient at getting around in the wheelchair, he wandered the halls to kill time in between therapy sessions.

"Find any of your guys yet?" he asked, lighting a cigarette.

"Give me a drag on that," Calvin said.

"Okay with you, Doc?" Morelli asked, looking at Andy.

"What the hell," said Andy.

"Here," said Morelli, handing the cigarette to Andy, "you'll have to do it. I can't reach from my chair, man."

Not wanting a battle with Calvin over a few puffs on a cigarette, Andy held it up to his lips so he could inhale.

"Sweet," said Calvin, holding it in his lungs. "Got anything stronger?" he asked after exhaling.

"Not today, my man," said Morelli. "Hey, I'm out," he said, shaking the empty pack. "Can you run down and get me some smokes, Doc. You're more mobile than the rest of us. I'll look after my man here while you're gone."

With reluctance, Andy agreed. Morrelli was probably faster in his wheelchair than Andy could walk, but he figured it did Calvin good to have someone to develop a friendship with.

"There's a PX outlet on the main floor," Morrelli said. "Thanks, man."

Waiting for the elevator, Andy kept tabs on the two patients, visiting amiably when the doors opened. Stepping in and pushing the ground floor button, it descended, making several stops on the way.

Customers lined up at the counter delayed Andy. Not knowing Morrelli's brand, Andy bought a pack of Camels, remembering that's what his friend smoked in the Nam. It seemed so long ago when Camel was alive and puffing on cigarettes with a desert scene pictured on the package. Amused that both whiskey and tobacco had labels with animals, he tucked the smokes in his pocket and returned to the solarium.

The first thing he noticed when stepping out of the elevator was the absence of Calvin and his Stryker frame. Figuring somebody had moved it, he looked in both directions. No sign of Morelli either.

Okay, he thought, *he can't just disappear.* Andy decided on a systematic search for his missing patient, returning to the elevators. The doors opened and Marilyn stepped out. Some of the nurses hung out on the solarium during breaks.

"Going somewhere?" she asked with a smirk. "Looking for a missing patient? Just in case you're interested, he's on the eighth floor roaming the hospital with a double amputee. I don't suppose you will be able to tell me why," she said sarcastically, "or how he's gotten there?"

"I think they're playing a practical joke on me," he said.

"A missing quadriplegic is no joke, and it certainly isn't practical," she said. "Can you tell me why you aren't with Calvin?"

"I went to do an errand for Morrelli, the amputee in the wheelchair."

"Is this Morrelli your patient?"

Andy shook his head no.

"Then I suggest you go and fetch Calvin immediately."

She stepped closer to Andy.

"Have you been drinking?"

"Not on my shift," he said. "I had a bit too much last night."

"You better clean yourself up, Parks. Your patient care is sloppy, and you smell of alcohol. I want to know immediately if you can't find them on the eighth floor. That's where they were last seen."

"Yes, ma'am," said Andy, thinking, *What are they, escaped criminals?*

He found them on the eighth floor. Still talking, they burst into laughter when they spotted Andy. Angry at first for getting him into trouble, he realized it was the only time he'd seen Calvin smiling since they met. It was clever, a double amputee in a wheelchair hauling around a quadriplegic in his Stryker frame.

"How long you been planning that one?" Andy asked.

"We just thought it up after you left," Morrelli said, proud of himself.

"Did Miss Prissy find you?" Calvin taunted.

They found that hilarious and burst into laughter again.

Andy smiled and threw the package of cigarettes in Morrelli's lap.

❋ ❋ ❋

After his shift, Andy changed into civilian clothes and left the base. He needed out of the Army for a couple of days. He'd only been at the Presidio a month, but it felt longer.

He kept his sleeping bag in the car, along with some camping gear from his trip across the country.

He drove south along the coast until he found the beach, deserted in December, where he'd spent the final two days of his leave before reporting to the Presidio. He spent all his days off there. He packed supplies the half mile to the sandy perch amongst the rocks that overlooked the ocean. Finding his camp undisturbed, Andy went for a second load of gear from his station wagon before gathering driftwood for a fire.

By evening his hangover had receded to a dull headache. The sound of waves breaking on the shore intermingled with the crackling of the fire glowing in the enveloping darkness. The last calls of the gulls ended with the daylight, but the wind continued blowing in from the sea. Andy faced the ocean and let the breeze swirl around him before returning to the fire.

Hungry for the first time in days, he heated a can of soup in an Army mess kit over the fire. Still hungry, he did the same with a can of beans and cut into a block of cheese.

The serenity of the ocean soothed emotions worn raw by Andy's year in Vietnam and the ongoing pain at Letterman's. The peaceful stretch of beach helped clear his mind of a persistent mental pain. He could think here, mourn properly for the Professor and Yardly. Andy knew the war hadn't ended for him with the completion of his tour. He expected it would when he left the Nam. He realized how naive he was to think that.

Andy grappled with his guilt. Just being alive triggered thoughts of unworthiness. He wanted to leave the war behind, but it raged on in his head.

Having faced the possibility of his death at a young age, Andy turned philosophical, a need to put all the killing in some context that made sense.

"It don't mean nothing" is how some of them expressed it in the Nam. Andy never knew what that meant, interpreting it as a simple statement with many layers. At a sober moment, an epiphany about war had come to him when he realized, deep down, that the Viet Cong meant to kill him. One aspect of his baptism of fire, this meeting death face-to-face, and witnessing the evil side of what man was capable of.

Waking that night to a full moon, Andy stood and surveyed the shoreline bathed in the unexpected light. With the tide low, the wet sand shone luminescent in the way it shimmered after waves retreated into the sea. Deciding to walk along the shore, he turned after half a mile and viewed the glow from the fire he kept going through the winter night. An orange-red light reflected off the rocks and gave him a fleeting sense of peace. A glimmer of well-being flickered deep in Andy, faint, but existing.

He fantasized about not going back, remaining on this beach for an extended stay before drifting off and starting a new life, maybe joining the draft dodgers in Canada.

Returning to the fire he stoked it with more wood, bringing the flames back to life. When only the red-hot coals remained, he opened a bottle of port and sipped on the sweet wine. He liked the taste of grapes fermented to a syrupy texture. Andy felt no desperate need to drink excessively on this night. Preferring a light buzz for remembering the Professor and Yardly, Andy crawled into his sleeping bag and went to sleep, the warmth of the fire a comfort in the night.

CHAPTER EIGHTEEN

ANDY RETURNED TO the barracks in time to shower before reporting to the ward. He wrapped a towel around his waist and walked towards the latrine. Renaldo ran after him.

"First sergeant wants to see you."

"About what?" Andy asked.

Annoyed at the intrusion, he stopped and faced the company clerk. Self-conscious about the remnants of boils and scars from his tour in Vietnam exposed in his nakedness, they embarrassed Andy even in the company of men. Resigned to the lack of privacy, he waited for Renaldo to continue.

"Some of the nurses are complaining. Top wants to see you before your shift."

"I'll be late to relieve the night medic."

"Top says it can't wait. Oh, and by the way, I got some info about the guys in Calvin's unit. You buyin' drinks tonight?"

"That was the deal," Andy said.

A gloom had come over him when he entered the barracks that morning. Choosing to spend a third night at his ocean camp and drive in early, he was already frustrated. Two days camped on the isolated beach had soothed emotions rubbed raw by the news of the

Professor's death. An hour back at the Presidio had erased that. He dreaded his shift on the quad ward where his inability to help Calvin Lake reminded him of his failure as a medic.

Sergeant Hastings got right to the point.

"I'm not liking what I'm hearing from the nurses, Parks. Care to have me elaborate?"

Andy stood without responding.

"I don't care what you've seen or done in Vietnam, or what kind of sloppy-assed habits you formed there. You are still in the United States Army and will behave accordingly. You're one of the lucky ones coming back in one piece. But I've seen your type before. You come back from the war all slack-assed and thinkin' the Army owes you some special privileges for being shot at. Not in my unit. If you think otherwise, let's hear it."

"No, First Sergeant," Andy said, knowing not to challenge his authority.

Hastings read from a sheet of paper he picked off his desk. "Leaving your patients while you wander the hospital. Giving them cigarettes. For Christ's sakes, Parks, they're quadriplegics, and prone to respiratory problems. And you're helping them smoke?"

"Not exactly," Andy said.

"One of the nurses reported she saw you holding a cigarette to his mouth. You deny it?"

"No, First Sergeant."

Hastings paced in front of Andy before getting close and glaring into his eyes. "You watch your step, soldier. I will not allow you to do damage to this man's Army, not on my watch. We haven't gotten to the drinking yet," he continued. "I hear you're doing plenty of that, too. Care to explain?"

"I only drink when I'm off-duty, Sergeant."

"The nurses say they smell alcohol on your breath and suspect you are drinking when you're on the ward."

"No," Andy said.

"I also have reports of you drinking heavily in the barracks."

"Yes," Andy admitted. "I didn't know it wasn't allowed."

"Well, I'm telling you now, Parks. Your behavior will improve, or your world will be one with a lot of hurt in it. Understood?"

"Yes, First Sergeant."

"And one other thing," he said. "You are restricted to the base until your conduct is befitting of a soldier in the United States Army. You are an embarrassment to the uniform. Under no circumstances will you be allowed to discredit the military with your behavior off this post. Dismissed," he said. "Now get out of my sight."

※ ※ ※

Andy left the orderly room in a daze. The tongue lashing wasn't pleasant, but the restriction to the Presidio devastated him. He'd been able to cope with his emotions by getting off the base and away from the quadriplegic ward and the Army. Two days on the ocean shore left him feeling refreshed enough to return to his duties until his next days off.

Already late, he decided to stop in the mess hall for a coffee and think things through. Marilyn must have complained about him. It wasn't enough that he'd developed a rapport with Calvin. They wanted more. He suppressed the urge to spike his coffee with a shot of whiskey.

Reporting to the nurse's station, Andy glared at Marilyn. She glared back.

"You're late," she said. "You've had two days off. I would think that's enough to make it possible to get to work on time."

Andy didn't bother explaining the delay.

"I'm here now," he said. *And not hungover,* he thought, *and you're still bitching.*

"Yes. Good thing. There's been an incident."

"Incident?"

"We've had a hard time with Calvin the last couple of days. Kenny will fill you in on the details."

Andy located Kenny on the acute ward monitoring the ventilator settings on a patient.

"Hey, man," he greeted Andy.

"Sorry I'm late. First sergeant needed to give me shit, remind me I'm still in the Army." He pulled Kenny aside and asked, "So what's with Calvin?"

"I don't know all the details, but one of the nurses ticked him off. She asked if he'd like to see the Christmas decorations in the lobby. He erupted and got her crying. Marilyn got involved. You know where that leads. She got all huffy and told Calvin the sooner he learned to accept his paralysis, the better it would be for everybody including himself."

Andy hated her. Maybe he should find a way to help Calvin out of his misery. The feigned cheerfulness and attempts to normalize things like Christmas angered him, too. Sometimes the pretending made things worse.

Calvin dozed in his Stryker frame, probably sedated. Not waking him, Andy gathered supplies for the daily bowel routine. No function had developed, and probably wouldn't.

When Calvin woke, his eyes had the look of a man staring at something far away, not visible to anyone else. Subdued, Andy wasn't sure it was from the drugs or just being defeated. He felt a heavy sadness for the man the war had taken everything from but his life. That was ebbing out of him as well, in a cruel and slow process.

A sense of hopelessness took hold of Andy. Trapped, depressed, angry, not one of the nurses on the quad ward understood the Nam. Nobody knew what a patient like Calvin must be feeling, so everybody just pretended things were normal, or would get better, or that some abstract concept like freedom or democracy meant something to a grunt just back from the war paralyzed from the neck down.

"You're back," is all Calvin said when he noticed Andy. Listless, he continued to stare at nothing, his eyes conveying a helplessness Andy had not seen in him before.

A voice in Andy's head told him, *Do the right thing. Don't let Calvin suffer with a fate he considers worse than death. Don't let him suffer like you let the napalmed Vietnamese girl linger, or the Viet Cong soldier spewing the remains of his blood with the last breaths of life at the Slaughter in the Ca Mau. Help Calvin. Do the right thing.*

Andy got busy with the morning bowel function. Halfway through the procedure Calvin started talking.

"You know what bothers me the most, Doc, about the war, about all of our dead, and about just lying here day after day? It truly don't mean nothin'. I'd like to say we fought the good fight, but who am I trying to kid? We were a bunch of dumbass cannon fodder, fighting our guts out just to survive and kill enough of them to get home. It didn't work out."

Calvin paused for a moment.

"You see the Christmas decorations they put up in the lobby?"

"Yeah," said Andy. "I saw them."

"I got some upset. Didn't know why at first but, I figured it out. I finally figured it out. Wanna know why?"

"Sure," said Andy.

"It's that everybody's going around acting like I should feel normal about stuff. But, hey, I'm not normal anymore and I'm not ever gonna be. So, tell me why I should feel good about Christmas? It just makes me feel worse.

"The fucking nurse with the Christmas shit acting so excited like I should be too. More than anything I want normal, Doc, but it ain't ever gonna be. I'm not accepting my new normal and never will."

Calvin stared at nothing for a while, then continued.

"So, what's next for holidays? New Years? How we gonna celebrate that? Have the nurses put stupid hats on our heads and wish us a happy New Year? Without the booze, of course. It's bad for our ruined bodies to drink alcohol, the only thing I would like about it."

He paused again, breathing heavy like he'd exerted himself.

"Next up, Valentine's Day. Somebody's gonna want hearts in the lobby, ask me to be her Valentine? It just reminds me I'll never have a normal relationship with a woman.

"Or maybe come spring a nurse will say, 'How are you today, Calvin? It's nice outside, so maybe we can roll you out in the sunshine for a bit while you continue to lay immobile for the rest of your life.

"And I'm supposed to say, 'Gee, that's swell,' go along with all the bullshit because it makes everybody else feel better. But not me, Doc. I want out of this body. It has me trapped. It's my prison. I need to escape, get out of here. Can you help me? There are ways we can do this, Doc. Just pick one."

※ ※ ※

Andy ordered whiskey at the Enlisted Men's Club waiting for Renaldo. A quick change into civilian clothes after work and he was three drinks into a buzz by the time the company clerk arrived.

"I missed you at supper," he stated. "Steak night. You should be there when they feed us good."

The chubby clerk didn't miss many meals.

"Not hungry," Andy muttered. It had been a long day. Any emotional benefits from two days at his ocean camp evaporated within an hour of returning to the base. In no mood to resist the only relief from the constant turmoil in his head, Andy ordered more whiskey.

Renaldo ordered a beer and handed Andy some notes written on a used envelope.

"Here are five members of the platoon I've been able to locate. The dead guys are always easiest to find," he said.

"Thanks," Andy said.

"One of the guys in there is still alive. I should have more for you soon. How'd it go with the first sergeant?"

"As expected," Andy said. "Hastings reacted like a lifer."

"He hates San Francisco. The city gets on his nerves, all of the long hair on the hippies, the anti-war protests."

Andy shrugged. "Told me this was a plum assignment."

"It's supposed to be. I'm just hoping to stay here and avoid the Nam."

Andy left the club and started to return to the barracks. Remembering a bottle he had stashed in the car, he walked to the parking lot adjacent to the living quarters. Hating the lack of privacy on his bunk, he crawled into the back of his station wagon and leaned against the seats looking out the rear window.

I'll sleep here, he thought. *Might as well.*

Andy crawled into his sleeping bag and sipped on the whiskey until he passed out—just like most nights.

The next day he bounded into the ward, hungover and bearing bad news.

"I've got five names for you," Andy told Calvin. "Like you expected, it's not good news. Renaldo says it's easier to trace the dead guys, so anyone who's still alive may not show up until later."

"I'm not expecting the news to be good, so let's hear it."

"Timothy Barker, your medic, died the day you were hit. Ron Mortimer and Pedro Delgado as well. Vincent Maltise is the fourth KIA on Renaldo's list."

"I knew about Maltise," Calvin said. "He was our LT. Not surprised about Barker. He took risks getting to guys and would have been exposed treating casualties after we were hit. Sorry to hear about Morty, a good guy, and Delgado, Brown Bird. So, who made it out? You said one of the five names you had was still alive."

"Delmer Edwards," Andy said, "alive but legless in Cleveland."

"Good for Delmer. We called him Black Eagle. He liked that. Good on the M-60," Calvin said before staring at nothing again, retreating into his thoughts.

※ ※ ※

Most nights, Andy preferred sleeping in his car to spending time in the barracks. It was his only escape from the grimness. The Army smothered him, and more than ever he needed out, uncertain he could survive the few months left on his draft commitment.

The Christmas season in San Francisco had barely penetrated his consciousness. He tried writing letters to his family like he promised, but they were awkward and stilted. What could he possibly say about the quad ward? He managed some notes about the ocean, but nothing he really wished to communicate. The most important thing about Christmas for Andy was Sammy's return from Vietnam. He breathed a sigh of relief with his friend back from the war.

Renaldo continued finding the names of Calvin's dead platoon members. Murcell, Dentwick, Chapman, Whitaker, and Martinez, all killed when the platoon was overrun. By the end of January all names were accounted for. John Kiner, the last man found, the only one to survive the attack unharmed. Knocked out by flying debris hitting his helmet, he woke not remembering what happened to the rest of the platoon.

Calvin kept repeating, "It's what I expected. I knew it was bad. It don't mean nothin.'"

Restricted to the base, Andy became increasingly bitter about his posting and the emotional toll it had taken. Unable to escape to his camp on the ocean on his days off, he drank even more heavily as his animosity grew; he got rebellious. Taking a bottle of Coke half filled with Wild Turkey to work with him, Andy dodged the nurses and allowed Calvin sips of the whiskey. As they bonded, Calvin's pleas for Andy to end his life intensified. Marilyn caught him red-handed with alcohol on the ward.

"I don't know what it is about you Vietnam vets," she began. "Why you can't just come back from the war and behave like normal people, like the World War II guys. My father served, and an uncle, and they are fine."

Barely able to restrain his anger, the first sergeant paced in front of Andy before speaking. The veins on his neck bulging, his eyes filled with fury, he looked like he would haul off and hit Andy.

"The goddamned nurses are complaining about you, again, Parks. And that's before this latest episode with the drinking on duty. They are fucking uncomfortable working with you. Brass is on my ass, and you will pay for that. I will quote from memos crossing my desk.

"Parks' job performance is poor. He is moody and sullen. He is hostile to the nurses. He is smoking with the patients."

Hollering the last accusation, he stopped shouting for a moment to glare at Andy before continuing. "For fuck's sake, Parks, they are quadriplegics and you are lighting cigarettes for them. It's not good for the patients."

Andy raged internally.

Not good for the patients? What would have been good for the patients is if they'd never been sent to Vietnam in the first place.

"Your actions will have consequences. You are in violation of several articles in the Uniform Code of Military Justice. If I have anything to say about it, you will not get off lightly. You are restricted to your quarters until further notice. Understood?"

Returning to the barracks, Andy knew what he needed to do. There was no way he could remain cooped up in his quarters while the Army decided what to do with him. Packing the few belongings stowed in his footlocker, he took them to his car. Already feeling guilty about his decision, he owed Calvin an explanation.

Not welcome on the ward, he walked past the nurse's station without looking at who was on duty. Finding Calvin's Stryker frame, he rotated it so the two of them faced one another, man to man, Vietnam vet to Vietnam vet.

"I'm leaving, man," Andy began. "You deserve to hear that from me. Sorry I couldn't help you, but I gotta get out of here. I'm in enough trouble that I doubt they would let me return to work on the ward. I'm here to say goodbye."

"What, Miss Prissy catch you drinking again, giving me sips of your Wild Turkey, or is it the smokes you're lighting for me?"

"Something like that."

"She give you the lecture about it being bad for my cardiovascular system?"

Andy nodded.

"I guess finding out about the drinking has put a strain on her cardiovascular pussy. How blonde do you think she is down there?"

Cheeky to the end. Andy smiled at the absurdity of the comment.

"Something like that," he repeated.

"I guess I'm a bad influence, Doc."

"I guess you are." He knew it would give Calvin pleasure to hear that. "You would have been a good platoon member, Eagle One."

"And you, Doc. Don't be so hard on yourself about surviving the Nam. I accepted a long time ago that I died over there. It's just taking a little while longer in my case."

"I know," said Andy.

"I think we got it covered, Doc."

CHAPTER NINETEEN

Late January 1970

WITH ONLY A vague sense of a plan, Andy drove on Highway One heading towards Southern California to find Sammy. *Maybe Sammy can help.* He'd saved Andy from the Viet Cong. Now he'd need to save Andy from himself.

Andy camped on the beach that evening. In the morning, he shivered in a light drizzle that dropped out of a grey sky. A familiar headache throbbed as he realized the gravity of his actions. He had thirty days to clear his head, figure out a way forward. Then, he would be classified as a deserter.

Andy walked in the rain while gulls circled overhead. Ever-present along the California coast, their cries pierced the dull bleakness. Simultaneously peaceful and unsettling, nature continued unabated on this isolated stretch of ocean, oblivious to Andy's personal agonies. A touch of melancholy echoed in the calls of the sea birds. Gliding with wings outstretched that caught the wind at angles kept them airborne with an ease Andy found mesmerizing.

He stopped at a large log of driftwood washed ashore during high tide, the remnant of a tree trunk worn from floating in the sea.

Andy sat, aware of a duality of feelings. The relief of not having to face the quad ward, Marilyn, First Sergeant Hastings, the barracks, calmed him while he pondered his future. The darker side of his guilt, magnified by deserting the patients who lay paralyzed for life, intermingled with the necessity of leaving. Was he going mad, or selfishly incapable of appreciating his good fortune to have survived the war?

Perhaps, but he knew he'd reached some kind of limit. Whatever the consequences, he needed time to sort it out before he could return to the hospital.

Gathering his gear, he loaded the station wagon and continued along the coast. Half Moon Bay appeared on his left just south of his camp. While the vehicle's heater warmed and dried him, he drove without stopping, viewing the ocean scenery from his car.

For the first time in his postwar life, he had no family trying to figure out why he wasn't the same, and no Army demanding he be a medic treating the human consequences of the Vietnam War.

Before noon, Andy arrived on the outskirts of the small coastal city of Santa Cruz. Finding the sandstone cliffs overlooking the ocean pleasing, he stopped to stretch and walk along the landscaped foot paths near the jagged contour of the coastline. No longer raining, the fog dissipated as the late-morning sun poked through the clouds. Noticing a pier in the distance, a long arm jutting from the shore into the ocean, he saw a car drive onto it. Andy continued watching until it parked near a slight crook in the structure a good distance from the entrance. Curious, he decided to see if he could do the same.

The scenic drive along the cliffs descended and took him to the pier. The town's name of *Santa Cruz* appeared on a sign with painted gulls. Two live ones perched on top, unconcerned by the vehicles passing nearby. Intrigued by driving onto the wharf, Andy traveled most of its length before parking. Supported by wooden pilings pounded into the seabed, rising twenty feet above the waterline, it extended a half mile out to sea.

Stores lined one side selling fish packed on beds of crushed ice. Some of the boats already returned from the day's fishing unloaded their catch on landings beneath the pier. Andy heard the barking of seals and watched as they swam near the pilings or rested on crossbeams above the water waiting for scraps or culls from the fishermen.

At railings overlooking the ocean, a few men had poles with their lines dangling in the water. Sitting on a bench, Andy sipped at a soft drink and watched from a short distance. Catching slender fish eight inches long, the anglers removed the wiggling bodies and put them in burlap sacks.

Maybe I could settle in a place like this, thought Andy.

A pang of realization followed. He would not be settling anywhere—for a while. Fascinated by viewing something normal and separate from the war, his sense of isolation returned.

An older man stopped for a rest on the bench and nodded a greeting.

"The smelt are running today," he said, placing a sack beside him. Sensing Andy's interest, he opened it and showed him the contents. Dozens of slender fish filled the burlap bag.

"My wife doesn't like it so much that I bring them home," he said with a slight Italian accent. "But I like to fish and can't resist keeping them for the freezer. Do you like to fish?" he asked.

Andy nodded. "I've only fished in lakes and rivers," he said. "I saw the ocean for the first time two months ago. I'm from Oklahoma."

"Just out of the service?" he asked.

Andy nodded again.

"This town," the man continued, "is full of hippies now. All we see is the long hair on so many of the boys. They are all against this war. Were you there?"

"Yes," said Andy.

"I thought you might be in the service because of your short hair," he said.

To Andy, it was a small thing, but another example of the Army isolating them from society.

"There was a murder under the entrance to this pier last year," the man said, pointing to where the pilings began at the shoreline. "A Vietnam veteran was accused of killing a homeless man. Two of his friends from the Army sat right where we are sitting and got a policeman to confess to the killing. Of course, the confession proved inadmissible in court, but the young man was acquitted. The local paper wrote a lot of stories on the case.

"One of the friends of the accused lost a foot in Vietnam and said the young man saved his life over there. It was big news in this town. There were drugs involved, so many drugs in this town. Everything is so crazy with the drugs."

Andy offered the man a lift, but he declined.

"I have lots of time," he said, "to clean the fish before my wife returns. She's babysitting the grandkids today."

Another encounter reminding Andy how separate his new existence would be. He'd never broken a law in his life but was now a fugitive in his own country. The authorities would have reported him AWOL by now.

Andy continued on Route 1 through Aptos and Watsonville, hugging the coast. At Castroville an archway over the road proclaimed the town as *Artichoke Capital of the World*. Not knowing what they were, he stopped and asked the attendant at a service station while filling his car.

"Yes, they're a vegetable," he told him. "Grow on a shrubby looking plant, kind of hard to describe what they taste like. You should see some in the fields just outside of town."

Everything in California intrigued Andy as it was so different from Oklahoma. Three of the guys he knew in Vietnam were from the state. Sammy, of course, and Paul Voight, whose address in

Fresno he'd kept from his time at the hospital. Doc Woski, also, the medic he replaced in the platoon. Maybe he could live here someday.

Andy intended to visit Voight on his way to Sammy's. Maybe he wasn't the only vet feeling empty and unconnected—and crazy.

Keeping to the coast, the highway wound through Ft. Ord, a large infantry and basic training facility near Monterey. Built among the sand dunes bordering the ocean, firing ranges and barracks were visible from the main highway. Andy caught glimpses of troops running in the cadenced rhythms of training exercises. He hoped for some emotional and geographical distance from his situation. A longing to be done with the Army gnawed at him as he sped by the base, the nation's militarism ever-present even along the scenic coast of California.

Monterey, forty miles from Santa Cruz, and on the opposite side of the same bay, looked refreshed in the afternoon sun after the morning showers. Warmer than San Francisco, Andy bought supplies for the night and drank a coffee offered at the store. He would continue driving on the coast and camp overnight before turning inland for Fresno.

South of Monterey the terrain turned rocky and the scenery spectacular. By the time Andy reached Big Sur, massive cliffs stood at the water's edge. A profusion of densely growing flora clung to the sides of mountains plunging to the shoreline. Collisions of waves against stone powerful enough to erode the craggy outcroppings pounded the shore with the ebb and flow of the tides. Andy had never seen such a rugged beauty before.

Camping one more night on the sands of a cove near Big Sur, he loaded his gear and headed east in search of Voight.

He entered Fresno on Route 99 and stopped at a gas station to ask directions. Finding the suburban neighborhood with Paul Voight's address, the houses looked similar and recently built. Arriving unannounced, Andy vowed to leave if he made the family uncomfortable.

A slender woman in her forties opened the door, surprised to see someone she didn't recognize. Andy introduced himself.

"I'm looking for Paul Voight," he said. "We met in Vietnam. Have I got the right address?"

"Yes," she said, "Paul is our son, but he's not in right now. You were in Vietnam together?" She hesitated for a moment before inviting him to come in.

Andy followed her to the kitchen where she offered him a coffee. She looked troubled. An uncomfortable silence followed. Andy was about to excuse himself and leave when she spoke again.

"You were in Vietnam together?" she asked a second time.

"Yes. Not in the same unit, but I was a patient at the 29th Evac where Paul was stationed. He gave me his address and said to look him up if I was in California." Sensing Mrs. Voight's distress, he asked: "Have I come at a bad time?"

"No," she answered, breaking into tears. "It's just that we don't know where he is. I'm sorry," she said, recovering. "He's home from Vietnam, but it's like he's a different person. He seems so troubled and irritable. We don't know what to do for him. He's been home a month, but we haven't seen him for a couple of weeks and are worried about him."

"I'm sorry," Andy said, not knowing what else to say. His family would be feeling the same way about him, especially once they learned about his AWOL. "Do you have any idea where he might be?" Andy asked. "I could go and look for him if you like."

"We've checked everywhere we can think of. Was he okay when you knew him in Vietnam? We know he was wounded, but he won't talk to us about it."

"I think so," said Andy, hesitating, realizing he was okay in the war, too. To his dismay, most of his problems surfaced after his return.

"You were also wounded?" she asked.

"Not exactly," Andy said. "I was in the hospital with a bad infection. Paul was working triage when I arrived. That's how we met. I'm a medic as well."

Worried, Mrs. Voight searched for answers. Andy had no idea how to help her.

"Paul's father came back from World War II just fine. He doesn't understand Paul's restlessness, his anger, why he can't just come back and be glad to get on with his life."

Andy nodded. *Paul's father wasn't dropping burning gasoline on children and calling them dead VC,* Andy thought.

"Maybe his anger will pass," she continued, trying to console herself."

Andy, the tongue-tied medic again, had no words for her.

"Mrs. Voight, let me leave you my address, and a friend of mine's where Paul can reach me when he returns. I hope he's doing okay. Please tell him I came by."

Andy handed her a slip of paper with his parents' address, and Sammy's.

"I'm sure he'll be sorry to have missed you," she said.

Mrs. Voight walked Andy to the door.

"Let me know if I can help in any way," he said.

Perplexed and shaken, Andy got into his car and drove. He needed to see Sammy.

The visit with Mrs. Voight made Andy realize the impact his behavior must be having on his own family. His mother would be anxious and worried. His disappearance, not just geographical, but emotional, had left the family bewildered. Since Andy couldn't explain it to himself, he had no idea of what to say to them.

He kept hearing about the World War II vets, how they had come back from their war and gotten on with their lives. *Why can't I do the same?*

What about his uncle, his namesake? Never giving Andrew's disappearance much thought, Andy accepted the family's version of events. Unusual, unfortunate, and a mystery, but explainable in a context his relatives could understand. Andy had questions for him now and wanted to have a conversation with him to hear about his war.

The missing uncle he'd never met began to take on a new importance in his life. *Do we share a defective gene?* Maybe not all the World War II vets returned normal. Andy vowed to find his uncle.

Continuing on Highway 99 south, 200 miles separated him from Sammy, home now in Barstow, California. More than anyone, he helped Andy survive his tour in Vietnam. Andy needed to see him with his own eyes, a final personal confirmation that he had really made it out of the Nam.

Andy drove into the darkness. Only the headlights of other vehicles illuminated the passing landscape while the white lines on the road flashed rhythmically as he rolled on. He felt more peaceful in the dark, hidden and at ease. At rest from the scrutiny of the day, he drove until arriving in Visalia, an hour from Fresno.

Hungry, he pulled into the parking lot of a roadside cafe. He had much to think about. After finishing a cheese sandwich, he munched on the fries that came with the meal. In no hurry because he had all night to get to Barstow, the friendly waitress filled his mug of coffee several times before Andy got up to leave.

"Where you heading?" she asked.

CHAPTER TWENTY

AFTER LEAVING THE cafe in Visalia, Andy continued south on Highway 99 and settled into the natural cover of the night. He liked the hours from midnight until dawn.

In Vietnam he'd preferred the nocturnal, once he'd gotten over the initial fear of being hunted in the dark by Charlie. Most nights, uneventful, he listened with an intensity that transferred to his private thoughts, much like he felt at that moment rolling down the highway towards Barstow, where Sammy would be.

For ten months they had shared every step, every hardship. The selflessness of a deep friendship formed amidst the savagery of men intentionally killing men, a paradox of war. They vowed to do whatever it took to get each other home and had succeeded in delivering on that promise.

Andy hoped to begin sorting out his new troubles with his trusted friend.

❋ ❋ ❋

He found Sammy in a two-room dwelling on the outskirts of town. Hearing the vehicle driving to a stop outside of the Spanish-style house brought his friend to the door. Recognizing Andy, a perplexed smile formed on the familiar face.

"Sammy," shouted Andy through the rolled-down window of his car.

"What the heck? My parents told me to expect a friend. I had no idea it would be you, Doc."

"I know," Andy said. "I phoned them to get your address but told them I wanted to surprise you. Well, we made it, bro, made it out of the Nam."

"We did, man, and look at you," Sammy said as Andy approached. "But don't you have some time left in the Army?"

"It's a long story," Andy said, throwing his arms around Sammy, then standing apart to look at him. Along with the lopsided grin, vestiges of the war remained visible in his eyes, warm in seeing Andy, but troubled as well, peering at the world with a wariness born of conflict.

"We'll talk about that later," Andy continued. "Things haven't gone so good and have gotten kind of crazy."

"Nothin' worse than we already went through, Doc. It'll all sort out."

With Sammy back a month, Andy recognized the euphoria of being home, but also the physical hardships of the war. Andy could spot a recently returned Vietnam vet by his appearance and saw it on his friend. The strain around the eyes, and the thin, almost emaciated look except for the wiriness of muscles needed to hump seventy pounds of gear through the mud and swamps of the Delta. After washing the grime of a tour of duty away, an imprint remained. The youthful wholesomeness gone; the normal vitality of young manhood snipped off at the roots left something old about the young veterans of the war.

"Come inside," Sammy said. "We'll catch up. Not all the news is good, but goddamn it's good to see you. And we made it. We goddamn fucking made it."

Sammy put the coffee on the stove to percolate and gave Andy an update on the platoon.

"The Professor and Yardly's deaths were hard on everyone. It even showed on Howitz. I think we all took it as a failure. Any death is difficult, but the Professor came such a long way from the time he first arrived in the platoon. We were all pulling for him. And what can you say about Yardly, a sixteen-year old Montagnard kid dying with an American infantry unit because we needed an interpreter? I think we all felt ashamed after it happened, not just about his death, but the fact he was even out there with us."

Sammy set two mugs of coffee on the small kitchen table. "Let's go outside," he said. Two chairs faced the sparse desert terrain behind the house. "I like sitting out here, especially at night and in the early morning."

With no other houses in sight, the fenceless backyard looked out on the expanse of an uninhabited landscape.

"It has its own kind of beauty," Sammy commented before continuing with news about the platoon.

"I guess Black Henry took it hardest. We were all bushed. Command was pushing hard to make contact with the remnants of a VC battalion chewed up pretty bad in a jitterbugging operation we were part of. Black Henry had his squad beyond the perimeter on a night ambush. They never made contact but kept hearing Charlie all night. None of them got any sleep. In the morning the Professor walked point. You know the rest of the story.

"After that, Black Henry kind of just withdrew into himself, wouldn't say a word to anyone."

Sammy got up to get them some more coffee.

"Want something stronger for that?" asked Andy. The urge to drink was with him all the time.

"Seriously?" Sammy said. "I thought you didn't drink?"

"I never developed the taste until I got back from the Nam."

"Fill me in, brother."

Andy walked around the side of the house and fetched the bottle of Wild Turkey from the car. Returning, he poured some into the mugs of coffee.

"I don't really know where to begin," Andy said. "You know how we used to dream about returning home? How some of the guys would go into great detail about what they would eat, brag about the girls they would meet, fantasize how they would be waiting for our return. If only they could make it out of the Nam. It hasn't turned out like that."

Andy told him about his life at the Presidio. He mentioned Calvin Lake but didn't tell him about his unwavering desire to kill himself.

"It don't make sense, but somehow it's worse than the Nam, all those men just lying there all day every day, trapped in bodies that aren't gonna heal. At least we had hope over there. The Nam turned into a life sentence for those guys."

"We'll figure something out, Doc," Sammy interjected. "It's not like you killed somebody. The Army can cut you some slack for a few weeks while we decide what to do. Stay here as long as you need to." Already Sammy considered Andy's problem one of his own. Strange, but Andy missed that about the Nam. Not the war, but the fact everybody experienced the same hardships and faced them together.

Andy wanted to say more but couldn't find the words. Staring straight ahead at the desert, he blurted out, "I'm so tired of not being able to help anyone, man. It's like the bodies keep piling up and I'm standing there watching, incapable of doing anything about it. And I'm the medic. I'm supposed to fix it."

"Are you kidding me, Doc? We felt so secure going out there with you as our medic. We knew you were there for us, would do your best. Nobody doubted you. After you left, we were all uneasy, more afraid. You saved lives, Doc. Don't you go thinkin' otherwise."

"I only feel like I lost people. All of the dead weight is crushing me."

"Come on," Sammy said. "I want you to meet somebody."

"What? Right now?"

"Right now. My sister has something she wants to say to you."

"But I've never met your sister."

"I know you haven't. I've got three of them, but this one has something to say to you. She's the oldest."

Confused, Andy followed Sammy to an old Volkswagen Beetle parked in front of his house. "This is hers," he said. "She lets me borrow it. She's home with her kids, so I do some of her errands for her."

Reluctantly, Andy tagged along.

"Don't worry," Sammy said. "We won't stay long. We still have some catching up to do, but now's a good time to fulfill a promise I made to her."

Without knocking, Sammy walked in the front door of his sister's place. "Amy," he shouted. "I've got someone you should meet."

"Just a minute," a voice from another room answered. "Be right there."

"Hi," she said, entering the living room with an armful of clothes to fold. Surprised to see her brother at this time of the morning, she looked as confused as Andy.

"Amy, this is Doc Parks, my best friend from the Nam. More responsible than anyone for making sure I made it home. I think you had something you wanted to say to him. I think he needs to hear it."

Amy set the clothes on the seat of a chair. Her long dark hair fell to her shoulders when she stood to approach her guest. Her brown eyes grew moist, like she was going to cry. Andy looked at her awkwardly, not knowing what to say.

"*This* is Doc Parks?" she said with a quiver in her voice, now unsuccessful in holding back her tears. She walked up to Andy and wrapped her arms around him, pulling him tight as she hugged him. "Thank you," she said, "for helping to bring my brother back from the war. We can never begin to repay you for what you meant to him. He wrote to us about you all of the time. And now we get to meet you," she said, sobbing. "We are so grateful."

Andy could not remember crying in the war, nor at any time since returning. He cried now with Amy holding on to him and not letting go, making up for all the times he'd had to hold it in. "You have no idea how worried we were. It was a great comfort knowing Sammy had such a good friend looking after him."

True to his word, Sammy excused them soon after, promising to bring Andy to dinner at the Donato household the following evening so the whole family could meet him. "That's just the way Italians are," he said. "Way too emotional. But they all want to meet you, so I guess it's good to go and just get it over with. They all love you already, so be prepared to get stuffed with food and drink, especially now that you're a drinking man."

Andy sat without saying much on the ride back to Sammy's, embarrassed by his emotional display, but feeling a little better at having let some of the hurt from the Nam out.

Sammy did most of the talking. "There's no way, Doc, you're in this alone. Nobody understands the Nam except for us who've been there. When you're ready, I'm taking you back. In the meantime, you can expect some Italian hospitality. Wait until my mother gets her hands on you. I told her you were on the skinny side. She'll want to do something about that.

"I've been doing a lot of thinking, too," he continued. "There's no explaining the Nam. I don't even try to. It's abnormal, the whole fuckin' experience. I just call them *the normals,* people who haven't been there. It'll take a lifetime to sort it out."

Sammy showed Andy around Barstow in the afternoon, taking him to the community college where he intended to enroll in the fall. "I'll stick around for a while and take advantage of the college benefits for veterans and the low tuition. I want to make sure I can adjust to being in school again. I'm thinking about becoming a teacher."

In the evening they cooked hamburgers on a grill Sammy rigged over a firepit in the backyard. After eating they broke into a cheap jug of California wine and the talk grew serious again.

"Black Henry should be rotating home now," said Sammy. "He was all fucked up after the Professor's death. I tried drawing him out, but he just stared past me like he didn't ever know what I was talking about. I'm not sure he heard a word I was saying. I'd like to try and contact him in Alabama soon, see how he's doing."

Andy asked about the LT.

"Howitz extended his tour another six months. He came and spoke with everyone individually after the Professor and Yardly bought it. Just like he did the time we almost got overrun near the Seven Mountains. He told me he almost lost his command right after arriving in the Nam. The platoon sergeant was getting reckless and usurping his authority. The LT told me he learned something valuable from the experience. Once he was prepared to lose his command rather than allow the more experienced platoon sergeant to act carelessly with the lives of the men, it sorted out. He's extending his tour because he feels a responsibility to getting everybody home, not any allegiance to the war."

Deeper into the jug of wine, Andy told Sammy more about Calvin Lake, how conflicted and hopeless his situation made him feel.

"It's the war, Doc, not you. We did our best. That's all anybody can ask."

The stars shone bright through the night desert air. Cool in late January after the sun disappeared, the two friends continued sitting outside, stoking the fire with scraps of wood from the sparse terrain.

"Think Black Henry will be all right?" Andy asked.

"Hard to say," Sammy responded. "I'll try and get in touch. We owe him a lot too. Weird, how the Nam stays with you even though we're home."

Andy grew pensive thinking about the war. "I don't know what to tell my family. How will I ever explain what I've done?"

"There is no explaining the Nam," Sammy repeated.

"But I'm home now and only had a few months left in the Army. It's all so crazy."

"The war's crazy, Doc, not you. Don't let it get to you."

They sat for long stretches without saying much, their friendship comfortable with the silence.

The night continued to cool in the desert. Sammy fetched two ponchos from the house, brought home with him from the Nam. Andy remembered the last time he wrapped one around him in the jungle, trying to stay dry beneath a Mekong Delta deluge. On this night, no rain fell from the Mohave Desert sky.

❈ ❈ ❈

In the morning Andy felt some emotional relief from having confided with the friend that knew him best. Beginning to understand they would carry the war with them for good, a resolve formed to start sorting through the confusing maze of his post-war life.

During breakfast, Sammy spoke against remaining a fugitive. He encouraged Andy to return to the Army—when he was ready. "Get over that hump in your situation," he told him. "You don't want to be lookin' over your shoulder for the rest of your life. There ain't any future in that. One step at a time."

Whether by personal weakness, or a confluence of events, he'd dug a hole for himself with no easy way out.

Before leaving for dinner at the Donatos', Sammy told Andy about his return.

"When I got back, my mom fixed a special meal for the family. I'm the only son, but my three sisters were there, and Amy's husband, Terry. I'm just out of the jungle, you know, not five days removed from my last patrol. I asked my mother to please pass the fucking potatoes. Everyone looked stunned for a moment, then burst out laughing."

Andy thought for a moment. "Yeah, I guess every other word was a profanity in the Nam. Like the war itself."

"So much stress," Sammy said.

"But you said 'please,' and not 'motherfucking potatoes'?"

"I did."

"Your manners are improving."

"Just warning you so you don't slip up and repeat my performance."

"I'm on my best behavior."

Mother Donato accepted Andy like a long-lost son, making sure his plate filled with tasty morsels specially prepared for the occasion. Sammy's father, at the head of the table, insisted "his boys" sit on either side of him, treating Andy like an honored guest. The wine flowed freely amidst the feast. Used to a Cherokee stoicism, Andy suppressed his embarrassment and enjoyed the evening.

Sammy's sisters, Amy, Dolores and Sally, came with husbands and a boyfriend. The meal lasted well into the evening. Toasts were spoken, and the women's eyes filled with tears. The men congratulated Sammy and Andy for helping each other survive the war, being good friends, and looking to a good future. Invitations to visit exchanged, the night of hospitality ended with hugs and handshakes all around.

"See, what did I tell you?" Sammy said on the way back to his place. "Italians are way too emotional. Hope you're okay with that because I think my family just adopted you."

Andy didn't say much. He was okay with that.

※ ※ ※

His visit fell into a routine. While Sammy looked for work to tide him over until the fall session began at the community college, Andy relaxed and drank coffee in Sammy's backyard, taking short walks into the desert. Some days he worked with Sammy at casual jobs cleaning construction sites of debris. Other mornings he visited Amy and helped look after her two children.

Andy's pending return to the Army loomed over his peace of mind. Some nights the war intruded. Sammy, rarely sleeping a full night, joined him for sips of whiskey in the backyard. The desert air, cool in the February night, was conducive to reflection while gazing at the stars.

"We have our whole lives ahead of us," Sammy said one evening.

"Let's get you back to the Army, Doc, so you can get it over with and start living again."

Andy knew his friend was right, but dreaded going back worse than he dreaded Vietnam.

❋ ❋ ❋

They camped along the ocean on the way to San Francisco. The coast of Southern California was in bloom with wildflowers, the yellow of the poppies bursting forth in patches protruding through the green winter grasses on the sides of hills. Lingering in the early mornings at their campsite, the friends brewed coffee over an open fire on a small grill Andy carried with them in his car.

Taking their time, they camped four nights, following Highway One to where Andy showed Sammy his favorite place on the ocean near Half Moon Bay. It would be his final night of freedom.

Always trying to make it easier for his friend, Sammy said, "It's not like the night before a patrol in the Nam."

No, it isn't, but I dread it just as much, thought Andy. *There is a lot between me and a normal life. This is just the first step.*

The base remained as he remembered it, green and neatly trimmed with a beautiful view of San Francisco Bay. They passed the hospital, ten stories towering above everything else. Packed with misery from the war on each floor, that would not be different either.

In the orderly room, Renaldo sat at a desk with a stack of papers spread on top. Surprised to see him he blurted, "Andy, where you been?"

Hearing the commotion, First Sergeant Hastings appeared from the filing room.

"Well, well, well," he began. "Look who we got here." Without pausing, he went to a phone and dialed a number without taking his eyes off Andy.

"Who is this?" he asked, looking at Sammy after hanging up the phone.

"A friend from my platoon in Vietnam," said Andy.

"My friend has been AWOL for a few days," said Sammy. "He was a good medic in the Nam. We were in the shit together. Why don't you cut him some slack?"

"You are both a disgrace to the Army," Hastings shouted.

"I'm no longer in the Army, Sergeant," Sammy said.

"Then I suggest you leave before I notify the civilian authorities and have them forcibly remove you from this base." Hastings paced a couple of steps, looking smugly at Sammy. "I've called the MPs," he said. "Your friend, Parks, is still deep in the shit as you describe it. He was the last person to see Calvin Lake alive."

CHAPTER TWENTY-ONE

BY THE TIME the MPs arrived, handcuffing Andy and roughly escorting him to a van used to transport prisoners, Hastings had called the San Francisco police about Sammy. Not intimidated by the sergeant, Sammy spoke his mind.

"Don't worry, Doc," he tried to reassure Andy as he was led away. "We'll get to the bottom of this."

Turning on the sergeant Andy heard him lay into Hastings as the MPs dragged him out the door.

"This how you treat a Vietnam veteran, you fucking REMF lifer," Sammy shouted. "You don't know shit about Doc Parks, what he did for guys in the Nam."

Hastings glared and shouted back, a mean glint in his eye. "You raggedy-assed Vietnam vets can kill all the gooks you like over there, but you don't get to choose who lives and dies here. You don't get away with murder in my Army."

That was the last thing Andy heard as the MPs dragged him out the door.

✳ ✳ ✳

When they arrived at the prison, Andy looked at the foreboding two-story structure. Tiny windows with bars ran along the top tier. To his right, a twelve-foot chain link fence enclosed a small courtyard, coiled concertina wire on top.

Hands cuffed behind him, an MP each took an elbow and rushed him up a set of concrete steps into the prison. Andy saw the number 1213 stenciled in paint on the building, a yellowing white smooth stucco finish.

Inside, noise reverberated off the concrete walls, men shouting obscenities, angry guards ordering, bullying, taunting. One of them told Andy to strip while he tapped his truncheon in the palm of his hand as if looking for any excuse to club Andy.

"Put these on," the guard said, tossing a set of Army fatigues. "You'll be here a while."

After dressing, two guards took him down another set of concrete stairs to a twelve foot by eight cell in the basement. He sat on the cot, the only item provided. Thoughts swirled, but mostly came back to, *How did this happen? Four months back from the Nam and I'm in prison being accused of killing Calvin Lake. I must be going crazy.*

He received no details of any charges. A sadistic guard hung around and taunted him. "Must have taken a lot of guts to kill that paralyzed patient. You'll hang for sure, Parks. Must be a fucking psycho to do something like that."

Isolated from the other prisoners, Andy paced the small cell in solitary confinement. For something to do, he took up smoking and read the New Testament, the only things allowed. He got no inspiration from the Bible. He thought about his mother when he read it, smoking as many cigarettes as permitted. *She'd be ashamed of me. What would the parishioners of Trinity Baptist think of me now?*

Confused, Andy began to doubt his innocence. *Did I kill Calvin?*

Andy's only reprieve from solitary was eating with other prisoners. But he was warned, "As long as it's easier to bring you to the food and not the other way around, this will continue."

❋ ❋ ❋

Sitting in the mess hall, a small, wiry prisoner stared at Andy. When he looked up the man asked, "You gonna eat that?"

"What?" Andy asked, emerging from his daze.

"That piece of bread on your plate. The one you ain't touched."

"Oh," he said. "Sure, go ahead."

"What you in for?" the prisoner asked, reaching across the table and taking the bread off Andy's plate. "You the guy killed that paralyzed patient?"

Andy didn't answer.

"The man ain't charged you yet?"

Andy shook his head.

"You don't eat much . . . or talk much either." Before leaving he held his silverware in the air for the guards to see he was finished. The MPs motioned for him to proceed to a large tub where a different MP accounted for each utensil.

Andy didn't eat much in the prison. It was vile. The toilets, filthy, and often clogged, overflowed onto the floors. Excrement, tracked into the showers, rarely got cleaned. The stench, nauseating, left Andy feeling dirtier after every use.

Andy had entered the latrine and saw an inmate puking. Unable to make it to an unused toilet, the inmate gagged trying to hold it in, then spewed vomit on the tiled floor. A guard rushed him and shoved him into his own filth.

"Dirty fucking puking bastard," he shouted. Andy glared at the MP before helping the prisoner to his feet and to a sink. "Finish your business and get back to your cell," the guard ordered Andy. "I'm done coddling you useless shitheads."

The guards, in thick-soled boots with trousers tucked into them, walked with wooden batons for protection, and threatened retaliation for any infraction, real or imagined. Andy ignored the order until the guard tapped him with the club he carried.

"Best do what you're told, asshole."

❋ ❋ ❋

He got most of his information from Roy Franklin, the prisoner he had given a slice of bread to in the mess hall. Despite the slender frame, Franklin gobbled up whatever extra food he could get. Only twenty-two, but experienced in prison life, he liked to talk, and told Andy about the stockade.

"You think this is bad? Conditions is way better than before. This is some crazy house."

Franklin told Andy about the 1968 mutiny, a prison protest instigated by abusive MPs that left one prisoner dead.

"Twenty-seven of those fuckers charged with mutiny and court-martialed. Man, they handed out some sentences, some up to sixteen years," Franklin said. "All over a sit-down protest because one of us was dead and conditions was so bad. Don't pay to mess with the man. Any black man tell you that."

Franklin took a liking to Andy. Always on the wrong side of the law, he knew a lot about it.

"You seen some lawyer yet?" Franklin asked. "Even in here they have to let you see one. Nothin' gonna happen without that."

That's right, Andy thought.

Days turned into weeks and he remained confined to his basement cell without word of any charges. Franklin gave him hope.

"They got nothin', Andy. Paralyzed guy dies, happens all the time. Don't let the guards mess with your head. The Army ain't executed nobody in years. Manslaughter is the most they can get on you."

Franklin had a point, but if guys were getting sixteen-year sentences for holding a sit-down protest in the prison's courtyard, then being executed for Calvin's death was a real possibility.

Roy's own story, one of living on the fringes, involved minor brushes with the law as a youth culminating in a judge giving him a choice between going into the Army and a jail sentence.

"It don't make no difference," he told Andy. "I still in prison, except now I got to get outta the Army prison, and then the Army, too."

Andy never got his full story, but it had to do with an underage girl, some marijuana, and, according to Franklin, "being black in the wrong place with circumstances beyond my control."

The guard in charge of Andy liked to hang around outside his cell and try and goad him with profanity. He continued reminding Andy of his situation. "How we feeling today, motherfucker? Enjoying prison life? You stupid motherfuckers are all alike, complaining all the time."

Andy hadn't said a word. Complaining or showing fear would only exhibit weakness. But inside a bleakness prevailed.

❀ ❀ ❀

Weeks after being locked in the stockade, the abusive guard arrived at Andy's cell and banged on the steel bars with his truncheon. "Lawyer's here to see you, fuckhead. If you ask me, all of you should just be sent to Vietnam, let the Viet Cong have a go at you."

Led to a small room next to the administrative office, Andy entered and found an officer sitting at a table, the only furniture besides two chairs. Motioning for Andy to take a seat, he finished making a note on a legal pad and introduced himself.

"I'm Lieutenant Marks. I've been assigned to represent you."

Andy nodded, not knowing what to expect. Marks, a few years older than Andy, had his tie loosened and his dress green jacket hanging on the back of his chair. He didn't look career military.

"Calvin Lake died of complications from a pulmonary embolism," Marks began. "Know what that is?"

"Basically, a blood clot in the lungs," answered Andy. "Quadriplegics are susceptible to them."

"That's right. The prosecutor is still fishing for a manslaughter charge. Even in the kangaroo courts of the military it's an imbecilic stretch, although nothing surprises me around here anymore."

Andy sensed he must have had something to do with the mutiny cases.

"Here's the murder weapon," he said derisively. Marks took a package of cigarettes out of his shirt pocket and threw them on the table. "You smoke?" he asked. "Feel free if you do."

Andy reached for the pack and removed a cigarette.

"Two of the nurses are willing to testify they saw you giving cigarettes to Calvin Lake. The blonde nurse is saying you also gave him alcohol."

"A few sips, not enough to do him any harm." Andy's stomach tightened, still deciding if he could trust his lawyer.

"So what happened?" Marks asked.

"I don't know," Andy answered. "I saw Calvin the night they say he died, but he was alert. We talked for a few minutes and then I left."

"What were you doing on the ward? Your first sergeant is claiming you were restricted to your quarters."

"I came to say goodbye," Andy said. "I went AWOL right after seeing Calvin, like I'd already planned."

"Your service record says you were in Vietnam until late October."

"Yes." Andy didn't see the relevance.

"The Army is having a huge problem with AWOLs right now, but it's guys trying to avoid Vietnam. You just got back. Why go AWOL? You only had a few months left in the Army. The prosecutor is making the argument you had no reason to go AWOL if you had nothing to do with Calvin's death."

The lieutenant's questions made him uncomfortable. He'd asked the same ones of himself. Andy decided to level with him.

"Calvin wanted to kill himself. He made no secret of that. He kept pestering me to help him end his life."

"And did you?"

"No," Andy retorted. "You been to Vietnam, Lieutenant?"

Marks shook his head. "I haven't had that pleasure," he said.

Andy sensed an anti-war sentiment in the comment.

"Maybe some think the killing gets easy," Andy said, "but it's not like that. I had enemy soldiers dying of the most grotesque wounds, struggling to breathe and spewing blood all over my face as their lives ebbed out of them." Andy thought of the Ca Mau. "Or kids dying horrible deaths from the napalm we dropped on them. I couldn't bring myself to play God even when I probably should have. I certainly wasn't going to with Calvin Lake. For most of us, even in a war, it's not easy to kill somebody."

Marks looked at Andy intently, allowing him to continue.

"In the Nam, everybody dreaded the kinds of wounds found on the quadriplegic ward. So there I am, just back from the same war, walking around on two legs, not even able to look at those guys in the eye because I feel so guilty about not only being alive, but physically able. There are too many bodies from the war already. I'm not going to add to the count. Explain that to your prosecutor and some of the guards in this shithole while you're at it."

Marks thought for a moment. "The blonde nurse, Marilyn Reese, is making a big fuss."

"That's odd. She hated Calvin. I would think she'd be glad to have both of us gone. You should ask her why, as the head nurse, she allowed Calvin Lake to lay there in one position long enough to develop deep vein thrombosis, precipitating the pulmonary embolism."

"Good point," the lieutenant said, writing on his note pad. "If I can get them to end this charade, drop any charges related to Calvin's death, they'll probably ship you to Fort Ord for a court-martial on the AWOL charges."

"What are the chances of that?" Andy asked.

"Right now, the Army is taking a lot of heat for the whole mutiny fiasco in '68. And the war grows more unpopular by the day. Higher command is tired of being embarrassed by the bimbos running this place. With the Army ripping apart at the seams with so many AWOLs, they have no idea how to regain control. As much as I'd love defending the charges against you in court, I can't see them proceeding on such flimsy evidence. A few puffs on a cigarette and some sips of whiskey killing Calvin Lake is a stretch."

※ ※ ※

Two weeks later, with Andy doubting the Army would ever let him
out of prison, a new guard opened the door to his cell and told him to
join a formation in the courtyard. Thirty prisoners stood waiting for
a sergeant to speak. Seeing Franklin, Andy fell in beside him.

"What's up?" Andy asked.

"Beats me. The man be about to speak."

A lot of boyish faces peered at the sergeant, looking too young
to be dangerous criminals.

Hands behind his back and pacing in front of the prisoners, the
sergeant began with a derisive remark. "If it was up to me, you'd all
be going to Vietnam."

"Not this shit again," Franklin muttered.

The guard shouted, "You have another opinion, Franklin?" They
all knew him by name.

"He's already been there," he answered, pointing to Andy.

"Then you really are a dipshit," he continued. "Unfortunately,
instead of Vietnam, the lot of you are being shipped to Fort Ord in
the morning. Your court-martials will be administered there. The
guards will bring you here at 0800 hours."

"Hot damn," Franklin responded, ecstatic at his good fortune.
"They must wanna be dischargin' me with some bad paper," referring
to a less than honorable discharge. "I guess that gets me outta prison,
the Army and goin' to the Nam." Roy knew everything about the
system.

"You know that guard givin' the bullshit spiel about the Nam? Saw
the motherfucker drag one of those kids down a set of concrete stairs a
few months ago, his head bouncin' on every one of them. Some mean
motherfuckers in here, Andy. Can't believe I get to go, too."

Charges linking him to Calvin's death never materialized. He
knew that much from being on the bus to Fort Ord. No handcuffs on
the prisoners or guns for the guards accompanying them on this trip.

Andy took a window seat near the rear, the vehicle a drab olive green inside and out. Otherwise, it reminded him of a school bus. Franklin slid in beside him as Andy looked at the stockade for a final time. The old building must have housed a lot of misery over the years.

Franklin bounced in the seat, anticipating the trip and telling everyone within earshot, "This be a better place, brothers, a hundred percent sure of that."

Andy remembered driving by Fort Ord on the way to see Sammy. One hundred and twenty miles to the south, the large and sprawling base trained soldiers in the sand dunes along the coast near Monterey. The Presidio, also on the ocean, marred its scenic setting with the tragedy and turmoil within its institutions.

Viewing San Francisco through the window, Andy looked at parts of the city he'd never seen. The rows of houses and apartment buildings stretched for miles. The concrete overpasses connecting complicated mazes of freeways would have interested him in different circumstances. Any plots of dirt not covered in asphalt or cement sprouted shrubs, bushes, trees and flowers.

On the road, with an unusually quiet Roy Franklin beside him, Andy appreciated looking at the sights without interruption. He owed a lot to the man, helping him cope with the solitude and uncertainty he faced separated from the other prisoners.

Thirty minutes from the Presidio, a shout from behind interrupted Andy's thoughts.

"Jesus Christ, he just cut himself! Sat right there and cut himself," one of the prisoners hollered to a guard.

Andy turned and saw an MP looking bewildered and unsure of what to do. "Medic, is there a medic on board?" he called out.

Andy walked to where a kid sat staring straight ahead while his wrist bled. Andy took his shirttail and wrapped it around the bleeding arm. "Can somebody rip part of my shirt off or find something I can apply pressure with?" he asked. "It can be anything, a handkerchief, a fatigue sleeve."

The bus pulled to the side of the road. Andy kept his palm pressed over the shirt wrapped around the wrist. The young man continued to stare straight ahead, zombielike. Another guard produced a pressure bandage from a first aid kit on the bus.

"Thanks," Andy said. He looked at the wrist to see if an artery or major vein was severed. The bus seat and the young man's clothes were bloody, but applying pressure stemmed most of the bleeding.

"You all right?" Andy asked the kid. "The bleeding's just about stopped now. I just want to tape the bandage in place so it's tight against the wound." His patient continued staring ahead without responding.

"I think we can go now," Andy said to the nearest guard, who looked relieved.

"Thanks for helping," he said. They weren't all pricks, at least not all of the time.

Andy sat next to the kid on the way back to the Presidio to make sure the bleeding didn't start again. The young man never said a word throughout the ordeal or as the bus retraced its route.

Arriving at Letterman's, Andy and a guard walked the patient into the emergency room. Nobody on duty recognized him.

Returning to the bus, he sat next to Franklin, who resumed his talkative ways unabated for the entire two-hour ride to Fort Ord.

When Andy spotted the sand dunes along the highway, he knew they were close. Catching glimpses of the ocean before entering the main gate, the prisoners shuffled in their seats vying for a better look out the windows. Driving through part of the large and sprawling base, they passed dozens of two-story barracks and a supply depot with loading docks a hundred yards long. Stopping in front of a compound surrounded by a chain link fence, a guard ordered them off the bus.

"They're all yours, Sergeant," he said to a tall black NCO looking them over after they assembled in the semblance of a formation.

"Thank you," he bellowed. "My name is Sergeant Gour," he began. "We will get along fine if you do what you are told. It's easy. Do what you are told, we get along. Understand?"

The response was half-hearted.

"You don't speak English?" he shouted. "This is the Special Processing Detachment, or SPD for short. Most of you will remain here until your court-martial."

Over six feet tall, Gour stood erect, using his lean, muscular frame to exude an air of authority. Enunciating his words loudly and clearly, he continued.

"I know that most of you are here because you have gone AWOL. Let me remind you that if you run away again, before your court-martial, you will be charged with desertion. Do I make myself clear?"

Not waiting for an answer, he proceeded with his introduction. "I'm sure you have noticed there are no bars or fortified gates in this compound. There are no armed guards that are going to shoot you. That don't mean you can mess with me or my staff. Understood?"

Andy understood perfectly and suspected the rest of the men did too.

CHAPTER TWENTY-TWO

July 1970

THREE HUNDRED MEN broke formation and formed a human chain to scour the compound for a few dozen cigarette butts. Nothing else among their possessions created any litter. Dressed in Army fatigues and boots, green baseball-style caps for head gear, they ambled through the grounds from one end to the other.

Nine double-story barracks surrounded by a chain link fence twelve feet high housed the collection of Army misfits. Andy viewed the exercise as an attempt to keep them busy. The activity provided structure to the boredom. With no abusive guards or jail cells, life at the SPD detachment allowed free movement within the compound.

Returning to the barracks, Andy and Franklin climbed the stairs to their second-floor bunks next to each other in the middle of two long rows of beds. A group of soldiers gathered at Franklin's cot to discuss the latest sentencing handed out at the daily court-martials. Just as the sergeant had said, most of the men in the SPD compound were up on AWOL charges.

Andy sat on his cot disinterested in hearing the latest news. He pondered how to make the inevitable phone call to his family. During his five months in prison, he'd written two letters, neither providing an account of what had happened.

Andy had scrounged enough quarters to make a long-distance call to Oklahoma from a payphone near the main dispensary.

His mother answered. "Hello."

"Hi, Mom."

"Andy, where are you calling from? We've been frantic with worry waiting to hear from you."

"I know," he said, "and I'm sorry. I just didn't know how to explain things. Everything got so mixed up at the Presidio. I'm at Fort Ord now waiting for a new duty posting." He left out any mention of his pending court-martial.

"We received your letters but were so confused about what was happening. We called the Presidio and spoke with a Sergeant Hastings. He told us you were in prison for killing a patient. I said that couldn't be my son harming innocent people. You were a medic in Vietnam taking care of a platoon. He said, 'That's probably where he learned to kill.' Then he told us you were drinking all the time. I knew that couldn't be you, but we didn't know what to believe." Andy heard her crying.

Fucking Hastings, thought Andy. Controlling his rage, Andy tried soothing his mother's concern.

"I don't know how to explain everything, Mom, but I'm okay and I didn't harm any of the patients. The Army knows that and have dropped all charges. The patient who died was paralyzed from the neck down. I looked after him." Andy left it at that.

"So, it's all just a big misunderstanding?" she asked.

"Yes," said Andy. Just a big misunderstanding explained it as well as anything.

"Sammy, your friend from Vietnam, phoned and talked to us. He told us you'd be okay and not to worry. You'd done nothing wrong."

"No, I haven't," he said, not sure exactly what the truth was anymore. Sammy had come through for him again. How many times had he helped him out of jams? He'd lost count.

"Mom, I have to go soon. I'm on a pay phone. Say hi to Dad. I miss you all."

"Wait, son. Don't go just yet. Hang up and place a collect call. Your father would also like to speak with you."

"Dad's home?" *He never misses work.* As long as Andy could remember, his father went to his job at the rail yard. Clocks could be set by the steadiness of the man's schedule. "Is everything okay?"

"Yes," Rebecca answered, vaguely, exhibiting a version of her own evasiveness. "But he would like to speak with you, son."

Andy hung up and placed the collect call.

His mother answered on the first ring.

"Before I put your father on I need you to promise me something."

Andy's stomach churned, uncomfortable with the direction of the conversation. "What is it, Mom?"

"I've already lost a brother," she began. "I don't know if I can bear to lose a son, too. You need to promise me that whatever happens you won't just up and disappear like your uncle Andrew." His mother began crying again.

The disappearance of his uncle had always been a family mystery. He sensed an eerie connection to this man he'd never met ever since he learned he'd been a medic in his war, too. Andy had already created a huge mess for everybody, mostly for himself, but he wanted to be a good son.

"I promise, Mom. I don't want to just disappear somewhere. I promise I'll come home after I get out of the Army." *I'd like to find Andrew for you,* he thought, *for all of us.*

"It will get better, son. You'll see. Everybody loves you and is praying for you."

"I love you, too, Mom." Praying wasn't going to help him, but he knew the importance of the church in his mother's life.

"Here's your father, son."

"Andy," Henry Clay began, "your mother's been frantic with worry about you."

"I know, Dad, I know." *Mothers are allowed to worry,* he thought, *but men, especially Cherokee ones, bear their burdens stoically.* Andy wasn't very good at that, either.

"Son, we don't understand what's happened. San Francisco was such a good duty posting, a chance to see a different part of the country. Then, the Army suspects you of killing someone. We know you didn't do it, but we don't understand."

"Dad, I don't know what to say. Like I told, Mom, I didn't harm anyone. One of the patients wanted to kill himself, and they thought I helped him do it when they found him dead."

"But why?" his father persisted. "Why did he want to kill himself?"

"Because he was paralyzed. He didn't want to live like that. He wanted me to help him end his life. They found him dead, but I had nothing to do with it. When I was in the stockade, I found out he died of complications from his paralysis."

"I see," his father said, but Andy sensed he didn't.

"Even in the war, I didn't kill anyone, Dad."

"The sergeant was so insistent. It didn't sound like you, but he had us all so worried when he said they were charging you with murder."

"All the charges have been dropped, Dad. I promised Mom I'd come home after I get out of the Army." He wanted to say more, explain how as the medic he tried to keep everybody alive, but it didn't always work out. "It's not easy to kill someone, Dad."

"I know, son."

"I'm sorry, Dad, for all of the worry I've caused everyone. I'll explain more once I'm home. How are Nancy and George?"

"They are fine, Andy. They'll be glad to know that you called, and everything will be all right."

Andy wasn't so sure, but he needed to go. The conversation troubled him, and another of the SPD soldiers stood nearby waiting to use the phone.

"Okay, Dad, give them my best. Goodbye."

"Phone when you can, son. You can place a collect call anytime. It will help your mother to hear from you," he said.

Andy hung up and brushed by the man waiting to make his own call. He recognized him from the compound, but they hadn't met. Embarrassed he might have overheard part of the conversation Andy didn't look at him.

He walked back to the SPD detachment, rehashing the conversation, and his life.

"Look at this, Andy," Franklin said. Finished with the daily search for debris in the litterless company grounds, they walked along the compound's fence on the way back to their barracks. His friend pointed at a hole in the chain link fence patched with wire. Roy put a leg through an opening. "Freedom," he joked. "One leg is free right now." Andy suspected Franklin would hatch a plan to get the rest of him out.

They ambled towards the barracks where each morning after police call a crowd gathered around Roy's bunk. Andy rarely participated but overheard a lot of conversations. While writing a letter to Sammy, Franklin interrupted him.

"Hey, Andy, this be my man, Derwin Dunne. Come all the way from North Dakota to get his court-martial. Knows a lot about this place."

Andy looked at the dark-haired Dunne, who nodded at him after Roy's introduction. He'd never met anybody named Derwin or from North Dakota. An upper lip with a humorous curl broke out in a smile at the introduction. Black-framed glasses magnified his eyes, and a thin mustache contributed to an impish impression. After acknowledging Andy, Dunne returned his attention to Franklin.

"My man Dunne is tellin' me there be a set of wire cutter's in the compound. And I been thinkin', what if we got your car brought down here? Could tool around Monterey."

"We could," Andy said tentatively, "but what if we get caught?"

"Caught?" exclaimed Franklin, the question a silly objection to his plan. "Ain't got no guns in this place, Andy. Can't shoot us if they ain't got no guns."

Andy saw a flaw in Roy's thinking. A lot of possibilities existed between driving around Monterey freely and not being shot for breaking out of an unarmed compound.

"'Sides, Derwin's sayin' nobody cares what happens after evenin' bed check. We show up for the mornin' formation, stay outta trouble, everything be fine."

"What about Sergeant Gour?" Andy asked.

"Gour?" Another silly fret of Andy's. "That motherfucker ain't gonna worry 'bout no skinny little black guy disappearin' with a skinny white guy for a few hours. Not if he don't even know we gone."

Andy wouldn't mind having his car brought down from the Presidio. He worried about it sitting in the parking lot for such a long time. No telling what Hastings might have already done with it. Renaldo would know.

"If I had the phone number of the orderly room, the company clerk might bring it down," said Andy. "He'd probably charge us."

"That's easy," Roy assured Andy. "I can get the number, even make the call."

"A good idea," said Andy, "in case that fucker Hasting answers the phone." He thought of the beaches near Monterey, remembering the cove he'd camped at in Big Sur.

Not wasting time, Franklin checked his pockets for coins. "I'm a little short," he said. "Who's gonna contribute?" Mostly dimes appeared out of the pants of the guys hanging around Franklin's bed.

"Should be enough," Franklin said, counting the coins. "Be back shortly."

"The motherfucker says he'll do it for a hundred dollars, plus expenses," Franklin said after returning to the compound. "I jus' asked Gour straight up if I could go use the phone," he told the group reassembling at his cot.

"I told Renaldo to bring it down on the weekend, we'd meet up with him on Saturday night after the evenin' bed check," Roy continued. "I'm taking up a collection to raise the money, guys. I think every five bucks is good for a ride to Monterey and back. Whatcha think, Andy?"

He simply nodded. Roy was setting up a taxi service for the inmates of SPD with Andy's car.

"What about getting him the keys?" Andy asked.

"Keys?" Incredulous, Roy looked at Andy like everybody knew how to hotwire a car. "It's taken care of," he said. "Derwin, you be organizin' the wire cutters?"

The logistical details taken care of, the resident philosophers came forward. Dunne speculated how much longer he might be inconvenienced by the Army.

"If I'm not out by Christmas, that's it, I'm gone." Under no circumstances was the Army to be taken seriously. "Think I'd miss being home for Christmas because the Army won't give me leave time? No way. Fuck that shit. Let them find me if they're so desperate to have somebody sit on their butt all day in some shithole base I'm supposed to be at."

"What if you get orders for the Nam?" a red-haired guy with a Carolina drawl asked.

Franklin jumped in. "Think they be sendin' this motherfucker to the Nam," he said, pointing at Dunne. "Ain't that right, Andy? You want this shithead next to you in a foxhole fending off the Vee-et Cong? Ain't gonna win no war that way. Even the fuckin' lifers know that."

"What about you, Franklin?" the same soldier asked. "What you gonna do if you get orders for the Nam?"

"Me? I don't need to be goin' all that way to pick a fight with some Vee-et Cong. Got plenty of fights here in this country."

"Besides," Dunne interjected, "it goes against our motto."

"Motto?" the red-haired guy questioned again.

"Everybody knows we're all up on AWOL charges," Dunne said. "We're the SPD Roadrunners. Here today, gone tomorrow."

"Yeah?" Red added, sarcastically. "You're sayin' we shouldn't worry? So, who's our mascot, Alfred E. Neuman?"

❀ ❀ ❀

Slipping out of the compound proved easy. Derwin Dunne, in charge of the wire cutters, came along. "Snip, snip," he said, cutting through the patch job in the fence. "It's easier, and the lifers don't mind as much if we use the same spot."

Nervous, Andy looked forward to retrieving his car. Part of him relaxed a bit knowing he'd survived the war and faced no serious criminal charges. The monotony of the last six months also factored into his decision to go along with Franklin's plan. Time spent in the stockade and the SPD detachment would not count as time in the Army towards his discharge, but after his court-martial he would have just two and a half months remaining. A touch of fatalism in his thoughts, he reasoned, *There's not much more the Army can do to me. I've done everything the country's asked of me. If they want more, it's somebody else's turn.*

Right on schedule, Renaldo had the car waiting for Andy and Roy Franklin on Saturday night. "Hi, Andy," Renaldo said cheerfully. "You got my hundred bucks?"

Franklin took a wad of bills out of his pocket and counted out 100 dollars.

"What about expenses?" Renaldo asked. "You owe me another twenty-five bucks."

"For what?" questioned Franklin. "You think I'm a bank?"

"For gas, meals, motel and a bus ticket back to San Francisco."

"Shouldn't be worth more than twenty," Franklin said, pulling another bill out of his pocket.

"Okay," said Renaldo, "I'll settle on the twenty if you give me a ride into Monterey."

❀ ❀ ❀

Andy hopped in behind the wheel and the four went into Monterey. It felt good to be driving again. He missed the sense of freedom his car gave him. Nothing since returning from Vietnam had given him as much contentment as driving his station wagon, whether it was the afternoon forays into the Oklahoma countryside, or the road trip to California.

The novelty of escaping the compound at night and driving around Monterey soon wore off. None of them had any money because the Army didn't pay a soldier while doing *bad time*. Andy hadn't had a pay voucher for six months. Tired of having to scrounge money for gas and only visiting Monterey in the dark, his car sat parked most nights.

Andy thought of a plan to ease the boredom while he waited for his court-martial. He approached Sergeant Gour. "I'd like to see if they need any medics over at the hospital. I could give them a hand, and it would get me out of the compound for a few hours."

Fort Ord, a large training center, didn't have the mangled bodies of returning Vietnam veterans needing extended care.

"I thought you worked in the hospital at the Presidio? You went AWOL. What's different?"

Andy shrugged. "I don't know, Sarge. I was just back from the war. You were there. Did you just return and get back to normal?" Andy knew Gour had been with the 25th Infantry Division by the unit insignia on his right shoulder.

"You were in the Nam?" he asked.

"Ninth Infantry," Andy told him.

"That's a rarity around here." The sergeant thought for a moment. "I'll tell you what. Go speak with Sergeant Garcia over at the hospital. We go back a long way. If he says okay, I'm good with it. And Parks," he added, "nothing ever gets back to normal. I been there twice. Get used to it."

Andy's court-martial took a month to arrive. He stood before a captain who looked bored and only mildly annoyed while shuffling papers around on his desk. After reading the charges of AWOL he pronounced a sentence.

"You have been found guilty of being absent without leave. Your rank shall be reduced by one grade, you will be docked two hundred dollars in pay, and shall be restricted to the base for thirty days." No lecture followed.

Andy had already struck a deal with Sergeant Garcia. In exchange for working on one of the wards prior to his hearing, the NCO agreed to have Andy assigned to the hospital permanently after his sentencing. Andy filled in on the flu ward, short of medics and full of stressed trainees doing their basic and advanced infantry training.

Gathering his belongings at the SPD detachment, he said goodbye to Franklin. "Let me know when you want to go into Monterey," Andy told him. "I'm on the flu ward at the hospital." The thirty-day restriction to the base meant nothing. Fort Ord, an open post, had no checkpoints for entering and leaving the base.

"I be gone soon, Andy. My hearing's next week. They gonna discharge me with some bad paper. Can't say that I mind."

"Where will you go?"

"Down to LA," Roy said. "I like it there. Lots goin' on and it's warm all year."

Andy sensed he wouldn't see him again. The Army was full of goodbyes. "Take care of yourself, Roy Franklin. And stay out of trouble."

"Don't know I can do that, Andy," he said. "Maybe try it for a while. Find some legit job or somethin.'"

"You do that. Good luck."

"And good luck to you, Andy."

At the admin office Andy signed out and looked for Sergeant Gour.

"I just wanted to thank you for speaking to Sergeant Garcia for me," Andy said. "It looks like I'll be at the hospital here until my discharge."

"Us Vietnam vets have to stick together." He smiled and offered his hand.

After shaking it Andy turned to leave.

"Just one more thing, Parks," Gour said, his smile broadening. "Will you be taking your car with you? We could use the space in the parking lot."

CHAPTER
TWENTY-THREE

A LONG ROW of shaved heads protruded out of the uniformly spaced hospital beds, which extended along both sides of the ward. Ready to begin his morning shift, Andy held a sterile canister of thermometers and began inserting them into the mouths of the patients on the flu ward.

"Andy, is that you? I knew you were in the Army, man, but I never expected to run into you."

The familiar face beneath the shaved head was Glen Avery, an acquaintance from Vinita, a neighboring town in Oklahoma. "I heard you were in the Nam," he continued. "I'm just finishing my advanced infantry training before going over. What's it like?"

Andy remembered being in Avery's shoes, desperate for any bit of information. But there was no way he could sum it up in a few words, none that would do him any good.

"You hear about Davey Buckley?" Avery asked. "He got killed over there just before I got drafted."

Andy knew the name but not the person. He could see the worry in Avery's eyes.

"All of the sergeants training us have been over there," Avery said, "but they don't tell us much. They keep sayin' we should pay attention and get in shape or Charlie will cut our balls off and shove them down our throats. Is it really that bad, or are they just tryin' to motivate us?"

"The war can't last forever," Andy said. "Maybe you won't even have to go." Despite Andy's ray of optimism, they both know Avery would end up in Vietnam. *Charlie isn't going anywhere*, Andy thought.

"Just remember conditions are the same for them," Andy said, repeating what Camel told him. "The year will pass. See you back home when we're out of the Army."

It was like saying goodbye to a doomed man. Even if he survived the war, Andy knew young Avery would suffer and bring it home with him.

* * *

Andy rented a one-room cottage off the base to avoid the barracks. The Fort Ord Hospital had trainees, not quadriplegics back from the Nam. He spent his days off camping in Big Sur, the natural beauty calming and connecting him to something peaceful yet powerful, more substantial than himself.

His drinking returned, though not as desperate as in the days on the quad ward when he needed absolute obliteration each night in order to sleep. Now it was a buffer, a layer added between himself and the Army and the war.

Camel still came in his dreams.

Andy searched for him in the rice paddy, finding him facedown next to the dike, a skeleton now. The paddy dry, the seedlings withered and scorched. Andy touched him, and he came to life, but had no flesh. He smiled and his teeth were prominent because there was no skin on his face. His eyes were empty sockets.

"What took you so long, Doc? I thought you guys were going to leave me here forever."

"We thought you were dead, Camel," Andy told him.

"I am, but where is the rest of the platoon? Some of the others must be dead, but I'm out here in this shithole of a rice paddy where you let me die. I had this wound in my side, but it's gone now." He showed Andy the ribs on his skeleton with long bony fingers. One of them was scarred where the bullet must have hit before tearing through his liver.

❊ ❊ ❊

When not camping on the beach, Andy explored California on his days off. Near Garberville, he walked among the giant redwoods. The massive trees dwarfed him, but as he hiked through the forest he connected to the constant cycle of decay and renewal. Saplings grew out of toppled trunks, the new nurtured by the old, no separation between the living and the dead. Each root tapped into sustenance from the ground while thick trunks reached hundreds of feet into the sky so tiny leaves could find the sun.

He continued until he came to a river. Emerging from the damp forest he sat on the bank and felt the sun warm him. It was peaceful there, and he allowed it to seep into him, fleeting, but aware of it. The flowing of the grey-green water was rhythmic, steady but always changing like life itself. He wanted to find an equilibrium with life, but didn't know how.

He thought of Sammy and his family. *Stay focused,* he told himself. *For now, keep goals simple. Finish with the Army and get on with my life. I'm strong enough for that.*

❊ ❊ ❊

One week before Andy's scheduled discharge he received a letter.

Dear Andy,

I am writing to you out of desperation. My husband and I don't know what to do. Paul is in the VA hospital here in

Fresno on the psychiatric ward. He's very sick with severe headaches, dizziness, and abdominal cramping. His body is covered in a rash none of the creams and ointments prescribed by the doctors will heal.

We don't know what it is that you can do, but we are desperate for anything that might help our son. The diagnosis given by the psychiatrist is a war related neurosis. Paul is certain he has some tropical ailment he picked up in Vietnam. He's very depressed. Can you help us?

Sincerely,
Brenda Voight

Andy had already planned to stop in Fresno before seeing Sammy and returning to Oklahoma. He hoped Paul Voight would help him make sense of his own isolation. Mrs. Voight's letter described a situation worse than Andy's. He wrote her a quick reply.

Dear Mrs. Voight,

I'm sorry to hear about Paul's hospitalization. I'm out of the Army in a few days. I will visit as soon as possible. Please say hello to Paul and tell him I look forward to seeing him.

Sincerely,
Andy Parks

❋ ❋ ❋

By mid-afternoon Andy arrived at the VA hospital, a multi-story facility in a suburban setting. The October sun, warm in the San Joaquin Valley, shone bright in a cloudless blue sky as Andy parked and walked inside. At the reception desk he asked a young woman for Paul Voight's room number.

"Give me one second," she said pleasantly. Her demeanor changed when she realized Voight was on the psychiatric ward. "Are you family?" she asked. "If not, I'll have to check with the nursing staff before you'll be allowed to see him. What is your relationship to Mr. Voight?"

"Look," Andy said, "we were in Vietnam together. His mother got in touch with me. She thought it might help if I could see him."

"I still have to check. Come back in an hour."

Andy returned to his car and sat for a moment. The sun had warmed the interior to an uncomfortable level. In his hurry to get to Fresno he'd skipped lunch. He found the hospital cafeteria and ate a sandwich while waiting.

"I'm sorry," the receptionist said at the information desk. "The doctor feels it would be best if Mr. Voight had no reminders of his Vietnam experiences at this stage of his treatment. If you were there together, it might trigger bad memories when he sees you. It could set his recovery back for some time."

Andy knew if Paul's experiences returning from the war were anything like his, he felt isolated and alone. Friendship with someone who knew what he'd been through would do him good. Surprised at his anger, he tried not to take it out on the young woman only following instructions. But he resented her officiousness and the emotional coldness that came with it.

"I know you're only doing what you're told, but my friend was wounded trying to reach a dead platoon member. Before he was properly healed, they sent him back to his unit. He couldn't pack the gear. Instead of shipping him home where he belonged, they assigned him to the triage unit of an evac hospital. That's where they bring the wounded from the battlefield. If he's feeling anything like I am, he could use a friend, not more isolation."

"I think the doctors know what is best for the patients," she huffed. "You are not allowed on the ward to see your friend." She busied herself with papers on her desk.

Andy glared at her. She didn't look up. Controlling his anger, he walked towards the doors leading out of the hospital. He paced in the parking lot craving a drink of Wild Turkey. He lit a cigarette instead.

Andy drove to the Voights' house. Paul's mother answered the door. Looking well-groomed in a blouse and skirt, signs of weariness appeared in the deepened lines on her face and a greying of her dark hair at the temples. She ushered Andy into the house.

"Thank you for coming," she said. "I'm just getting ready to return to the hospital to see Paul. Can you come with me?"

"Of course," said Andy, "but I just came from there and they wouldn't let me on the ward."

Brenda Voight, dismissing any pretense of small talk in her worry and concern about Paul, waved off Andy's inability to see her son with a flick of the wrist.

"They'll let you in with me."

On the way Brenda Voight brought Andy up to date on her son's condition.

"It's gotten so crazy," she began. "We are at our wit's end trying to figure out what's wrong. Paul is in pain and the psychiatrist is telling us it's all in his head. A mother knows when her son is suffering. Paul is not himself and insists he's not imagining his symptoms. They have him so doped up most of the time he's not always coherent. He says it's the drugs, not his mental state. He's depressed. Anybody would be, cooped up on a ward full of troubled young men."

Andy kept quiet, allowing Mrs. Voight to continue.

"Paul has these horrible rashes all over his body. He has migraine headaches and is dizzy most of the time. Nothing they are treating him with is helping, so they figure it must be caused by his war experiences. Does any of this make sense?"

The tongue-tied medic again, Andy shrugged and continued listening as Brenda Voight spoke of Paul's troubles.

"After you came to visit, we didn't hear from Paul for two months. You can imagine how worried we were. Then, he just shows up and doesn't want to tell us where he's been. He seemed confused by our questions. He said he was so depressed sometimes he couldn't move. He's thinner than when he returned from Vietnam. He doesn't eat much because it upsets his stomach. If he doesn't vomit, he has diarrhea."

Brenda Voight, still clutching the steering wheel, put her forehead on it and sighed after taking a deep breath. "Nobody can tell us what is wrong with our son. He knows it must appear like he's crazy. He's convinced he has some tropical disease he picked up in Vietnam."

※ ※ ※

There was no checkpoint on the ward for Brenda Voight. The nurses all knew her and said hello.

"This is our other son, Andy," she lied. "They are very close. Maybe seeing his brother will help Paul." They nodded in agreement.

They found Paul propped up in bed, expressionless, staring straight ahead. He looked at his mother first.

"Hello, dear," she said. "A friend of yours has come to see you. Do you remember Andy Parks? You knew him in Vietnam."

"You came," he said.

At his bedside, Andy gazed at the grimace on the gaunt face. Handsome, even in Vietnam, the appealing brown eyes and sandy-colored hair looked diminished by the pain and ravages of whatever plagued him. Andy noticed the lack of muscle tone as one of Paul's forearms reached for the remnants of the wound that smashed his collarbone. He rubbed it without looking where the ugly scar remained above the internal damage that still ached. Paul's arm, a stick remnant of what it should be, exposed the rash his mother described.

"How's it going, Paul?" Andy asks. Realizing the foolishness of the question, Andy shook his head. "Sorry, man, a stupid thing to say."

"I'm glad you came, Andy," Paul said, ignoring the awkward start to the conversation. "It's been a nightmare since I've been back. At first, I thought I was going nuts. I avoided questions about the war and got angry when anybody brought it up. I'd start thinking about guys I lost as a medic and get depressed. Nobody understands shit about the war."

Andy nodded. He knew exactly what Paul described. He thought he'd coped fine until he didn't, ending up in prison.

"I thought the dumb questions triggered the headaches, until they became more frequent. Some were so intense no amount of over-the-counter painkillers helped. I got so desperate I considered scoring some heroin just to get relief from the pain. I finally got some codeine prescribed. If I took enough pills that helped, but I was always running out. The doctors here in outpatient started suspecting I was an addict faking my symptoms to get more codeine. Something's very wrong with me. Most of the time, I can't eat because my guts are on fire. I'm a physical mess. Now they've got me on the psych ward because they think it's all in my head."

Andy moved closer. "Can I have a look?"

"I picked something up in the Nam, man. Look at this rash." He unbuttoned the front of his hospital pajamas. "Sometimes it goes away on some parts of my body but reappears. None of the creams the doctors prescribe do any good."

Andy looked at Paul's chest. "I've seen something similar in the Nam." Andy remembered Black Henry and the Professor showing him the same tiny black dots sprinkled amongst the raised and reddish outbreaks on the skin.

"Something else," Paul continued. "I found work for a few days clearing brush for a farmer near Fresno. A couple of the Mexican guys I worked with invited me for beers after finishing the job. After drinking my first I fell violently ill like I had a massive hangover. I had to leave my head was pounding so bad. I started vomiting on the way home, all from one beer. A friend of mine helped me recover. She brought me cold compresses for my head and fed me soups. It took two days before I could get out of bed.

"One of the doctors suggested a liver biopsy. I'm thinking it should show something, give some reasons why I'm so sick. We're waiting on the results."

Paul's mother entered the room looking upset. "There are some things I need to do this afternoon, dear. I'll be back tonight with your father."

Andy sensed Brenda Voight needed to get off the ward. He wished he'd driven his own car so he could stay longer.

"Do you have to go?" Paul asked Andy.

"I came with your mom," he said, "but I'll be back, too."

Andy knew Paul wanted to tell him something more, but not in front of his mother. "I'll catch up to you, Mrs. Voight," Andy told her.

She nodded and kissed her son goodbye.

"What happened to the guys in your platoon with the rashes?" Voight asked.

"I don't know. One of them was killed, but the other should be home in Alabama. It gives me an idea."

"Can you do me a favor?"

"Sure. What do you need?"

"Can you check in on my friend, Sheila, let her know what's going on? She doesn't have a phone, so you'll need to go to her place. Here's the address."

Andy ran and caught up with Brenda Voight as she walked towards her car. She waited until they were inside the vehicle before speaking.

"I ran into the psychiatrist while you were visiting with Paul," she began. "He asked if he could speak with me. I thought he might have some news about Paul's condition. Instead, he asked if I knew what kinds of drugs Paul was taking. I told him he would know that better than I because they were the ones prescribed by the doctors. He said, 'No, what kinds of illegal drugs is Paul taking?' He thinks my son is a drug addict." She leaned her head into her hands and shook it. "This is all too crazy. None of it makes any sense. My son is not a drug addict."

"Mrs. Voight, Paul told me they did a liver biopsy, but the results aren't back. I've seen that kind of rash in Vietnam but don't know what it's from. Paul is not an addict. He couldn't have functioned as a medic if he were drunk or stoned all the time. There is a physical cause for his problems."

Nodding, she said, "It's just that we were so glad and happy when he got back from Vietnam. He seemed fine. Then, he's angry, and disappears for two months. When he returns he's so thin and sick. We have no idea why this is happening."

Ronald Voight arrived home from his office while Brenda and Andy sipped coffee. Andy saw a resemblance to Paul in the brown eyes and light brows on a broad forehead, but with a stockier frame. He was direct, motioning for Andy to join him at the kitchen table.

"We have wondered if there were things we could have done differently," the elder Voight confided. "It's just that we never expected any of this. Paul was safe and out of the Army. Then, it all just deteriorated. So different from when I got back from World War Two with the whole country celebrating and wanting to get things back to normal. We were so optimistic then and were for Paul when he returned. Of course, I never got a scratch and Paul was wounded. Maybe that's what made a difference."

Ron Voight looked at his wife before continuing. "We got our hopes up when Paul went into the hospital thinking he would get better. It's just never good news."

The Voights put Andy in Paul's old room. He excused himself after supper and lay stretched out on the bed, thinking. *Maybe Sheila will have some information . . . Paul looks horrible.*

Andy craved sips of Wild Turkey. He bought cigarettes instead and went to find Sheila. He usually liked being in new places, observing, wondering about the lives of strangers. He chain-smoked while driving to her address, a tiny house in an older and poorer part of the city. Mature elm trees lined the street.

"Yes?" she asked, answering the door.

"Hi," Andy said, "I'm Paul's friend. We were in Vietnam together. He asked me to come by and see how you are."

"Come in, please. Is Paul okay?"

Andy sat across from Sheila in her living room. Plump, but pretty, her black hair fell around her shoulders in a sleeveless dress. Andy found her attractive. He worried about Sheila noticing how appealing he found her.

"I don't mean to alarm you," he said, "but he's pretty sick. They have him on the psych ward at the VA hospital because they don't know what's wrong with him. Do you know anything that might help?"

She shook her head and averted her gaze, not wanting Andy to see her tears. "I met Paul in high school. He used to pal around with one of my brothers. I'm a couple years older, but I had a crush on Paul before he went into the Army. I wrote to him in Vietnam. I guess I was hoping to get together when he returned. When he did get back it was like Paul needed someone to talk to. I guess he felt comfortable with me. We had this intimacy that was special, somehow, without being lovers."

Andy sat without interrupting.

"I wanted to be, and maybe we would have, but Paul got so sick he just wasn't interested in sex. He would get so terribly depressed and just lay in bed for days at a time. I would lay down with him, stroke him, hold him, kiss his face, whisper how much I cared about him. I felt so close to him, but he would pull away sometimes, not angry with me, but so deeply troubled. He would say he was 'damaged goods.' I loved him anyway. Then, the headaches would come, the dizziness, the rashes on his body. We tried everything to treat them. Paul would soak in the bath and I would massage creams and ointments into his skin He was still in some pain where he'd been wounded. You say you were in Vietnam with Paul?"

"Yes," said Andy, "we were both medics."

"He got so sick I knew he needed to get some medical care. I took Paul to the VA hospital, but after they admitted him, they wouldn't allow me on the ward. It was selfish of me to keep him here so long. I guess I'm in love with him." Sheila wiped her tears.

"It sounds like you were giving him better care than they are," Andy said. "Paul wanted to make sure I got in touch with you, tell you he's thinking of you. They wouldn't let me see him either, until I pretended to be his brother. I promise I'll keep you up to date."

❋ ❋ ❋

When Andy saw Paul the next day his friend looked depressed, staring at him with less expression. Self-conscious, Paul tried to explain.

"With some of the nurses it's possible to fake taking the tranquilizers. I don't like what they do to me. One of the sticklers was on duty this morning. I feel doped up."

"I saw Sheila," Andy said. "You should marry that girl."

"Maybe in some other life," he mumbled. "Nothing's gone right, has it? The psychiatrist came by this morning. The results of the biopsy are back. My liver is inflamed and showing signs of damage. Here, you can feel it's enlarged." He pulled his gown aside for Andy.

"Now they have a new explanation for why I'm so sick. I'm either an alcoholic or a heavy drug user. I told them I can't drink, and have never done drugs, just a little pot in the Nam. Shit, Andy, you were a medic. Just when were we supposed to do all those drugs over there and still function? I'm twenty-two years old, can't drink a beer without getting violently ill, and they're telling me I have the liver of a fifty-year-old alcoholic. The shrink told me the sooner I admitted to my addiction issues and stopped denying them, the sooner I'd recover."

Andy had a sinking feeling. The psychiatrist would have known the results of the biopsy when he spoke to Brenda Voight. Feeling like the medic who should be able to "fix it," Andy stared at his friend. Frail, weak, depressed, and without answers, Paul looked like a defeated man. A familiar despair from the war gnawed at Andy. *If the doctors don't know how to help, how am I supposed to?*

They chatted for most of the day. One of the nurses kept checking on them, acting like Andy should go. He ignored her, an older and uglier version of Miss Prissy.

Paul told him more of his experiences before he'd gotten to the 29th Evac. Neither of them had saved enough platoon members to feel good about their tours. Paul was also in the defoliated zones and got the shit sprayed on him. Nobody knew his platoon was there—or it didn't matter.

Just before he left Paul asked, "What will you do now, Andy?"

"Go back to Oklahoma, I guess. I'm gonna check on something first, though. It's a long shot, but you're sick for a reason and it's got nothing to do with your head."

"You'll stay in touch?"

"I will."

Andy had a bad feeling when he left the hospital that day. He'd return to Fresno and see Paul before leaving for Oklahoma. He wasn't sure he'd have any information to help him.

Mrs. Voight hugged him when he stopped to say goodbye. "We'll see you in a few days," she said. "You are always welcome."

Andy knew the chances of finding Black Henry and finding any answers were slim, but he needed to try. Sammy would help, foolish quest or not.

That night, he made it to the coast and built a fire on the beach. He smoked the last of the cigarettes he'd bought before meeting Sheila. He drank most of a bottle of Wild Turkey.

Camel came to him again in his sleep, still in the rice paddy and asking when the platoon would come for him.

"Fat chance of that, Camel. Don't you know we're on our own?"

CHAPTER
TWENTY-FOUR

ANDY SPENT THE night on the coast to clear his head. Again, he retreated into a bottle of Wild Turkey. No answers emerged, just another hangover. Disgusted with himself, he packed his camping gear into the car and set out early in the morning.

A fog blanketed the coast during the night, restricting visibility, matching the lack of clarity in his thinking. The cloud cover lifted as he drove inland, and the sun's warmth broke through in streaks of light piercing the grey. His gloom lifted slightly when he arrived at Sammy's.

"Remember the day Black Henry and the Professor came into our hooch with those rashes?" Andy asked Sammy. "Paul has the same thing, only he's been out of Vietnam several months. The rashes are the least of his problems, but I was wondering if we could find Black Henry and see how he's doing? Maybe he knows something that might help."

"I know he made it out of the Nam," Sammy said, "but I haven't been able to find him. After the Professor got killed, he kept to himself and nobody has heard from him."

Sammy sat in the same backyard overlooking the desert. Nearly a year out of the war, the outward scars healed, he'd put on a little weight and grown his hair longer. His eyes had the same intensity, but his smile came easier and softened his face. Enrolled at Barstow Community College, he'd begun to put the war behind him and get on with his future. He fidgeted with his hands while looking at the ground, a gesture Andy remembered from the Nam, thinking about what he wanted to say before speaking.

"I know someone who might be able to help, at least with information."

"Really, about the rashes?"

"Broader than that. I'm taking a class in modern US history, but most of the course is on the Vietnam War. I'm the only veteran in the class. My prof and I talk quite a bit. He asks about my experiences in Vietnam. His son's a lawyer in Los Angeles and working on a class action suit with some vets back from the war who are having health problems. They're getting nowhere with the VA, running up against a stone wall. Some of their problems sound like Paul's."

"Can we talk to him?"

"I don't know why not? He's interested about the war. His course puts what's happening in Vietnam into a global context. I'm sure you could sit in on some of the classes if you want."

❋ ❋ ❋

They found Sammy's history prof in his office. Books on shelves lined the walls, with magazines, mimeographed copies of articles, and newspapers piled in stacks among more books on his desk. Absorbed in a copy of the *Berkeley Barb*, he didn't notice Sammy until he knocked on his open door.

"Interesting stuff," he commented, looking up at his student. "The Vietnam War has spawned a whole subversive culture of young people saying no to their government. They want nothing to do with the war or the values that spawned it. So what can I do for you, Sam?"

"Professor Bernstein, this is Doc Parks, my best friend from Vietnam. He stopped by for a visit on his way back to Oklahoma. One of his medic friends is sick with symptoms like the veterans your son is representing. I thought you might be able to help with some information."

Andy offered his hand across the cluttered desk. The older man's firm grip and attentive eyes signaled an interest in what Andy had to say.

"What kind of problem is your friend having?"

"He's in the psych ward at the VA hospital in Fresno. His liver is enlarged and inflamed, showing symptoms of alcohol abuse, except my friend can't drink or he gets violently ill. The doctors don't believe him. They think he's either a drug addict or an alcoholic. He's also got skin rashes that won't heal. A psychiatrist has diagnosed him with some kind of war neurosis."

Bernstein thought for a moment, then removed a sheaf of papers from one of the stacks. He skimmed the mimeographed sheets in his hand.

"Sam says your platoon came in contact with some of the defoliated areas in the Mekong Delta."

Andy nodded. "My friend was north of where we were, a platoon medic with the First Infantry Division. The Army told us it was just some herbicides that were harmless. We were more worried about other kinds of stuff."

"Like staying alive," Sammy interjected.

Bernstein tossed the paper in front of him and leaned forward. "A year ago, a young man came into my son's law office wanting legal advice concerning a dispute he was having with the VA. He'd spent most of 1963 as a military advisor to the South Vietnamese Army. Discharged the next year, his wife gave birth to their first child in 1965. It was stillborn, probably a good thing because it was horribly deformed. At that point, the couple figured it was just bad luck and tried again. They had a baby girl born with a cleft palate and a hand missing some fingers. By then, the husband had recurring rashes diagnosed as chloracne, a skin condition caused by exposure to toxic chemicals. The veteran became convinced the birth defects of his children were linked to Agent Orange when one of the guys he was in Vietnam with had a child with similar problems. The government, and the VA, are denying any links between the chemical defoliants and health problems, except for the chloracne, which they say poses no long-term risks."

Andy stood mesmerized by the professor's detailed knowledge of the sprays used in Vietnam. Bernstein got up and removed the stacks of books on two chairs and motioned for Andy and Sammy to have a seat.

"My son asked if I would look into the history of their use in Vietnam. What I found was disturbing. Records show as early as 1952, Monsanto informed the government some of its farm chemical, 2-4-5-T, which makes up half of what you know as Agent Orange, contained dioxins—one of the most toxic molecules known to man. Further scientific studies linked exposure to dioxins with birth defects in mice."

Andy sat stunned. "So why was it used?"

"That's the question, isn't it," replied Bernstein. "The science says it never should have been, but it was, something like twenty million gallons worth. And there's more.

"Dow, the other major manufacturer, is saying they can't be held responsible for any damages because they were only doing what the government requested in ramping up production for use in Vietnam. Who's to blame?

"It gets even more complicated. In 1966 the first resolution against its use in Vietnam was brought forward in the United Nations because it violated the 1925 Geneva Protocol banning the use of chemical and biological weapons. The US defeated the resolution by arguing Agent Orange is an herbicide and as such is not a chemical weapon. Our government used as a precedent the British use of 2-4-5-T in Malaya suppressing a rebellion there in the 1950s.

"Several countries around the world have used these chemical defoliants, including our neighbors to the north in Canada. Three provinces cleared forests and cut lines with it. In northern Ontario areas of crown land were cleared using students as markers while planes flew overhead spraying the chemicals. Canadian soldiers also tested it around Gagetown, a military base in New Brunswick.

"The concentrations used in Vietnam were often dozens of times stronger than what the manufacturers recommended. I fear we're only seeing the tip of the iceberg on this issue."

"Paul mentioned the defoliants were sprayed right on top of his platoon," said Andy.

"We were all in the defoliated zones," Sammy said, "filling our canteens from the streams and any crater that held water."

Professor Bernstein wrote his son's telephone number on a slip of paper. "You are both okay?" he asked.

"So far," said Sammy.

"It might be a good idea if your friend contacts my son. It won't cost him any money. His firm is gathering cases for a class action suit."

"Not as harmless as they told us, is it?" Andy said as they walked back to his car.

"What are you gonna do now, Doc? Contact the professor's son?"

"I want to go see him, get as much information as possible. Then I'll go back to Fresno and give it to Paul. I think he needs to get off the psych ward. It's doing him more harm than good."

❋ ❋ ❋

Andy got through to Michael Bernstein the next day.

"Is it possible to meet with you in person?" the lawyer asked Andy. "I have an information package that might be helpful, but easier to explain face-to-face. Let's see . . . it's Thursday. Can you make it to Los Angeles on Monday? If not, I can send it in the mail."

"No," said Andy, "I can come."

"Good. We also have a doctor familiar with these toxins. I'll include his contact information along with some legal documents to fill out if your friend decides to proceed. Have him try and remember everything he can about any exposure to the Agent Orange."

"Okay. He's already mentioned some stuff."

"Be sure and have him write it down. Unfortunately, he's not the first vet to be misdiagnosed with psychiatric problems from the chemicals that are physical in origin."

Andy got off the phone feeling positive about helping Paul and relaxed a little. Sammy's family expected him for supper on the weekend. Amy insisted he stop in for a visit with her husband and children. Free of the Army at last, he hung around Sammy's place and visited the college campus.

"You could enroll in school here," Sammy encouraged. "I'm getting two hundred and twenty dollars a month in veteran's benefits to attend college. We could split the rent and live pretty good on that, concentrate on our studies and work in the summer."

"Let me get Paul squared away and then we'll talk more about it."

First he needed to return to Oklahoma, but guessed his parents would be pleased if he enrolled in college.

※ ※ ※

On Saturday Andy took a long walk in the desert, giving Sammy time to study. He searched for cactus in the sparse terrain and noticed a variety of flowering plants not seen from the backyard. He avoided a rattlesnake sunning on a flat rock that paid him no mind as he walked past. A desert coyote with pups hunted mice near a dry streambed. Graceful in her movements, the young emulated her hunt for food. Light of foot in the parched landscape, their playfulness reminded Andy of children. Mother coyote prodded them with a look and nip when their concentration waned.

On his return, Andy looked through the books Sammy needed for his classes. Andy took a book off the shelf and began reading about a man building a cabin near a pond in the woods and living a solitary life. Not understanding all the author's philosophy, it expressed a peacefulness that appealed to Andy. A few pages into the book Andy set it beside him and fell asleep on an old couch in the living room.

Awakened by overhearing a conversation at the door, Andy sat up. A woman's voice told Sammy they needed to come to his parents' house as soon as possible.

"What's wrong?" he asked Sammy, looking stricken at the door.

"We need to go to my parents' place. Something's happened."

"To your parents? Are they okay?"

"Paul is dead," said Sammy. How many times had they told each other of somebody's death? They ought to be used to it by now. *How would Sammy's parents know?* Then he remembered giving Mrs. Voight the Donato number before leaving Fresno in case they needed to get a hold of him. Sammy didn't have a phone.

A sick feeling lodged in the pit of his stomach. He dreaded more details but couldn't get to the Donatos' fast enough. Sammy drove.

Mrs. Donato stood by the lone tree in the front yard waiting, a daughter near her. She came towards the car, crying softly, understanding and feeling the grief of another mother without knowing the child.

Andy began crying when he saw Mrs. Donato's tears. Becoming a blubbering mess around Sammy's people, he couldn't hold back when she put her arms around him.

"This war is no good for you boys, and not over yet," she said, crying softly.

"What happened to Paul?" Andy asked. "What did the Voights tell you?"

"He took too many pills," she said. "His mother phoned. She wanted you to know how much she appreciated your help. Her son was very sick and took a lot of pills."

Andy pulled away from Mrs. Donato and slumped against the tree, knowing exactly what had happened. In his stupidity he'd missed all the clues—Paul's depression and anger about the war, how sick he was, the false accusations about the alcohol and drugs.

That's why Paul avoided taking his meds. He was saving them up for one final dose.

"I'll go with you to Fresno, Doc," Sammy told him on the way back to his place.

Andy nodded, starting to pull himself together. "We still need to find Black Henry," he said, "make sure that motherfucker's okay."

"We'll find him," Sammy assured him, "make sure he's doing okay."

Andy couldn't stop thinking about the Voights and how devastated they would be, getting their son back from Vietnam, then losing him.

"What a clusterfuck it's turning out to be," he told Sammy. "Nothing but a goddamned clusterfuck."

"That pretty much sums it up," Sammy said.

❋ ❋ ❋

The pews of the church filled with Paul's aunts, uncles, cousins, former teachers and friends in the community. The Voights tried to be stoic. Andy held back, watching, not wanting to intrude. Mrs. Voight cried often while those around her consoled her grief, putting their arms around her and hugging her while she clung to them.

Sheila Hernandez, the only other person Andy recognized, spoke to him about Paul. Dressed in black, her pretty face etched in sorrow, she wiped at her eyes in the same way she had when Andy visited her.

"He knew he was really sick. It's not normal for a twenty-two-year-old man to be unable to eat, breaking out in ugly rashes all over his body. It did something to his mind. He was so isolated, spending days at my house without going outside. I loved him. I think he knew I loved him." She broke down and sobbed.

Subdued on the way back to Barstow, Andy reflected on the war coming home with him. *Difficult to shake this melancholy,* he thought. *Death following me like a black shroud. How long will the bodies continue to pile up? I'm powerless to help. Just like in Nam.*

Seeing the grief Paul's death caused the Voights had brought his own parents into focus. And he wanted to find his namesake, his mother's missing brother, the WWII medic who just might be as messed up as Andy. There might be clues to his disappearance in Oklahoma.

Andy said his goodbyes to Sammy early in the morning. He sensed it would be a while before they'd see each other. Andy had the same empty feeling he had when he rotated out of the Nam, leaving his friend with two months left on his tour. In the rearview mirror, he saw Sammy waving a last farewell.

The road loomed ahead, the desert sky a soft blue in the early morning. Getting out of the Army was supposed to fix Andy's emotional distress. He knew it wasn't going to be that easy. He could drive all the way to Oklahoma and not outrun the turmoil in his head. It would ride along with him.

CHAPTER
TWENTY-FIVE

November 1970

THE PARKS FAMILY gathered after church in their Afton house. Visiting before the Sunday meal, Andy chatted with his brother-in-law, Ben Kinecky, a former Marine, football player, and married to his sister, Nancy June. Andy hoped for a job in Ben's construction business.

"It's kinda slow right now," Ben said. "Maybe in the next couple of months something will open up."

"I have an idea," Andy said. "What if I had a truck? Maybe you need supplies at the lumberyard and don't want to take the time to go and pick it up. I could do that. It wouldn't cost you much."

"It might work," Ben said. Andy's mother, Rebecca, looked hopeful as the family discussed the possibilities for her son's employment "I could mention you to some other businesses, too," he added.

Not needing further assurances, Andy sold his station wagon and bought an old pickup, hoping it would run long enough to provide him with a job. He advertised two numbers where he could be reached for his light hauling service—his parents' home, and Kinecky and Sons Construction.

Andy's mother told everyone her prayers were answered, but Andy knew she still worried about his state of mind. Andy deftly refused to talk about the war or what happened at the Presidio and deflected questions with vague statements. By suppressing his feelings and not speaking of the Nam, Andy wanted to signal to his family that the horrors he'd experienced in war were behind him.

Rumors of Andy's imprisonment had preceded his return to Oklahoma. He ignored that, too. Accompanying Rebecca to church, he noted the congregation of Trinity Baptist acted more uncomfortable than hostile. A superficial politeness prevailed. Andy could do that. No standing ovations for his second return, but he hadn't liked the first one. Conscious of his other reason for returning to Oklahoma, Andy asked about his uncle after church.

"Why did he disappear?"

Rebecca, in a good mood after the Sunday sermon, reflected for a moment before answering. "Nobody knows, dear. We just realized one day that he was gone. There was tension in his marriage when Andrew came home from the Navy, but his wife was not on good terms with the family. She left soon after Andrew."

"Aunt Ruby has a picture of Andrew with the Marines."

"Yes," said Rebecca. "That was puzzling at first, but as you have explained, the Marine Corps uses Navy medics."

"Why do you think Andrew disappeared, and where would he have gone?"

"Really, dear, we have no idea."

"So, what was he really like? You told me he liked to build things and draw. You showed me some of his sketches."

"Actually, son, he was a lot like you."

Great, thought Andy, *a disappearing urge is in the genes. He probably hated football like me, too.*

❊ ❊ ❊

Andy hung around his brother-in-law's construction office, drinking coffee and waiting for business. He got calls to remove trash from local yards. A local businessman hired him to clean a vacant lot scheduled for a building project. Not the most satisfying work, but he was making money.

On one of his runs to the Vinita Lumber Yard, a girl approached while he tied his load.

"Andy Parks, is that you? I heard you were back in town."

It was Lila Mayes. They'd dated briefly in high school until Andy lost out to one of the Vinita boys.

"Hello, Lila. I got back a few weeks ago." They were distant cousins, having common ancestors on Andy's grandmother's side. Andy found her attractive. She had more Cherokee than him, and a little Mexican heritage. Her brown body, thick and strong, showed through her skirt and short-sleeved blouse.

"What are you doing here?" he asked.

"Working in the office upstairs," she said. "I saw you through the window so came down to say hello. I heard you were in the Army and in Vietnam. I guess you're back." She wore glasses now, softening her tough-girl look.

"Maybe you could take me to lunch sometime and we could catch up on what you've been up to." She moved closer to Andy and looked into his eyes. Hers were dark, and large. The scent of her rose perfume swirled in the air.

"Just phone the office and ask for Lila," she said, touching Andy's arm. "I guess I better get back to work. You'll call?"

❊ ❊ ❊

Lila sat across from Andy in a Vinita steakhouse. Wearing a denim jacket opened in the front exposing a white blouse underneath, her bosom stretched the fabric fastened by a row of silver buttons.

Andy chewed on a tough cut of meat, self-conscious about how long it took him to swallow each piece. The conversation lagged while Lila picked at a salad between glances at Andy.

"When did you get back from Vietnam?"

"Over a year ago now," he said, not sure if Lila was really interested or just wanted to break an awkward silence. He stopped chewing and looked at her, hoping their talk didn't veer towards the war. She'd taken her coat off, exposing her brown arms. Andy watched her fidget with a ring on her little finger, a band with tiny gold threads woven into a circle.

"It's probably not good dinner conversation," he said. "I don't like talking about it."

"I had a cousin over there. He doesn't mind talking about it."

"What's his name?" Andy asked.

"Desmond Mayes," she said. "Everyone calls him Desi. He was in the infantry, then a door gunner on a helicopter."

Andy didn't recognize the name.

"A lot of guys from here have gone over," she continued.

Andy nodded. "Would you like to go for a drive?" he asked, hoping to change the subject and salvage the date.

"Sure," said Lila, letting Andy help her with her coat.

Arriving at Andy's truck she asked, "Have you got anything to drink?"

Andy pulled a bottle of Wild Turkey from behind the seat. "This okay?"

Andy opened the door and helped her into the cab. She scooted over next to him. Sharing swigs from the bottle as they drove, Andy headed towards Grand Lake.

"Pull over here," Lila instructed two miles from the lake. She put the bottle on the floor and kissed Andy. The whiskey on her breath tasted good and mingled with her perfume. Lying on the seat, Andy pressed against her. When she wiggled out of her coat, Andy caressed the smoothness of her bare arms. Things went no further.

"Let's drive around some more," she suggested.

Sobered after all the kissing, they drank from the bottle again as they started towards the lake. Finding a stretch of shore to walk along, Lila pressed against Andy as they stopped and watched the moon reflect off the lake.

"I guess I should go home," Lila said, leaning into Andy for a final kiss before walking back to his truck. "Let's do this again next Saturday."

❋ ❋ ❋

Andy sat in the cluttered office of his brother-in-law's construction business. A radio with the volume turned low played Hank Williams singing "I'm So Lonesome I Could Cry." Ben got up from his desk to turn up the sound. Oklahomans liked a good-hurting country song.

News of Nixon's planned troop withdrawals came on when the recording ended. Andy listened in silence. Ben shook his head.

"I want to believe Nixon, but nobody seems to have figured out how to win this war." He looked at Andy like he wanted him to comment. When he didn't, he asked, "Time for a break?"

Anita's Grill featured booths along the walls and ten-cent mugs of coffee. Functional tables and chairs filled the rest of the room. Ben sat across from Andy while the waitress filled their cups.

"The thing is," Ben said, still not finished with his opinions on Vietnam, "Nixon wants peace, but with honor. We wouldn't be in this situation in the first place if they'd've just let you boys fight the war with whatever it took to win it."

Andy ignored Ben's comments, hearing that point of view frequently in Oklahoma. His brother-in-law probably believed it, and that it expressed support for Andy.

Instead, it triggered images of the war.

Lack of firepower? The B-52 strikes pulverizing the jungles, the napalm setting kids on fire, not hard-nosed enough?

"Andy?" Ben said his name, bringing him out of his thoughts.

"Do you want anything else?" A waitress stood at their table, order pad in hand.

"No, thanks," he said, "just coffee."

Ben ordered a sweet roll. "You free this afternoon?" he asked Andy. "We could use some two-by-fours and plywood for the Harmon Ranch project."

Andy, still in Vietnam, nodded. They sat in silence while Ben concentrated on his food. Someone bumped Andy from behind.

"I see you made it back," the voice said.

Andy turned, not recognizing the face at first glance. A compact and well-muscled Indian stood with arms folded. Sunglasses obscured his eyes. A leather medicine bag hung from the man's belt.

"Vietnam," the Native American said. "You hitched a ride on my helicopter. I thought it might be you dating my cousin, Lila. She told me she was going out with some skinny medic who'd been in the Nam."

"Tahlequah?" Andy said, surprised.

"That's where I'm from," the man said, pulling up a chair and sitting down. He nodded at Ben like he knew him. "Desmond Mayes is my name."

"Lila's your cousin?"

"That's what I said. She's my uncle's daughter."

"You knew one another in Vietnam?" Ben asked.

"We crossed paths," Andy said.

"You must have been in the Mekong Delta, too," Ben said.

"Ninth Infantry," Talequah said. "Fuckin' wet. Never could keep my feet dry, so I put in to be a door gunner. Up high . . . where it's dry." He smiled. "Charlie still messed with us, but we had better angles up there. Could unload a shitload of firepower on his ass."

Too late for Andy to avoid a discussion about the war, he opted for trying to cut it short. "I should probably get going," he said to Ben, standing, then remembering they'd come in his brother-in-law's truck.

"Hang on, Andy, we'll go in a minute."

Andy sat again, realizing Ben was not going to miss an opportunity to talk about the war.

"How often would you make contact?" Ben asked.

"Whenever Charlie wanted," Tahlequah said. "Sometimes he just disappeared, but you could feel him, always watching, waiting for you to fuck up and stop paying attention."

"I was in the Marines," Ben said. "Missed the war by a couple years."

"That's too bad," Tahlequah said, unimpressed. "Everybody should have a war to go to." He leaned back in his chair and folded his arms. Growing his hair thick and long now, it reached his shoulders. He kept his sunglasses on in the cafe. "Sometimes I miss it."

With Tahlequah's eyes hidden, Andy couldn't tell if his comments were sarcastic.

"Didn't you play football?" Andy asked, hoping to change the subject.

Tahlequah just smiled again and stood to leave. "See you around," he said to Andy. "Make sure you take good care of my cousin."

"I know him," Ben said. "Dizzy Mayes. He used to be a hotshot linebacker."

"I think his name is Desi," Andy corrected.

"No," Ben said, "they called him Dizzy because he hit so hard, he'd ring a player's bell. I'd stay away from him if I were you. There's talk he's runnin' drugs."

❋ ❋ ❋

Andy continued seeing Lila, and his crush on her deepened into infatuation. Her femininity engulfed him. They dated on weekends and saw one another for lunch or a movie during the week.

Desi Mayes answered the door to Lila's apartment when Andy arrived to pick her up on a Friday night. Andy was surprised and leery.

"Lila will be right out," Desi said, letting Andy in. "Care for a drink?"

"Sure," Andy said.

"Lila and I are more like a brother and sister than cousins," he said, handing Andy a beer. "I lived with her family for a while when we were kids."

"I didn't know that."

"So, you work for Ben Kinecky? I figured you must when I saw you in the restaurant with him."

"He's my brother-in-law."

"No shit?"

"You know him?"

"We played football against each other. A friendly rivalry." He smirked.

Uninterested in football, Andy didn't press for details.

"So how long you been back from the Nam?"

"About a year," Andy said. "You?"

"I did two tours," Desi said. "My second ended a few months ago. I thought about staying in the Army but decided to get out. No reason to be in the Army if there ain't a war going on. This one won't last forever."

"I guess not," said Andy.

Lila came out of her bedroom dressed in a white blouse, tastefully low-cut, and wearing a bead necklace. The contrast with her brown arms and black hair stunning, red lipstick completed her appeal.

"Desi says you met in Vietnam," she said.

"Sort of," Andy said.

"He surprised the hell out of me, thanking me for a ride on my Huey in Cherokee."

Andy smiled, Desi's tough exterior softened in Lila's presence. "My nickname for him was Tahlequah," Andy said. "He told me about his medicine bag, and how they used to clobber Afton in football."

Lila laughed and sat next to Andy on the couch, placing her hand on his thigh, the scent of her perfume filling the air. "I like it," she said, smiling at her cousin.

"Then Tahlequah it is," Andy said. "I like it, too."

The next evening Lila had Andy take her home early. She kissed him passionately before he dropped her off.

"Come by about ten tomorrow morning," she said. "My roommate will be at church."

When he arrived, Lila opened the door wearing a pair of denim shorts cut high above the knees and a yellow tank top without a brassiere. Her apartment, above a bakery, got warm when the family-owned business used the ovens. The aroma of yeast and fresh bread permeated the room.

"It's hot in here," she said, fetching two beers from the refrigerator. She handed one of them to Andy and sat close to him on the couch. Andy finished half the bottle while his mind raced. He put his hand on her bare thigh. She brushed her lips against his cheek before kissing him. Her mouth tasted of beer and whiskey.

"I want you to make love to me," she whispered in his ear. Standing before him, she took his hands and placed them on her hips. Bending down to kiss him again, she pressed her breasts into his face while she slipped her top off.

"Come with me." She led him by the hand into her room, pushing him gently onto the bed. She slipped out of her shorts and stood before him naked, allowing him to look at her. Lila joined him and while kissing she began unbuttoning his shirt. Taking her time, she examined Andy's chest. Only remnants of scars remained from his days in Vietnam.

"What's this, darling?" she asked, tracing a finger along some forgotten gouge taken out of Andy's flesh by a thorn or jagged branch in the jungle.

Self-conscious, Andy didn't know how to reply so just shook his head indicating he didn't remember. Lila continued removing his clothes until Andy lay naked with her.

They pressed against one another and Lila freed a breast and offered Andy a reddish-brown nipple with one hand while she reached for Andy's penis with the other. She tried guiding him into her.

Andy's failed erection betrayed his desire for Lila. She tried stroking. Humiliated, Andy felt Lila pulling away. She stood again, her brown body glistening with perspiration as the sun shone through a window in the warm room. Despite the heat, goose bumps formed beneath the little brown hairs on her arms. Tears welled as she glared at him, feeling humiliated that Andy did not find her attractive.

Lila fetched a robe from the closet and hurried into the bathroom. Andy dressed and left Lila's feeling hollow and ashamed.

CHAPTER
TWENTY-SIX

ANDY RETURNED FROM Lila's expecting the house to be empty, figuring his parents would be at church. Instead, he found his father munching peanuts and watching a football game on the television in the living room.

How do they do it, thought Andy, *remain so content?*

Miserable, Andy retreated into his room. Lila had rejuvenated him, but now he felt like a moth attracted to a hot bulb only to be burned. Without her, he faced a gloomy future.

In the bottom drawer of his boyhood dresser, he fetched the bottle of Wild Turkey. Sitting on his bed, back against the wall, he sipped while pondering his future.

What future?

Andy swigged on the whiskey until he felt the familiar buzz, the welcomed buffer between his unsettled core and thoughts, which made sitting alone in his room tolerable. Into that zone, it dulled the emotional pain and delayed the urgency of figuring out what to do with himself.

He sat on his bed until he'd drunk enough whiskey to doze. A knock on the bedroom door intruded.

"Andy," his mother said on the other side. "Someone's here to see you. Are you awake, dear?"

"Yes, Mom, I'll be right out." Thinking it might be someone from the church visiting, more a friend of his mother's, Andy took his time. In the bathroom he combed his hair and gargled some of the whiskey out of his breath.

In the living room, an unlikely visitor sat chatting amiably with Henry Clay, figuring out which ancestors they had in common. Tahlequah had removed his sunglasses for the occasion. Quite at home, he looked up when Andy appeared.

"I guess we're related, cousin," he said, smiling. Henry Clay beamed.

"The two families intersect right after Nanye-hi," his father said.

Andy knew as much from Lila, and the fact that if you shared Cherokee blood with someone in northeastern Oklahoma you were probably related. He thought of Lila and his failure as a lover.

"Would you like to stay for dinner, Desmond?" Rebecca asked, standing in the doorway to the living room.

"No thanks, Mrs. Parks," he said, full of charm. "I actually came by to see if Andy wanted to go out for a while. We were in Vietnam together, you know."

"Yes," said Henry Clay, "it's quite the coincidence."

Not really, thought Andy. *Lots of guys from Oklahoma were in the Nam . . . Tahlequah is really turning on the charm.*

Tahlequah's car, a red Pontiac Firebird, sat parked on the opposite side of the street. Still not sure why he'd come, Andy got in the passenger side and waited for him to speak first.

"Lila's worried about what happened," Tahlequah began.

Not sure what he knew, Andy wasn't going to blurt out his dysfunction.

"You know, it was nice that you and Lila were going out. She really likes you. I don't think much of the creeps in this town that might be taking her out if you weren't. I mean, us Vietnam vets gotta stick together. You're even part Cherokee, and related." He flashed Andy a grin.

All facts, but the part about Lila was what interested Andy.

"She doesn't understand why you left so suddenly. Are you breaking up with her?" Tahlequah sped towards Vinita. "Want to go get something to eat, maybe grab a beer?"

Andy nodded. Of all he'd thought about since his failure, breaking it off with Lila had not occurred to him.

"I thought she was upset with me," Andy said.

"Naw, not really," he said, increasing the speed of the Firebird. "She just got her feelings hurt thinking you thought she was ugly."

So, he does know.

"It happened with my Peggy once," he said. "Just once, but I can tell you from experience it won't happen again."

Peggy, Tahlequah's Choctaw girlfriend, had won an Indian beauty contest. *An unusual name for a Choctaw girl,* thought Andy, *but not as bad as Andrew for a Cherokee.*

"Cheer up," he told Andy. "Watch this thing go." He pressed the accelerator. "Peggy and I want to take you guys out next Friday, our treat."

The Friday night date with Peggy and Tahlequah went well for Andy. Reuniting with Lila, they had fun eating pizza and drinking enough beer to feel uninhibited. Taking Tahlequah's words to heart, his failure with Lila not permanent, Andy became her lover that night.

The evening had not gone as well for Tahlequah. Peggy drank too much beer and openly flirted with one of the guys at a nearby table. Tahlequah glared at him, a fight averted only because the man's buddies intervened and ushered him out of the restaurant.

He told Andy later, "I should have known better than to date a Choctaw. Some of their women will break your balls every time."

Peggy and Tahlequah broke it off for good that night, but Andy gained a friend in Lila's cousin.

❀ ❀ ❀

Tahlequah's passion was fishing on Grand Lake where he had a small cabin and kept a boat. He had mentioned it and asked Andy if he'd like to join him the following day.

"There's some record-sized paddlefish out there. Let's see if we can find some," Tahlequah said. Not long afterward, they hooked into a giant.

The two men stood in the boat struggling to hold the full weight of the sixty-pound paddlefish. The small dingy rocked in the shallow water where the giant species of catfish liked to bottom feed. While Tahlequah wrestled the fish on board, Andy tried steadying the boat by spreading his legs wide in the stern.

"Take a picture." Tahlequah smiled, struggling to hold the fish upright. "Hurry, this ugly sucker's too slimy to hold for long."

Tahlequah let go of the fish and it slid onto the bottom of the boat.

"Forget it," he said, "we'll take a picture on shore."

Tahlequah's cabin came into view 200 yards beyond the point where they snagged the spoonbill. At the shore, Andy hopped out of the boat and dragged the bow so it rested on the sand.

When in the area, Tahlequah resided in the cabin, which was shaded by the overhang of a cottonwood tree. A stand of scrub willows grew in a clump nearby. A firepit halfway between the cabin and lakeshore roasted some of the day's catch on an iron grill placed above the open fire. Chunks of a striped bass and several of the smaller crappies filled a large skillet.

"Check this out, Andy," he said, flipping the fish to fry on their other side. "I got a new recipe from my aunt for the fish batter." Andy took a chunk of the bass out of the pan and tasted it.

Tahlequah treated Andy like a member of the family, trusting him with looking after his boat and cabin while away on "business trips," a world he kept separate from Andy and Lila. Andy had heard some of the rumors about Tahlequah's "business," but as their friendship grew, he saw no evidence of anything illegal.

Tahlequah drank only beer with Andy, who'd never seen him smoke anything except tobacco. Occasionally, when sitting by the fire, they would discuss Vietnam.

"In my first contact with Charlie I never fired my rifle," he told Andy one night. "The squad thought it was funny to put a new guy out on an LP. Of course, they had two experienced guys with me, not happy about having me along. Thought I might get them wasted by doin' something stupid. One of 'em said, 'Now listen here, Chief'—he actually called me that—'we ain't out here to have some fucking new guy get us killed. You cause us any trouble and I'll fuckin' shoot ya myself. Comprende?' The fucking moron didn't know the difference between an Indian and a Mexican. That got sorted out *real* quick.

"So, the three of us was out there beyond the platoon's perimeter all cozy-like and not even breathin' so's we can hear each other. Pretty soon I do hear something, a kind of slitherin' sound movin' through the mud. You know the fuckin' Delta always so wet from the rains and the swamps. But this was no sound from an animal. I knew that much. By this time, I'm wonderin' why my partners out on the LP aren't hearin' it too, so I lean in to the one next to me and I can hear him just starting to make a snoring sound. The motherfucker's asleep. I figure his dumb grunt friend is too because I can see his head nodding and looking at the ground. Now, I don't want to startle them cause they're probably gonna give our position away if I try and wake them. I'm just hoping the one guy doesn't start snorin' louder."

Andy looked at Tahlequah's face, the light from the fire illuminating his cheeks and the whites of his eyeballs, reflecting the outlines of his long hair and stubbly beard. He rocked back and forth while telling the story.

"By now I don't want to shoot the Charlie. That'd have all his buddies onto us real quick. So I get my knife ready. The whole platoon had this thing for carrying these Bowie knives and spending time sharpening them. One of the guys showed me how to get it sharp as a razor. It worked out good that first night of contact.

"By now I can see the Charlie's outline, still slitherin' through the mud. I don't know how he's not noticin' us, but he's maybe angled wrong, movin' kinda diagonal to our LP and breathin' heavy, and wheezing, like he's got something wrong with his lungs. I'm afraid to let him get any closer. Soon as he sees us, he's gonna shoot. So here I am the FNG, and these dorks have nodded off in our foxhole."

Tahlequah paused for a moment, staring at the fire, which crackled, sending red sparks popping.

"I pounced on the motherfucker and drove my knife right through the back of his neck. He stopped wheezing.

"I had my hand cupped over his mouth real tight, and I pulled him into our foxhole. Of course, my dumb fuck partners are awake now. Even in the dark I can see their eyes big as saucers watching the Indian haulin' a dead gook into our hole. Nobody says a word because we're all afraid we've already made too much noise. The really dumb one gets busy double clicking on the radio, our signal for spotting Charlies. Pretty soon a firefight starts on the platoon's perimeter, and we have to stay low because rounds are comin' our way, too. It don't last long. All's quiet again and we spend the rest of the night not sayin' a word with a dead gook in our foxhole.

"Later, the really dumb one says, 'Thanks, Chief, you really helped us out there.' I just got up close in his face and glared at him. 'You ever do that to me again and I'll kill you,' I said. 'Same goes for callin' me Chief.' That platoon wasn't like yours, Andy. Not as tight, you know, and the LT not runnin' it good."

With just the two of them, Andy sometimes talked about the war. He thought about taking a trip to Missouri and looking up White Henry, but a routine developed, and Lila beckoned.

✻ ✻ ✻

Totally in love with his brown girl, Andy sought no wider connection with the world than what she brought to his life. Everything else remained an emotional desert devoid of interest or feeling. Andy came alive again through Lila. Her love outshone anything he'd ever experienced. Peeling away the dead zones without feeling, Lila affirmed them and filled them with joy, the smitten boy, fleetingly, tentatively, becoming whole through her.

Lila enjoyed sunning herself on the sand when the lovers were alone at Tahlequah's cabin on Grand Lake. Her darker skin browning further in the summer heat, she lay on her back and closed her eyes while Andy stole glances at her.

"I don't need to be any browner," she said, laughing. "I just like the feel of the sun on my skin. Can you rub some cream on me, sweetheart?"

Andy adored every inch of her. Massaging the lotion into her skin, he took his time and included her toes. The nails, painted different colors, were just as feminine as the rest of her.

Not shy with her body, Lila turned over so he could do her back. She wore only a bikini bottom, plunging in the lake when she wished to cool off. Andy couldn't get enough of her.

Tahlequah's camp provided privacy for the lovers. Lila's cousin liked having them watch over the place during his frequent absences. Disappearing for days at a time, he never told Andy or Lila the nature of his business. "Looking after my properties," is all he would say.

Andy learned the lake using Tahlequah's boat, finding remote coves for romantic rendezvous, impressing Lila. Thirteen hundred miles of shoreline surrounded the massive body of water. Concentric circles encapsulated their world in ever smaller orbits until only the one they inhabited remained.

Tahlequah's absences became longer and his explanations obscure. Andy, immersed in his love for his girl, barely noticed the changes in his friend. Lila, cleaning the cabin before returning to Vinita, found two pistols hidden beneath the mattress, and a loaded rifle underneath the bed.

"Did you know these were here?" she asked. "It is Oklahoma, but kind of creepy loving one another with loaded guns right underneath us."

Andy didn't know about them. He cleared the chambers of all three weapons and put them back where they'd found them. A further search revealed hundreds of rounds of ammunition in the cupboards behind the food stores and dishes.

"Is Desi okay?" she asked. "It just seems kind of strange to have so much ammunition for three guns."

What worried Andy was the number of clips they'd found, many of them loaded. He didn't mention it to Lila.

"I'll talk to him," Andy said. "We haven't seen him for a week. He should be back soon."

❉ ❉ ❉

Evasive, Tahlequah tried to make a joke of his weapons cache.

"Phew, glad you told me about my guns not being loaded. That could leave a guy in a lot of trouble, you know . . . Lila find them? Sorry, Andy, I didn't mean to scare her. I like having you guys look after my place while I'm gone. I'll make sure they're put away better."

That was all he said until later, their familiar campfire burning late into the night. Reflective, Andy discerned a difference, an agitation in his friend, his words hovering around something he couldn't articulate.

"You know, I miss it, Andy, the fact every step was important in the Nam. It clears the mind of clutter. What's left is all that matters. Don't you ever want to go back and do it better?"

Andy related to part of that, a chance to redeem himself with Camel, assuring his dying friend instead of remaining tongue-tied. Maybe he could have even saved his life, and a lot of others. The men he knew were all home now—or dead.

"I don't see much purpose in going back," Andy said. "Too late for that now, anyway. The news says the war's winding down."

"No, no, Andy, that's not what I mean. Fuck the war. I never felt as alive as I felt over there, risking it all in a firefight, matching wits with Charlie. He can have his Mekong Delta. I just want that feeling again of having everything so on the line my every step is important. It's just that I feel dead sometimes, you know."

CHAPTER
TWENTY-SEVEN

HORACE THORNBILL WALKED to the pulpit and the congregation rose. Thick, with hair greying at the temples, the pastor looked more like a truck driver in an uncomfortable and ill-fitting suit, his occupation during the week in between sermons. He smiled at the faithful before giving thanks to the god they gathered to celebrate each Sunday.

Andy tuned out the moment the pastor uttered, "Let us pray." Living with his parents because his light hauling service lacked the income to rent a place of his own, he still accompanied his mother to church occasionally.

The preaching begun, Andy retreated into daydream, hypnotized by the droning voice of the minister's reverence towards a god Andy wasn't sure existed. Out of the corner of his eye, he could see a nodding congregation affirming the words of Horace Thornbill. Andy's own nods were ones of dozing after a late night in Lila's arms.

The word *atheists* registered in Andy's consciousness, then *foxhole.* The pastor rambled on about the fact that there were none in the trenches of war because of a soldier's reliance on God in situations of grave danger.

Andy, attentive now, remembered cursing himself for not digging in deeper during a mortar barrage that killed the new guy, Calhoun. Pressed against the earthen wall while hearing the *whump, whump, whump,* and waiting for each blast to land, he swore some more for making the hole so wide. *What protection is this, leaving so much room for a shell to land beside me?* Worried about Sammy, exposed by pulling guard, it was Calhoun that died from a direct hit.

Rather than finding God in the foxhole, in despair, Andy searched for pieces of the grunt's body amidst the gore. Not sure at first who'd been killed, he looked at the faces of platoon members at dawn. Finding Calhoun's dog tags in the slime, Andy knew for sure. Mechanically, he sifted through the splattered blood and tissue, confused about how much of it should be placed in the body bag. Did it matter? Angered by the death, he became determined to gather what he could of Calhoun.

As Horace continued, Andy noticed the eyes of the congregation furtively looking his way. Not acknowledging the pastor or any glances, Andy stared at the back of the wooden pew in front of him, immersed in his memory of foxholes.

Waiting for the last word of the sermon, he bolted to the car, knowing the after-church chit-chat would depress him. He sat and waited for his mother and Henry Clay, trying to compose himself so they wouldn't notice the degree of his withdrawal.

"Are you feeling under the weather, dear?" Rebecca asked while Henry Clay drove home in silence. *Maybe Dad has an inkling?* Andy just wanted to be alone and regain the outer equilibrium needed to face the world. How silly a simple-minded sermon about atheists and foxholes had the power to reduce him to a quivering mess on the inside.

The episode ended his church attendance. Two months later, another incident deepened the chasm between the *before* and *after* since resuming life in Oklahoma.

❋ ❋ ❋

Andy and Tahlequah turned into the drive of his aunt and uncle's pecan farm. Five striped bass, gutted and cleaned, filled a tub in the back of Andy's pickup. The largest, a twenty-pounder, intended for his aunt Ruby.

"An impressive fish," Tahlequah said. "Sure you don't want that one yourself?"

"Naw, my mom's already got plenty in the freezer, and Dad's not too keen on the taste. Besides, I'm still trying to find information about my uncle. I've got more questions for my aunt Ruby."

"You still trying to track him down?"

"Trying."

He wanted to ask his aunt about the Marine who came looking for him and left the photograph of them in a jungle in the South Pacific.

Grabbing the bass lying on top of the ice, Andy lifted it by the tail and put it in a burlap sack. Not the prettiest of fish, he liked the striped markings on the thick body running down the side away from the large eyes and gaping mouth.

Knocking on the door, his uncle Roland answered gruffly. "Yeah?"

"It's Andy. We brought you and Aunt Ruby a fish."

"I don't want your fish," he said.

"Who's that at the door, Roland?" he heard his aunt say. Appearing behind her husband, she pushed by him and saw Andy. "Well, come in, nephew. Who's this you have with you?"

Andy introduced Tahlequah.

Ushering the guests into the kitchen, Aunt Ruby offered them cups of coffee from the pot she always kept on the stove.

"Roland," she hollered, "Are you having coffee?"

"No," the same gruff voice shouted from another room.

Tahlequah glanced at Andy with a puzzled look. Noticeably embarrassed, his aunt said, "Honestly, I don't know what gets into that man."

Not understanding why their presence was irritating his uncle, he awkwardly said, "We brought you a twenty-pound bass."

"And you can take it with you when you leave." Roland stood behind them in the doorway to the kitchen. "I already told you I don't want your fish."

"What on earth has gotten into you?" Aunt Ruby asked, confronting her husband.

"Your nephew's tellin' Georgie and all the other relatives to avoid going to Vietnam. No wonder the country's going to hell. With that kind of attitude, it's no surprise they can't whip a bunch of skinny-assed Viet Cong wearing sandals."

So that's it, Andy thought, *World War II again.*

Roland's Army had taken on the Germans and the Japanese, defeated them both, but a bunch of underfed guerillas held the same Army to a standstill in Vietnam.

"It's humiliating. That's all I got to say." Roland turned and walked away.

Ruby sighed. Andy, uncomfortable staying, rose before leaving.

"Thanks for the coffee," he said, not knowing how to exit gracefully. His aunt, obviously embarrassed by her husband's rudeness, walked with them to the door. Not the kind of woman to let Roland dictate which of her relatives could visit, Andy figured she'd have a few words to say to him after they left.

"What the fuck's his problem?" Tahlequah asked on the way back to the truck.

Andy shrugged, embarrassed that he'd brought his friend along to witness his uncle's behavior. He thought Roland had always liked him.

※ ※ ※

The first full summer of his love with Lila waned in northeastern Oklahoma. Only sporadic news of the war reached Andy, mostly during the news breaks on the country radio station his brother-in-law kept tuned in the office. Ben Kinecky still gave an occasional opinion but had given up trying to engage Andy in discussions about Vietnam. The war seemed less personal now that all of the guys Andy knew would be home. The entire Ninth Infantry Division was part of US troop withdrawals.

As Andy's love deepened for Lila, the months passed quickly as the lovers created their own special world. Mesmerized by his girl, Andy thought no further than fulfilling his need to be with her, more content than he'd been since the war. Lila became his focus. Her presence seeped into his being.

As the New Year came and the winter greys turned into the greens of spring, Andy experienced a renewal stirring within where only dead zones had existed. He thought about a future with Lila and expanded his light hauling service into agricultural commodities. He planned for a larger truck and consulted with Ben Kinecky on how to grow his business. He dared to include hope as part of his emotional landscape.

The war came less in his dreams, and the drinking gradually subsided. With Lila in his life, Andy began to feel whole and connected again.

He still exchanged occasional letters with Sammy. No news of Black Henry surfaced. Not far away in Missouri, White Henry had returned to farm with his father. While Andy got on with his life in Oklahoma, Sammy did the same in California.

❋ ❋ ❋

On October 26 of 1972, three years to the day after Andy returned from Vietnam, Henry Kissinger declared "peace was at hand." Andy had no idea what that meant for the country, only that his brother, George, and others like him, would not have to go to the same war. Otherwise, nothing changed for Andy. He felt no elation about the war ending. *What has been gained?* Remnants of his experiences remained. Lila's presence had tamed the worst of the demons pushed into the recesses of his mind.

All of that changed in November.

❀ ❀ ❀

Lila's roommate away for a weekend meant the lovers had her apartment to themselves. Enjoying the privacy with his girl, Andy looked forward to just staying in for her days off. Lila snuggled beside him on the couch. Dressed in a white blouse and matching pair of shorts, he put his arm around her and smelled her rose-scented perfume. He loved her affection.

When the phone rang, she bounced off the couch to answer it, her long black hair floating behind her as she hurried across the room. "Maybe I shouldn't answer it," she joked, giving Andy a coquettish sway of her hips before turning to pick up the receiver. "I don't want anything to interrupt our plans, darling."

Andy still couldn't get enough of her. Whatever she wore, or cooked, or said, enthralled him. He watched as she turned and picked up the receiver with the same delicate hands that caressed him, the red-painted fingernails visible across the room.

"Hello," she answered. Andy watched as her shoulders sagged, not hearing what Lila mumbled into the telephone. Sensing bad news, Andy got off the couch and came up behind her.

Turning to him with a blank expression she spoke.

"Desi's been killed. The state troopers shot him this afternoon. We have to go." She burst into tears.

Hurrying past Andy, she went into her room. Andy followed. Hearing her sobbing, he tapped on the door.

"Lila, what happened? Can I come in?"

"I'll be out in a minute," she called out between sobs.

"We need to go over to my uncle's," she said. Lila barely looked at Andy as she hurried past him. The tongue-tied medic returning with the emotional shutdown, Andy followed her out of the apartment.

"What happened, Lila?" he asked on the drive.

"We don't know yet," she snapped, fully angry now, her reaction to Tahlequah's death. Andy drove the rest of the way in silence.

At the uncle's, the family crowded around a table in the kitchen. More anger. Some of the men downed shots of whiskey, the women quietly weeping.

"The fuckin' state troopers shot him from behind," one of the men said. "He was just out drivin' his car."

"Some dirty cocksucker must have turned him in," someone else said.

"Who's this you got with you, Lila?" the uncle, Tahlequah's father, asked. Andy had not been introduced. Raymond Mayes, slumped over his glass of whiskey, holding it with both hands, looked like he wanted to erupt.

"One of Desi's friends," she said. "They were in Vietnam together."

An angry murmur went through the men. Andy felt very white, an intruder even though Tahlequah was his friend. Lila made no attempt to ease the situation. Andy felt out of place and that he should go.

Speaking to Lila, quietly, gently, in her ear, "Call me when you're ready to go and I'll come and get you." His girl, looking straight ahead, barely acknowledged him.

Returning home, his mother heard him come in. Sensing Andy's distress, she hovered around him. Andy knew the look well. He'd given her a lot to be concerned about these last three years. He just didn't know how to fix it—the intense isolation, the separation from his family.

"You seem troubled, dear," she said. "Did something happen?"

"A friend of mine just died," he leveled with her.

"There was a police chase on the news over by Tahlequah," she said. "Did it have anything to do with that?"

"I expect it did."

"The police haven't released any names yet," she said.

"It was Desmond Mayes."

Rebecca gasped. "Your friend? That nice young man you were in Vietnam with?"

He nodded.

"The news says there were drugs involved."

"I suspect there were."

Rebecca sighed. "I'm so sorry, dear. I will pray for the family."

Andy nodded again, resigned to his mother's turning to prayer in every crisis. "I think I'll turn in, Mom."

In his room, he resisted the urge to drink freely from the bottle of Wild Turkey. He wanted to blot the world out, but he worried about Lila. He could feel her slipping away.

At eleven o'clock, he called her uncle's. The line busy, he kept trying every few minutes. By midnight he still couldn't get through.

Venturing through the dark, immersed in the black cavern of his mind, Andy drove like a blind man retracing a route. On the porch, Raymond Mayes sat surrounded by family. Where Andy's mother turned to prayer, Tahlequah's father chose drink. Not alone in his drunkenness, several men squinted as Andy approached.

"It's that white kid again," one of them said, "sniffing around for Lila." The alcohol fueled the crude reference and anger.

"She doesn't want to see you," someone said. "You best be on your way."

"Can I at least speak with her?" Andy asked. "Desmond was my friend."

"I never knew you," the elder Mayes shouted.

Two of the men on the porch approached Andy, now standing on the lawn. He had no choice but to leave.

The house quiet when he returned, he sat in the dark in his room, choosing drink to obliterate pain.

Three years out of his war and the loneliness returned.

Most of the story of Desi's death came out in the following days. Ben Kinecky knew two of the state troopers involved.

The chase had been wild. Tahlequah made a run for it, heading for the lake. One of the trooper's chase vehicles overturned in the pursuit. The official report said shots were fired at the police. Drugs were found in the car along with two pistols, a rifle and ammunition. The chase, described as high speed, ended when Tahlequah's vehicle skidded off the road.

Andy wondered how Tahlequah, by himself, could fire a gun behind him while driving at high speeds.

Two properties were found on Grand Lake linking Tahlequah to their ownership. Andy only knew the camp where the friends liked to fish and cook their catch right out of the lake.

A day after the funeral, Andy drove by the cabin. Oklahoma State Troopers had the area roped off, posting it as a crime scene under investigation. With no trespassing allowed, he drove to some of Tahlequah's favorite sites where they'd caught the spoonbill catfish he loved. The record size eluded Tahlequah, but he'd come close.

Andy walked on the shore, the sky grey in November, a chilly breeze blowing in off the lake. Thinking how different his friend's life would have been without the war, Andy pictured the star football player laying out opposing players with hard tackles on the field. He also dwelled on Lila and the love lost with Desi's life.

Lila barely spoke to Andy at the funeral, surrounded by her family, angry about the death of Desmond Mayes. "I need to be around my own people for a while," she said, not explaining more.

Andy left it at that, the best part of his life since returning from the war over. He returned to his isolation, another body added to the dead weight he carried.

CHAPTER
TWENTY-EIGHT

LILA NEVER CAME back to Andy. Deep into November the skies remained as grey and bleak as his mood. Withdrawing further into himself, his behavior resembled his last days on the quad ward when internal pressures overflowed into overt expressions of despair. The drinking returned while awake, and the dreams when he slept.

The jungle burned every night.

Six children from the napalm, laid out in a row, peered at Andy. He'd forgotten his aid bag. Nothing in it that would save the kids, but he needed the morphine to ease their pain. He searched while each in turn pleaded in agony.

"Now you have really done it," the girl from the mortar team rebuked him. "Now that you have burned them with your napalm, can you not at least ease their pain?" Andy didn't know how to explain to her that he didn't drop the napalm on the children. He just wanted to help.

"Then do something."

She scowled and disappeared, shaking her head in disgust.

Five of the kids were already dead, and a little girl was having trouble breathing. He asked if they expected him to bring them back to life.

The disturbing dream woke Andy. Sitting up in bed, he breathed deeply, trying to ease the turmoil from the nightmare. He rested his back against the wall. Reaching for the never-empty bottle of Wild Turkey, he remembered the day the children burned.

He had confronted Howitz, his only run-in with the LT. He knew the lieutenant was hurting, too, but Andy, full of despair, could not hold his frustration.

The platoon returned to Dong Tam soon after, all of them dirty and exhausted, in need of rest. Andy, cramping from dehydration and a lack of salt, wanted only to find his cot and rest. His body a mess of jungle rot and infected leech bites, he headed for his hooch. On the way, he overheard an exchange between Howitz and the company commander, waiting for the platoon.

"So, what was the final body count, Lieutenant?"

"Sir?"

"How many dead?"

"Six unarmed kids, Captain. Count them if you like. One little girl was still breathing so we medevaced her out." Howitz, as weary and filthy, was in no mood to rehash the incident.

"I'll put down six kills, Lieutenant."

"They're dead all right, Captain, but they weren't armed, and they were kids."

"Don't get soft on me, Lieutenant. They grow up to be VC anyway."

"Not now they won't."

"Are you unhappy with the way things are done in my company, Lieutenant?"

"No, sir," Howitz responded. "Are you unhappy with my command and combat record?"

"At ease, Lieutenant. No need to get teary over a bunch of gook kids. Understood?"

"Perfectly clear, sir."

"Then that will be all."

"Yes, sir." Howitz saluted and continued walking to his quarters.

The body count was the big thing in Vietnam. Andy just wasn't expecting it to continue once he got home. Calvin Lake, the Professor, Yardly, Paul Voight, and now Tahlequah were gone. They began showing up in his dreams.

The Professor sat next to him on a dike bordering a rice paddy.

"You know, it's pretty here, Doc, but I want to go home. The platoon shouldn't have left me in this field. It's lonely."

"Where's Yardly?"

"His people came and took him home. Why can't you take me with you?"

"You have six months to do on your tour."

"How come you got to go home but I can't? Why won't anyone come and get me? I don't want to end up a skeleton like Camel. The platoon left him here, too."

✳ ✳ ✳

The dreams came with more frequency, some convoluted and surreal, others so vivid and real it was as if Andy was retracing his steps in Vietnam. He became increasingly chastened, isolating himself with whiskey and the solitude of his truck and room.

Driving along the lake, everything reminded him of Lila and Tahlequah. He never realized how much they had in common.

The family, noticing his deterioration, tried intervening.

"Andy, you need to talk to us, honey. You can't go around with everything bottled up inside. You're likely to explode. We need to know what happened to you over there. We're worried about you," his mother pleaded.

Mothers don't like hearing about burning kids in the jungle.

✳ ✳ ✳

The Professor was near a mound of dirt, which must be from digging a foxhole. "When you die in the Nam you never get out," he told Andy. "*I don't want to end up like Camel.*"

"*Professor, you and Camel are dead. I'm sorry you didn't make it out of the Nam, but only your body came home.*"

"Get me outta here." The Professor beckoned, reaching towards Andy . . .

He heard his mother's voice. Why was she in Vietnam?

"Andy, what are you doing out here?" His mother was shaking him.

Andy came to. Embarrassed, he noticed the heap of soil in the backyard his father had brought in to fill a low spot. Henry Clay was there, too.

"Come inside, son, we need to talk."

Noticing his clothes were filthy from the dirt, he brushed at them. Still embarrassed, he stood and asked, feebly, "What time is it? I must have been dreaming."

"Outside?" his mother questioned. "It's three in the morning."

Suddenly chilled, Andy began to shiver.

"Let's go inside," his mother said. "I'll put some coffee on."

Henry Clay began. "Son, who were you talking to in the backyard?"

Andy, still shivering, had no intention of telling them the details of his dream. When he didn't answer, Rebecca took a different approach.

"Dear, why can't you just tell us what you're feeling? It's not normal to be wandering around in the backyard in the middle of the night talking to yourself."

Andy sat stoically.

"We need to get you some help," Rebecca continued. "The Veteran's Administration in Tulsa told us they would see you if we book an appointment. I think you need to go."

So they've been plotting this, Andy thought. Still silent, he sipped his coffee.

Rebecca began to cry. "You need to promise me, no matter what happens, son, you just won't up and disappear on us."

"We're worried about you, Andy," Henry Clay added. "You're here but you just seem so aimless and unsettled."

Andy nodded. He owed his parents that. What a mess he'd created by not being able to return to Oklahoma and get on with his life.

"I'll go see them at the VA," he said, not knowing what good it would do.

✸ ✸ ✸

The drive to Tulsa took two hours. Mostly silent in the car, he regretted agreeing to come.

"Try not to be upset," his mother said. "Just be honest with the doctor."

About what? he thought.

At the reception desk in the clinic a young woman looked up and said, "Yes?"

"I have an appointment," he said, "for Andrew Parks."

She pulled a file from the stack on her desk and opened it. "So, what's the problem?"

Caught off guard by the question, Andy stood for a moment without answering. "Problem?" he repeated.

"Yes. Why have you driven all the way to Tulsa to see a doctor? I need to put something on your chart before he sees you."

"It's kind of private," he said.

"Look," she insisted, "I need to put something on your chart, so why don't you just tell me why you're here."

"I'm having . . . bad dreams," he stuttered. "My family thinks I need to get checked out."

"Bad dreams," she repeated as she wrote on the chart, saying it loud enough for Andy to worry the whole waiting room heard it. "Have a seat and the doctor will be with you in a few minutes."

A middle-aged nurse came into the waiting room and called his name. Dressed in the traditional white uniform of her profession, she ushered him into an examining room. Business-like, she took his blood pressure and wrote it on a chart. "He'll be with you in a few minutes," she said, and left. Andy felt trapped.

The doctor entered and said hello. In his fifties, somewhat overweight and smelling of tobacco, he sat on a stool near Andy and looked at his chart.

"You look okay," he said in a friendly manner. "A little thin, but what's the problem?"

"My parents want you to check me out," Andy said. "They think I'm having bad dreams." Feeling self-conscious, he added, "They found me in the backyard talking in my sleep."

"So, when did these bad dreams start? Everybody has them from time to time."

Andy nodded.

"You were in Vietnam?"

Andy nodded again.

"When did you get back?"

"Three years ago."

The doctor looked surprised. "You wounded over there?"

"No."

"You were one of the lucky ones," he said, putting the chart down and standing up. "What did you do in Vietnam?"

"I was a medic."

"A medic helping the wounded," he said. "That must have felt pretty good, helping your fellow soldiers out. It makes me feel good here at the VA." He made it sound like they were in the same business. "You working?" he continued.

"Self-employed."

"Young man, upstairs in this hospital are several amputees and burn patients that have it much worse than you. My advice is to go home and get on with your life. You are fortunate to be able to do so. I can give you a prescription for some sleeping pills if you like, but if a few bad dreams is all you're having trouble with, then I think you are adjusting well. Time will heal the worst of it."

Andy declined the medication and returned to the waiting room where his mother waited. On the way to the car, she said, "Andy, you seem upset. What did the doctor say?"

"He said to go back home and forget about the war." He hastened the pace to the car. They had driven to Tulsa for nothing.

"That's all? Did you tell him about being in the backyard in the middle of the night?"

"He said everybody has bad dreams from time to time."

Rebecca stopped and looked at Andy. "I'm not leaving Tulsa, honey, until we get some answers. I'm going back and speaking to the doctor myself. We didn't come all this way to be told it will be fine when it's not."

Andy's mild-mannered mother turned and headed towards the clinic. Inside, she walked to the reception desk and asked to see the doctor.

"That won't be possible," the woman on duty told her.

"A mother knows when something is wrong with one of her children," she persisted. "My son has not been the same since returning from Vietnam. He needs help from the VA, not some runaround."

"Have a seat, then, if you insist," the young woman said.

Embarrassed, Andy went and found a vending machine to buy cigarettes. Outside, he smoked several and could see his mother through the window sitting with her arms crossed.

When the doctor came out, Andy saw her walk across the room and confront him. He could see his mother gesturing with her hands and shaking her head at the doctor. The VA was the VA, established to help veterans but with a reputation for putting cost-saving measures ahead of its clientele.

Outside, Rebecca wiped at her eyes, attempting to compose herself.

"I'm sorry, Mom," he said. "I'll do better."

Too emotional to say much she said, "I know you will, honey. We'll get through this."

Walking to the car Andy told himself, *I have to keep my guard up better. Nobody can ever know how I'm really feeling.*

❄ ❄ ❄

Nearing Christmas, Andy's mood failed to improve. He remembered enjoying the holidays in the past, the festivities of gift-giving and visiting relatives. Now he dreaded the season, having to make conversation and pretending to be happy. It took a lot of effort hiding his gloom.

As he sat in the office of Kinecky and Sons Construction, the news was full of the B-52 raids on North Vietnam. The walls closed in on Andy every hour as each broadcast related the latest tolls of civilian deaths. Officially named "Linebacker II," the football reference was not lost on Andy. Dubbed the "Christmas Bombings" by the media, the closest he'd been to the destructive power of the 500-pound bombs was in the Seven Mountains. With up to 108 of the missives freefalling on Hanoi from each plane, more than the intended military targets were hit. Along with the electrical plants, fuel storage tanks and supply depots, 2,000 homes were destroyed, and 1,624 civilians killed.

In the Nam, they'd called the monstrous bombers BUFFs—big ugly fat fuckers. As Andy sat in silence, picturing the devastation, he decided to leave Oklahoma. He might be taking his troubled mind with him, but he could no longer stand the stilted parameters of his life. He would reiterate his promise to his mother to always stay in touch, but he needed to get away from the constant expectations of him to return to the boy he had been before Vietnam. That Andy no longer existed. A man now, he needed to chart his own course.

According to the newscasters, Nixon's bombing raids were not playing well in the rest of the world. By December 29 of 1972, international outrage contributed to a halt.

Winning had no meaning for Andy. He'd already lost Camel, the Professor and Yardly, Boy Red, Calvin Lake and Paul Voight. He wondered what Tahlequah would have said.

The body count continued. America was running up the score, with civilians now, but still losing the war.

Andy left Oklahoma for good.

PART THREE

HIDING OUT

CHAPTER
TWENTY-NINE

Crooked Creek, Alberta, Canada
1982

IT WAS OCTOBER and snowing, early even for northern Alberta. Andy tapped the snow off his boots outside, removing them in the entry porch.

"Sammy's on the phone," Lisa called, motioning for Andy to come into the house. Andy's wife had warmed to her husband's friend over the years. He often had her laughing when he called. Today, her expression was serious as she handed Andy the phone.

Sammy normally called around Christmas, so it was too early to be sending his seasonal greetings.

"Hi, Doc," Sammy began.

"What's up?" Andy asked. "Is everything okay?"

"I've located Black Henry . . . but it's not good news."

"So what's wrong?"

"He's in Atmore, Alabama, at the Holman Correctional Facility."

"In prison? So when's he get out?"

"Doc, he's on death row."

Hanging up the phone, Andy looked at Lisa.

"What is it?" she asked. "You look like someone's died."

"It's Black Henry," he said. "We've been looking for him since he made it out of Vietnam. He's scheduled to be executed next year."

Lisa gasped. "Oh my God, what happened?"

❋ ❋ ❋

In the ten years since leaving Oklahoma, Andy had not stayed in one place for more than a few months before settling in northern Alberta. He'd lived in Hawaii, duplicating his light hauling service on Oahu. Taking boats to Fiji, New Zealand and Australia, he worked enough to keep traveling. If he had a plan, it was to keep moving, escaping the narrow confines of what might be expected of him. By 1975, the year the last American left the US embassy in Vietnam, Andy boarded a ship in Sydney Harbor bound for Honolulu.

A young woman, traveling with friends, sat at a table near Andy's. Too shy to introduce himself, he'd admired her quiet demeanor. Noticing her in a deck chair, he stood at the ship's railing looking out at the ocean. He turned to see the girl looking at him.

"It's quite a lovely perspective, isn't it," she said, smiling, "being this far out on the ocean."

Andy nodded his agreement and moved closer to where she sat.

"I'm Lisa," she said, extending her hand.

❋ ❋ ❋

Wanting to sit down after hearing the news from Sammy, Andy looked out the window from the kitchen table. The snow, swirling in the wind and accumulating in drifts, continued to fall.

He'd tried to put the war behind him, establish something normal in his life. Events kept bringing it to the surface. The news about Black Henry shook him, penetrating the thin veneer between his life now and in the past.

"He was an important platoon member," Andy began, owing Lisa some explanation. He'd thought the body count might be finished this many years after the war. As a Canadian, Lisa hadn't watched any brothers or cousins doing a tour in the Nam, or any friends and acquaintances in her community not returning from it.

"Sammy got a call from White Henry," he said. Andy could see by her expression even the nicknames confused her. "They were close in the Nam. Black Henry was never the same after the Professor and Yardly got killed. It happened after I rotated home."

Lisa wanted him to talk to her about the war. He never could. Incapable of understanding his own feelings, how would he explain them to someone else? And like his mother, she wouldn't want to hear about burning young kids in the jungle with napalm. He would keep that secret.

"He killed somebody?" she asked.

"He says it was self-defense." Andy realized how feeble that sounded. *That's what all murderers say.* But he knew Black Henry. He'd protected the Professor, and Yardly. A paradox of war, but he'd shown strength and kindness amidst the brutality.

"They are about to begin executions again in Alabama. White Henry saw a newspaper article about a condemned black man named Henry Jones. He'd wanted to find him, but not like that. Sammy says White Henry visited him in prison. He doesn't want to die alone, wants both of them there for his execution."

"You're not thinking of going?" Lisa asked. "Please tell me you're not."

❋ ❋ ❋

After three years of wandering, Andy met Lisa. He admired the graceful way she carried herself. Shy and unassuming, everything about her complemented her understated beauty. Her auburn hair matched the tone of her skin perfectly, framing a face that peered at the world with blue eyes with just enough green to enhance a wholesome appearance. Andy found her farm-girl practicality appealing. It was the intuitive side of their love which drew them together.

"We are from different places," Lisa had told him, "but we understand each other deeply." They shared long hours of conversation without need of others. She soothed something in Andy, which he couldn't define. For the first time since leaving Oklahoma his restlessness eased.

After meeting, they had not wanted to part. Their romance, begun en route to Honolulu, continued when they landed. From two countries, they found ways to be together until Andy traveled no farther, finding a home with Lisa in Canada.

After marrying, they settled in the Peace River Region of Alberta, working in Grande Prairie, ten miles from the farm where Lisa grew up. Five months later, a chance encounter had a big impact on Andy's life.

Invited to a barbecue, Andy and Lisa turned into the driveway at her parents' farm. Several neighbors and family mingled near a large firepit in the middle of a stand of mature poplars near the house. Lisa's stepdad, Reed Fitch, presided over the gathering, directing friends to a table with snacks and an ice cooler with beer and soft drinks. Sociable and well mannered, he stood among the guests, visiting and making sure everybody was looked after. Events at the farm matched his easygoing nature.

Seated across from Andy at a picnic table during the meal, a slender man in a ball cap about his father-in-law's age introduced himself.

"I'm Leonard Davis," he said, offering his hand. "Reed says you came all the way from Oklahoma to marry his daughter."

Andy laughed. "We met on a ship sailing from Sydney to Honolulu."

"That must have been romantic," the woman sitting next to Leonard said. "I was stuck hauling bees on my honeymoon," she added, poking her husband in the ribs with her elbow. "And nothing much has changed in thirty years of marriage."

"My wife, Shirley," he said. "Just getting you used to what you were in for marrying me," he added, looking at her.

"Bees?" Andy asked.

"Why, yes, honeybees," she said. "My husband keeps them for a living, a lot of them."

"Interesting," Andy said. "So how long have you been a beekeeper?"

"Pretty much all of my life. My grandfather kept them on the farm. When sugar was rationed during the war, we expanded the numbers of colonies and started selling a lot more honey. They interested me more than the cows, pigs or chickens."

"So how many do you have now?" Andy asked.

"Two thousand hives," he answered.

Intrigued, Andy pestered him with questions until Leonard's wife intervened.

"Enough with the bee talk. I live with it all week. It would be nice not to hear it while I'm trying to have a visit. Why don't you invite young Andy to come and have a look for himself?"

❋ ❋ ❋

"Every bee has a function," Leonard explained as he took what looked like a miniature crowbar and pried the cover off a hive. A large cluster of bees formed on the surface of the wooden frames sitting in a neat row inside the opened box. The sun shining on them created a shimmering luminescence as the light shone through the transparency of their wings, which fluttered as if a gentle wind moved over them. The bees moved about the crowded cluster without any apparent urgency or hostility.

"The queen lays the eggs," Leonard said as he took the hive tool and skillfully removed a rectangular frame solid with bees. "I'll show you." He pointed to the hexagonal honeycomb in the center. "Look in the bottom of these cells. You'll see what looks like a miniature grain of rice. That's a newly laid egg. The young workers nurture them, and the older ones go out foraging for pollen and nectar. They'll go two miles if they have to in order to find a source of honey."

Andy stood mesmerized. Many of the hives, painted white, were placed nearby, contrasting beautifully with the greens of the grass and leaves in the poplar trees behind them.

"We call this a bee yard," Leonard continued. "We usually place forty colonies in each location. Bees have a highly sophisticated eye structure that orients with the movement of the sun, making it possible to find their way back to their exact hive. Let's see if we can spot the queen."

With so many bees, Andy wondered how that would be possible. "So, how many would be in this hive?" he asked.

"Around fifty thousand," Leonard said, as he pulled another frame out of the box, looking for the queen. "Do this all day and it'll make your eyes tired, but I think we can find this one."

With ease, Leonard continued pulling frames out of the box.

"This is the brood nest where the queen lays all of the eggs, up to two thousand a day. She'll be in here somewhere. It takes three weeks for an egg to reach maturity. There's one chewing its way out of a cell right now." A bee from underneath a light-brown capping ate the thin membrane covering it. As soon as the opening was large enough, the bee walked out and joined the rest of the workers.

"She'll spend two or three weeks inside the brood nest nurturing the eggs and larva, eventually capping the cells before she joins the foragers bringing back nectar . . . look, there's the queen," Leonard said, pointing to a bee with a thicker and elongated abdomen.

"I see her," Andy said. Her golden abdomen shone in the light of the sun. Dozens of workers moved about her as she walked across the frame.

"We don't want to spook her," Leonard said, putting the frame back in the hive.

"They're very calm," Andy said, fascinated with how the bees didn't mind their hive opened.

"This helps," Leonard said, blowing some smoke gently on the cluster from a canister he held in one hand that had a spout and small bellows attached to it.

"It's called a smoker," he said, "a rather primitive device, but it calms the bees, activating a nonaggressive urge to protect the brood nest by clustering tighter around it."

❄ ❄ ❄

Andy hung around Leonard's so much that first season he worried about being a nuisance. He spent most of his days off helping him. He learned how to bring the boxes of honey, called supers, in from the bee yards and extract them. He helped Leonard move the bees to different locations where they had blossoms to forage on. He watched with fascination as the frames filled with honey.

"How much do I owe you for all of the help?" Leonard asked at the end of the season.

"I just appreciate learning about them," Andy said.

"Well," the beekeeper pondered, "come see me in the spring and we'll talk about it some more." He sent Andy home with two thirty-pound pails of honey.

That winter Andy read books on beekeeping, occasionally phoning Leonard with questions. In April, Leonard called him.

"Come by my place tomorrow morning first thing in that pickup of yours. I wonder if you could haul something for me?"

"Sure," Andy said. "Is the season starting?"

"You might say that."

Five hives in newly painted boxes stood gleaming in a row outside Leonard's honey house. "Your wages," he told Andy. "Now that I've got you hooked, you'll be needing your own bees."

Andy went to work for Leonard that season, who taught him about bees in a way only someone who'd spent a lifetime working with them could. Leonard's 2,000 beehives required a crew of four to look after them. As a novice, Andy was just part of the crew, but Leonard took a special interest in him because of his fascination.

Andy had never been so enthusiastic about anything in his life.

Leonard showed him how to take his five hives and make them into twenty-five by the end of the first year. He worked in the woodshop over the winter building hive boxes and thousands of wooden frames to go in them for the bees to build their honeycomb in. The smell of the pine equipment mingling with the warmth from the woodstove was as intoxicating as the nectar in the summer.

Andy sat and watched the snow accumulate. While a gloom descended on him, he noticed the irony of the date—October 26, 1982—thirteen years to the day since he'd returned from Vietnam.

Normally inclement weather didn't bother Andy. He simply worked inside his small woodshop, enjoying it as much as working with the bees. He had a lot of supers and frames to build that winter. In the five years he'd worked for Leonard, he'd accumulated 500 hives and planned to add another hundred the next season.

He sat, unable to go back to the shop, as powerless to move as he was to help Black Henry. That was the trouble with the war. It kept resurfacing, triggered by events beyond Andy's control. Northern Alberta could not be farther from Vietnam geographically or climatically. Yet the war always seemed to return.

CHAPTER THIRTY

BEEKEEPING SUITED ANDY. From the moment Leonard Davis opened a hive for him, he wanted to keep bees for a living. The nurturing rhythms of the season appealed to him as it unfolded in the northern climate.

With the receding snow in April came the fuzzy catkins of the willows. Growing in low-lying areas where pools of water formed from the snowmelt, the scrubby stands of trees sprouted puffy fluffs of white buds contrasting with the stark greys of the leafless branches. Hints of green appeared on the sun-warmed ground where no snow remained. When tiny yellow stamens grew out of the white fluff, the bees foraged on the first nectar and pollen of the season.

Andy liked watching as they hovered near the tiny blossoms before landing to access the nectar with their tongues. On their rear legs, balls of pale-yellow pollen formed as each bee gave the appearance of floating between the minute blooms. A distinctive hum filled the air, the collective sound from thousands of pairs of wings carrying the nectar gatherers to and from the willow trees.

During May, the dandelions came into bloom, leaving a yellow blanket of color in the hayfields. Andy observed individual bees rolling in the blossoms bursting with nectar and pollen. As the frames of the brood nest filled with honey, a yellow hue formed inside the hives where traces of pollen dust accumulated from the combined efforts of the foragers. The strong, medicinal aroma of dandelion honey emanated from the colonies swelling from the abundant source of nectar.

Andy sensed the bees at their most content during the dandelion flow, the anthropomorphic observation having some scientific basis in the way a hive cleansed itself with spring foraging. The rear legs of the workers bulged with orange-tinted pollen, which the bees packed into the hexagonal cells in the brood nest, a colony's source of protein for nurturing the hive.

In June the clover and alfalfa plants began their bloom, and the bees started filling the honey supers with an extractable surplus. While the clover emitted the sweet aroma of their blossoms, Andy stood beside fields of pinkish white flowers teeming with the fecundity of nature. Content listening to the steady hum of bees foraging in a sea of bloom swaying in the summer breezes, Andy felt the satisfaction of his work. Throughout July and into August, the bees, with business-like efficiency, packed the white boxes of the hives with nectar while the honey flow continued, enhanced by occasional rains.

The long days of summer in the far north combined with the bountiful acres of forage produced excellent crops. Andy's beehives averaged a yield of 205 pounds of honey in the 1982 season. News of Black Henry put a pall over his good fortune.

Black Henry was scheduled to die in the electric chair in June 1983. Sammy, a teacher now, had visited their friend on death row just after Christmas. Andy talked with Sammy shortly after the visit, replaying the conversation over and over as the countdown to Black Henry's death continued.

"He's real sick, Doc, been in Holman five years. It's hard to say how much is physical or mental. He won't talk about it. The doctors have him on some painkillers, but I think everybody just wants to get the execution over with, including Black Henry. The NAACP is involved trying to get his execution stayed, but I think he wants to die.

"Jesus Christ, Doc, they're really going to kill him. He just sits in that tiny cell all day rocking back and forth. Every time the white guy they're executing in April passes by his cell he tells him, 'I'll warm it up for ya, nigger.'

"'You'all do dat,' Black Henry yells back. It's the only thing they have to say to one another."

Lisa noticed a change in Andy's mood after receiving the news about Black Henry. "What's going on in that head of yours? You seem so quiet. Is it about the man you call Black Henry?"

Andy refused to discuss it, shutting down just as he had with his parents. Her persistence frustrated him. Lisa wanted to discuss Andy's troubles with the war, but rarely her own childhood. After meeting, they'd talked about their lives, establishing an immediate affinity. Andy told her details about the war; she insisted on more, without fully divulging her own past. It took him years to get her story, not always from Lisa, but from her family.

An alcoholic father, terrifying in his abusive rages, had threatened to kill them all. Lisa's mother bundled up four daughters at night and drove away, her husband sleeping off another drunken spree. Lisa worried about leaving her father, and didn't want to go. She was nine years old and it was the last time she saw him.

The next day, by himself on the abandoned farmstead, a crop in the field waiting to be harvested, her father blew his head off with a shotgun. Lisa cried sometimes with the memory. She had abandoned him, blaming herself for his death. She once told Andy, "Maybe if we hadn't left?"

"I think we are drawn together by each other's pain," she said. "You understood things other young men didn't." She had not spoken of specifics, leaving Andy to figure it out.

Andy recognized the guilt that weighed Lisa down because of his own. Perhaps that was the glue that bonded them. They shared in the shame of leaving the dead behind. They should have been able to do more.

❄ ❄ ❄

Lisa arrived home from work early and found Andy in the shop at a table saw, the blade's teeth filling the air with a steady high-pitched whine, an opened bottle of whiskey on a workbench. It triggered the worst fight of their marriage.

"I will not live with a drunk," she hollered. "I had enough of it as a child. Drinking never solves problems. And I can't even begin to understand why you would be standing at a saw and drinking. What would you do if you cut yourself?" She broke down, crying.

"I know this is about that man Black Henry. Maybe he shouldn't have killed somebody. Has that ever crossed your mind? Some things are just wrong," she shouted.

Andy stood, stoically, unable to explain how the news of Black Henry could impact their lives so long after the war. Andy thought Lisa's own story should give her some understanding.

"My father's family blamed my mother. Maybe I did too, a bit. I hated how patronizing everyone acted, telling me to be brave and strong, be a big girl. All of the talk about my father 'being in a better place' confused me. Nobody actually told me he was dead. I wondered where he had gone and why he couldn't just come back to us."

Lisa cried with the memory. Her rage softened with the tears, Lisa embraced her husband.

"I know you love me," she said. "I've never had that before. Not in that way. I mean, Reed Fitch married my mother and rescued us. He's been good to us, but I have you now, my own love."

Reed Fitch had met Lisa's mother, Cora, in England, "bomber command" as her mom always referred to it. Lovers during the war, they'd returned to Alberta intending to marry. Cora broke it off after meeting a dashing young man who'd also returned.

Andy only got parts of the story about Cora's first husband. For fifteen years, the party never wound down, ending in alcoholism and despair. When Lisa's father pulled the trigger that ended his life, he also destroyed any vestiges of normalcy for Lisa and her sisters. Reed Fitch re-emerged in Cora's life, and he had never stopped loving her. He had put the broken family back together with kindness and stability.

Lisa approved of Andy's beekeeping. They had helped one another, finding a common purpose in building a life apart from their troubled pasts. Lisa didn't understand why the news about Black Henry upset the equilibrium in their marriage. And Andy couldn't explain the hold Vietnam claimed on his life.

"My parents were both in World War II. They don't have a problem living a normal life and talking about it," Lisa told him.

"What about your father?" Andy asked. "He had all kinds of troubles."

"You leave him out of this," Lisa demanded. "It's not fair to bring him up. I don't know what caused his drinking, but there are plenty of veterans from my parents' generation who aren't alcoholics."

The World War II vets again, thought Andy.

Andy didn't want to lose Lisa, or the life they had. He stopped drinking in the shop around the saws, becoming more secretive and careful to hide it when he needed a release.

❊ ❊ ❊

The winter before Black Henry's execution dragged on for Andy. He forced himself to work, but without his normal sense of accomplishment. Ever since the war, he'd never slept for more than four hours at a time. Waking in the night, he felt for Lisa, a sound sleeper. He lay in the dark next to her and pictured their little house set back from the gravel road that ran by their farm.

Together, they'd seeded a large area with grass. Lisa dug flower beds and filled them with petunias, lupines, and pansies. The blue monkshood and hyacinths filled in asymmetrical areas dug out of the lawn, red poppies sprinkled throughout. Varieties of annuals and perennials provided an oasis of color amidst the green of the grasses and poplars bordering the yard. Finding young spruce in the forest, they transplanted them between the house and the road, the evergreens giving color against the white of the winter snow. With every tree and flower planted they shaped their own lives, creating beauty and distance from the turbulence of the past.

Andy's practical bent drew him to the vegetable garden beside the house. He enjoyed the lettuces, beets, carrots, tomatoes, turnips, squash and cabbages, but liked growing potatoes best. The northern climate, suited for the root crops, was perfect for the red norland, netted gem and golden russet potatoes.

Closer to the road, Andy built his woodshop. Not as elaborate as Leonard's, it created a practical refuge for the woodworking projects that expanded the size of the beekeeping operation.

Late in April, just as the last snows receded and the poplars were about to leaf out into an explosion of green against the blue skies bright with sun, Andy struggled with his emotions. Six weeks remained until Black Henry's execution. The fact paralyzed him. His inability to do anything ground him to a halt. The image of his former platoon member sitting in a hot and cramped cell waiting for death dominated his mind.

Drained of motivation by a sense of powerlessness against forces greater than his ability to influence, Andy sat motionless for long periods trapped by his thoughts. It was like weight added to him, preventing him from moving. He had much work to do.

The bees needed moving into their spring locations where the willows bloomed. Each hive had to be checked for fresh eggs, the sign of a viable queen. New summer locations had to be found and new hive boxes painted. Two thousand frames remained unassembled. Normally, he worked with enthusiasm and a sense of accomplishment. During the spring of 1983, Andy resembled a condemned man himself waiting for the inevitable day in June when everything ended.

Sleep only came with exhaustion. Troubled dreams of netherworlds appeared, preventing rest: *dead platoon members assembled in a withered rice paddy; Camel becoming a skeleton; Vietnamese soldiers*

with bent and mangled weapons from the Slaughter in the Ca Mau;
the five women shot by the gunship huddled together, their conical hats
adjusted to hide their faces; Calvin Lake's head cradled in the crook of
his arm . . . Black Henry bent from the weight of his shackles.

Andy moved closer to help Black Henry remove his chains, but
the locks were thick and heavy. "Be too late for dat anyways, Doc,"
he said, shifting his position, trying to rest his burden on the ground.
"Way too late for dat."

Andy surveyed the gathering. They either didn't see him or were
ignoring him. He was ashamed in Black Henry's presence. "Is it wrong
to want to live?" he asked them. "I need to know."

The crowd all turned at once and looked in his direction. Their
eyes so different in death. They saw right through him. He wanted to
go back to the living now but was paralyzed and unable to move. He
cried out.

"What is it, Andy?" It was Lisa, shaking him in their bed.

Confused for a moment, he said, "It's just a bad dream."

"You need to talk to me, darling," Lisa said, with sympathy, but
also not letting him off the hook with a vague explanation. "Your
moods are scaring me."

Andy moved next to Lisa and put his arm around her. She rested
her head on his shoulder. He smoothed her hair with his hand while
she nestled against him. Sensing he wanted to try and talk about
what was happening to their lives, she gently prodded. "What is it,
honey? Please talk to me."

Andy didn't want Black Henry's plight to intrude on what they
had built together—but it had. He decided to tell Lisa what he knew.

"You remember how you felt about leaving your father when you
were a little girl, how guilty it made you feel?" Andy felt Lisa's tension
at the mention of her parent.

"This is not about me," she bristled, pulling away slightly.

"No," Andy said, "but let me explain. You were a little girl, powerless
to change anything, but you still felt guilty. Just being a part of events

that night has left you feeling responsible for what happened.

"It's the same with Black Henry," he continued. "We were all just thrown together, all of these guys from all over the country, having to depend on each other to survive. Black Henry helped me do that. I owe him my life, but I can't help him now. It eats at me, just the same, even though I know events are out of my control. Deep down I keep searching for some way to help, but I keep coming up empty."

"But he must have killed somebody to be in prison," Lisa said. "Why do you feel responsible for that?"

"I don't," Andy said, "other than Black Henry getting a raw deal in life. He told Sammy what happened. There was a dispute over a job at one of the hiring centers for agricultural work. During the argument things got out of hand. There was some pushing and shoving, a knife got drawn, and Black Henry just reacted. It wasn't his knife, but the dead guy's friend said it was.

"I know Black Henry. He's not a killer. We were all under such stress in Vietnam. I know on the surface it doesn't make sense."

"So how do we get through this?" Lisa pressed. "You can't keep it all bottled up inside."

Andy remembered his mother saying the same thing.

"I don't know," Andy said, "maybe after the execution." His heart sank after uttering the words. "I'm doing the best I can."

"I believe you, honey, but you have to promise not to shut me out of your life. I need to know what's going on in that head of yours."

"Okay," Andy said, not knowing if he would ever understand enough about himself to do that.

CHAPTER
THIRTY-ONE

ON THE DAY of Black Henry's execution Andy didn't know what to do with himself. His bleak mood, building in intensity all spring as June approached, had a mind-numbing effect reminiscent of his days in Vietnam.

"Are you okay?" Lisa asked before leaving for work. "Would you like me to stay home today? The garden could use some attention, or I could help you with the bees."

Andy didn't. He appreciated Lisa's concern, but hiding the extent of his depression took tremendous energy. It was easier being alone.

Sammy promised to phone that morning from Alabama where he and White Henry had arrived to be with their former platoon member.

Expecting his call at nine, Andy paced between the kitchen and living area in their tiny house. He felt isolated and a long way from Alabama—and guilty, of course, always guilty. *I should be there too.*

"Hi," he answered, knowing it was Sammy, right on schedule. "Any chance of a stay?"

"Not likely," Sammy answered. "It's a frenzy down here. We may not know for sure until closer to midnight when the execution is scheduled, but it doesn't look good."

"How's Henry?"

"Terrible, Doc. He's so sick he can barely walk he's so crippled up with the pain. Nothing's been diagnosed, but he's a physical mess. He can't weigh more than a hundred and fifty pounds. He won't eat anything, says it hurts his gut."

"You've been able to visit with him?"

"Just twice; everything's so locked down in the prison it's hard to move. There's a crowd gathering outside to cheer on the execution. It's sickening, the whole spectacle."

"Yeah, and it's our guy at the center of it. I should be there," Andy said.

"I don't know what you'd be able to do. Only two of his people are allowed at the actual execution. Black Henry doesn't want any of his family to see him die that way. He doesn't want to be alone, either. I guess he thinks we're used to it, but I've never seen anything like this."

"I don't even know what I'd say to him," Andy said. "Nothing's appropriate."

"Nothing," Sammy agreed. "White Henry is with him now."

"How's he doing?" Andy asked.

"You know White Henry. He hasn't changed. He'll be there for our guy, but he's having a hard time with it, the execution and all."

Andy ran out of words but didn't want Sammy to hang up yet. "I don't know what to do with myself," he blurted.

"There's nothing to do, Doc."

"You'll call tomorrow?"

"Of course. I'll spend a couple of days with White Henry, and then I'm coming to see you. But I'll phone tomorrow."

"And find something to say to Black Henry for me, let him know how much it meant to me knowing him. He saved my life you know."

"We all saved each other's lives," Sammy added, "but I'll make sure I pass on your words."

Andy hung up the phone feeling like he should have had more to say. Claustrophobic inside the house, he wanted something panoramic and soaring to clear his head. All he could think about was Black Henry being strapped into a chair and bolts of electricity surging through his body when an executioner flipped a giant switch on a wall. Sammy, a high school teacher now, sent him a book on the history of the electric chair.

"There are a lot of people working to prevent this," Sammy had told him. "The barbarity of the method is under scrutiny and there are too many aspects of Black Henry's case that don't warrant the death penalty."

❋ ❋ ❋

Knowing he would not get much work done, he chose to drive to each of his bee yards and check on them. The time alone in his truck provided solitude. Riding through the countryside reaffirmed his new life.

Two miles from his farm he turned south on the gravel road and continued until he came to an alfalfa field with a farm gate at the edge of it. Unfastening the latch, he entered and followed a trail through the crop and pulled up beside a yard of his bee colonies. The alfalfa, beginning to form buds but not yet in bloom, filled the entire 300 acres. The darker green of the established plants contrasted with the lighter new growth, translucent in the summer sun as Andy checked for blossoms. A tree line of poplars at the opposite end of the field marked its edge.

The foragers returning with yellow balls of pollen on their legs indicated the bees were into the hawksbeard, a weed in the dandelion family growing in clumps throughout the hayfield. Satisfied the bees had enough nectar and pollen to keep them healthy and raising brood until the main honey flow, he walked through the yard and watched at the entrances of several colonies. With nothing more to check he returned to his truck. Noticing white clouds forming in the west with a tinge of grey, he gazed at the horizon above a stand of spruce at that end of the field. A slight breeze caused plants to sway to the rhythms of each gust.

Continuing along the trail towards the tree line, he parked again at the western edge of the alfalfa field. Walking towards a steep bank high above the Simonette River, a gap in the poplar trees allowed a view of the valley with the waterway winding through a rock-strewn bottom. A mix of poplar and spruce left no gaps in the flora along the steep banks, except where the sheerness of rock facings remained bare. Andy sat for a long while, grateful for the seclusion, trying to come to terms with Black Henry's fate.

He spent the rest of the day driving to his bee yards spread over a twenty-mile radius from his place. Farmers needed the bees for pollinating the clover grown for seed and regenerating the pastures and hayfields with new growth.

Closer to home, he pulled into the site of an old homestead. The log structure intact, except for a collapsed roof decaying where it had fallen in on itself, his bee yard fit nicely into a sheltered space behind the abandoned house. Originally a garden, rhubarb still grew at the edges of the clearing, where poplar saplings had already begun to reclaim the untended ground.

Getting out of his truck, several agitated bees buzzed around his head. Before he could investigate, two stung him on the face. Retrieving his bee veil from the truck, he slipped it on and lit his smoker before walking into the yard.

Andy saw three hives knocked over, each teeming with bees clustered on the exposed brood trying to keep it warm. Others circled in the air on the lookout for further intrusions. Andy noticed a light trail through the grass with three damaged frames, the beeswax partially eaten out of them by a bear. Two piles of scat with undigested barley hulls gave further evidence of the intruder.

He wondered how the bears did it, smashed into a hive and then sat amidst the angry bees and ate, swallowing mouthfuls of the stinging insects along with the honeycomb filled with brood and pollen. Despite the damage, Andy experienced an exhilaration living among such an observable prevalence of wildlife.

Using the bellows attached to the canister on the smoker, Andy fanned the lit burlap inside until a thick smoke poured out of the spout at the top. Blowing it over the bees clustered on an upended super, he turned the bee box to its normal position, careful not to crush many bees. Setting it on the hive's bottom board, he arranged the individual frames in between blowing more smoke on the colony. Angry bees continued to bump at his veil and sting through his coveralls. Repeating the process with each of the six overturned supers, he gathered the damaged frames and knocked the remaining bees off by giving each a hard tap on the ground.

He would need to put up a bear fence around the yard. He worked quickly, driving posts into the ground every fifteen feet until the outline of a rectangle emerged. He threaded a thin cable wire through insulators attached to the posts until he had four strands on the fence. Driving a ground rod deep into the soil, he ran another wire from it to a solar panel set on a small square of plywood. Attaching a second wire from the fencer to the bottom strand, he wove it through all four before switching it on. Power surged through the wires.

Activating the electricity reminded Andy of the day. Closing the palm of his hand on the top wire to test for the current sent an uncomfortable jolt through his body, the worst of the charge mitigated by the thick soles on his leather boots. He thought of Black Henry.

All day Andy fought the desire to swig from a bottle of Wild Turkey, but Lisa would be returning from work soon and expecting to find him sober. When she pulled into the drive, Andy was at a shed replenishing the bear fencing supplies he carried with him in his truck. He greeted her in the yard.

"I don't know if you will understand," Andy began, "but I need you to realize how difficult this is for me tonight."

Lisa nodded for him to continue.

"Every time I think the war is behind me, it pops up again, and someone else dies. I need for you to know that I want a life. I want us to have a life. I'm trying to have that for us, but this thing with Black Henry is driving me over the edge with anger, and frustration, and grief. I want to lash out and hurt whoever is responsible for the raw deal he's gotten in life. But I don't even know who or what to direct it at. And it leaves me feeling hopeless."

"I know, honey," she says. "Maybe not everything, but enough to know how it has hurt you. It scares me sometimes, the hold that war has on you, but I'm trying too. And I believe we will be okay. What we have here is full of hope. We have worked too hard for it not to be."

"I'm gonna need to be alone tonight," he said. "Please don't be hurt by that, or think I'm shutting you out. I don't know what to do with myself, or how to sort these feelings out. It will be okay, just not tonight. I always find some equilibrium."

"Okay," Lisa said, but Andy could sense her tension. "It's just that you've been so different ever since Sammy phoned about Black Henry. I don't know where you go in that head of yours."

Andy nodded and looked into her eyes, more blue than green now in the afternoon sun. "I'll walk you into the house." He put his arm around her waist. Lisa did the same.

"Will you be wanting supper?" she asked.

Andy shook his head.

※ ※ ※

When troubled, Andy often sat in his woodshop or walked in the warehouse and extracting facilities, thinking. On this night, he pulled the chair out from an old desk in the shop and sat. In the bottom drawer he found his emergency stash of whiskey.

He liked best the initial buzz the Wild Turkey gave when it first took the edge off raw emotions. In that place, it altered his perspective without losing clarity. Sometimes a better equilibrium emerged.

He thought about how Black Henry and the Professor used to look after Yardly. It didn't seem so strange at the time that a Montagnard boy would be with an American infantry platoon. They used to share a foxhole, all three of them, Yardly so small he took up little space. Black Henry, the mother hen, fussed over their supper. Some of the guys went to great lengths trying to spice the C-rations, carrying seasonings in their gear and combining the cans of beef stew, a favorite, with the ham and lima beans, which almost nobody liked.

Black Henry would have them take all of their C-rats out of their packs and, like a chef, muse over which combinations would create the best meal. Yardly always seemed delighted by the ritual and pleased to be included.

After choosing the ingredients, he mixed them in a steel helmet with the camouflaged cover removed, spicing the concoction and tasting it with his finger as he went. When ready to heat, he ignited a small tab of C-4 underneath the improvised pot.

Andy, often resting with Sammy in the foxhole next to them, would watch as the trio enjoyed their meals. "This is the best ever," the Professor would say to Black Henry.

Yardly and the Professor never made it out of Vietnam. Black Henry would be dead in a few hours.

The whiskey helped to at least suspend those thoughts of loss.

Andy staggered from the woodshop wanting to be somewhere else. Near the house, he knelt on the ground and vomited.

Lisa hovered over him. Sensing not only her disgust at his condition, but her sympathy, they staggered together into the house. Exhausted and fully spent, Andy made it to the couch in the living room where he collapsed. He caught a glimpse of Lisa crying as she covered him with a quilt, the last thing he remembered from the evening.

CHAPTER
THIRTY-TWO

ANDY PACED WHILE waiting for Sammy's flight to arrive in the Grande Prairie Airport. In the aftermath of Black Henry's execution, he recognized the familiar numbing of his emotions. With invisible layers between him and his surroundings, he mechanically went about what he needed to do, hopeful Sammy's visit would alleviate his emptiness. The guilt of being alive dominated his mood.

Right on schedule, the small plane carrying his friend landed on the concrete runway and taxied to a stop. They had not seen one another for three years. This would be Sammy's first visit to Andy's farm.

When Sammy entered the terminal, Andy waved a greeting. Not much had changed in his appearance. A few pounds heavier, filling out his frame and face, he moved with the ease of a mature man as he walked into the waiting area.

"Am I ever glad to see you," Sammy said. "It's been a rough few days."

"It has," Andy said, "but I didn't have to witness it. Let's grab your bag and get out of here. My place is about an hour from here," he said, placing Sammy's bag in the back of his truck.

"I'm looking forward to seeing it. From the plane, it looked like nothing but wilderness between Edmonton and Grande Prairie with a bit of farmland thrown in."

Andy nodded. The main highway passed through poplar and spruce forest with tamarack and willows growing in the marshy areas. The rivers, streams and creeks spread elaborate tentacles through the green of the massive forests studded with ponds and small lakes. Closer to Grande Prairie, land cleared for farming expanded in all directions from the city of 30,000, the main hub of the Peace River Region.

"How's Lisa?" Sammy asked. They had met on a visit to Barstow not long after Andy married, and often exchanged pleasantries when Sammy phoned. "I'm not sure I can talk about the execution in front of her. It's even worse than the Nam, if that's possible."

"Lisa's always trying to get me to talk about the war figuring it will lead to understanding. What can I say? It just makes me feel worse."

"Nothing can," Sammy confirmed. "I mean, we were there and can't make any sense of it. How is anybody else supposed to?"

"Things are kind of tense right now. This whole thing with Black Henry had me reeling. I got totally plastered on the night of the execution. She hates it when I drink. Her father was a drunk."

"Lots of guys are having trouble, Doc."

"Are you?"

"I keep busy."

"It's like I just need a release sometimes, take the pressure off."

"We all do."

Heading east from Grande Prairie, the land remained flat with newly seeded crops blanketing the fields with shoots of green. As they rode in silence, Andy sensed Sammy wasn't quite ready to talk about the execution. He looked out the passenger window, taking in the terrain.

"How's White Henry?" Andy asked.

"How are any of us, really? We're all trying to make sense of it. White Henry was always so steadfast. In the Nam we relied on that. That part of him hasn't changed, but it was hard on him, too, seeing Black Henry at the mercy of forces beyond our control and not being able to help."

Andy had never made the trip to Missouri to look him up. Plans to visit after the war, sincere in their intentions, never materialized. Unanticipated realities dominated his agenda.

"He said to make sure and say hello. The invitation to visit is still open. He's farming, too, you know."

Thirty miles from Grande Prairie, the Smoky River Valley came into view. From the top of the hill the highway could be seen winding through the heavily treed terrain to the waterway. After crossing the bridge, Andy turned off the road and took a dirt trail to the water's edge. The spring runoff from the mountains continued to swell the banks with a swift-flowing current.

Not wanting to return home before they'd had a chance to talk, Andy parked by the remnants of a campfire ringed with stones.

"It's pretty here," Sammy said.

"My place is ten miles farther. Lisa has dinner planned for your arrival. She gets nervous when we visit, afraid it'll bring back bad memories. Her folks reminisce about their war all the time and enjoy it."

"Then they weren't on the front lines."

"They had a purpose beyond surviving it."

Sammy watched the river flowing before continuing. "We saw some bad shit over there. Maybe that's the problem . . . no purpose to it."

"So now Black Henry's dead, too."

"Can we take a walk?" Sammy asked.

The branches of the poplar trees near the bank reached out over the river. Large for the region, their thick trunks gnarled with age, the boughs branched into newer limbs forming leaves in the June warmth. Andy looked at the far side of the river 200 feet away. A sandy bank saturated by the rise in the water level from the continued snowmelt in the mountains slid into the swift current.

They followed an animal trail along the river's edge. Blossoms from the wild roses, prevalent in the area, bloomed among a profusion of shrubs. Andy recognized a clump of wild raspberry bushes with their prickly stems growing next to some lowbush cranberries, neither bearing fruit this early in the season.

They sat on a log as Sammy was ready to talk.

"It was horrible, Doc. They brought him in all bound up in some sort of straitjacket, sat him down and strapped him into the chair. He found us with his eyes and never looked away."

Sammy, restless, stood and stared at the river. Tears formed as he tried to maintain composure. Andy had never seen Sammy cry.

"The executioners had a bucket with a sponge in it, a salt solution they doused his shaved head with before . . . before—" He took a deep breath. "Before they put a metal skullcap on his head with the electrodes on it. Black Henry was hyperventilating. He looked at White Henry, then me, back and forth every few seconds, nodding at us. We nodded back, our eyes locked into his. White Henry kept repeating over and over 'You're not alone, you're not alone.' But he was alone.

"The executioners were moving quickly to get it over with. The warden asked Black Henry if he had any final words. What was to be said? He'd already told us how good knowin' us in the Nam had been. And told the warden, you know, in that accent of his that he didn't want 'none o' that God stuff. Jesus ain't made nothin' good for me in this life, don' expect much in the next one.'

"Then they put a cover over his face so we couldn't see him. Right away the first jolt had our guy jerking, then rigid. That's the one that's supposed to send enough voltage into the brain to render him unconscious.

"The next jolt sent smoke out from behind the hood over his face, and one of the prison guards gagged and threw up. We couldn't smell anything behind the glass partition, but we know the smell of burning flesh from the Nam.

"A doctor came over and listened for a heartbeat and shook his head. They had to blast him again.

"White Henry is glaring at the scene, grinding his teeth. After the third blast the doctor said there was no heartbeat. Mercifully, the curtains closed, but I'm feeling totally empty and drained. I haven't said a proper goodbye, haven't known how to under the circumstances. And it's too late."

Sammy sat on the log again and fiddled with a small branch he had picked off the ground. Andy's insides churned.

"And that was it, Doc. A guard walked with us through the locked gates. I'm feeling claustrophobic and needing fresh air. By the time we're outside, the crowd there to celebrate the execution was quiet.

"We walked to White Henry's pickup. Neither of us spoke. I just wanted to get the hell out of there, and so did he."

Sammy stood again and threw the branch he was holding into the river.

"You know, Doc, I think that Agent Orange really fucked up a lot of us over there. I think it made Black Henry sick; I think he was gonna die anyway. Black Henry deserved to be in a hospital with proper painkillers and somebody giving a damn about his condition. It was a horrible death, Doc. He suffered right until the end.

"We went and saw Henry's mother, you know."

"After the execution?" Andy asked.

"Yeah, Black Henry asked us to. He wanted us to tell her two things—that he died a man, and that he's sorry they are so poor. That's what a life comes down to? Being poor, but trying to die with dignity while the man sends a thousand volts of electricity surging through your body?"

Sammy picked up a stone and rolled it in his palm before tossing it into the river.

"White Henry's told me more about how the NAACP got

involved. They were saying Black Henry's arrest was racially motivated, that Alabama executed a sick black man who never should have received the death penalty in the first place. The jury recommended a thirty-year sentence. But Alabama allows a judge to override a jury's sentencing decision. That's what happened. Some nutcase judge with a penchant for using the electric chair handed it down. Jolt-'em Jerry is what they call him. It turned into a tug of war, a giant clash of forces all centered around the death penalty, each side thinking the case has implications going forward. But the injustices were already in place long before Black Henry set foot in Holman.

"It's too late for a lot of things, isn't it? Ever wonder what your life would be like without Vietnam?"

"I try not to go there," Andy said, "beyond it being a lot different because of the war."

"Maybe you have the right idea, Doc. Get as far away from it as possible."

"It comes with you. The difference living here is I don't have the everyday reminders that rubbed me raw in Oklahoma. All the people for it or against it, the whole nation's self-identity wrapped up in it. Here, I don't have that stuff—until something like this comes along. I just work hard and try to create my own situation on that bee farm of ours."

Sammy thought for a moment. "Ever tried to count the number of dead bodies we've seen?"

"I call it my 'dead weight,' carry it around in my head," Andy said. "I really thought the war would be over after we got home, but the bodies keep piling up."

"It's the same for me," Sammy said. "Ever wonder what's happened to guys like Eli?"

"Sure. And I still have an uncle I'm trying to find from the Second World War."

"The one who disappeared?"

Andy nodded. "So, you saw Black Henry's mother?"

"He was from a little place called Demopolis, not even in the town itself—what they call the Black Belt Region of west central Alabama. The name refers to the dark, rich topsoil, and the high percentage of blacks in the population.

"We had trouble finding Henry's mother. Two white strangers looking for an older black woman raises suspicions. We found her in the middle shack of five at the edge of a cotton field. A young black man came out on the porch and yelled, 'What you white boys want?'

"'We're looking for Rachetta Jones,' White Henry says. Before he could say anything more, the young guy tells us, 'You be leavin' that woman be. She jus' had one of her own killed up at Holman yesterday.'

"'We're here to pay our respects,' White Henry told him. 'Henry asked us to stop and see his mother.'

"'How you be knowin' Henry?' he shot back, still angry. 'You white folks jus' always intrudin' on people's bis'ness.'

"'We were in Vietnam together,' White Henry says.

"Without saying anything more, he went inside. Two minutes later a middle-aged black woman came out on the porch and looked at us. 'You knows my Henry from Vietnam?'

"'Yes, ma'am,' White Henry says. 'He asked us to pay our respects. He died a man. He wanted you to know that.'

"Rachetta Jones started weeping and motioned for us to sit down with her on the porch. She smoothed her faded cotton dress against her lap and wiped at her tears.

"'That boy was never right after gettin' back from that war you boys was fightin.' Goin' off by hisself all de time, not tellin' his mama what was wrong. Never understood what kind o' quarrel us black folks have with no Viet Cong. That boy would try and work, but he be sick all de time, vomitin' if he was in the sun any, his skin full of ugly rashes an' itchin' somethin' fierce. Sez his head was hurtin.' Never could afford to see no doctor.'

"We sat there for an hour or so and told her some stories about Black Henry in the Nam. We talked about his courage, and how he saved a lot of lives. I left Alabama wondering if the war will ever really be over."

Andy looked at the swiftly flowing current gurgling along with the rushing of water over rocks and fallen branches pressed against a large tree that had fallen into the river.

They had talked enough for the moment and were comfortable in their silence.

"Let's go see your place," Sammy finally said.

"Lisa will be expecting us," Andy said.

CHAPTER
THIRTY-THREE

ANDY POURED HIS coffee and went outside to the deck beside his house. Two weeks from the summer solstice, the sun's rays sparkled off the dew-saturated grasses in the yard.

He liked the early mornings of summer in the north, peaceful yet coming to life with warmth. A pair of robins searched for worms, hopping from spot to spot while their beaks probed the damp ground. Rising earlier than Lisa, he utilized this time to sit and plan the day.

Over dinner the night before, Sammy told them he expected to help during his visit. Lisa had laughed at his insistence. "Are you really going to make him work?" she said, looking at Andy. Then, turning to Sammy she told him, "Not everyone finds the bees as fascinating as my husband."

Talk during the evening had been lighthearted, avoiding mention of the execution. Andy would busy himself in work now, burying his anger and guilt about Black Henry.

Sammy joined Andy on the deck. "I helped myself," he said, referring to the cup of coffee in his hand. "Maybe you have the right idea. Just leave it all behind as much as you can. You and Lisa have your own world here."

Andy nodded. "It's a good place for hiding out. It helps some of the time getting far enough away."

"We sort of knew that in the Nam, I guess, that it would always be with us, but didn't want to acknowledge it. We needed to have hope."

"Wait until I put you to work with the bees," he joked. "Are you serious about wanting to work while you're here? You only have a few days."

"Absolutely. You have one of those things that covers the head so I won't get stung?"

"A bee veil," Andy said. "It will at least keep the bees off your head."

❀ ❀ ❀

Andy, behind in his spring work, fitted Sammy with a pair of coveralls hanging on a hook in the honey house. The bee veil, attached with a zipper across the shoulders, hung from the back. "Just flip it over your head when we get to the bees. I'll make sure it's zipped up properly."

"Why are the coveralls white?" Sammy asked.

"It's partly traditional," Andy said, "but white is neutral to the bees. They don't react aggressively to it. But don't expect that to keep them calm if we do something stupid. Leonard Davis, the man who got me started, used to joke, 'The worst thing that ever happened to bees was beekeepers.'"

"So, what are we doing today?" Sammy asked.

Turning east onto the gravel road in front of Andy's farm, they drove two miles to the first location. Thirty fenced colonies appeared near the road. Andy pulled into the field and parked the truck next to them. A stand of willows several acres deep protected the colonies from the predominant west wind.

"One second," Andy said, "while I turn off the power." He hopped over the top wire, taking a mild shock when his legs briefly straddled the fence. "The bears get a better jolt. They don't wear boots. There are a lot of them in the vicinity of this yard, but all of the willows nearby are an excellent spring source of pollen and nectar for the bees." After turning off the switch on the solar panel, he opened the gate for Sammy.

Some bees were already in the air circling around the hives. More could be seen milling about on the small wooden landings below the hives' entrances. Others were still, giving the appearance of sunning themselves. A steady hum emanated from the colonies.

"Here," Andy said, "we better get your veil zipped up." He checked Sammy out. Satisfied, he told him, "Once we start working the hives, there will be a lot more bees in the air. A few will be bouncing off the outside of your veil and landing on you to rest. Don't worry about it. They won't be able to get inside.

"I have to make up some nucleus colonies from the strong ones," Andy said, taking a wad of burlap out of the pocket in his coveralls. Holding it away from him, he lit it before stuffing it into the canister of the smoker and closing the spout. "Just tag along. It's easier explaining as we go, but essentially we'll be removing frames of brood from the strongest colonies to form new ones."

Andy blew smoke around the edges of the hive cover before prying it off with a hive tool. "The bees gum it up with beeswax and propolis," he explained.

A cluster of bees formed on top of the hive, and the fluttering of wings and movement intensified the hum coming from the colony. Andy gave them more puffs of smoke.

"It has a calming effect, making the bees want to hover around the brood."

He loosened the outer frame in the top super with the hive tool before lifting it out, laying it upright against the bottom super. Most of the bees remained on the frame.

"The queen will be somewhere on the brood, so we always remove the outer frame first, so we don't roll her. Now we can simply move each one over one slot after looking at it.

Andy removed the next frame. "This has a lot of pollen in it. See those cells with the pale yellow in them? That's from the willows. They take the balls of it from the rear legs of the foragers and pack it tight. This is from the dandelions." He pointed to cells full of orange pollen. Most of the frame's hexagonal cells were filled with the bees' source of protein.

"This is what we're looking for," Andy said, removing the next frame. "These brown cappings covering the cells are what we call capped brood. Underneath are bees in the pupal stage. Look right here," he said to Sammy. "One's emerging now." A bee inside the cell chewed at the thin capping. In seconds it emerged and joined the other bees.

Andy took the frame of capped brood and shook the bees off it into the opened hive, then tapped it on the ground in front of the entrance. Few bees remained. He set the frame in the middle of an empty super. After replacing the frame of capped brood with one the queen could lay eggs in, he put the hive back together, except for the cover.

On top of the hive he placed a rectangular metal grate with thin bars across the length of it. "It's called a queen excluder. The worker bees can move freely through it, but the queen, with a thicker abdomen, cannot. That will keep her in the brood nest. Now all we have to do is put the super with the frame of capped brood on top and close it up with the hive cover. Enough worker bees will move up and keep the brood warm. Early tomorrow morning we'll come back and remove the frames of capped brood above the excluders. There will be lots of bees on them, but because they're above the excluder, we'll know the queen isn't with them. We'll put them in pre-sorted brood chambers with two empty spaces, haul them to another bee yard, and introduce a queen. That will start a new colony."

Andy looked at Sammy, nodding in the bee veil. "You'll get the hang of it. To start with, just pack the equipment for me."

By noon, they had completed working two bee yards and had isolated fifty frames of brood above queen excluders. Andy noted the totals in a logbook.

"This time of year, we can start the nucleus colonies with two frames of capped brood, so we have enough for twenty-five new hives."

They were eating lunch at the edge of a large clover field. Sammy walked into it a few yards and looked back at Andy.

"I can't even see where this field ends. How many acres?"

Andy joined him and pointed to a tree line visible on the horizon. "I have another bee yard at that end. This whole section of land is in clover. That's six hundred and forty acres, one square mile."

"All in clover?"

"Yeah."

Sammy walked a little farther into the field. "I guess the bees can make a lot of honey here."

"When it comes into bloom," Andy said. He stooped and picked a bud beginning to form. "By July this field will be white with blossoms, the scent of nectar sweet and strong, especially with a light breeze blowing."

❄ ❄ ❄

"This feels really good, Doc."

Andy smiled at Sammy sitting in the passenger seat, his veil off, perspiring after finishing work on their third bee yard of the day.

"What?" he said, noticing Andy looking at him.

"You know, you're the only one in the world that still calls me that."

"Do you mind?"

"Of course not. I think Lisa finds it amusing."

"Doc Parks, that's how you were introduced when I arrived in the platoon. I didn't even know your first name until we started sharing a hooch."

Andy thought for a moment. "In some ways it seems like a long time ago, sometimes like yesterday."

"Yeah, like this thing with Black Henry."

"I dreamed a lot about the war, you know, before the execution, and felt a jolt of electricity right at midnight when the first surge would have been going through his body. Do you and Carole talk much about Vietnam?"

Andy knew Sammy's wife in the same way his friend knew Lisa, mostly from occasional chats on the telephone when the wives answered.

"I guess it's yes and no. So much of it doesn't make sense to her. I try and answer her questions, but I don't know if I explain it well. Are you and Lisa okay with it?"

"That's a hard question for me to answer, too. We're fine when the war is in the background and we can just focus on our lives. I don't like talking about it, and she's hurt and thinks I'm shutting her out when I don't. But it's impossible to explain something when you don't understand it yourself."

"I'm impressed with what you've done here. I wish I could stay for the whole season."

"This is only your first day of beekeeping."

"Yeah, but it's so peaceful."

By three in the afternoon they had pulled enough frames of brood to make forty-seven nucleus colonies. "We have time for one more yard," Andy said as he pulled out of the clover field. "There's one just south of here."

Dust from the gravel road billowed in their wake as they drove to the next location. "It gets pretty dusty on these roads without any rain," Andy said, slowing before a bend. After making the turn he looked out the window. A thin tree line of scraggly poplars between the road and a bee yard came into view. Andy pulled to a stop.

"Something doesn't look right."

"What?" Sammy asked.

"I'll go check it out. You stay here."

"No, I might as well come too."

Andy walked across the gravel road and got to the ditch by the entrance to the field. He heard something thrashing in the trees and the sound of branches breaking. He saw movement as a large black bear climbed fifteen feet up a small poplar, and in a rage snapped off the top. When Andy took a step back towards the truck, the bear, noticing him, began snapping its jaws. The bear rushed down the tree and charged.

"Run to the truck," Andy shouted. He had heard that bears were highly agitated when they snapped their jaws but had never seen it. Not sure they had time to reach the cab, he hollered at Sammy to dive under the truck. Andy did the same.

The bear, too large to fit, pounded the ground with its paws and reached for them. Dust flew along with bits of gravel making a tinkling sound as the small rocks hit the side of the truck. Andy felt some pebbles hit his legs through his coveralls.

"I don't think he can get at us," Andy said, out of breath. He saw a stone near Sammy. "Hand me that rock." Pounding on the undercarriage of the truck, and hollering, he hoped the noise would spook the bear. It had no effect. Snarling, teeth bared and still snapping its jaws, it continued circling the truck looking for a way underneath. It began clawing at the road. Andy had seen bears dig under fences. He took the rock and smashed one of the bear's paws when it reached for them again. It only enraged the animal further.

Huddling together, there was nothing more they could do.

"I don't suppose there's much traffic on this road is there?" Sammy asked.

"No," Andy said. "We'll just have to outwait him and hope he doesn't keep digging."

Catching their breath, they watched as the bear circled, not able to see anything but the bear's feet and claws.

A sharp report sounded from behind them. The bear dropped to the ground, and they watched it thrashing and growling. A second shot put an end to its movement. It shuddered, letting out a final gasp, and was still.

"Jesus Christ," said Sammy. "What the fuck just happened?"

"Someone shot the bear."

"Well, I guess it's our lucky day."

"Still find beekeeping so peaceful?"

"And I thought Vietnam was dangerous."

Andy scooted out from under the truck and looked at the bear. On its side now, blood trickled out of its nostrils and mouth, pooling in the gravel road. Andy looked up while he brushed the dust off his coveralls. An older man walked towards them with a rifle cradled across his arms. Andy didn't recognize him.

"Dash Holybrooke," he stated with a trace of an English accent, sticking out his hand to shake.

"Andy Parks," he replied. "This is my friend Sammy Donato."

"Are those your beehives?" Dash asked, pointing towards them with his rifle.

"They are, and by the way, thanks for helping us out of a jam."

Holybrooke, short, and a bit portly, merely grunted like it was nothing.

"You don't carry a rifle to protect your bees? If you ask me, this country has too many bears. They could stand to be thinned out. Look at the coat on this one. He's not missing many meals. We better get him drug off the road."

"We can do that," Andy said, motioning for Sammy to help him. They each took a rear leg and dragged him into the ditch.

"Over three hundred pounds, I'd say," Holybrooke commented, "large for a black bear."

"Do we need to bury him?" Sammy asked.

Holybrooke scoffed. "What for?" He looked at Andy. "Your friend ain't from around here is he? Between the coyotes, wolves and ravens, there won't be nothin' left of him in two days. Even the bones will disappear."

"Oh," Sammy said, looking sheepish.

"I better go and have a look at those hives," Andy said, "see if there's any damage." Sammy and Holybrooke followed.

"So where are you from?" Andy heard Holybrooke ask Sammy as they walked behind him towards the bee yard.

"California."

"Your friend, too?"

"No," said Sammy, "he's originally from Oklahoma. We met in Vietnam."

"Ah." Holybrooke nodded, seeming to understand. "He doesn't have a rifle? He must know how to shoot one."

Sammy shrugged. "He was our medic. I know he carried one, same as the rest of the platoon."

"Ah," Holybrooke repeated. "He should think about carrying one here."

Andy stood at the fence around the bee yard. Several saplings lay across the top. He brushed one of the wires with the back of a finger and felt it spark. The solar unit, its connections intact, continued emitting a current.

Along the north side of the yard, the bear had dug two large holes underneath the fence. One of the posts leaned but was held up by the wires. Not a blade of grass remained from the bear's digging and pounding along that side. Several of the small poplar trees had their branches shredded and trunks broken.

"I've never seen a bear this angry before," Andy said. "There's some damage inside the yard, but it must be from a younger bear slipping underneath where the larger one's dug his holes." He picked up a frame lying nearby on the ground, the wax eaten out of it, leaving only the wooden rectangle.

"Scraps left by the smaller bear," Holybrooke said. "It must have enraged the older one to watch him eating from the hives while he went hungry."

"Yeah," Andy agreed. Three hives lay knocked over, and a few frames littered the ground. "It fits the pattern of a young bear. If the larger one had been inside, he wouldn't be so tentative about smashing into the colonies."

"You looking for more places to put your bees?" Holybrooke asked.

"Sure," Andy said.

"Come and see me when you get the chance. Go back around that bend and go east at the first crossroad and follow it several miles till you get to the end of the road. That will be my place."

Andy watched Holybrooke return to his truck through the thin tree line. Turning towards Sammy, he saw a rip at one of the knees in his coveralls. His friend covered in dust, he noticed a cut on an elbow bleeding, and his bee veil hanging askew and dangling from his shoulder.

Brushing more dust off his own coveralls, he looked at Sammy and asked, "Had enough of beekeeping for one day?"

※ ※ ※

Lisa walked into the house and found Andy sitting at the kitchen table tending to Sammy's torn and bleeding elbow. After cleaning the worst cut, applying hydrogen peroxide and an antibacterial cream, he scrubbed the abrasion on his forearm extending from the elbow to his palm.

"At least you have a useful skill from the war," Sammy said. "The only time mine might have come in handy and I don't have a rifle."

Lisa hurried to the table. "Do I need to ask what happened?"

"We ran into an angry bear at the Stevenson location. Do you know Dash Holybrooke?"

"I know of him, but we've never met. Word has it he's pretty reclusive."

"Well, he came along at the right time and shot the bear."

"Oh my God," Lisa gasped. "Where were you?"

"Underneath the truck."

Lisa just shook her head and took a closer look at Sammy's elbow. "Shouldn't we take him to a doctor?"

"I'll be fine," Sammy said.

Andy nodded. "We've got it cleaned up and this cream will prevent any chance of infection. I've got the coveralls in the wash. They'll need repairing. I better get started on that," Andy said. "After supper I've got to sort a few more brood chambers. We pulled enough frames for forty-seven nucs." He looked at Sammy. "That's beekeeper jargon for nucleus colonies. We'll have to start at about five in the morning. There'll be a lot of bees on those frames covering the brood in the coolness of the morning."

"I'm here to help," Sammy said.

Lisa looked at Andy. He sensed her disapproval and that she was about to say something. "What would have happened if Dash Holybrooke wouldn't have come along? Does he always carry a rifle?"

He thought for a moment. "I did have a plan to get us out of there." Sammy and Lisa both looked at him now. "The bear couldn't stay that angry forever. If he didn't leave, I was going to try and hop in the cab when he was pawing the road on the other side. Blowing the horn might have spooked him. Failing that, I could have distracted him and given Sammy a chance to climb in and we could have simply driven away."

"Simply?" Now it was Lisa's turn. "I take it the bear chased you under the truck? It must have been a close call or you would have gotten in the cab and *simply* driven away to begin with. Now you're going to take your injured friend along with you tomorrow and do it all over again?"

"I can't leave those frames of brood above the excluders for long," Andy said.

"And I am here to help," Sammy reiterated. "Five in the morning sounds fine. A few scrapes is not a worry."

"Can our guest at least have the evening off?" Lisa protested.

"Sure," Andy conceded. "It won't take me long to finish sorting the brood chambers."

Later, in bed, Lisa scooted beside Andy, took his arm and put it around her. Snuggling against him she asked, "What really happened today? I don't want my husband eaten by a bear."

"No," Andy told her, "that would be humiliating, forever being *the woman* whose husband got eaten by a bear."

"The truth," she demanded. "I always have to pry things out of you."

"Well, he was pretty worked up. They're usually timid. I'd never seen a bear snapping its jaws like that. The fence was keeping him out of the bee yard, but he was trashing everything around it, pounding the ground, breaking small trees in half and shredding what was left."

"Oh. You be careful, Mr. Parks. Maybe you should carry a rifle."

"Yeah, but you know I haven't touched one since the war."

"I know, honey, but that was a close call. The bear is dead. Does it really matter who shot it?"

"I guess not."

"You'll at least consider getting one."

"Okay."

❊ ❊ ❊

By a quarter past five they were in the loaded truck and retracing their route of the day before. Close to the solstice, the sun provided plenty of light for working the hives so early. The northern climate still cooled to a few degrees above freezing in early June, causing heavy dew that moistened their boots as they worked.

The frames of brood, covered with bees keeping them warm in the morning chill, were easy to lift out of the top supers above the queen excluders. Andy worked quickly removing them, handing them to Sammy, who placed them in the space provided in the brood chambers already on the truck.

"It speeds it up with two of us," Andy said. "We have to take them out of the hives early before they get active. We want a lot of bees on that brood for starting the new colonies."

He examined one of the frames. A thick layer of bees hung on as he removed it from the colony. "If we did this later, the hive would be breaking cluster in the heat of the day to begin foraging. That's a good amount of bees for our purposes."

Sammy just nodded and followed instructions.

By nine they had all forty-seven nucleus colonies unloaded and situated in a new yard. "We need to move bees at least two miles from their original hive so they will orient to their new location. That will prevent them from returning to the old one. How's the elbow holding up?"

"Ready for any new crisis. What have you got planned for the rest of the day?"

"Let's go back to the farm for some breakfast. I'll change your dressings while we're there before we head back out. We'll pull some more frames of brood. You sure you don't want some time to relax?"

"The bees are interesting," Sammy said. "I'd like to see as much as possible. Did Lisa talk to you about a rifle?"

"She brought it up."

"You gonna start carrying one?"

"I haven't touched one since the war. Have you?"

"No," Sammy said, "but I haven't got enraged bears chasing me."

"True, but that's the first time it's happened. I told her I'd think about it."

"You don't have to use it unless you absolutely have to."

"Honestly, I'd rather not even have one in the house. They make me uncomfortable. We know what they can do to people."

"Everything is always so complicated," Sammy said.

"What do you mean?" Andy asked.

"Well, like you carrying a rifle. Most people wouldn't hesitate after what happened yesterday. Because of your experiences in the war, there's more to consider."

Andy thought for a moment and nodded.

"Or a normal thing like having kids. You and Lisa planning on having any?"

"We've talked about it. You?"

"Carole really wants to, but I've known too many vets that have had deformed babies from the Agent Orange. I could never live with myself if I passed that on to my child."

"Yeah, I don't know what to do. You had any problems? We were all exposed."

Back at the house, Andy put a pot of coffee on the stove. "We'll take a break." He motioned for his friend to have a seat where they would be more comfortable.

"I haven't noticed anything," Sammy answered.

"I've had a lot of trouble with my teeth since I've been back," Andy said. "Within a year I had lost three, and no matter how much I brushed I kept getting cavities. I didn't know what was going on until I saw a Vietnam vet interviewed in a documentary about the war. He worked loading the planes with the defoliants. Said he'd lost all his teeth within a year of being back. I knew then what the problem was."

"You hear about a vet named Paul Reutershan?" Sammy asked. Andy shook his head and poured them coffee. "Back in '78 he appeared on *The Today Show* and announced, 'I died in Vietnam but didn't know it.' He was riddled with cancer and died a few months later. He flew through clouds of the chemicals all the time during his tour. The guy was a health nut, even in Vietnam. It's all documented by his mother. Two days after his death she received a letter from the VA requesting that his disability check be returned."

"Does Carole know about this stuff?"

"Most of it. She still wants to have children. I'll be stressed the whole time she's pregnant and will be counting the fingers and toes of my kids as they're coming out of the womb."

❋ ❋ ❋

"Five days goes quick," Sammy said, standing at the gate to catch his flight. "I'm glad I came and got to see your place. I still envy you getting to keep bees for a living, although it's not quite as peaceful as I first thought—and is more dangerous," he joked.

The visit had gone well, subtle transformations shaping Andy's outlook. He could say goodbye to Black Henry now. Having Sammy around for a few days helped put things into perspective. Their days together in a foxhole had formed the basis of a lifelong friendship. They'd helped each other survive their tours as boys, and they were helping each other get through life as men. Sammy had a knack for showing up at the right time.

"Come again during the harvest and I'll show you how we pull honey," Andy said.

"Thanks for saving my life—again."

"Anytime," Andy said, "although it was probably a preventable catastrophe. Give our best to Carole. We may be down to see you for a week this winter."

"Things are going to be okay, Doc. We've made it this far."

Andy realized they had. He had been fortunate in his own way to survive the war and be able to start a new life. He hadn't had a drink since the night of Black Henry's execution and was feeling strong, any cravings easy to resist.

Sammy turned one last time as he exited the terminal and waved.

Friendships like that weren't formed every day, Andy realized. Their lives had taken different paths since the war, but the bond remained. Andy would go home and get to work. The season, in full swing, demanded his attention. Lisa would be home soon. Maybe he could have one of those talks with her now that he understood things better. Sammy had given Andy a sense that maybe he'd chosen the right path. Life could be good sometimes, certainly worth living with friends like that.

On the drive home from the airport Andy noticed the crops were off to a good start. They grew quickly with the length of the days in the far north. At the Smoky River Valley storm clouds gathered overhead. A good rain would be timely for all the farmers, including beekeepers. He would stay in tonight, not go and work in the shop, maybe fix supper for Lisa and give her a break. He had a glimmer of hope for the future. *Life can be good.* Sammy helped him realize that.

CHAPTER
THIRTY-FOUR

JUNE MERGED INTO July, and what beekeepers called the main nectar flow began. Andy, looking for last-minute locations for the nucleus colonies, remembered Holybrooke's offer. On the way to his farm, Andy checked on the yard where the bear had been shot.

The colonies stood tall with three and four honey supers on them. The white of the freshly painted boxes gleamed in the sun against the green glow of the hayfield. Andy got out of his truck and watched the bees returning to the hive entrances. He'd filled in the holes where the younger bear had scooted underneath the fence and saw the animal had not returned.

On peak days each colony could gather twenty pounds of nectar. The season unfolded quickly in the long days of the north. Anticipating a heavy flow of honey, and giving the bees enough room to store it, became essential to making a good crop.

Busy with the season, and satisfied the young bear had moved on, Andy followed the directions Holybrooke had given to find his farm. As he drove east the gravel road inclined gradually as it entered low-lying foothills. Poplar forest bordered both sides of the road after passing the Stevenson home place tucked in amongst a stand of mature spruce. The occasional cleared field exposed a grey-wooded soil more suitable for cattle operations growing hay instead of grain.

Andy reached Holybrooke's place at the end of the road eight miles from his bee yard. With no buildings visible, he turned onto a trail that wound around a hill and brought him to a small farmhouse beside a pond. Beyond the dwelling he saw an outbuilding with a swather and an old combine parked beside it. Holybrooke worked repairing a wooden granary nearby.

"Ah, young Andy," he greeted him. "You must be wanting some bee locations. I have just the spot for you."

Andy liked most of the farmers whose land provided locations for his bees. They often expressed an interest beyond the pollination benefits of the colonies.

Holybrooke set down his hammer and walked towards Andy. "Having any more bear problems?"

"Not so far," Andy said. "I just checked the yard where you shot the bear. The young one's moved on."

"Ah." He nodded. "Come inside for a minute. Have you got time for a tea before we head out?"

Andy didn't, but he rarely refused a farmer's hospitality.

"Your friend go home?" Holybrooke asked while he put the kettle on to boil.

"A couple of weeks ago."

"He told me you'd met in Vietnam."

Andy nodded, still uncomfortable discussing the war, especially with someone he didn't know well.

"You're lucky," Holybrooke said.

The statement surprised Andy. He'd heard negative comments from people when they learned he'd been to Vietnam, but never *lucky*.

"How so?" Andy asked.

Holybrooke left the kitchen and went into a small sitting room next to it, returning with a framed photograph. "My best friend," he said, handing it to Andy.

A young man stood looking at whoever had snapped the picture. A serious expression, except for the hint of a smile, his posture was erect and confident. In the uniform of the Canadian Army, he held his hat tucked in the crook of his arm.

"Before shipping out," Holybrooke said, "Randall Crenshaw. We pretty much did everything together. That photograph was taken just before we were off to give the Germans hell. Friends like that don't appear every day. Of course, the Germans had friends of their own, and shot back. Randy didn't make it. Your friend Sammy did."

Holybrooke's eyes watered slightly before turning away and bringing the tea. Andy did a quick calculation. Forty years would have passed, and he still grieved his friend's death. Andy thought of Camel and the Professor. What would he have done if Sammy had died?

During tea, the conversation turned to the normal pleasantries of new acquaintances. How did young Andy of Oklahoma come to keep bees in northern Alberta?

"Ah," Holybrooke acknowledged, "marry a Canadian girl. I never was much for hitching up like that. I had this crazy notion to homestead, own a farm of my own. I didn't figure it was a life any woman would be happy with. Now, mind you, beekeeping sounds interesting. Maybe I should have considered it, sweetened me up enough to marry."

Outside, they got into Holybrooke's pickup and took a trail beyond the row of wooden granaries he'd been repairing when Andy arrived. At the crest of the field the forested foothills below them continued until they merged with the horizon.

"It was this view that convinced me to stake my claim on this section of land." Holybrooke parked. "I should have been more mindful of the poor soil with too many rocks to pick, but we all have foolish notions as young men."

Andy noticed a large-blossomed variety of red clover seeded in the field before them, some of the blooms mature and lush, bursting with nectar. The contour of the land sloped gradually towards the forest of mixed poplar and spruce a half mile in the distance.

Andy broke a stalk off a plant and squeezed one of the blossoms, the juices oozing onto his finger. "The clover adds nitrogen to the soil," Holybrooke said. "I'll be taking it for seed. Your bees won't have to worry about me cutting it for hay before they get a chance at the honey in those blooms."

He walked towards a wind row of brushed trees formed when the land was cleared. The continuous pile, twelve feet high and five yards wide, ran the length of the field, the strong scent of drying sap pungent in the air. Andy marveled at the conversion of wilderness to cultivation still in progress.

"I thought this would be a good spot for the bees," Holybrooke said.

Andy walked with him and nodded. "This is good. It offers protection from the west wind. I'll need to put a bear fence up, though."

"We'll make sure the bears don't bother your bees," Holybrooke said.

In beginning to know Holybrooke that summer, Andy experienced an affinity with a World War II vet he'd never known. They'd always exhibited such certainty of cause. In Andy's life, he'd never heard anyone question the morality of participating in the Second World War. Vietnam was different, like an open wound that failed to heal because of continued irritations. As different as their wars were, Andy realized Holybrooke had some of the same lingering troubles about his experiences.

"I got placed on an Ontario farm in 1936," he told Andy, "during the Great Depression. England had a surplus of poor children, orphans and abandoned, on the streets of London. Canada needed labor for its farms.

"The program got started in 1869, but I was among the last to arrive before it shut down. I was eleven years old. I was what we used to call a tough kid, getting into trouble, but only because I was fending for myself. Begging, really, and the authorities frowned on it, but I needed to eat.

"The farm wasn't so bad. A lot of hard work. I looked forward to attending school in Canada, but it was the Depression, and everybody was more concerned about eating. We did get fed pretty good on the farm, and book learning wasn't a necessity. I wasn't mistreated, but I always regretted the farmer reneging on the deal and not allowing me to get an education.

"To get off the farm, I lied about my age and joined up at sixteen. In 1941 Canada was already in the war and enlisting was easy."

Holybrooke's story explained the trace of an English accent.

"I was christened Dashiell Holybrooke, a little pretentious for a London kid of the streets having to hustle to keep myself fed. Calling me *Dash* was an early abbreviation of the name and fitting.

"I joined the Hastings and Prince Edward Regiment in Bellevue, Ontario. I became Holybrooke of the Hasty Ps. That's what we called ourselves. We trained in England for a while before participating in the Allied invasion of Sicily as part of the Canadian First Infantry Division. That was in '43. Most of us were anxious to get into some action. The training in England seemed to last a long time, kind of ironic for me to be back where I was born.

"I saw five months of combat before being wounded and captured. I remember crawling up to a row of hedges, thinking I was well concealed. The Germans must have spotted me because a grenade, one of those potato mashers we called 'em, came flying over the top and landed to my right. The blast stunned me. The shrapnel caught me on the side.

"My ears were ringing so bad I couldn't hear, and I couldn't move at first, or think straight. That's when Randy tried to rescue me. When he came forward the Germans fired several rounds through the hedges and one of them hit him in the forehead."

Every time Holybrooke mentioned his friend he became emotional. Andy recognized it as Dash's *dead weight*, something he could relate to from carrying around his own.

"I lost consciousness at some point because the next thing I remember is coming to and being a prisoner of the Germans. Well, a new phase of my war began."

As the two men grew closer they visited more often and Holybrooke's story dripped out. Andy learned of Howard and Bergand, Simpson and Kreiken, unfamiliar names attached to the familiar wounds of war. Holybrooke heard about Camel and Boy Red, the Professor and Yardly.

Speaking about their wars, Andy recognized similarities linking them that transcended their individual experiences. There was something in Holybrooke that reminded Andy of the uncle he was named after, but had never met.

He had told Lisa about Holybrooke's experience.

"Does he have any family?" Lisa had asked. "What about the farmers in Ontario? Wouldn't they have adopted him?"

"No, he was just brought over to work. He hasn't stayed in touch. The only time he's been back to England is with the Canadian Army. They trained there before going to Sicily. The only photograph in his house is of a friend he lost in the war."

"Canadians wouldn't do that, would we? That's child labor."

"I don't know," Andy said. "Didn't you learn about it in school?"

"No, we didn't. That's so sad, not having any family. People say he doesn't have many friends, either."

"He's friendly to me, and he likes having our bees on his land. If he was an orphan in England before coming to Canada, and never married, he wouldn't have any family. I guess he just got busy with his farm."

"We should make sure that doesn't happen to us," Lisa said.

"What?" Andy said, perplexed by Lisa's comment. "Your family is here, and we know lots of people."

"I'm just saying we need to think about having children if we are going to."

Busy with the season, Andy had not had the conversation with Lisa about birth deformities linked to Agent Orange.

❊ ❊ ❊

Holybrooke visited them on their farm, interested in the bees and their production. Andy showed him the processing facilities. With the circular extractors whirring at high speeds, the machines emptied 100 frames of honey with each load, the centrifugal force throwing it against the stainless-steel walls before it pooled into a tank beneath.

"How much honey in there?" Holybrooke asked, having to shout to be heard above the noise.

"Two thousand pounds, when it's full. We use gravity to this point, but we need to get it into the settling tank."

A two-inch line attached to a honey pump on the floor arced upward and disappeared through a circular hole in the ceiling.

"It comes out here," Andy said, showing him a larger tank mounted on a steel frame in an enclosed room. The thick liquid flowed out of the line and disappeared into an opening at the top. A sturdy tap at the bottom was still high enough off the floor to place a food-grade barrel underneath.

"Can I watch you fill a drum?" Holybrooke asked.

Andy took one and popped the lid off. Easing the tap open, the honey flowed in a three-inch stream of golden liquid. The barrel filled within a minute.

"So how much honey would that be?"

"Over six hundred pounds."

"And in the tank?"

"Close to twenty thousand."

Outside, where they could speak without shouting again, Holybrooke said, "Ah, young Andy, did I tell you about finding those urns of honey in Sicily? We could barely lift them but were craving something sweet. Some of the guys in the platoon came and helped when word got out. We weren't supposed to be looting stuff, but most of the guys ate their fill.

"Farley Mowat, you know, the famous author, wrote about it in his book, *The Regiment*. Wrote a couple of them on the war and then about the environment. Farley was my platoon commander, good with a map. With him every step of the way until I was wounded. Never did look him up."

Andy heard more of his story.

"The first time I tried to escape, I didn't get far. It was automatic to be brought before a firing squad. I could sense the German commandant didn't want to have me shot. 'Why is a young lad like you fighting against Germany?' he asked. I was fair-haired and boyish looking. 'Where are you from?' I just had this feeling he wanted to spare me. I told him Germantown, Pennsylvania. It just popped out. I'd never been to the States before, didn't know a thing about the place, but it probably saved me. They put me back in the camp.

"I made good on my second attempt. A patrol of Negro soldiers from the American Army found me. They fed me some of their rations, tried to fatten me up a little. Had a jolly good time asking me about Canada. None of them was even from any of the northern states, maybe just one guy from Chicago. They repatriated me back to the Canadians. The war was just about over, so I never went back to a combat role."

❀ ❀ ❀

The supers steadily filled with nectar. When Andy checked on the progress of the bees, the full cells of honey in the frames glistened when the sun reflected off the thick liquid. The full boxes weighed up to eighty pounds and were sent back to the hives again after being harvested. Extracting began in the middle of July, and the nectar flowed into September.

The locations on alfalfa came into a second bloom after the first cut of hay. The weather stayed warm and the new blossoms filled with nectar. The bees produced a good crop, 220 pounds per hive,

Andy and Lisa realized after tallying the final numbers.

The workload of the busy season demanded Andy's attention. He still thought about Black Henry's death, but it gradually receded into the background and merged with the other dead of the war, joining the memory of Camel and Boy Red, the Professor and Yardly, Paul Voight and Tahlequah. Working to exhaustion with the harvest, if they visited Andy in his sleep he didn't wake or remember.

Septembers for a beekeeper in the Peace River Region were even busier than the harvest, which had to be wrapped up before feeding the bees. He had thousands of honey supers to bring in and store after extracting. The length of the nectar flow into September delayed preparing the hives for winter. October could not always be relied on to be warm enough, like the previous year when the snows and cold temperatures arrived early and he'd learned about Black Henry's pending execution.

In November, Andy loaded his truck with buckets of honey to distribute to the farmers who had provided locations for his bees. Not finding Dash Holybrooke in his house, he looked for him in the outbuildings, then on a hunch drove to where he'd kept his bees. At the crest of the field Holybrooke sat in his pickup overlooking the view where the wilderness bordered his farm.

November in the far north was often bleak, turning cold and damp. The leaves of the poplars, a brilliant yellow in October, had succumbed to the cooler weather and lay as mulch on the forest floor, the trees barren beneath grey skies that threatened freezing rain.

Not acknowledging Andy's presence until he tapped on the window of his truck, Holybrooke sat behind the wheel. After motioning for him to get in, he returned his gaze to the view overlooking the field he had carved out of the wilderness. Andy noticed Holybrooke's rifle against the seat. Not unusual, the somber mood more of a concern than the gun.

"Seeing this view is what made me homestead this land," Holybrooke said.

Andy kept quiet.

"It took a lot of effort to clear. I'm still trying to improve it, planting clover, picking the rocks out of the soil, burning the brush in the wind rows. Sometimes I ask myself 'What for?' Some days I no longer feel connected to it, like all the work I've done has drained the life right out of me. And there's no one to pass it on to, young Andy.

"Don't think I'm feeling sorry for myself. I had opportunities to maybe marry, have a family. I guess it scared me. Not coming from one myself I wasn't sure I would know how to start one, or what to do once I had one. Who doesn't have a mother or a father? Other orphans, like me, but the homes for children were horrible places. I was always running off, never knowing what I was looking for but needing to keep searching. Maybe if I'd been adopted, things would have turned out different.

"It was the same with leaving the farm in Ontario. At least I was well fed, but is that what a good life is, just getting enough to eat? So, I'm restless again at sixteen and into the Army and then the war. And it took the best friend I'll ever have, and while he was trying to rescue me."

Holybrooke shook his head slowly. Neither spoke for a minute. Andy, tongue-tied like he was in the war sometimes, searched for the right words to help.

"Do you have time for tea?" Andy asked. "I brought you some honey."

Holybrooke, his thick fingers wrapped around the steering wheel, reached for the ignition with his right hand and started the truck. "Sure, let's go have a tea, young Andy."

In the house he opened the wood stove and threw some kindling in to reignite it, the coals nearly extinguished. "Nothing like a fire and a cup of tea to warm us. Is this honey from the clover field?"

"Some of it will be. It's clover, but it all gets mixed together in the settling tanks."

"How's your friend Sammy?"

"He's okay. I don't get to talk to him much during the harvest we're so busy. I don't think I told you why he was visiting."

"I don't recall that you did."

"A friend from our platoon in the war had just died."

"Ah, you'd stayed in touch?"

"No, we'd just found him before he died."

A new phase of their friendship began that day. Holybrooke's somber mood receded over conversation, which led to more reflection. Andy told him about Black Henry's execution and how he'd saved his life late in his tour, putting his hand on Andy's shoulder so he wouldn't go after one of the new guys screaming and panicked from his wound. The fight soon shifted, and Andy had gotten to him soon enough. Nobody died. He spoke of the helplessness of not being able to prevent his execution or ease his suffering, and of the guilt over his death.

He told Holybrooke of the sorrow from many deaths, how they came to him in his sleep, the napalmed children and the women in the rice paddy.

Holybrooke nodded, and Andy knew he understood with a depth emanating from his own experiences.

Andy spoke of his missing uncle. Holybrooke poured more tea.

"You don't know where he is?"

"I don't know where to look for him," Andy said. "He was a medic, too, but with the Marines in the Pacific. That's all I know."

Holybrooke sat without saying more, looking pensive. "Probably at the end of a road somewhere," he said when he finally spoke. "You say he grew up on a pecan farm?"

Andy nodded. It had already crossed his mind.

❋ ❋ ❋

The idea came to him on the way home. Like a flickering flame that suddenly bursts into a raging fire, it consumed him. He didn't know if it would appeal to Lisa. He would have to proceed carefully, pick a good time to have the conversation with her. He didn't know why he'd not thought of it before, but now that he had, it gave him a purpose like he hadn't experienced since being introduced to beekeeping. This went beyond choosing what to do for a living. This would soothe his demons. Excited, he couldn't remember feeling this content.

"Ah, young Andy," Lisa teased him when he walked through the door, late for supper. She seemed to know he had just come from Dash Holybrooke's.

CHAPTER
THIRTY-FIVE

California Coast
February 1984

SOUTH OF BIG Sur Andy turned onto a trail off Highway One. Following the contours of a stream cascading through a boulder-strewn course to the ocean, the roadway ended where the creek emptied into the sea. A beach stretched for a mile between two mountains which jutted against the water at the shoreline. Waves pounding the rocks nearby foamed in the turbulence and sent a salty spray into the air, which the wind carried to where Andy and Lisa stood looking at the view.

"This is so incredible," she said. "Let's walk along the shore."

The sand, wet and smoothed from a higher tide and a light drizzle, extended undisturbed before them. Their steps left imprints, leaving a meandering trail erased by incoming waves.

As the remnants of a morning fog dissipated, Andy heard the bark of a seal and saw a herd resting on the beach. They approached quietly and walked among the animals, close enough to look into their eyes. Not wanting to disturb them, they sat on a log that had washed onto the shore.

"There is something so intelligent when you look into their eyes," Lisa said. "They know we are not here to harm them, but just be quietly among them, share something special, at least for us."

They sat tightly against one another, not interrupting the moment. Andy could tell Lisa was enthralled. She'd grown up around cows, and her fondest memories were of the annual cattle drives taking the herd by horseback to their summer pastures. Seeing so many seals basking on the sands of the California beach triggered strong emotions.

"That was perfect," she said, as they walked towards their vehicle. "I think we should come here again."

Arriving in Morro Bay by early afternoon, they found a cafe overlooking the harbor and ordered lunch. Neither Andy nor Lisa had seen the ocean as children. They had taken two extra days to spend time together on the scenic coastal route on the way to Sammy's. Driving along the ocean reminded Andy of his California days in the Army. Now, only a few hours from Barstow, he grew pensive thinking about the reason for their visit.

After lunch, he pulled into a Union 76 service station for fuel, remembering the bright-orange neon lights of the logo so visible in the San Francisco skyline during his days at the Presidio. The attendant, a man about his age, walked out of the garage with a slight limp and began fueling the vehicle.

"You want it filled?" he asked.

Andy nodded. Something familiar in the man's manner reminded him of Eli from the war. He hadn't thought of him for years but wondered where he might be.

"Where you headed?" he asked Andy.

"To see a friend," he said, vaguely.

"From the war?"

Andy nodded a second time, not even surprised at the question because he already knew the attendant was a veteran.

"It's nice that he survived. What unit you with?"

"Ninth Infantry," Andy answered.

"Americal," the attendant said, continuing to fill the vehicle. "Where you all coming from?"

"Northern Alberta," Andy said.

"How'd you get all the way up there?"

Andy shrugged, the answer too complicated for a short explanation.

"I've moved around quite a bit myself," the man said, seeming to understand. He hung the nozzle back on the dispenser. Andy paid him the exact amount and thanked him.

"You have a good visit with your friend, now, brother."

"Take care of yourself," Andy said.

When they were back in the truck Lisa asked, "How did you know he was a veteran?"

"I just knew," he said. "Something in his manner, I guess, maybe in the eyes?"

"That's weird," she said, "how you guys know."

They drove for a while comfortable in their silence.

"Do you think he will like us?" Lisa asked.

"He might need some time to adjust," Andy said. "He's experienced a lot of trauma, won't say a word to anyone. They figure it's temporary because he seems to have normal intelligence, but nobody knows for sure. He's not likely to get placed. He's four, doesn't speak, and has a deformity on one of his hands. They figure that's from birth."

Lisa sighed. "I'm so nervous. Are you having any doubts?"

"I'm not. It's something I need to do. Thank you for understanding that."

Sammy kept Andy informed of veterans' issues. He wanted to show him the new center opened in San Bernardino for the soldiers of the Vietnam War. They would meet a man named Tran there, an acquaintance of Sammy's.

"Don't be fooled by Tran's unassuming manner," Sammy told him. "He's well-connected in many circles. He survived the war as a Buddhist monk treating the casualties of both sides. He likes the fact you were a medic."

Sammy, an American version of Tran, had a lot of contacts in the veteran community and the steadily growing number of Vietnamese fleeing their homeland. Andy had turned to his friend for help once again.

"This boy is special to Tran. They don't know any details beyond the fact he has suffered great trauma. He arrived in Malaysia without parents on one of the boats. All Tran knows is what the survivors told him. The boy's mother was raped, then killed by the pirates, and his father thrown overboard when he tried to help her."

Andy shifted uncomfortably in his seat. Boat people fleeing Vietnam had been in the news.

"Tran doesn't know what to make of your request for a hard-to-place child. His deformed hand is consistent with the birth defects from Agent Orange. Because of that and his muteness, he just wants to be sure the boy is going to a good home. And you want to know something interesting?"

Andy looked at his friend. Sammy was as proactive as Andy was passive, beginning to come out of his shell only after deciding to try and adopt a Vietnamese child made homeless by the chaos his original country had helped create.

"They call him 'Henry.'"

"Henry?"

Sammy looked at Andy, grinning. "Yeah, figure that one out."

All of these Henrys in his life. Now all the way from Vietnam the name reemerged in an orphaned child. *How strange*, Andy thought.

❋ ❋ ❋

The vet center, on the ground floor of a strip mall, looked nondescript from the outside. That changed after entering through the aluminum-framed door. The presence of the Vietnam War was everywhere.

A printed sign in bold letters—*WELCOME HOME*—stood out above a display case with paraphernalia from the war. A helmet laden with graffiti on the camouflage cover rested on the top shelf. Inscriptions of *short* alongside the peace symbol adorned one side. A bullet hole piercing the metal had a circle drawn tightly around it. Larger ones concentrically placed completed the *bull's eye*. Names were written beside it—*WILL, JIMMY, MEMPHIS, BRETT, CRAWFORD.* Andy searched the helmet for more hidden meanings. Mesmerized and transported back to the war, he gazed at it until his concentration was interrupted by Sammy, who had his fist raised in a black power salute to the vet manning the reception desk in a wheelchair. Returning the gesture, the man rotated his wheels with his free hand to face the visitors.

"Hey, brother," he said to Sammy. "How's my man."

"I brought somebody I'd like you to meet," Sammy said. "This was my doc in the Nam."

"No shit, the one living in Canada? Welcome home, Doc," he said, the greeting common among veterans who'd not been warmly received right after the war. "I'm Vernon Tucker." Andy reached across the desk and shook hands.

"Vernon was Fourth Infantry," Sammy said, referring to a division north of them operating out of Pleiku. "We're here to meet Tran," Sammy said, getting down to business.

"Oh yeah," Tucker said, "the head witch doctor wants a word with you two before Tran arrives. He's in his office, room 303."

Andy followed Sammy past a row of cluttered filing cabinets to four offices in the back. Three had their doors closed, but Andy saw through the windows they were occupied. In each, a man sat at a desk facing the lone visitor in a chair opposite him.

Sammy stopped in front of the last door and tapped on the outside before entering. A casually dressed man in corduroy pants and a clean but faded green shirt stood and greeted them.

"Sam." He nodded. "Good to see you." He offered his hand to shake across the desk. "You must be Andy Parks," he said, not waiting for any further introductions. "I'm Doctor Terrence Wynn, head clinical psychologist. Welcome to the San Bernardino Vet Center."

Andy noticed a photograph with him in jungle fatigues, rifle slung over his shoulder, displayed prominently on the desk, answering any questions about his combat bonafides before they arose.

"Tran wanted me to speak with you before he arrived. He's self-conscious about his English, fluent, but accented. He has a few questions."

"An interrogation," Sammy joked.

Andy's stomach tightened.

"A screening," Dr. Wynn said, "and as a favor to Tran. We go back to Vietnam. He's doing good work. We don't normally involve ourselves with adoptions. We have no jurisdiction with US Immigration, certainly not Canada's."

Dr. Wynn paused for a moment like he was searching for the right words. "Tran's very Buddhist, a former monk, and quite frankly, the most compassionate man I've ever met. We're not looking to stand in the way of this boy finding a home, especially a good one. We'll keep it relaxed. You don't mind if Sam stays?"

"Of course not," Andy said, his tension easing.

"Sam has done a lot of outreach in the vet community. The fact that he approached us about you has a lot of sway."

Andy nodded.

"You're married, and have a farm in Canada?"

"A beekeeping operation," Andy said.

"That's good," Dr. Wynn stated. "How long have you had your farm?"

"Seven years."

"Any alcohol or drug issues?"

"He never even smoked any pot in the Nam," Sammy answered. "And I've visited his bee farm. There's too much work to do much drinking."

Wynn laughed and looked at Andy. "You have to understand what we are dealing with here. I have guys literally coming out of the hills twenty years after their tours," he said.

"To some, we're all a bunch of ticking time bombs about to go off at any moment," Sammy joked.

Dr. Wynn laughed again. "I know the type. You've done well," he said, looking at Andy. "Sam says you were a medic?"

"Yes."

"Why adopt?"

"I'm worried about all of the birth defects caused by Agent Orange. I couldn't live with myself if I had a deformed child because of my exposure."

Wynn shook his head in the affirmative, not making eye contact for a few seconds. Andy sensed a wistfulness in the doctor and wondered if the issue had struck close to home.

"There's that, too," he said. "The half-life for the chemical is eleven years, but that's only when it's exposed to the elements. None of us knew that right after the war."

Andy felt shame and guilt for how American forces destroyed the Vietnam countryside. They had dropped everything on the landscape and its people—napalm, defoliating chemicals and B-52 bombs—all meant to maim and destroy even the insect and plant life.

By the end of the interview it was three veterans of the same war talking.

They waited for Tran in a visitor's lounge. Not sure what to expect, Andy pictured everything from an emaciated Vietnamese man in orange robes to a scholarly-looking man in glasses and a Western suit and tie.

Tran matched none of the images in Andy's head. Tall for a Vietnamese, and slender, he wore no glasses. He stood erect without the appearance of being uncomfortable. Dressed casually in a pair of tan pants and white shirt without a tie, he bowed slightly before shaking hands.

In accented English, easy to understand, he got right to business without being abrupt.

"Thank you for coming," he began. "It is about the children we are concerned. It is good that you see that." He bowed slightly towards Andy again while seated. "This boy is very troubled, but a good boy," he emphasized. "We don't know all of his story. You are married?"

"Yes," Andy said. "My wife, Lisa, very much wants to meet this boy. He is named Henry?"

"Henry Vong," Tran replied.

"It is a special name for me," Andy said.

"We shall have to meet your wife, Lisa, of course. Henry doesn't speak. His left hand is without a middle and index finger, probably from the chemicals," Tran said. "You are in Alberta. We can contact the proper agencies. Canada is accepting many Vietnamese refugees. The children are everybody's priorities."

Standing again, Tran excused himself. "We are very busy with the children." He bowed, slightly, shook hands, and left as quietly as he had arrived.

※ ※ ※

Tran arranged to meet them at a house in Glendale, a suburb next to Los Angeles. Lisa paced, then brushed her hair and checked her outfit in a hallway mirror before they left. Andy kept his emotions hidden, saying little, but suspected he felt like Lisa.

"This is a big change for us," she said on the drive. "I try and put myself in his shoes. The news has pictures of how crowded those boats are, full of desperate people, hungry and thirsty. Most of them are attacked by pirates before they land. Nobody knows how many are lost at sea. I can't imagine seeing my parents killed. I mean, I lost my father when I was nine, and that was bad enough. But I didn't witness his death."

Tears formed. "I think about it, though, my father, alone, in such despair that he sees no way out but to shoot himself. How it came to that. What he must have been feeling. But I still had my mother, as difficult as she can be at times." Lisa laughed, nervously. "Here I am anxious over meeting a four-year-old child, babbling away, making all kinds of connections to our experiences before we have even met."

Lisa pulled a tissue out of her purse and wiped her eyes. "This is my way of giving back too, you know."

"I know," he said.

"You are a good husband . . . most of the time."

Andy smiled.

"Just don't let it go to your head."

"Tran has an amazing network of connections," he said. "I think he already knows this is a good fit, for the child and us. He's such a warm person."

"He's a Buddhist monk?"

"A former monk, I think. You will meet him today. He was a medic during the war, treating a lot of the civilians who were wounded on both sides."

"Like you?"

Andy thought for a moment. "Yeah," he said, "I guess it was kind of the same thing. Here we are." Andy parked on the street in front of a newer house similar to the others in the neighborhood. "There are five children being cared for here, all orphans. Little Henry is the oldest."

Tran met them at the door with the foster parents, a couple who looked a few years older than Lisa and Andy.

"Welcome," she said, in accented English. "I am Mai Linh, and this is my husband, Thomas."

Andy recognized the name as Vietnamese. Her husband stepped forward and offered his hand to shake.

"Thomas worked for the State Department in Vietnam, where we met," she said, explaining their mixed-race marriage. "Please come in."

Tran, standing inconspicuously behind Mai Linh, came forward to greet Andy with his slight bow before shaking hands. He introduced himself to Lisa.

"You come from a farm in Canada," Tran said to her. "In Vietnam we grow much rice, of course. My family farmed near Hue, an ancient capital in our country. Too many sons for the land, so I became a monk." He laughed.

Andy could see how at ease Lisa felt with him. "Yes," she said, "and my family has five daughters, and very much land to grow wheat and barley." Tran smiled warmly and invited them to meet the children.

All five were playing in an area of the large living room set up for them with toys, the most noticeable being large plastic blocks of different colors. An elderly Vietnamese woman sat on a sofa nearby watching them. She smiled shyly and spoke in Vietnamese to Mai Linh.

"My mother wishes to welcome you," she said. Seeing the guests, three of the children came closer, and a little girl wrapped her arms around Lisa's leg and clung to it. Lisa knelt and hugged her and when she stood held the child in her arms. Andy recognized Henry immediately. By himself, he turned away from the adults and continued concentrating on pushing one of the plastic blocks near a playpen while the toddler in it watched him.

Andy stood for a moment looking at him. Before he moved towards Henry, another toddler had attached himself to Andy's leg, and the memory of a Vietnamese orphanage on the outskirts of Can Tho came back to him.

There had been many children in raised cribs in the large room of a Catholic church. Several Vietnamese nuns cared for them. The grounds were pleasant and filled with young children who could walk. A wading pool had been filled with water where some of them cooled themselves while they played. Andy walked among them and sat on a bench where several crowded around him wanting to sit close to him and in his lap. He realized later he had come for the human warmth and innocence of the orphans, everyone in need of what the war had taken from them, the simple grace of human affection.

Andy bent and picked up the child at his feet, a boy of about three. He carried him to a couch near where Henry Vong played, set him down, and kneeled next to the boy they were hoping to adopt. Unable to make eye contact, Andy remained quiet, not wanting to force the boy to interact. He noticed the deformed hand, the left, looking claw-like with the index and middle finger missing. A deep affinity with the child came over him, and he reached for the incomplete hand with both of his. He felt a power now that had failed to save all the wounded from the war. *These hands could heal now,* he thought. Little Henry, not looking at him, leaned against him without pulling away.

Andy looked up and saw Lisa still holding the little girl, her head resting on his wife's shoulder, while she watched them. Snug in her arms, looking content enough to stay there forever.

CHAPTER THIRTY-SIX

Crooked Creek, Alberta
February 1985

THEIR ROUTINE REPEATED itself every morning. Andy stepped outside, held the door open for Little Henry, the dog followed them out.

Wearing winter sets of coveralls, the man and the boy trudged through the path made in the snow from numerous trips to the shop set up in the honey house.

Bella, a golden retriever, established her routine within theirs. Initially taking the lead on the path, she circled back behind Henry once satisfied no dangers lurked ahead.

In the months since Little Henry's arrival, he followed Andy everywhere. Still mute, Andy knew from looking into his eyes that he absorbed information like a sponge. He indicated needs with two simple tugs, and mimicked Andy's every movement.

He duplicated everything for the boy. Shedding their blue winter coveralls in the heated shop, they put on a lighter pair for their inside work, hanging on hooks next to each other and in the traditional white worn for beekeeping. Lisa had altered a pair to fit Little Henry.

She had balked at the boy being around the saws, but Andy set up a separate workstation for him in the corner and bought a set of protective covers for his ears. Two tugs from the boy, and Andy, who never wore them, understood that Henry expected him to have a pair, too.

This week they sorted brood chambers in preparation for the spring. Henry had his own hive tool, smaller, and busied himself scraping excess wax off the top bars on the frames while Andy arranged them into the supers.

"The frames we use in the middle of the brood chambers," he explained, "need empty cells for the queen to lay her eggs. Then we need some pollen and honey in the ones on the edges." He showed everything to the boy, who remained mute.

The frames fit perfectly in the gap of his deformed hand where the index and middle finger should have been. Andy wasn't sure what he was going to do with the boy when he got busy with the bees.

"You have your little beekeeper," Lisa told him. "Just remember there are child labor laws in the country. Isn't that what Dash Holybrooke regretted? Having to work so hard as a boy? Our Little Henry is only five."

Andy was pleased that he showed an early interest in the farm. They collected tools that fit his small hands, a hammer and screwdrivers and pliers. Lisa worried, but when Andy did need to use a saw, he made sure the boy was safely at his bench wearing protective ear and eye ware and out of the way of any possible kickbacks.

Andy and Lisa did not know Henry's exact birth date. They picked one suggested by the doctors.

"The most important thing is security and stability for the children right now," the child psychologist had told them. "In Henry's case, we don't recommend school for another year. Given time and the love and stability every child needs, he may resume speaking. We think his muteness is trauma induced."

Andy liked the psychologist, a kindly woman in her fifties assigned by the immigration officials to monitor their adoptees.

Their caseworker in Edmonton expressed concern the children would be so far from a speech pathologist in the larger center.

"But he doesn't speak yet," Lisa told the psychologist during one of their monthly treks to Edmonton so officials could monitor the child's progress.

"City people," the psychologist confided in Andy and Lisa, "would do well to visit a farm and get their hands dirty. Trust me, your children are fortunate where they are."

Hong Kim, the little girl who had rested in Lisa's arms the day they had met Henry, had come home with them, too. Not on that first trip because there were official procedures and channels to contend with, but it had progressed smoothly. Lisa had cried at their parting.

"I have never believed in love at first sight," she told Andy, "but that little girl is making me rethink that. We need to adopt her too. Can Tran look into that?"

A year younger than Henry, they had to choose a birthday for Hong Kim also. She stuck as close to Lisa as Henry did to Andy. "You are my golden rose," Lisa whispered in her ear, the literal translation of her name into English.

Bella, the golden retriever, proved to be worth her weight in gold. Every evening, when Andy tucked Little Henry into bed, she hopped up with him and stayed for the night. Henry delighted in her.

"That dog is so good for him," Andy told Lisa. "I think she knows more than we do about helping him."

"It's certainly an upgrade in her sleeping arrangements," Lisa joked, "a nice warm bed off the floor. You know Henry saves part of his supper for her and feeds her a snack before they go to sleep."

Henry's first sound was laughter at Bella burrowing beneath a snowbank at the scent of a prairie chicken nesting. As the front of her disappeared, her tail straightened, and she vanished in the soft snow. The boy pointed and squealed with excitement when a bird flew out, disturbed flakes shimmering in the air as the winter sun, low on the horizon, shone on them.

Andy read to Henry each night after tucking him into bed while Lisa did the same for Hong Kim. The boy would often be asleep before Andy finished, but he continued speaking softly and watched him slumber, his intense dark eyes hidden in sleep. Andy knew he would never know his complete story. How strange the boy had experienced the terrors of modern-day pirates while other boys his age only knew them through stories of adventure.

After patting Bella, Henry would switch places with Lisa for a few minutes to say good night to Hong Kim. Unlike her brother, she was speaking like any four-year-old and asking questions.

"Why doesn't Henry talk?" she asked one morning at breakfast.

"He will," Andy answered, "when he is ready. Not everyone has something to say all of the time."

"Will his hand get better, too?"

"No," he answered, searching for the right thing to say. "Sometimes we are born with some things missing."

"Oh," she said.

Andy, relieved Hong Kim seemed satisfied with his answer, watched for Henry's reaction. He continued to eat his porridge without showing any outward signs of understanding the conversation. Andy felt like he needed to say more but couldn't think of the right words.

"I can talk when I want to," Henry said in perfect English, "and still do things with my hand."

Andy, inwardly stunned, glanced at Lisa, who was already looking at him. Struggling not to show surprise and make Little Henry self-conscious and revert inside his shell, Andy searched his mind for what to say next. He didn't need to say anything.

"What do you do in the honey house?" Hong Kim asked Henry.

"Sort brood chambers," he answered, matter-of-factly.

"How do you do that?"

"You have to find frames the queen can lay eggs in and have

pollen and honey in some of them."

"Oh, can I sort brood chambers, too?" she asked.

"You have to learn something about bees first," Henry told her.

Andy and Lisa continued glancing at one another without being obvious about their surprise. Overjoyed that Henry not only spoke, but carried on a conversation with his sister, Andy kept quiet until the conversation lagged.

"Well, little man, is it time to get to work?"

Henry shook his head in the affirmative.

Lisa accompanied them to the door. "You're not taking my little girl out to sort brood chambers," she whispered to Andy.

"How else is she going to learn?" he teased. "But Henry says she needs to know more about bees first."

"Just a normal family having a conversation at breakfast," she said, pulling Andy aside before he went out. She smiled broadly and squeezed Andy's arm. "Now I'm speechless."

Andy pulled into his best spring location two miles east of their home place. Little Henry sat in the passenger seat of the three-ton truck, his bee veil already zipped into place on his modified set of coveralls. That was the deal struck with Lisa.

Appalled that Andy even considered taking the boy beekeeping with him, she had insisted on specific conditions.

"I can't believe I'm even considering this," she said. "He's five years old."

"He's a precocious child," Andy said, "totally fascinated with the bees. I've tried reasoning with him, but he insists he will be fine."

"Who are the parents here? It's irresponsible. What if something happens?"

"He'll be in the truck for the unloading. Bella's coming too."

"That makes a difference?"

"She's really good with him."

"At beekeeping? Honestly, Andy. He's to have his veil on at all times. I know he goes around mimicking your every move, so you might have to actually wear yours once in a while."

The willows were in bloom, and the bees needed moving to their spring locations. He had gone over and over with Little Henry how he would have to follow all the rules set down. If he forgot, Andy would bring him back to the house.

So far so good. Andy could see him from the Bobcat as he set the bee pallets in the yard. Henry watched, veil on, through the window of the truck.

Finished unloading twenty-five pallets with four colonies on each of them, he drove the forklift back on the trailer. A few bees circled, orienting to their new location. The cool of the early spring morning kept most of them inside the hives.

Andy took a solar fencer from the cab and told Henry he could come out.

"Come on, Bella," Henry said, speaking like a normal five-year-old. The dog hopped out but crept underneath the truck. "What's wrong with Bella?" he asked.

"She doesn't want to get stung," Andy said. "Sometimes they're a little bit angry after we move them."

"Oh." Andy could see him thinking. "But they aren't stinging us."

"No," Andy said, "but Bella doesn't have a veil on and snaps at them when they fly close to her, and that gets them mad. Come with me so we can connect this solar panel to the fence, so the bears won't bother the bees."

"Don't they snap at the bees and get stung?"

"Well yes, but they eat the brood and break into the hive, so I guess the bee stings are worth it when they're hungry. We put an electric current through the fence to keep them out of the bee yard."

Henry looked at the thin wires on the fence.

"It doesn't have electricity in it until we hook this up," Andy said.

"Then it keeps them out, but the bee stings don't hurt the bear?"

Andy marveled at the same thing. A bear could take hundreds of stings on the nose and in the mouth and throat while swallowing mouthfuls of brood, but a little electricity in a wire was enough to keep them from getting into the yard.

"I guess they just don't mind bee stings as much as they do electricity."

"Oh," Henry said. *Finally,* Andy thought, *an explanation the boy accepts. There's absolutely nothing wrong with his intelligence.*

That evening, Andy sat on the edge of Little Henry's bed, as proud as any father. Their week of moving the bees into their spring locations had gone smoothly. Attentive and well behaved, the boy had exceeded Andy's expectations.

He continued looking at him after he fell asleep, tired from the early mornings and busy week. When Henry rolled onto his side, his deformed hand came out from under the sheet and rested on the covers.

Andy felt gratitude that Henry, safely tucked into a warm bed, had come into his life. *What is your story, little man, the dangers and tragedies you have already faced in your life? Such courage and resilience you have shown.*

Seeing the incomplete hand, anger surfaced and coexisted with the love he felt for Henry. Alarmed at the emotion, and aware of its duality, a memory transported Andy back to Vietnam fifteen years ago.

His platoon had been in a firefight at the edge of a village. White Henry walked point and spotted movement behind a row of shrubs near several thatched dwellings. Both sides opened fire, the contact fleeting. The element of surprise taken from them, the Viet Cong vanished into the jungle next to the village.

They found a casualty in their search through the huts, a young boy lying on a mat with his intestines spilling out of his abdomen. When Andy knelt to have a look, his dark eyes stared into his. He couldn't believe the stoicism of the child, fully conscious and not emitting a whimper.

An older woman wailed in the background as Andy did the only thing he could think of, dousing the intestines with a saline solution from an intravenous pack and placing them back in the boy's abdomen before using a large bandage to hold them in place. He waited for a medevac.

No way the child lives, he thought, *another senseless casualty in the war.*

Andy left Henry's bedroom and searched through a box of old photographs and papers, piling stacks of folders and packets of developed pictures on the floor as he rummaged. Lisa heard the commotion and came into the room.

"Andy, what are you looking for? Is everything okay?"

Barely acknowledging her presence, he uttered a quick response and continued digging through his files.

"It's in here somewhere," he muttered.

"What's in there, honey? What could you possibly need to find tonight? Andy, you're scaring me."

"Don't be," he said. "I get it now. After all these years, I'm starting to get it."

He rummaged some more and found a newspaper clipping from the Nam Sammy had sent him. A picture taken at the 29th Evac showed Miss New Jersey of all people with her arm around a Vietnamese child, shirtless, but with a large bandage over his abdomen. They were both looking into the camera. Below, the caption read, *HIS LUCK'S IMPROVING.*

Tran Van Hay, 5, is the envy of thousands of Vietnam servicemen who only wish they could be held by Miss New Jersey, who is accompanying Miss America on a tour of Vietnam. Tran is a patient at the U.S. Army's 29th Evacuation Hospital in Binh Thuy in the Mekong Delta, where he is recovering from stomach wounds.

Andy stared at the clipping, cut out of the *Stars and Stripes*.

Nothing was too crazy for the Nam, he thought. *First, we wound him with our firepower, save his life by medevacing him to our field hospital, and Miss New Jersey arrives to make it all better.*

"I'm not the crazy one," he said, handing the article to Lisa. "He was Henry's age when I put him on a medevac. The stomach wounds they're referring to were actually his intestines ripped open by a bullet that sliced through his abdomen."

"Then you saved his life," Lisa said.

"It never felt that way," he said. "We never should have been there in the first place. It took a lot of people to wound him, and a lot of people to save him. I was just one part of a great big mess.

"But I get it now. Our Henry is just doing the same thing I am, trying to create stability from the chaos and pain. Only I was a young man, not a boy. He has experienced unspeakable traumas, and we are going to give him a good life, deformed hand and all."

"Yes we are," said Lisa, "and Hong Kim, our little girl. We'll keep them safe and they will have a good life."

Andy moved a stack of papers off a chair and sat down, suddenly exhausted. "I don't know how I could have forgotten. Seeing Henry sleeping, so vulnerable, and with his deformed hand triggered the memory. They were the same age."

"You must have repressed it," Lisa said.

"I suppose."

"The beekeeping is so important to him," Andy said, "the glimpse into such an ordered and structured world. The bees are so determined, such a healthy part of nature. I'm so glad we didn't keep that from him."

"I see that now," she said.

Andy started organizing the mess of papers from the folders, then stopped. "The heck with it, I'll put everything back in the morning. We need to talk some more."

"Would you like a cup of tea before bed?" Lisa asked.

"Sure."

While Lisa made the tea, Andy peeked in on Henry again. Bella raised her head and her tail thumped on the bed twice before resuming her own sleep. His little beekeeper slept on.

"I don't think the two Andys ever reconciled, not completely," he told Lisa after they sat down with their tea. "The person before the war has never been the same since, and the two have never been in harmony. Nobody got the same person back after I came home. Things are better now. I'm more content than I've ever been, but I don't suppose I'll ever be the most normal guy you could have married."

"I suppose not," Lisa teased, "but I get the complete Andy now, the one who is new and whole again, the best Andy."

"Don't get carried away." He smiled.

"We've carved this reality out together, you know. Now we have Little Henry and Hong Kim to complete it."

"Yes we do," he said. "I suppose we should introduce them to their grandparents in Oklahoma this winter, if we have any kind of a year."

"Okay."

"Henry Clay is pleased to have a grandson with the same name, although he's perplexed, wondering how he came by it in Vietnam."

"I guess none of us will ever know. There are a lot of Henrys in your life."

"Yes, and ours is a child prodigy in beekeeping," he joked.

"Now don't you get carried away," Lisa said. "I think that mostly applies to music and mathematics."

"Are you sure you're ready for a visit to Oklahoma, meet the rest of the relatives?"

"They can't be any worse than mine."

"There's only one way to find out."

CHAPTER
THIRTY-SEVEN

Afton, Oklahoma
December 1985

ANDY HAD KEPT his promise to his mother. Even though he'd established a life far from Oklahoma, he'd stayed in touch, visiting occasionally and writing letters, just as he had from Vietnam. With his uncle's whereabouts still unknown, Andy tried not to broaden the hole left in his mother's life.

Arriving during the Christmas festivities with the grandkids was a good time to visit. While Rebecca fussed over the children, hugging them and showing them the brightly decorated Christmas tree, Andy and Lisa chatted with Henry Clay. Nearing sixty, his father had lost some of his stoicism, greeting Lisa with warmth. She reciprocated and sat amiably answering questions about her family and life in northern Alberta.

Overwhelmed by the attention, Little Henry joined Andy on the couch, his three-fingered hand tucked into a pocket. Andy worried about overprotecting the boy. His shyness concerned him, but he had shown a remarkable resilience in his young life to even survive. And his affinity for the bees exhibited amazing maturity. He intuitively understood their complex nature. While many adults scurried from even the possibility of a bee sting, the boy accepted them as part of beekeeping without fear or complaint.

Once the children were bathed and in their pajamas, Rebecca stopped fussing long enough to allow Lisa to excuse herself to tuck them in for the night.

"It's been a long day," she said. "They were so excited about meeting their grandparents in Oklahoma. It's all Hong Kim could talk about on the trip."

"I won't be long," said Andy.

"She's lovely," said Rebecca after Lisa had left.

Henry Clay dozed in his chair.

"Your aunt Ruby would like to drop by in the morning to meet Lisa and the children," Rebecca said.

"How's she doing now that Roland's died?"

Rebecca shrugged. "You know Ruby. She doesn't let on much about personal things. She's staying on the farm for now. I worry it's too much for her, but she insists she has the help she needs."

Andy nodded. He sensed his mother wished to say more.

"She always felt bad about the way Roland treated you and your friend just before you left Oklahoma, like maybe she was partly to blame."

"She talked to you about that?"

"Yes, after you'd left. We were all so afraid you'd just up and vanish like my brother. You were so troubled after the war and none of us knew what we could do for you. It was the most hopeless feeling."

"There were a lot of things going on," Andy said. "I don't know what any of you could have done. The changes were in me and I just couldn't adjust. I didn't understand them myself."

"I guess we never understood much about how all of these wars can change a person. Thank you for keeping your promise. We are so glad to see you and Lisa, so thankful you're doing well."

Andy smiled at his mother. "I just needed to find some equilibrium after Vietnam. Friends who'd been in the war kept dying even after it ended. Tahlequah's death had a big impact. My world had compressed around me so much that I was living entirely in my head. I wanted out of it, too. I drank to blot out the bleakness that prevailed. Deep down I knew that I wanted to live and have a life, but something needed to change. The only thing I could do to relieve the pressure was to leave."

"Do you think that's what happened to Andrew?" His mother's question surprised Andy.

"I didn't come back the same person that everybody was expecting. I suspect it was the same for Andrew. His marriage was also failing."

"Yes, I remember them having terrible arguments and everything being so turbulent. Andrew wouldn't talk to anyone about it."

"He may not have known how. It was easier to just disappear than to talk about. I also kept things from you because I was ashamed."

"Ashamed? I don't understand, dear. Whatever could you be ashamed about?"

"I don't know that I can fully explain it. It's like a taint that comes back from the war with you for even being near the barbarity. I didn't want any of you to know about what I had witnessed, let alone participated in. It's not how I was raised."

Rebecca was near tears as she looked at Andy. "But you were a medic, dear, helping people."

"Yes, after we'd set the jungle on fire. Both sides were killing people, children among them. There were too many casualties that could not be put back together. I did my best, but the brutality was overwhelming. Right and wrong got blurred and it disturbed me at the deepest level. I just wasn't the same person."

"And that's what we were all trying to do, restore the Andy we knew before the war. I'm so sorry, dear, that we didn't realize."

"Don't be. It's nobody's fault, not within the family. None of us could have known. You can't be blamed for wanting your son back, or for not understanding he would not be the same."

"I didn't know your father before the war, but he and Andrew were so different. Your dad just wanted to get back to normal. Most of the country was feeling that way. It was like your uncle had no normal to get back to. He became so restless and just disappeared. Without admitting it, I think we saw the same in you."

Andy nodded and thought for a moment. He felt great affection for his parents in that moment and admired their ability to be content with their lives. He'd never doubted their love for him.

"Your aunt Ruby has heard from Andrew's friend from the Second World War again."

"Recently?"

"October, I think. She's got his telephone number and address. She thought you might like to talk with him yourself. There are so many unanswered questions. Ruby thinks Andrew may have married again without divorcing, making him a bigamist. He may be in trouble with the law, although that isn't the brother we knew."

Andy thought of his time in prison, also out of character.

"I don't think we'll ever know all of the reasons," he said, "unless we find him, or he gets back in touch. The war has long tentacles that hold on to you and keep pulling you back to it. Some things you don't realize until years later."

"You have a family now. That must feel good."

"Yes, but I was even afraid to have children. Many of the vets were having babies with birth defects caused by all the chemicals used over there. How do you explain to your wife that some things would never be normal because of what happened before we even met? Adopting Little Henry and Hong Kim changed a lot."

"I couldn't imagine life without my children. Lisa has been understanding about not having her own babies?"

"We've had our ups and downs, but she fell in love with Hong Kim at first sight. It would have broken her heart if we couldn't have adopted her. We couldn't have loved our own children more."

"The true meaning of Christian love," Rebecca said. It was the first reference to her religion that she had made.

"I've had a vasectomy," Andy said, "so there's no chance of passing on a deformity from my exposure to the defoliants. Any health problems will be restricted to me."

Rebecca shook her head slowly as tears flowed. "We had no idea. Your friend, Sammy, he is well?"

Andy nodded. "They have a healthy daughter." Andy thought of Black Henry as he told his mother this, deciding not to upset her further by mentioning his death. He remembered Rebecca praying for him, Yardly, and the Professor right after Andy returned from Vietnam. None of them were alive now. He realized he still hid things, preferring to keep them private to avoid more grief.

"Adopting Little Henry and Hong Kim has given more to Lisa and me than we can ever give to them."

"We are so thankful," Rebecca said. "They are delightful and our grandchildren in every way."

❋ ❋ ❋

Ruby arrived in the morning while Rebecca and Lisa were feeding the children. Still overwhelmed by the attention, Little Henry focused on his plate of eggs and potatoes while Hong Kim smiled at the new visitor.

"You must be Lisa," Ruby said as she hugged her. "We are so glad to finally meet you. And who are these darlings?" she asked, kneeling beside the children.

Standing by the doorway, Andy came forward and said hello.

"Aren't you a sight for sore eyes, nephew," she said. "We've missed you." She hugged Andy and stood back to look at him before focusing on the children again. Never at a loss for words, she spoke to Little Henry.

"I hear that you have a dog," she said.

Little Henry looked at her and nodded.

"Does she have a name?"

He nodded again.

"Well, what is it?"

"Bella," he said. "She had to stay at home."

"Would you like to meet my dog?"

Little Henry shook his head yes.

"What is your dog's name?" asked Hong Kim.

"Buddy. Do you think that's a good name?"

They nodded, Little Henry looking serious and Hong Kim smiling, continuing to charm everyone.

❋ ❋ ❋

"This is the number here," Ruby said, handing Andy a notepad.

Lisa and Little Henry were outside getting acquainted with Buddy, an aging but good-natured border collie. Hong Kim sat on Andy's lap in his aunt Ruby's kitchen.

"Richard Fremont," Andy said, reading the information. "He's in Chicago."

The photograph of his uncle in the jungle lay nearby. Andrew was in the middle, flanked by his friends, his aid bag between his legs. Andy always had his nearby.

"Do you know which man is Fremont?"

"I think it's this one, although look at them—they were all just boys."

Andy studied the picture again. More than their youth, he noticed something not hidden by the slight smiles on their faces, which were ones of friendship. The eyes, even in a grainy photograph, showed pain. Andy knew they had already seen and participated in the killing. He'd ask his aunt for a copy on this trip and wondered why he hadn't before.

"When I spoke with him on the phone, I asked him. He remembered bringing the picture years ago, but not any specifics. Said he would be the one with the ears so far off his head. I remember Andrew enlisting in the Navy after Father died. In those days, sixteen was considered old enough to make your own way.

"He was so good with your mother after Dad died. He stood in the middle at the gravesite, an arm around each of us. Rebecca cried and cried. Andrew consoled her as best he could.

"After the funeral we gathered at the farmhouse. We weren't sure yet what was going to happen to the three of us. Father just worked for the Fredericks, the owners. That was when they told Rebecca she could stay with them and that I would go and live with the Harmons on a neighboring orchard.

"Not long after Pearl Harbor was bombed, Andrew went off to war. Life goes on."

Andy thought of Dash Holybrooke, also sixteen, leaving his farm in Canada to sign up. Millions of men were doing the same thing throughout the world.

Andy looked at his aunt, still staring at the photograph. Darker haired than his mother, and greying, sadness in her eyes contrasted with her normally bold manner. The middle child of the three orphans, part of her role would have been as surrogate mother. Vestiges of it remained.

"You look so much like him," she said. "Even the way you speak and rest your chin on your hand resembles him. Your moods and how unsettled you were after returning from Vietnam were so reminiscent of Andrew.

"I understand why you want to find him," she said. "You have so much in common. It came to me the day Roland behaved so badly the last time you were here. We were all so worried about you, and then Roland has to go and pull a stunt like that. He got a piece of my mind afterwards, but I'm so sorry for his behavior."

"The whole country was torn apart by the Vietnam War," he said. "Roland couldn't figure it out any better than anyone else. We were all trying to make sense of the changes going on."

"He didn't have to be so pigheaded about it."

Andy smiled. His aunt had a way of abruptly cutting through nonsense.

"What's pigheaded?" asked Hong Kim, still sitting on Andy's lap.

"It's when men get something foolish in their heads and won't let it go," Ruby told her.

"Oh, can I go play with Buddy, too?" she asked.

Still smiling, Andy lifted her off his lap, and she ran out of the kitchen.

"Should we call Richard Fremont?" Andy asked.

"Time's a wasting," Ruby said.

❊ ❊ ❊

The phone rang twice before a woman's faint voice answered. "Hello."

"May I speak with Richard Fremont?" asked Andy, trying to hide his nervousness.

"I'm afraid that won't be possible," the woman said. "My husband is very ill and cannot come to the phone. May I ask who this is and the reason for the call?"

"Of course," said Andy. "I'm terribly sorry. My name is Andy Parks, the nephew of a good friend of your husband's. My uncle and he were in the South Pacific together."

A long pause followed. "Perhaps I should get Richard."

"This is Richard." A gasping man's voice came on the line, coughing after getting the words out.

"Mr. Fremont, I believe you were in the South Pacific with my uncle, Andrew Elrod. We are trying to locate him. None of the family knows where he is. Can you help us with any information?"

Another long silence interspersed with a coughing fit. "Andy saved my life," he finally said.

So, he went by Andy, too.

"Do you know where he might be or how we can find him?"

"It's been a very long time. I can't say."

"Mr. Fremont, can you tell us anything at all about when you knew my uncle. My mother knows nothing and is heartbroken that she has lost touch with her brother. She would be grateful for any information. You have said he saved your life?"

"At Edson's Ridge," he stated. "That's where we were both wounded."

Andy was unfamiliar with the battle. "That was in the South Pacific?"

"Yes, in the Solomons, Guadalcanal. We had landed during a storm and took the airfield easier than we thought. I think we surprised the Japanese. We held on to it for a month before the Japs got serious about trying to take it back. They had to go through us to do that, on the ridge they named Edson, after our battalion commander.

"I was shot in the arm and bleeding badly. The Japs were all over us and Andy shot one just before he stabbed me with his bayonet. He couldn't get it in very far before he died. I remember your uncle kneeling beside me getting the bleeding stopped, telling me I'd be okay. Then, he went down, shot somewhere in the gut. That's the last I remember. I woke up in the hospital. Don't remember how I got there. I thought Andy had died. A few days later we saw each other on the same ward. I was never so glad to see another person in my life. We hurt ourselves laughing we was so glad, till we nearly busted our guts open again."

Andy wanted to keep the conversation going as long as he could but was concerned about Richard Fremont's coughing and shortness of breath. "I'm so sorry to impose, but my family didn't know any of this." Aunt Ruby looked down at the pad Andy scribbled notes on.

"I had a great respect for your uncle," Fremont continued, "my best friend. I'm sorry I can't be of more help, but I must go. This cancer has laid me low."

"No, please," Andy said, "stay on the line a bit longer; there is so much we don't know. Why did you get in touch with my aunt Ruby in October? Have you heard from Andrew?"

"I guess I just wanted to make sure your family knew that he saved my life. I'm grateful. He gave me another forty-five years."

"You haven't seen him?"

"Some confidences must be kept. I'm dying. He can't return. I'm sorry, that's all I can say."

Andy heard the receiver click into its cradle.

"What was that all about?" Ruby asked. "You look stunned."

No closer to finding his uncle, he felt deflated.

"I think he's been in touch with Andrew but won't say. Mother was talking about him being in trouble with the law?"

"Rumors and speculation," she said. "It's hard to know the truth. An old buddy of Andrew's told Roland your uncle nearly beat a man to death for making a pass at his new wife. It's so out of character for him."

"What's Mother think?"

"I don't know that she's heard all of the rumors. I don't tell her everything. She was so close to Andrew. I don't want to hurt her any more than she already is."

Andy thought of Black Henry again. *Gentle men caught up in violence after the war.*

"I think he's still alive. He was at Guadalcanal, but we still don't know why he doesn't want to see anybody."

"And maybe never will," his aunt finished his thought for him. "Sometimes it's best to let sleeping dogs lie."

❈ ❈ ❈

All of the Parks gathered at the house on Fourth Street to celebrate Christmas. George had arrived from Dallas where he now fixed planes for a major airline. Nancy June and Matt lived in Vinita a ten-minute drive from their childhood homes. With two children of their own, the house filled for the rare Christmas that Andy could be with them.

When Ruby arrived with Buddy, as promised for Little Henry, he fed the border collie a sausage saved from his breakfast.

"Stop by this week at the office for old time's sakes," Matt told him. "I'll give you a tour of the town."

"I think he would have seen the town by now," Nancy June chided her husband, "but you'll have to come for dinner before you head back."

"Come by anyway," Matt insisted. "We'll catch up."

It proved too much for Little Henry, who found a spot on the couch near Andy. Buddy followed and curled near his feet.

Henry Clay delighted in the festivities, more relaxed than Andy remembered him. Hong Kim sat in his lap soaking up all the affection in the room and beaming it back at everyone with her smile.

The sign outside the office of his brother-in-law's construction company still read *Kinecky and Sons*. The newer office, expansive, brightly lit and with a secretary, looked prosperous. Upon entering, the cramped feeling it triggered in Andy remained the same.

His visit in Oklahoma had gone well. He would not stay long. The week after Christmas, and he already felt the pull to return to Alberta. Little Henry felt it too, asking about Bella and wondering how the bees were overwintering.

At home the land would be blanketed with snow and frozen, the bees clustered in their hives. Andy welcomed the rest during winter and worked on projects in the shop, patiently waiting for the arrival of spring. The cycle would begin again with the snowmelt and emergence of the bees to forage on the willows.

In Oklahoma he had completed a cycle too, not of seasons, but of family. He knew there would always be a duality to his life, and two Andys to reconcile. Healing from the war was a process, not something he would ever complete with an arrival point—equilibrium between the two Andys the goal, not a complete merger.

"Let's take a drive," Matt said, emerging from his own office within the larger one. "What do you think?" he asked, waving an arm expansively at the new facilities.

Afton had not changed much, 900 people housed within a few streets. The elementary school bordered the south end of the town, the elm trees in front impressive even leafless in the Oklahoma winter.

"Most of our construction is over by Grand Lake these days. As you can see, Afton hasn't grown any."

Andy remembered his days on the lake with Tahlequah and Lila, the happiest he'd been during his return to Oklahoma after his discharge from the Army. It had all come crashing down around him after his friend died.

Matt had the radio on in his truck as he drove, a habit Andy remembered. Talk radio had replaced the country music station his brother-in-law used to have tuned. Andy caught brief bits of the conservative host's jubilation over the landslide reelection of Ronald Reagan the year before.

"The country will stay on the right track now," Matt said. "Ever wonder if Vietnam would have been any different if Reagan would have been president during those years?"

Andy had not.

He did remember Reagan calling for a chemical weapons ban the year before, while continuing to ignore the Vietnam veterans' Agent Orange issues. The government still viewed it as a harmless farm product. *It's all about patriotic slogans now,* he thought, *empty ones devoid of substance.* He would keep his opinions to himself, not undermine a good visit.

In a few days the family would head home. Little Henry and Andy could check on the bees and start preparing for spring. Barrels of honey in the warehouse needed shipping.

As he drove with Matt, he viewed the Oklahoma countryside through the window of the truck. He doubted he could have had a happy life here after Vietnam, which stayed with him in layered ways, filtering through his consciousness with fleeting glimpses of understanding.

Grand Lake came into view, the sun low in the western sky reflecting a glare off the water. Andy felt an intense desire to be at his farm. There was no future in reliving the past, only in understanding it.

CHAPTER
THIRTY-EIGHT

Crooked Creek, Alberta
October 1990

ANDY TOOK A break and waited in the house for Little Henry to get off the school bus. Drinking coffee while his son changed clothes, they walked to the honey house afterwards. Bella, aging, followed, still included in their activities.

Busy with the end-of-season cleanup, Little Henry liked running the power washer while Andy scraped the final beeswax and honey residues from the extracting equipment.

Andy knew beekeeping had been good for him and his son. He'd not sentimentalized the importance of bees in his own life, but understood they provided more than a livelihood. Glimpsing the inner realms of the natural order, the symbiotic relationship between insect and plant, soil and water, wilderness and farm, gave Andy a sense of participation in something greater than himself.

Andy believed Little Henry intuitively benefitted from the same thing. His deformed hand became the perfect fit for a beeswax frame. At ten, he remained a precocious child, insisting on working with the bees alongside his father when not in school.

Lisa called out to Andy, who barely heard her above the noise of the pump on the power washer.

"Sammy's on the phone," she called.

"What's up?" Andy answered.

"White Henry's not doing well."

"What do you mean?"

"I don't think he's going to make it."

Confused, Andy remembered the platoon member from Vietnam, the man they all relied on, strong and confident. He'd never made it to Missouri to look him up.

"He's dying, Doc. I spoke with his wife, Elizabeth. They don't expect him to make it past Christmas. His lymph nodes are full of cancer and his heart's giving out. She said it would mean a great deal to him if he could see us."

None of what Sammy said made any sense. Twenty years out of his war, life had settled into a routine for Andy.

"Is there any way you can get to Missouri for a few days?" Sammy asked.

❊ ❊ ❊

Andy waited in the St. Louis Airport for Sammy's flight to arrive. Airports put him in a reflective mood. He'd never been on an airplane before induction into the Army. Flying had always carried him towards life-changing experiences.

As he noticed young men in uniform walking briskly towards their destinations, he grew pensive and remembered his own experiences. A Marine looking precise in his dress greens stood gazing at the planes on the tarmac. Hair trimmed and full of youthful vigor, Andy didn't have to look for any decorations or a unit patch to know he'd never been to war.

Able to travel incognito now, Andy observed from a distance. Preoccupied with his pending visit with White Henry, his thoughts drifted back to Vietnam, to that day in the booby-trapped swamp. Above the waterline, clouds of mosquitoes were thick around their heads, oblivious to the war, participating in their own frenzied blood-feast. The muck sucked at their feet and mired them in the mud. Underneath, the leeches, bloodsucking, also took their share before the war emerged.

Boy Red had triggered the grenade that blew most of his face off. Dragging his body wrapped in a poncho through the swamp left a dissipating trail of blood in the murky water. Discovering more trip wires, some of the men started to come unglued. White Henry had given them hope and courage that day by leading them out of the swamp.

Andy recognized a familiar pattern after the war, repeating itself even after twenty years. Unable to save those who had saved him, he would watch them die.

❊ ❊ ❊

Andy looked at the Missouri countryside through the bus window on the two-hour ride south to Jackson. Cattle grazed in pastures interspersed with mostly harvested cornfields. During the drive, Sammy told him what he knew.

"White Henry came back from the war and farmed with his dad. That's all he ever wanted to do. He married a local girl and bought more land near Jackson, growing corn, expanding a herd of cows, keeping some hogs. They still farm together but have expanded the operation.

"His parents want to meet us and offered a place to stay. I thought it best if we just booked a hotel in Jackson. Henry's in the hospital there."

They found a room near the bus station and dropped their bags off before searching for a cafe in the small town. A light drizzle wet the sidewalk as they looked for a place to eat.

With the evening dinner crowd thinned out, Andy felt more comfortable talking. "What's really going on here?" he asked. He still relied on his friend to keep him abreast of veterans' issues.

"A whole lot behind the scenes. The VA and the government are still denying almost all the links between exposure to Agent Orange and any health problems. It's not just the birth defects in our children. All kinds of cancers are showing up."

"What's this about a heart condition?"

"Premature aging," Sammy said, "another item to add to the list. The dioxins in that shit are hard on all of the body's organs."

"I won't know what to say to his family," Andy said, the tongue-tied medic surfacing.

"His kids are fine," Sammy said.

"Until their father dies," Andy interjected.

"It's a mess. I think the government's waiting for us to die. That's when the war will be over."

"So we just wait for the cancers to show up?"

"You're the medic. What do you think?"

"I'm just a beekeeper. I haven't kept up," Andy added.

Satisfied, Sammy moved on. "There's been a class action suit settled out of court for one hundred and eighty million. It works out to about thirty-six hundred per claim."

"That's what a life is worth?"

"A lot of sick veterans aren't even aware they're entitled to anything. Most of the health issues from exposure are not being accepted. We're not through with that shit yet."

※ ※ ※

Their reunion with White Henry happened in the Jackson County Hospital nearly twenty-one years to the day after Andy had returned from Vietnam. He learned that Henry Wyatt, born on February 17, 1948, in the same hospital where he now lay dying at the age of forty-two, had never strayed far from home except to do his tour in Vietnam. His goals were simply to go back to the farm after the war, marry, raise a family, and make a local success of his life.

In another war he would have been considered a hero. With the Ninth Infantry Division in the Mekong Delta, he received a silver star for the day he led the platoon out of the booby-trapped swamp, and a couple of bronze stars on other operations. His presence in the platoon had meant more to Andy than any medals represented.

They found him in a small hospital room on the second floor. He recognized them immediately.

"Sammy, Doc, you guys made it," he said.

They walked to opposite sides of the bed to greet him, each grabbing a hand and awkwardly embracing him through the IV tubing in his arm and the one carrying oxygen to ease his breathing.

Andy had not expected White Henry to look good, but the deterioration disturbed him. The once-powerful frame had shrunk to a sunken image of the man he'd known in Vietnam. The hair left after the chemo treatments had turned grey and exaggerated his drawn face. His hands, still prominent, protruded from the hospital gown, a bony remnant of the strength they used to convey.

Straining to catch his breath he told them, "This is not how I would have liked seeing you guys all these years later, but I'm glad you came."

They exchanged information on their families for a few minutes. White Henry, in obvious pain, closed his eyes. A nurse entered the room with a pretty dark-haired woman.

"It's time for Henry's medications," the nurse said. "He should probably rest for a while after I administer it."

Sammy and Andy moved away from the bed, allowing some privacy with her patient. "You must be Elizabeth," Sammy said to the other woman. "We spoke on the phone."

"Yes, of course. I'm sorry," she said. "Where are my manners? Please, call me Liz. We are all in such a state. Thank you for coming. It will mean a great deal to Henry."

Andy introduced himself and shook hands.

"I have to run some errands before picking the kids up from school. I'll leave you to visit. Henry's parents would like to invite you for dinner tonight so they can meet you. I can drop by around five to pick you up?"

"We'd love to meet White Henry's folks," Sammy said. Realizing he'd called him by the platoon's nickname, he awkwardly added, "I'm sorry, that's what we called him in Vietnam. I hope you know how much having him with us has meant to Doc and me."

"Yes, it's a shock to everyone. Our world's been turned upside down. Five o'clock?" she added before leaving.

"Of course," Andy said. "We'll be here."

They drank coffee in the hospital cafeteria for an hour to allow White Henry the time to rest and have the pain medications take effect. When they returned, he had them adjust the hospital bed so he could sit upright.

"Charlie never got me," he began. "It looks like my own government has. I'm just thankful it's me and not my kids." He caught his breath again.

Andy could not help but wonder, *Will we all get cancer?*

"I need to ask a favor," White Henry said. He paused to take a breath. "First, I want to make sure you know some things from our time together in the Nam." He looked out the window before continuing.

"I tried to extend my tour before I left. I wanted to make sure everybody got home. I guess I thought I could help do that. Howitz would have none of it and wouldn't submit the paperwork. He told me, 'Get the hell out of here and don't look back. There'll just be more guys to look after when your six-month extension ends, and then what will you do? Extend some more, or get yourself killed?' I felt responsible the Professor didn't make it. I've carried that around with me ever since."

"We all have," Sammy said.

"I was already home, too," Andy said. "It hit me hard. I guess we all failed him."

"You know how scared he was when he first arrived," White Henry said. "He came such a long way. I thought he might make it. I know Howitz felt responsible."

"And Black Henry did," Sammy said. "He wouldn't speak to anyone for weeks afterwards. Howitz had the whole platoon to look after. All of the guys wanted to go home."

"It was the LT who kept extending," White Henry said. "He stayed in the Army for a while, tried to make it a career, but it was never a good fit. When he heard about what happened to Black Henry he got out and went to law school. He works on a lot of vet issues. He's in Asia right now working on behalf of a Vietnam veteran who never returned from the war. The guy is married to a Vietnamese woman and has been on the run for twenty years, mostly in Thailand."

"Incredible, the way the war has impacted so many of us," Sammy mused. "It's as endless as the Mekong River."

They had visited the entire afternoon. White Henry dozed. It was almost time for Liz to pick them up.

"We'll see you tomorrow," Sammy said as he reached out to touch Henry's shoulder. Andy wasn't sure he'd heard him, but he opened his eyes briefly and nodded. A slight smile acknowledged he knew they'd be back.

※ ※ ※

Roy Wyatt met them at the door. The father, an older and more compact version of White Henry, stuck his hand out and introduced himself. "It's so good to finally meet you boys. Come in, come in."

"Henry has told us so much about you," Helen Wyatt said inside the door, drying her hands on her apron. "Make yourselves at home. I'll leave the three of you to visit while I finish getting supper ready. Can I offer you anything, some coffee or tea?"

Andy declined, feeling awkward about arriving at the Wyatts' in good health while their son lay dying in the hospital from the chemicals they'd all been exposed to.

After a courteous bit of small talk to get acquainted, the conversation turned more serious, reflecting the somber mood of the household.

"I don't know what's happening to this country," Wyatt began. "They send you boys halfway around the world to fight a war and then don't look after you once you're home. The government's refusing to cover one dime of Henry's medical bills. Liz is having to sell their cattle herd just to cover the hospital costs."

Wyatt stood and showed them a photograph. White Henry leaned on a wooden fence while cows grazed in the background.

"This was taken two years ago. We couldn't believe it when Henry first took sick. He was barely forty and fit from working this farm. He never smoked, hardly ever drank. He liked watching some of the college football in the fall and might have a couple of beers."

"It's the dioxins that were in the chemicals," Sammy said. "They were in his body. We're so sorry, Mr. Wyatt, for what's happening."

"It just don't seem right," Wyatt continued. "I can take you down to the local bar and show you some of the boys Henry went to school with. They're still doing the same thing they were while Henry was in Vietnam, drinking and smoking and raising a ruckus while they shoot pool and chase girls. None of them get sick.

"Henry goes off to the war, comes home and marries Liz, they have Scotty and then little Becky and all of a sudden Henry's dying." He paused and took a deep breath. "I'm sorry for going on about it," he said. "I told myself I wasn't going to do that while you were here. Nobody told me life was going to be fair, but you boys already know that."

Conversation lightened during the meal. The Wyatts asked Andy about beekeeping and living in Canada. He told them about his own Henry helping with the bees. They related to that.

Liz arrived to pick them up and stayed for a cup of tea. Roy and Helen Wyatt fussed over Scotty and Becky. "You are so thin, dear," Helen said to Liz. "Can one of us drive our guests back to town for you?"

"That's all right," she said. "I need to stay busy."

Andy sat in the back seat with Becky on the drive to Jackson. Sammy talked quietly with Scotty, who sat between him and his mother in front, asking the twelve-year-old about the things he liked to do. The boy wanted to know more about his father.

"Did you really know my dad in Vietnam?"

Sammy kept it simple. "Yes, we were in the same platoon."

"Did you know my dad has some medals from the war?"

"Yes," Sammy said. "Did you know he got them saving us?"

"How did he do that?"

Sammy told him about the swamp without any of the gory details. "Doc and I are here today because your father is so brave."

In the back seat, Becky started to talk. "I like cows. Sometimes I help my dad feed them when they're little. Do you have any cows on your farm?" she asked Andy.

"Just bees," he said, "and a dog."

"I like dogs," she said, "but why do you keep bees?"

"So we can collect the honey."

"Oh, I like honey."

Outside the hotel they thanked Liz without lingering. "She must be exhausted," Andy said. Not ready for sleep, he suggested a walk to unwind from the day. The cooler crisp air of the evening felt good on his face, soothing the intense emotions accumulated during the day.

"Let's get a beer," Sammy said.

Andy rarely drank anymore. The urge to obliterate the emotional pain he carried diminished with the degree of purpose established in his life. The hurt remained, but empathy replaced much of the anger. The war had shown him the impermanence of life. He would always feel guilty for surviving it, but now saw his good fortune as a gift. That had really begun with adopting Little Henry and Hong Kim. The broadened perspective in loving them gave him the equilibrium he needed to move on from the war. *What's happening to White Henry could happen to me,* Andy reasoned. Each day became important.

❋ ❋ ❋

The tavern could have been anywhere in Missouri, Oklahoma or

Alberta. The smell of stale cigarette smoke and beer hung in the air, while the sound of a country and western song played on a juke box. Loud conversation and colliding pool balls reverberated.

They picked a table farthest from the crowd in the half-empty room. Andy drank part of a beer before either of them spoke. Reflecting on the day, he assumed his friend was doing the same.

Two men about their age played pool at one of the tables on the other side of the room. A woman stood nearby and drank a beer. Cigarettes dangled from the mouths of all three, and boisterous laughter followed many of the shots.

Some of the boys White Henry would have gone to school with, mused Andy, *probably the ones Roy Wyatt referred to.*

"You have any problems from that shit?" Sammy asked, referring to Agent Orange.

"Just my teeth," Andy told him. "I never knew what the problem was after I got back. I couldn't keep them from decaying. Then I saw a vet being interviewed who'd done his tour filling the tanks on the planes doing the spraying. He said his teeth had fallen out within a year of returning from the war. You?"

"Not yet. You ever wonder about the other guys in the platoon like Eli and Minnesota?"

"Sure. White Henry's the last guy we're still in touch with."

Sammy nodded.

"I ever tell you about Calvin Lake, the kid on the quadriplegic ward?"

"Some of it."

"He lost his entire platoon in one day. He didn't want to live any more paralyzed from the neck down. He kept asking me to help him kill himself."

"I guess we're the lucky ones." Sammy looked at Andy from across the table. "Should we get out of here?"

They spent three days with White Henry, visiting, reminiscing, and saying their goodbyes.

"The hardest part is leaving my children, not being there to make sure they're doing okay in the roughest patches of life."

Andy made no trite comments about how they would be fine. He mentioned the conversation he'd had with Becky about the cows.

"She was Daddy's little girl," White Henry said. "She would follow me around at calving time wanting to mother the newborns. Just this spring one of the cows had twins and only looked after one of them. She wouldn't let the other suckle or get close to her. He wound up a mess from scours and malnutrition and we had to feed him from a bottle. Becky lay next to that sick calf and talked to it, petted it like a dog.

"It did get better and we got another cow to accept it. But he always came to greet us when we made our rounds that spring. W-6 is what we called him from the tag in his ear. It was pretty special having my little girl help her daddy."

At the end of their visit White Henry had one more thing to ask.

"I don't want to, but it's time to let go. I'm proud to have known you. I've asked the doctors to discharge me so that I can go home to die. They're advising against it, but I need to get out of here, spend my final days with my family."

In the morning White Henry was going home.

Andy pulled the IV out of his arm and they helped him get dressed, bundling him up against the cold. White Henry put an arm around each of them, and they carried him down the stairs in one final act of camaraderie, getting him to safety like they would have if he'd been wounded in the jungles of Vietnam.

Liz had the car waiting by the curb. There was no time for any long or sappy goodbyes. Andy opened the door, and he and Sammy slid White Henry onto the seat and embraced him one final time.

A familiar empty feeling came over Andy, like he'd just placed a wounded member of the platoon on a medevac and would never see him again. He looked at Sammy, tears forming. Andy put his arm around him, and they walked that way for a while. He remembered the day White Henry had left them in Dong Tam to rotate home.

The ache was heavy, deep inside Andy, but he knew he had much to live for. It was good to see Sammy again, spend time together, but he, too, needed to get home.

EPILOGUE

Crooked Creek, Alberta
2015

IN WINTER THE poplar were bare in northern Alberta. Andy liked the view from his study, where a few spruce added green to the grey-and-white landscape. A foot of snow has accumulated on a grassy area between the house and a tree line. He was comforted by the stillness of the cold and the cover of night. The moon often reflected off the snow, and the silhouettes of the trees could be seen out of the second-story window.

Forty-five years later, sleep patterns ingrained during the war allowed only a few hours at a time.

The photographs on the wall included one of Andy with the Professor. A glare reflected off his friend's glasses as they stood in front of a sandbagged bunker in Dong Tam. They were skinny—and young—boys sent to do a man's job in war. Yardly, even younger, was in the background. The Montagnard looked unsure of how he was supposed to pose, suppressing a smile that was normally on his face.

The two Henrys and Sammy stood in front of the entrance to a barracks, leaning on the ubiquitous sandbags that surrounded the buildings in Dong Tam. Andy remembered taking the photograph when the platoon had a two-day break to resupply and recuperate from a grueling patrol in the Ca Mau.

Only Sammy and Andy remained. He had no pictures of Camel, or Boy Red, or Square One, casualties who died despite his efforts to save them. Memories were all that was left. Camel no longer visited Andy regularly in his sleep.

Little Henry shunned his Vietnamese heritage for most of his years. As an adult, he searched for his roots, visiting the country of his birth frequently—as a beekeeper and an Agent Orange survivor. In doing so he closed a circle for father and son.

Beekeeping was all Henry ever wanted to do. He grew curious when Vietnam began developing a larger beekeeping sector and exporting honey. At an apiculture conference in Edmonton he had met a man attending on behalf of the Vietnamese Beekeeper's Association. Intrigued that one of their countrymen would be keeping bees in such a place as Canada, and impressed with Henry's knowledge, the man extended an invitation to present a series of lectures and demonstrations in the country of his birth.

While visiting, the language came back to him and he spoke with many Vietnamese. They told him of others with similar deformities and of a *Friendship Village* near Hanoi, which cared for those born with serious problems from the chemicals, an issue that continued in subsequent generations. Formed by American and Vietnamese veterans of the war as a place to come together in fellowship, it was where Henry met his wife. Lan Nhu, with a hand missing two fingers that matched Henry's, worked in the village caring for such children. Andy's Vietnamese-Canadian grandchildren were healthy and living on the bee farm that Henry never wished to leave.

Hong Kim, healthy, and a mother of two, married a local boy with whom she went to school. They graduated together in 1998 with their class of eighteen students. They now had their own farm, and she had never been back to Vietnam. Delightful as a child, she was no different as an adult.

Andy never located his uncle. Perhaps his namesake could have helped him figure a few things out about life in the aftermath of war.

Sammy remained a constant friend. He and Andy talk frequently, and always on the anniversary of White Henry's death. It was fitting that the platoon member to whom they looked most to guide them to safety and out of the war would be remembered in this private memorial.

Andy came to believe that the survivors were like the Mekong itself, branching into ever-changing tributaries and waterways moving towards the expanse of the sea to join with the rest of humanity. Once a death zone, the Mekong now nourished and filled the rice paddies where the renewal of each crop continued to sustain life while diluting the poisons dumped years ago on the unsuspecting landscape.

So it was in the sea of humanity where the Vietnamese had taken their place in the world, and the American veterans of that war who had joined with them were now forever connected by this place, this country called Vietnam.

GLOSSARY

Agent Orange: Slang for the most common of the chemical defoliants used in Vietnam. A 50/50 mixture of the common farm chemical 2-4-D and 2-4-5-T; the latter contained dioxins, one of the most toxic substances created by man. The term originated from an identifying orange stripe around the fifty-five-gallon drums it was shipped in.

AK-47: The most common assault rifle used by the Viet Cong and NVA.

Ao baba: A common loose-fitting blouse worn by the Vietnamese, especially prevalent in the Mekong Delta.

Arty: Slang commonly used for artillery by grunts in the field.

ARVN: An acronym for Army Republic of Vietnam, the South Vietnamese Army. Usually pronounced "Arvin," they were allies of the Americans in fighting the Viet Cong and North Vietnamese Army.

Base Camp: A permanent camp where a division's headquarters are located.

Battalion: There are generally four to six companies in a battalion with 300 to 800 troops and commanded by a lieutenant colonel.

Battalion Aid Station: Generally, set up for minor ailments in a base camp.

Boonies: The most common slang used by American infantry troops in Vietnam for areas patrolled beyond the relative safety of a base camp.

Brass: Slang for officer corps, usually used in the context of concerns about higher command coming to inspect or require something of troops of a lower rank. "Brass isn't going to be happy with this." Or, "Brass will be all over us for this."

Bronze Star: A US Army award for gallantry on the battlefield, below a Silver Star, the Distinguished Service Cross and the Medal of Honor.

Buying the farm: Common slang for being killed in action. The origins of the expression are linked to a $10,000 life insurance policy paid to the family of the deceased soldier. It is often shortened to "He bought it."

C-4 explosive: A putty-like substance that is highly explosive when ignited.

C-Rations: Meals in a can. The most common form of rations for American infantry units in Vietnam.

C-Rats: Slang for C-rations.

Charlie: Slang for the Viet Cong. The term originated from the Military Phonetic System where a "V" was "Victor" and a "C" was "Charles." Hence, Victor Charles for Viet Cong and shortened to "Charlie" by American troops.

Chieu Hoi: Literally translated as "open arms." The *Chieu Hoi* Program was designed to entice defectors from the Viet Cong to come over to the South Vietnamese side in the war. Leaflets were often dropped from the air offering rewards for defecting.

Claymore Mine: A lightweight mine used by infantry troops to establish a nighttime perimeter in the field. Seven hundred steel balls were embedded in a layer of C-4 explosive. Usually command detonated, it was deadly at close range.

CO: An abbreviation used for a commanding officer. It was also used to designate a conscientious objector.

Cobra Gunship: A helicopter designed for combat with a lethal arsenal which included rockets and Gatling guns.

Company: Normally comprised of three to six platoons and commanded by a captain.

Cracker: Slang for "poor white trash" and implied the white person was racist when used by black soldiers.

Cutdown: A medical procedure devised to expose a vein in order to get an intravenous started on a casualty whose veins are collapsing from shock.

Deuce and a half: A two-and-a-half-ton Army truck common in Vietnam.

Doc: Most medics were called "Doc." The term was so common that medics often used it when addressing each other.

Dog Tags: Metal tags worn around the neck on a chain or tucked into a boot with a soldier's identification and blood type.

Dress Greens: The formal uniform of the US Army.

Dust-off: A term used for a helicopter outfitted for medical evacuations of wounded troops in the field.

ETA: Estimated time of arrival.

FNG: Fucking new guy.

Foxhole: A two or three-man hole dug in the field for protection while spending the night in the field, referred to as "digging in for the night."

Gook: A racial slur for Vietnamese common amongst US troops.

Greased: One of the uglier terms for getting killed by enemy fire.

Grunt: Slang mostly used by infantrymen to refer to themselves as foot soldiers.

Hooch: Slang for living quarters in a base camp.

Huey: A common helicopter used by Americans in Vietnam.

Hump: The term commonly used for being on patrol. "Humping" through the "boonies" looking for "Charlie" was what the infantry was all about.

Jitterbugging Operation: A Ninth Infantry Division term used for the tactic of surrounding an area suspected of harboring Viet Cong and tightening the circle of troops to find the enemy.

Jungle Rot: A common foot infection of troops in the field exacerbated by the tropical climate, wet conditions and the myriad bacterial and fungal infections which thrived in the unsanitary conditions.

KIA: Abbreviation for "killed in action."

Kit Carson Scout: Vietnamese nationals attached to an American unit to act as interpreters of language and customs. They were called "Tiger Scouts" in the Ninth Infantry Division.

Klick: A kilometer.

LP: A listening post. A two or three-man team placed beyond the perimeter at night to monitor for enemy activity.

LT: A lieutenant. Each letter is pronounced and was used to address or refer to a soldier's platoon commander. It denoted respect but also familiarity.

LZ: A landing zone.

M-60: A common and important machine gun used by American infantry troops. The weapon was also mounted and used by door gunners on helicopters and strategically placed to protect the perimeters of a base camp.

MAT Team: A Mobile Advisory Team. A five-man American unit set up in a Vietnamese village to organize a Popular Force Militia of the villagers.

MEDCAP: An abbreviation for "Medical Civilian Action Program." Medical personnel were dispatched to rural villages for a day to provide medical treatments as a way of fostering goodwill between the civilian population and the Americans.

Medevac: A term for a helicopter extracting casualties from the field.

Montagnard: An indigenous people of Vietnam living in the Central Highlands of the country.

MOS: Military Occupational Specialty.

Napalm: Jellied gasoline dropped from the air in drums that explode and catch fire on impact. Flamethrowers use the same basic ingredient.

Night Ambush: A squad- to platoon-size ambush set in place overnight that attempts to intercept enemy troop movement.

NVA: North Vietnamese Army.

OR: Operating room in a hospital.

PBR: Patrol Boat, River. A US Navy boat, small and lightweight, yet heavily armed, manned by a four-man crew. A double-barreled machine gun was set in a turret at the bow, and an M-60 was mounted in the stern. It displaced little water, ideal for patrolling the rivers and canals in the Mekong Delta.

Platoon: Commanded by a lieutenant and usually comprised of twenty to thirty men in Vietnam.

Point Man: Often referred to as "walking point." Somebody had to go first on a patrol. A good "point man" was important to an infantry platoon.

Popular Forces: A village-based indigenous platoon organized by the South Vietnamese government and US military personnel.

PRC-25 Radio: Pronounced "prick twenty-five," each infantry platoon carried one for communicating in the field; essential for calling in air strikes, medevacs and artillery.

Psy Ops: Slang for "psychological warfare."

Punji Stake: A sharpened stick, often made from bamboo, placed in a camouflaged pit or attached to a booby trap. Several stakes are normally used in each pit or device.

Purple Heart: Awarded for being wounded or killed.

REMF: Rear echelon motherfucker. The term was used by grunts in the field to refer to troops in the rear. It is pronounced the way it is spelled.

RPD: A machine gun used by the Viet Cong.

RTO: The term stood for "radio telephone operator." Every infantry platoon had an RTO responsible for carrying and maintaining a PRC-25 field radio.

Short: Slang for not much time left on a tour in Vietnam.

Slick: A Huey helicopter without any armaments other than one or two door gunners.

Tiger Scout: What the Ninth Infantry called its Kit Carson Scouts. They acted as interpreters of language and culture for American infantry units.

Tracer: Bullets that leave a visible path through the air after being fired from an automatic weapon, allowing the shooter to "trace" where his shots are going. At night, these rounds are eerily visible in a firefight.

Wasted: Slang for "killed in action."

ACKNOWLEDGMENTS

POISONED JUNGLE IS my first published book. Much work beyond the writing goes into bringing a novel into print. This is an opportunity to acknowledge the contributions of others.

Many thanks to fellow writers in the Edmonton area who have read the manuscript and offered valuable and constructive suggestions. Instrumental among them are members of "The Breakaways," Robert Hunting, Kimberley Howard and Laura Hanon. They have all offered valuable insights. I am particularly appreciative of Kimberley and Laura's female perspectives on a novel exploring the ramifications of war. And to Robert's insights into writing and literature, explored weekly in our Tuesday-morning coffee sessions. Two old retired guys still writing and exploring the world.

My thanks to Don Levers, who has read every manuscript about Vietnam I have written. His support and comments as a friend and writer have been invaluable.

My son, Nathan Ballard, has also read most of his father's manuscripts. The many discussions they have generated from the personal to the philosophical have an added dimension, the pride of a father participating in intelligent and meaningful discussions with his son. It was always difficult to talk about the war. I never knew if I told too much or too little about my experiences. This has been an opportunity to answer many questions for father and son. Nathan's support has been unwavering, and for this I am profoundly grateful. The enthusiasm and help he and his wife, Shandra Ballard, have provided reaches beyond the publishing of a book.

A special thanks to Lilliane Andrews, partner in love and all things. Not one complaint about the stacks of manuscripts that often spill over into all areas of the house. There has not been a cranky word about the hundreds of hours it takes to produce just one book. There has been nothing but love and support on the home front.

Finally, Koehler Books has given me the opportunity to publish my first novel, at age seventy-one. Thanks to Greg Fields for his belief in the manuscript, Joe Coccaro for his editing, and John Koehler for making it happen. *Poisoned Jungle* has indeed been a collaborative effort.